SUMMER PASSAGE
OF '66

Steven S. Foster

Dedication

I dedicate this novel to my lovely wife, Sandi, who has been my muse, confidant and best friend.

CONTENTS

1 DEADMAN

Something was not right on that scorching June day in 1966. I tapped the fuel gauge on the dashboard of my red '56 Chevy. The needle pointed to empty. It had to be at least half full. I stared at the straight Arizona desert road and saw nothing but flickering heat waves on the hot asphalt. Desperate to find a gas station, I anxiously gripped the steering wheel.

A bright orange sun glared through my windshield. I lowered the visors and adjusted my sunglasses. Beads of sweat began to stream down my face. I was sure the engine would sputter and die. Far from home, I worried about my chances of survival. Desert sun burned into my flesh. I spotted a road sign—gas five miles ahead. I glanced at the fuel gauge again. Empty. I held my breath. Could I make it?

I drove on. It was like going in slow motion. A long road lay ahead. Finally, I pulled into a run-down station with two pumps. Relieved, I stepped out and looked at the dust-covered windows of a small office. I beeped the horn. No one came to help. I strolled to an attached garage and called out, "Hello! Anybody here?"

A dingy, gray Ford sedan sat forlorn up on a rack, and tools were scattered on the floor as though someone had tossed them into the air. "Hello!" It was eerily quiet.

An oscillating fan whirred in a corner while circulating warm air in my face and a lingering smell of grease. "Hello!" I walked outside and looked around. Behind the garage, old wrecks were left in the dust of desert wind. "Anybody here?"

No answer. I only heard my heartbeat. The sun glared down. I lowered my Padres baseball cap and walked to the front office door. It was wide open, and I stepped inside. A cigarette butt smoldered in an ashtray. Someone had been here.

A cash register drawer sat wide opened on the counter and it was empty, except for a few small coins in a tray. Wary, I turned and faced an old metal desk. On the floor, was a body of a thin gray-haired man. Dried blood stained the back of his head. Next to him was a tire wrench.

Sickened, I stood there, not knowing what to do. I had never seen a dead man before. I grabbed the phone on the desk and dialed. No sound. Pulse raising, I glanced at the cord. It had been cut. No way to call for help. I rushed to the gas pump and filled up my tank until the meter showed a total of four bucks and eighty-three cents.

Without another thought, I ran back inside and plopped a five on the counter. I picked up a pencil and wrote a note on a grease-stained pad. "Found body," I glanced at my watch and continued, "at 1:15 p.m. Tried to call police. Phone cord was cut. Going east for help." I signed, "Richard Thomson." I took one last look at the dead guy lying there stiff like a fallen tree. Nauseous, I ran back to my car and drove on.

Ahead was a long, straight road, and I had time to think. Early that morning, I left the comforts of my boyhood home in San Diego. At 18, I just graduated from Pacific Ridge High School. With my parent's blessing, I was on my way to work with my two uncles on their cattle ranch north of Flagstaff for the summer. After that, I planned to travel and see the country while I had the chance.

The Vietnam War was heating up. I knew I was supposed to serve my country but I figured I needed to see some of it first. In fact, my dad, a World War Two Navy vet, encouraged me to take this journey. If I had to go, I'd have a better idea of what I was going to fight for in a far-off land. Still, I hoped it wouldn't come to that point.

Before I left home, Dad smiled and said, "Live free while you can."

Mom hugged me. "I'm glad you'll have a chance to work on the ranch where I grew up."

After I waved to my two younger brothers and my 16 year-old

sister, I drove away. Excited about being free, I wanted to experience life to the fullest.

Then I found myself somewhere south of Kofa National Wildlife Refuge on highway 95, and I'd already seen my first dead guy. In the blur of heat waves, I spotted a man about 20 or so, and he stood alongside the road with his thumb out. His left hand gripped a two-gallon gas can. Cars whizzed by as though he didn't even exist, and I pulled over.

When I stopped, the hitchhiker opened my passenger side door and smiled. "You saved my life, man. I thought I was gonna die out there." He slid in the seat, placed the gas can on the floor between his knees and said, "Thanks."

"Glad to help." I drove back on the road and said, "I'm in a hurry!" I looked straight ahead and gripped the steering wheel. "I need to call the cops!"

"What happened?"

"I found a guy murdered at a gas station back there!"

"You know who did it?" His voice was firm and direct.

"What?" I glanced over, "No, of course not."

"Well, I do!"

A sharp blade pierced my side. "Hey!" I saw a hunting knife.

"Shut up!" He pointed ahead. "Turn on that dirt road!"

In pain, I tried to stay calm. "Take it easy, man."

"Keep driving!" He pointed to a parked car about a hundred feet ahead. "Pull over there!"

I did as I was told and stepped on the brake as a plume of dust billowed from behind my car. "Now what?" I asked.

"Don't do anything stupid!" He poked my skin with the blade again. "Now slide out real slow like."

Warily, I got out, stood by the open door and glared at his fierce, dark uncaring eyes.

He grinned and chuckled, "You want to kill me, don't you?"

"Put the knife down and you'll find out!" My jaw tightened.

"I got a better idea."

"What are you talking about?" I stalled and tried to think of a way out of this madness.

"It just so happens that I need a dummy!" He stared at me like a wolf about to go in for the kill. "You're my size. No one will ever suspect it."

"What?" I didn't like the tone of his voice.

He grinned and nodded to the inside of my car. With the door still opened, he ordered, "Now, move real slow and get that gas can out!"

"Okay." As I bent over and reached in, the blade jabbed me again. I glanced at my side. I was bleeding. "Just take it easy, man!" I noticed the can was heavy. "Hey! You already got gas in here!"

He grabbed the can. "Go on." He pointed to the other car parked in front of us.

I walked to the driver's side door of his vehicle. "Now what?"

"Get in, dummy!"

I slid into the seat, faced the steering wheel and looked for the keys.

His weird chuckling sounded like a hyena. "Forget it! I ain't that stupid!"

"What are you up to?"

"It's simple, dummy!" He smirked and leaned in so close, I could smell stale cigarettes on his breath. "I'm AWOL, man! The Army was about to ship me out to Nam!" He chortled, "I got other plans!"

"What the hell are you talking about?"

"Life and death! I'm getting out of this God-forsaken country! I ain't dying in no stinking jungle. So, I escaped. Trouble was, I needed money."

"You're crazy!"

"Yep!" He laughed. "The Army trained me to kill, man. It was so easy to knock off that old codger back there. Now I got enough to hide out in Mexico."

"Alright I get it." I glared at his twisted expression. "Just let me go. I won't tell anybody." I realized I was begging. I didn't care.

The deserter laughed wildly again. "I know you won't talk!" He paused and stared at me. "You see...I'm dead! It turns out

4

you're my dummy, sittin in my car!" Dog tags dangled from his hand. "See this? Now you're me." He dropped them in my lap.

"Hey!"

His fist slammed into my jaw. Stunned, I tried to regain my senses. With his hip against the door, he lifted the can and poured gasoline in the back seat. I smelled the stench of fuel. He tossed a lighter. Flames erupted. I hit his hand. He stumbled back. I tried to open the door. He kicked it shut, then took off running. Flames grew hotter.

I pushed the door open and stumbled out. Fearing an explosion, I ran as far as I could, then dropped to the ground and covered my head. At first, nothing happened. I looked up to see my Chevy speeding away. Enraged, I glanced at the burning car. Suddenly it exploded. Charred pieces of metal blew up. The hood landed within inches of me.

Far from any human contact, I lifted my shirt and saw blood dribbling down my side from a half-inch gash. Thirsty, weak, overheated, I staggered toward the main road. Somehow, I had to stay alive.

Left alone to die in the vast Sonoran Desert of Arizona, I pressed my fingers on the oozing knife wound to stop the bleeding. Stabbing pain shot through my side. Overhead, the sun glared down at me like an eye in the sky. Dizzy, I saw a figure coming through swirling heat waves on the road ahead of me. I blinked and opened my eyes wide. It came closer. Was it the killer returning to finish me off?

Struggling to stay alive, I picked up a rock with bloody fingers. Too weak to run, I'd fight.

Light-headed, I tried to make out the blurry image coming at me. I started to throw my weapon. But my knees buckled and I blacked out.

2 DOWN AND OUT

I awakened in the cool night air, gasped and sat up. A large hand gripped my shoulder. Slowly, I focused on a faint image. It was the face of a stranger. He wore a sombrero that was slightly tilted back on his forehead. In the glow of a nearby fire, I saw his reddish-brown shoulder-length hair and thick beard. He smiled through several missing front teeth.

"It's alright," he whispered softly. "Take it easy. You're safe now."

"Uh...where am I?"

"You're in the Sonoran desert." He gently nudged my shoulders. "Just lay back and relax."

I leaned on a pack. "I should be dead." My voice was gravelly.

"Yep." He smiled. "But you ain't."

I looked into his hazel eyes and said, "You saved me. Thanks."

"I'm glad I was nearby."

I reached out my hand, "My name's Rick."

He gripped my palm and shook it, "Call me, Dusty. Soon as I saw the smoke, I came a runnin. Here, take a swig of this." He put a wine skin to my parched lips.

It tasted bitter. I choked on it. "What is that?"

Dusty grinned and nodded, "Good medicine." He reached over with the liquid again. "Now, drink up. I made it myself. It's fermented wine from the cactus fruit. It'll help you sleep."

I took another sip and swirled in my mouth, then gulped it down. My tongue began to feel a little numb but I needed to talk. "A guy tried to kill me."

"Yep, looks like it." He turned on a flashlight and shined a beam at my wound. "Just relax. Okay, roll over."

I moved to my side and groaned.

Dusty lifted up my shirt and shined the light. "Lookin good.

That poultice oughta heal you up right nice." He smiled. "You're lucky that knife didn't go in too deep."

Numb from the cactus juice, I said, "I need to get to a phone and call the police."

"That'll have to wait. You just get some rest." He covered me with his blanket and handed over the wine skin. "Here, take a few swigs. We'll talk in the morning."

I tilted my head and drank. Weary, I yawned, closed my eyes and drifted into a peaceful sleep.

When I awoke early the next morning, I heard a cracking and scratching noise. Startled, I quickly stood up and called out, "Dusty!"

"I see you're awake," he said. "I'm right behind you."

I turned to my side and saw him with a long pole in his hands. He knocked down two red fruit from a tall cactus and they plunked to the ground.

"What are doing, man?"

"Gettin breakfast." Dusty picked up each fruit and brought the red morsels over, then squatted on his haunches. "Here." He handed me one. "Bite into this."

I hesitated. "What is it?"

"Sa'waro." Dusty took out a pocket knife and sliced off a small chunk and slowly ate it. While savoring the juices, he grinned with his mouthful. "Try it...you'll be glad to get your fill." He placed the blade handle in my palm.

I liked his cool earthy style. "Sure." I cut and ate a piece, and with my mouth full, I said, "Mmm...this is good." I glanced at the cactus. "What'd you call this?"

While still munching on his fruit, he looked at the nearby cactus towering over us. "This here blessed savior of the desert is what the Tohono O'odham Indians call a sa'waro." He walked over to the tall cactus. As he stood beside it, I estimated it had to be at least 30 feet high. Dusty stared at it and sighed as though he admired a great masterpiece. "Without these giants, many people would have a tough time surviving out here."

"How do you know so much about all this," I waved a hand in

7

the air and scanned the terrain with hundreds of cacti in every direction.

"I learned a lot from the locals out here." Dusty strolled back to the firepit and picked up a steaming coffee pot with a glove from his back pocket. "You want some?"

Without waiting for an answer, he poured the hot brew in a tin cup and handed it to me. "Sorry," he seemed mildly embarrassed. It's the only one I got." He shrugged, "You don't mind shar-in, do ya?"

I sipped it and handed the cup back to him. "That's not half-bad." I tried to recognize the flavor. "Doesn't taste like coffee, though. What is it?"

Dusty drank some and handed it to me. "Mostly chicory with a little bit of this and that," he chuckled and wiped his bushy red beard with his fingers.

"How long you been out here?"

"Well," He paused like he was in deep thought. "Ya see…" He seemed to weigh his words carefully. "I came out here a few years after the Korean War. I had enough of fightin and killin, man."

I drank from the cup and stood next to the fire. "Why come out here?" I poured from the pot and handed him the cup. Somehow, I felt stronger.

Dusty waved his hand wide. "This here's my home now."

Amazed, I couldn't help to ask, "I don't get it. How can you make it out here?" The sun glared down, and I lowered my cap over my eyes.

"Simple," said Dusty. "I spend a lot of time liven among my friends, the Tohono people. They taught me everything I need to know about survival." He nodded for me to follow him. o" Come on. I'll show ya a few tricks of the trade." We strolled over to what appeared to be a dead cactus with long spines pointing like thin fingers toward the bright blue sky. "Ya see that?"

"Yep." I looked at the barren trunk.

Dusty pulled out a machete he kept in a sheath on his belt and sliced off a spine about 20 feet in height. He walked over to a live cactus and pointed to the lush ruby red fruit at the top. "Now, the only way I'm gonna get that food way up there is to use a tool." He sliced a thin piece of cactus with needles on it and stuck it on the tip of his pole. "Now, watch." He reached high and gently poked the fruit. One fell to the ground. The other stuck to the needles, and he set his harvesting tool down. "We always show respect and don't hurt the plant."

"Hey, that's cool."

"Come on over to the fire." He nodded. "I gotta check that wound of yours again."

When I sat on the ground, I noticed that I felt no pain. Dusty examined it carefully like a doctor, then he smiled with a look of satisfaction. "You're doing fine. You'll heal in no time."

"Good, I need to find a phone and call the cops." I scanned the campsite. "Say...where are your wheels, man?"

Dusty stood up and stomped his boots on the ground. "This is it." He grinned and held up his thumb. "I can always hitch a ride if I got a mind to."

"That's it?"

"Sorry, it's all I got, Rick." This was the first time he spoke my name.

Seeing his sincere, caring expression, I liked his genuine, wild nature. "That's okay."

"Come on." He nodded to me. "Let's sit. We'll figure something out."

Together, we shared another cup of chicory and talked. Dusty had an easy-going way of getting me to relax and not worry so much. "Hey, I got an idea," he said with a twinkle in his eye. "We'll send up a smoke signal."

I laughed at his joke but winced at the pain in my side. "Hey, take it easy, man."

Dusty handed me the wine skin and smiled. "Here ya go. Take a few more swigs of this and you won't feel a thing."

"I took another sip."

"Don't move," he whispered.

"What?" I noticed his light-hearted expression had changed.

9

He was seriously focused on something on the ground. It was a rattlesnake slithering toward us.

I froze.

Dusty held up his machete. Like lightning, he sliced down. "Got it!"

The blade had cut the rattlesnake's head clean off. Its decapitated body still wriggled in the dirt. Without a word, Dusty picked up the twitching reptile while the head and poisonous fangs were left on the ground. It's cold, green eyes glistened as though it was still alive.

"Wow!" I jumped to my feet. "That was fast!"

"Sorry, snake. I didn't want to hurt ya." He paused to admire it. "Yep, you sure are a mighty handsome fella. But, you see, it's like this, we're gettin mighty hungry, and we need meat."

I stood there and watched as Dusty whispered strange words that I could not understand. Slowly, he moved about with his boots stirring up swirls of dust. It appeared to be a dance. I had never seen anything like it before.

With his eyes gazing into the crystal blue sky, he said, "Thank you for the nourishment we're about to receive." He placed the body on a rock, then looked up again. "You are the great provider." With his machete in hand, he skinned and gutted the reptile.

Soon, we had our cooked meat over the flames. While I chewed, I realized how hungry I was and savored every morsel with delight. "Hey," I chuckled, "Tastes like chicken."

Dusty busted out in a warm, hardy laugh, "That's what they all say." He continued to delve into his breakfast as though it was his last meal. After he finished off all but about six inches, he grinned and rubbed his belly happily. "Thank you, snake." He picked up the last piece, reached up and placed it at arms-length on a healthy saguaro.

"What's that for?" I asked.

"Well, my friend, it's best to only take what you need and no more. Always give something back. Soon, the birds will be attracted to the meat. If they don't get it, an owl may find it. No matter what, nothing's ever wasted."

"Sounds good to me."

"Ya hear that?"

"What?"

He turned to a nearby cactus. "Look," he pointed to beautiful white flowers with yellow stems filled with pollen. "See how those honey bees are flying in and out. They're all part of what makes this country so connected to a greater good, man."

For the first time in my young life, I sincerely listened and observed the steady of hum of desert life. "Wow!" In awe, I stood there and let my spirit soak it all in.

"Those tiny creatures, need pollen to make honey and keep their hive alive." He paused to admire them. "The sa'waro can't spread and grow without those bees, the pollinators. Also, the birds and even the night owl helps by passing all that good stuff around."

Dusty reached into his pack and pulled out a small tin can. "That reminds me, honey is good for wounds." He nodded to me, "Lift up your shirt, and I'll check that gash of yours."

As I did so, he removed the poultice. "Lookin good." He opened the can, then scooped a little honey on his fingers and rubbed it on my skin. "This'll help to heal you."

"I can see why you like it out here, Dusty."

"Yep, it's my home."

I thought of that rattlesnake again. "I still don't know how you survive out here." I glanced at the bloody head on the rocks. "When I saw that snake about to strike, I was so scared, I froze."

"Fear is only natural," Dusty impaled the snake's head and tossed it over to a mound of ants. They immediately set upon it. "When faced with danger, we have two choices. Run like hell. Or stand and fight."

Still disappointed in my reaction, I groaned, "But I froze, man!"

"Yeah, you did." He sat down cross-legged, looked up and patted a spot in the dirt in front of him. "Come, sit."

I plopped my rear, crossed my legs and faced him. "What?" I laughed. "Are you going to lecture me now?"

"Looks that way." He paused and gazed at me sincerely. "In this case, you did the right thing. That snake couldn't see so good. But he sure as hell sensed the slightest movement. When you're faced with a situation like that, just stay calm. Don't react. Think."

"Yeah, you took care of the rest."

He smiled, "It helped to have my machete handy at the time. Anyway, we'll talk more later." He stood up and pointed at the firepit. "Let's put this out. We'll head over to the highway."

Just as I started to pour a handful of dirt on the dying embers, I noticed a strange bird call, "A-hoo-a"

"What's that?"

Dusty looked up at the top of a cactus and nodded, "That's a white-winged dove," he whispered softly. "Listen."

"A-hoo-a!" Its call was louder. "A-hoo-a!"

Dusty slowly turned and looked steadily at me. "Okay, stay calm."

"What?"

He held a finger to his lips.

"A-hoo-a!"

"He's warning us of danger. Don't move!"

We heard a low growling sound. Wary, I kept my focus on Dusty as he turned slowly to his right. I looked in the same direction and spotted a male coyote staring at us from about 10 paces. Saliva dribbled from sharp canine teeth. With ears flared back and head lowered, it appeared ready to attack.

Dusty faced the animal. "Rick, stay calm," he whispered. "Don't look directly into his eyes." He pulled out a machete from the sheath on his belt. Cautiously, he knelt, picked up a cactus fruit and stood straight. "You look hungry, fella. Here ya go." He tossed the red morsel over and it landed a few feet away.

The coyote cocked his head warily. After the animal sniffed it several times, he finally stepped forward, bit into the fruit, backed away several feet and ravenously chewed the food.

Dusty watched, shook his head and sighed. "That poor guy is real sick." He glanced at me, "He's got a bad case of mange. Most likely, he's got parasites and too weak to hunt."

"Looks like he's got rabies." I stepped back.

"Nah, that critter would've attacked by now." He pointed with the tip of his machete. "Take a good look, Rick. "He ain't frothing at the mouth. He's just skin and bones. Besides, a coyote normally wouldn't attack a man."

For a moment, we watched that starving animal while he ate all the fruit. Then he sniffed, turned and walked over to the cactus where Dusty had impaled the snake meat on the needles. Hungrily, the coyote looked up and stared at the tempting morsel that was about eight feet above the ground.

"It's alright, fella," Dusty spoke softly and slowly picked up his harvesting pole. "Just take it easy. I'll get it for you." He reached up and knocked down the meat. "Eat up. That's all I got."

The coyote lunged, gripped the food in his jaws and ran off.

An hour later, I smothered the fire while Dusty packed up his gear. He slung a heavy backpack over his shoulders and handed me one of two canteens. "Here, keep this with you."

I took a sip and realized it was almost empty. "How do we get more water?" I shook it and worried.

"Come on," he grinned confidently and waved a hand toward the east. "There's a water hole that a way."

"But the highway is in the opposite direction. I still need to call the cops."

Dusty opened his canteen and drank the last drop. Then he held it upside down to illustrate a point. "We need to survive first."

Without another word, he turned and walked away. I realized how much I depended on my new desert friend, so I followed him deeper into that wilderness he called home. I glanced behind me and noticed the coyote was following us. After about a mile, he disappeared.

Another hour passed and we continued over rocky terrain. Hot and thirsty, I licked my parched lips and stripped my T-shirt off.

"Hey. Don't do that." Dusty glared at me, "If you want to stay alive, you need to follow a few rules out here."

Surprised by his stern tone, I stopped in my tracks and groaned wearily. "Well, what am I supposed to do, man? I'm thirsty!"

"From now on, you'll do exactly as I say," Dusty stood with his arms crossed. "You got that?"

Realizing that he was serious about my survival, I nodded, "Okay. What do you want me to do?"

"First, put your shirt back on." He glanced at the bright sun. "You'll get fried without it."

While I covered myself, he waited, then raised his arms, "You really need a loose-fitting long-sleeve white shirt like mine. But you'll just have to make do." Dusty took a red bandana out his back pocket, then placed it on my head. "Now put that Padres baseball cap on and let the rag hang down over the back of your neck. It'll protect your skin." He tapped the rim of his sombrero and softened his tone, "That's why I wear this."

I did as I was ordered and looked up for approval. "How's that?"

"Better...now let me see you breathe in and out."

I opened my mouth and inhaled the hot desert air. This made me even more thirsty.

Okay, Rick." Dusty placed his hands on my shoulders. "Out here, when we're trekking, keep your mouth closed and breath through your nose. No matter how tempting it is to lick your lips, don't do it. You'll have dry, cracked lips. It'll make you feel worse." He turned and started walking. "Come on. Let's get that water I promised you."

When we hiked to a rocky hillside, I noticed the sun was further to the west. As we climbed over some boulders, I asked, "What time is it?"

Dusty glanced at the sky, "Oh, about 3:00 or so. Almost there."

Minutes later, we knelt at a water hole below massive car-sized boulders and filled our canteens. While we sat down and drank, I scanned the gurgling flow of a spring along the rocks. Curious about its origin, I asked, "Where's the water coming from?"

"It's from an underground aquifer." He lifted his sombrero and let it dangle behind his neck from a string. "This land may seem empty at first. But when you look long enough, you'll see it's filled with plenty of life-giving sources to keep a man alive." He reached into the water, scooped out two-hands-full and splashed it on his face. "Ah, that's good."

I followed his lead. After taking several sips, I filled my canteen and scanned the rugged landscape. "Man, I don't know how you live out here. There's no way I could've found this water by myself."

Dusty looked up and smiled. "Like I said, it's my home. Got plenty of open space. Out here I'm free. Nobody's telling me what to do." He took off his shirt and splashed water on his chest. "Yep. After the Korean war was over, I needed to get away from all the madness of city life. Now I got what I need in the desert."

I noticed several scars running across his chest. "Did you get those wounds from the war?"

"Yep." Dusty put his shirt back on.

"What happened?"

He took a handful of water and slurped it. For a moment, he leaned against a boulder under the shade of an outcrop. He exhaled and said, "It ain't easy to talk about."

"Sorry, I shouldn't have asked."

Dusty tilted his head with a curious expression. "How old are you?"

"I'm 18. I'll be 19 next month."

"Well, looks like you're ripe and ready for the pickings." He shook his head and frowned.

"What do you mean?"

"Them damned war-mongers in Washington are looking for kids like you." Dusty folded his arms across his big chest and studied me. "Every generation, they send the next batch of boys out to get slaughtered in another war."

"You sound like my Dad. He was in the Navy during World War Two."

"Yep. Now it's your turn."

"I worry about getting drafted."

"All right, then." He let out a deep sigh. "You might as well know what it's like." He lifted his shirt. "See these scars?"

"Yeah."

"That's from hand to hand combat. It was kill or be killed. I survived. He didn't. After it was over, I looked at the knife in my enemy's chest. He was just kid. Not more than 18. I watched him gasping for his last breath with his wide eyes still staring at me." Dusty let out a deep sigh of regret and a tear streamed down his face. "I never want to harm another living soul again."

"Sorry, Dusty. I shouldn't have brought it up. That was stupid of me."

"It's okay. You need to understand what war is like before you get drafted into Vietnam." Dusty slung his backpack on, adjusted the straps and glanced at me. "Ready?"

"Yep."

"Okay...let's get to the highway and hitch a ride."

We hiked to the west along a rocky embankment, and I lowered the brim of my cap to cut out the sun's glare. Suddenly Dusty halted and said, "Hold it."

"What's wrong?"

3 SONORAN JACK

D usty looked to the south and pointed to a jagged ridge. "Ya see that?"

I turned and saw what appeared to be large birds circling overhead. "Yeah."

"Buzzard. Could be trouble. Come on."

We took off running and came to the edge of a dry, rock-strewn gulch. There, we spotted a man on the ground, and a mule was standing next to him with a full load of gear on its back.

As we got closer, Dusty halted in his tracks. "It's Sonoran Jack!" He ran over and knelt beside an old white-haired man with a shaggy beard. "What happened, Jack?" My friend lifted the fellow's head and cradled him in his arms.

The old guy's face was badly swollen and puffy. He blinked and gasped, "Got a snake bite!"

Dusty examined his cheek, just below the left eye. "Ah, Jack!" His voice cracked sorrowfully, "You look bad!"

Jack's lips were swollen but he tried to talk. "I just sat on a rock to rest a bit." He coughed. "When I put my hat back on. That's when a baby rattler slithered out and got me on my cheek!"

"Well, damn it, Jack!" Dusty was in tears and he sniffed. "You've been prospecting out here for over 20 years now... searching for silver and copper. How the hell did this happen?"

Jack coughed again. "I'm tired. Gettin old. I reckon I got careless."

I handed my canteen over, and Dusty put it to Jack's lips. "Here, take a sip."

Jack pushed it away. "Nah, don't bother!" He tried to open his puffy eyes and lifted his hand. "Say...do me a favor and get out a notepad and pen from my saddle bag. Write a note."

Dusty nodded to me, so I rummaged and found them. Since he

was holding Jack, I knelt and prepared with a pen in my hand.

"Write this down." Jack wearily tapped his finger on the pad. "Um…Dear Linda…sorry I left you when I did. Just remember I love you. Your far-away husband, Jack." He stopped and stared at the sky.

Dusty sighed and looked at his friend. "Damn it, Jack! You never told me you had a wife! Hell! You never even told me your last name!"

"It's Spencer." He wheezed and struggled to speak. "Linda's in Baltimore, I think."

While Dusty cradled Jack's head with his right arm, he reached over with his left hand, then abruptly ripped the paper off the pad, folded it and shoved in his shirt pocket. "Okay, Jack, I'll give it to the Sheriff, and he'll see that she gets it."

"There's a small bag of silver." He weakly tried to point to the saddle bag. "It ain't much. See that she gets it."

"All right."

"Dusty?"

"Yeah, Jack?"

Jack lifted his hand up. "I can't see your face."

Dusty gripped his palm. "I ain't much to look at anyway."

"Get out my bible in the saddle bag, will ya?"

I reached in, as the mule fidgeted. "Here, I found it."

"Who's that talkin there?"

"That's my buddy, Rick." Dusty nodded to me.

So, I leaned in closer. "Hi Jack."

He reached up and tried to shake my hand. "Glad to meet…"

A leathery palm dropped on his lap. He was dead with his eyes wide opened to the sky.

We buried ole Jack on a hill and piled rocks over his grave to discourage any scavengers, like coyotes. "This is a good spot with a nice view." Dusty pounded in a wooden cross with a shovel and scooped up stones, then patted them around it. When he was done, he said, "Well, that's it." He tied the tool back on Jack's mule and tightened the ropes.

With the bible in my hand, I glanced at the burial site. "What do we say about Jack?"

He stared at the mound and sighed, "This is my friend, Jack. He was a good, honest man. He loved this land." Dusty looked at me, "See what you can find in the book and read it."

I thumbed through the pages and stopped in Psalm 103. "Says here, 'As for man, his days are like grass; as a flower of the field, so he flourishes. When the wind has passed over it, it is no more.'" I paused as a cool breeze fluttered the pages. "'And its place acknowledges it no longer. But the lovingkindness of the Lord is everlasting.'"

That night, we decided to camp at the water hole, and Dusty said, "I'll guide you back to the highway in the mornin." He stood up and stretched his arms out. "You can hitch-hike from there." He handed me the note and bag of silver. "Give this to the Sheriff. Tell him what happened out here. Mention my name. He'll know how to handle it."

"What are you going to do?"

Dusty patted the mule's neck. "I'll look after this ole fella. Jack would've wanted it this way." He reached in the saddle bag and pulled out a can of beans and beef jerky. "Let's eat."

After we ate our meal, we rested on blankets that Jack had in his gear. As I leaned back and gazed at thousands of stars, I thought of the two days I'd been in the desert. Already I'd seen the body of a man who was murdered. Then I watched Sonoran Jack take his last breath. I glanced at my desert friend beside me. "Dusty?"

"Yeah?"

"What did you know about Jack?"

"Not much. We'd see each other whenever he'd drift in. We shared many a campfire over the years. Out here, a man doesn't talk about his past. Jack always said he'd strike it big someday, but he never did." My desert friend paused. "Oh, he'd find a small amount of silver and pay for his provisions, then be out again. Jack was on the move." Dusty waved a hand in the air, then added, "like the wind. He loved this land, though."

I sat up and looked at his red-bearded face all aglow from the light of the fire. "Dusty?"

"Yeah?"

"I worry about you. Do you ever get lonely out here?"

He sat up and stared at the stars. "Sometimes..." He paused like he was in deep thought. "I stay with the Tohono people for a few days. When I do, I bring some harvested sa-waro fruit and we share it all. We'll ferment it and drink together."

"Do you ever think of settling down and having a family"

"I had a wife in Nogales about eight years back." He paused again and let out a sigh. "She got real sick and was coughing up blood. Turned out she had cancer. Juanita died three months later."

Saddened by this, I looked over and said, "I'm so sorry." I didn't know what else to say.

"Don't be sorry, Rick. She was a good woman and she always made me smile. Every time Juanita looked at me, I'd melt. We were happily married for three of the best years of my life. I can still hear the way she giggled when I told a joke. I loved her so much." He patted his chest. "I'll always have those memories." He paused. "I have no regrets."

While I gazed into the night sky with all those bright stars, I thought about Dusty, the wild man of the desert. I could see that he was a deeply caring human being, who cherished all life.

At dawn, we packed our gear on Jack's mule and snuffed out the fire. Dusty held the reins, and I adjusted the strap of a canteen on my shoulder, then strolled alongside my friend.

"How long will it take to reach the highway?" I looked to the southwest and saw an endless desert.

"Couple hours or so." Dusty glanced at me. "If all goes well, you'll catch a quick ride and get off at Casa Grande. You can get in touch with the Sheriff there." He reached into a leather bag on the mule and pulled out a small paper bag. "Here take this."

"What is it?" I opened the sack and peeked inside at what appeared to be biscuits.

"Hardtack." He chuckled and said, "Ole Jack always kept a

stash. They're hard as a rock." He opened his mouth to reveal several gaps in his teeth. "As you can see, I'm better off without them. Try soaking them in water before you bite into one. At least you won't starve." He handed me Jack's backpack and bedroll. "Most likely you'll need these."

We walked on further, then Dusty glanced over. "Got any money?"

"Yep. Got plenty to reach my uncle's ranch north of Flagstaff. That's where I'll be working for the summer."

"Good," he said. "No need to worry about you then." He walked further, then added, "You'll be fine. Just remember some of the things I taught you."

I laughed. "You're starting to sound like my dad again."

"Yeah…it's becoming a bad habit of mine."

We continued to walk alongside the mule and listened to the steady clump, clump of its hooves over a rocky escarpment. I glanced at my friend and wondered more about his lifestyle. "Dusty?"

"Yeah?" He trekked on and looked ahead with a steady rhythm.

"I still don't understand how you make it out here. Do you ever need money?"

"I barter mostly." He kept walking. "Sometimes I find stuff out here and exchange it for food or whatever I need." His pace continued. "After I'm sure you safely get a ride, I'll have a look see at that burned out wreck and salvage a few pieces. I've learned to go with the flow of living out here."

When we finally reached the highway, I looked to my left and watched the passing cars in silence. I turned to my right and stared at the straight highway that disappeared over the horizon. For a moment, we just stood there knowing our journey together was over. We would have to say goodbye. It was strange. Although I'd only known my desert friend for a couple of days, it wasn't easy to leave. So much had happened during our short time together, I didn't know what to say. I adjusted my new backpack and hesitated.

After several minutes of standing beside the highway, he reached out and shook my hand. "Well, Rick, I'll take the mule and mosey on back a ways. Don't want to spook the drivers. I'll keep watch until you get a ride." He smiled. "Adios, my friend."

As he started to turn away, I had difficulty in just letting it go at that. "Uh…I have to ask you something."

"Yeah?"

"I just know you as Dusty…um…what's your full name?"

He rubbed the mule's forehead and hesitated.

"Come on, Dusty," I begged. "Once I get a ride out of here, we'll probably never see each other again." I waited as he continued to pat the pack animal. "I'm not leaving until you tell me."

"All right," he blurted out. "Ever since I was a kid, I hated my name." He groaned and shook his head. "It's Gunther P. Bartholomew."

Surprised by the sound of it, I nodded and started to repeat it, "Gun…"

"Don't," he interrupted and winced, "I can't stand it."

"Sorry…what's the P for?"

"Percy."

I paused and scanned the desert. "Well, Dusty suits you." I reached out and we shook hands again. "Now that I think of it, maybe I should have a nickname too."

"It'll come to you when the time is right." He waved a hand toward the highway. "Now go on. Get."

"Goodbye, Dusty." I stepped closer to the road, stuck out my thumb and didn't look back.

Moments later, a pick-up truck pulled over. An elderly woman rolled down the passenger side window, smiled and asked, "Where ya heading?"

"Casa Grande," I said.

"Hop in the back." She smiled.

"Thanks." I tossed my gear in the back and climbed aboard. While the truck sped away, I watched, as Dusty headed back into the wilderness with the mule at his side. That was the last I saw of my desert friend.

4 THUMPS UP

I sat in the bed of a dingy grey pickup truck. Behind the steering wheel was an elderly man, and a gray-haired woman sat quietly next to him. The driver wore a straw hat and rested his tanned left arm on the rolled-down window. I leaned against a wooden crate and took my cap off as the fresh air blew in my scruffy brown hair. Ah, this is the life of a hitchhiker, I thought. I'm as free as the wind. Nothing could be better.

In my mind, I heard my Mother's stern voice calling out to me, "Richard. You get in here right now."

I remembered the time when I was 10 years-old. I had been playing basketball with my friends on that summer night as we ran around in the white glare of a street light. Although I didn't want to go in, I knew that when Mom called out like that, she meant immediately or face Dad when he got home from work. Not that I had anything to fear or complain about. He was a great guy. Since I was the oldest of us four kids, I had to help Mom with the dishes.

Dad always said, "Son, you're the man of the house when I'm gone. I expect you to look after your two brothers and baby sister." Then he'd smile, place his hands on my shoulders and say, "Remember, son, I'm counting on you to keep everything ship-shape."

I'd nod and grin with respect and remembered that he was a battle-hardened Navy war vet from World War II and Korea. By the time I was 16, he had retired with the rank of Senior Chief Petty Officer. For a long time Dad wouldn't talk about his experiences until I turned 18.

Then one day he said, "Son, the military is drafting more young men to fight in Vietnam. "It's time you learn the facts about combat." He placed his hands on my shoulders and looked into my eyes. "If you get called up, you'll have to follow orders. Even when you think they make no sense. There's a lot of hurry up and wait. That's when you'll get bored stiff. In the heat of battle, fear will be your constant companion. Your buddy next to you could get his guts splattered all over you. It's hell. Do you understand?"

"Yes sir."

"I've seen the worst in humanity," he said. "Now it's your turn to face another war. In this case, we shouldn't be involved there in the first place. Hawks in Washington are making a terrible mistake and our young men are being slaughtered for no good reason."

Dad went on to tell me about facing death and losing his friends in combat. As he continued, I learned that a Kamikaze had hit his ship and it almost killed him. The only thing that saved him was that the blast had thrown him over board. His life vest kept him afloat for the next 16 hours until he was rescued by another destroyer.

After he told me, I thought hard about the fact that he almost died out there in the Pacific. That shook me up, as I realized that if the unthinkable tragedy happened, I would not have been born. Nor would any of my siblings. My dear mom would be left all alone—a lonely widow. Since he survived to raise our family, I was more grateful for each day of my young life.

Still, I was glad to be on this adventure. After my high school graduation, I was 18 and I didn't mind that I was bouncing along in the back of the pickup on a Sonoran Desert highway.

On each side of me, I observed the passing saguaro cacti, standing tall like sentinels. Rugged mountains edged toward the horizon, and reminded me of dinosaur bones. I noticed a small adobe house, and two cows in a corral. Along a river glistening in the sun, a tall man wearing a sombrero rode on on his brown horse. A woman hung clothes on a line while several dogs sat in the shade of mesquite trees. I wondered if they were members of the Tohono O'odham people that Dusty talked about.

With my hair blowing in the wind, I spotted a sign that said,

"Gila Bend Welcomes You."

I thought maybe I could call the police from there, but we passed right out of town in the blink of my eye. At first, I wondered why Dusty didn't mention the spot, and then I remembered he clearly stated that I should stop at Casa Grande. There, the Sheriff would know what to do. So, I relaxed and lowered the brim of my Padres baseball cap over my eyes and dozed off.

I awoke to a sudden jolt, then I realized that the pickup truck had pulled over at a dirt road. While a plume of dust swirled around the tail gate, I stood up to see what was going on.

"This is as far as we can take you, son." The elderly woman smiled through a rolled-down window. "Our ranch is down that a way." She pointed to the north.

I hopped out, slung my gear on my shoulders and stepped over to her side door. "Thanks for the lift," I said.

She smiled again, then reached in her purse and handed me some cash. "Here, young man. Get yourself some breakfast. Remember, God loves you, son."

"I appreciate that," I said. "But I already have enough money."

"Keep it anyway." She patted my arm. "Maybe you can give it to somebody else in need."

Admiring her generosity, I gladly accepted the five bucks. In that moment, she reminded me of how my mom was always helping strangers. "Thank you." I waved goodbye and listened to the slight grinding of the gears, while the old man drove away.

That frail woman's simple act of kindness along with my experience with Dusty, helped to restore my faith in the goodness of mankind. In fact, their compassion overshadowed the evil I had witnessed earlier.

Back on the main highway, I rode in the bed of a large truck loaded with a dozen migrant farm workers. No one said a word, but I still felt welcomed as I rubbed elbows with these hardworking people. While we bounced along, a smiling Mexican woman reached into a basket and passed out apples to the group. She wore a colorful red scarf under her straw hat and her brown wrinkled skin was aged by many years in the sun. After she made sure each person had fruit, she held up the last one and cut a slice with a pocket knife. With a warm smile, she handed it to me and gestured to eat it.

Moved by her simple act of kindness, I took the piece of apple and said, "Gracias." This was about all I knew of her language. I bit into the apple as we looked at each other in brief moments of her tender sharing. Gratefully, I savored the juices on my tongue and admired the joyful sparkle in her hazel eyes. Ancient lines crinkled on her face as she smiled again.

It wasn't long before the truck turned into a dirt road, and the driver stopped. A man sitting next to me nudged with his hot, sweaty arm and spoke in broken English, "You get off now."

I glanced at the woman and she nodded with her straw hat tilted back on her white hair flowing below her red scarf. She smiled warmly and pointed at the dirt road to let me know they were heading that way.

I leaped out with my bedroll still on my shoulder, then adjusted my backpack and waved. As the truck drove along the dirt road, dust swirled behind it. When it disappeared into a field, I was keenly aware of the silence. I adjusted my Padres baseball cap and tried to figure out my next move. It was beginning to get dark, but I noticed a slight orange glow to the west.

I stuck out my thumb and waited for another ride heading toward Casa Grande. An endless stream of cars and trucks whizzed by. No one stopped. In between the ebb and flow of traffic and blinding headlights, I remembered those quiet moments in the desert with Dusty. Through him I learned to relax in the solitude.

Another car passed. I heard the voices of little children giggling and laughing in their own backseat world of play. This sparked a flash of homesickness. For a brief moment, I missed the warmth of my close family.

An hour went by and the sun dipped below distant mountains. Cars sped on. Still, no one pulled over, and I began to wonder about this foolish idea of hitchhiking in the middle of nowhere.

Then in the darkness, bright headlights temporarily blinded my tired eyes. A Volkswagen bus pulled up and stopped about 50 feet ahead of me. Hopeful for a ride, I adjusted my bedroll and backpack, then I ran to it like a curious puppy. In the beams of passing cars, I saw a red peace symbol and pink flowers painted on the side. A door slid open with a loud thud.

"Hop in, man!" A long-haired guy about my age grinned and gestured with a hand, "Join the party!"

A plume of pot smoke billowed out. I peeked in and saw a half-dozen guys and girls in the back, all laughing and high while sprawled out on a mattress. I hesitated. A topless girl with perky young breasts leaned forward, smiled and beckoned, "Come, sit with me."

I sensed trouble. That's when I started to say no. But I didn't. Foolishly, I climbed aboard. Next thing I knew, hands were groping. Lit joints were being passed around like candy. Music on the radio burst in my ears, "Shout! Shout! Knock Yourself Out!"

A half-naked girl giggled and tried to hand me a joint. I said, no.

She said yes and snuggled closer. "Come on, relax. You're too uptight."

In the dim red overhead light, another topless girl with flowers in her auburn shoulder-length hair leaned over. She pressed her flesh against my chest and kissed my cheek. Weakened by youthful temptation, I held her in my arms.

"Oh, I like that," she said with a giggled. "We're getting low on pot." She groped to get into my back pocket. "You got cash?"

Realizing that I was about to get robbed, I pushed her away. "Hey, take it easy."

More hands groped from all directions. Everyone wanted what was in my wallet. Music blared; "Wipeout!" Ears bursting, I had to get out fast.

"Look out!" I shoved hard on the driver's seat in front of me. "There's a deer!"

Brakes slammed hard. The VW bus screeched to a dead halt. Kids flew forward. I ducked and caught myself on the front seat. "Get out!" I yelled. "We're on fire!" Girls screamed. Guys swore.

We all stumbled out on the roadside.

With everyone breathing heavily and looking nervously at each other, I paused. One doped-up shirtless dude stared and said, "Whoa! Far out, man!" Then I pointed at glaring oncoming headlights and yelled, "It's the cops!"

Suddenly the whole strung-out mob scampered back in the van like roaches running to hide in their dark crevices. Tires screeched, the engine backfired and the exhaust pipe farted in a black plume of smoke. I never saw a VW speed off that fast in my life!

After a good chuckle, I sighed, stared at thousands of twinkling stars in the sky and asked myself, "Now what?"

More headlights flashed in front of me. As cars sped on by, I turned and watched red tail lights seeming to mock my existence without any care of my well-being. Exhausted after three days of being away from the comforts of my loving home, I just wanted to lie down for a while.

I remembered Sonoran Jack's flashlight in the backpack, pulled it out and strolled into a field of desert scrub. With a beam shining, I looked for a place to rest and spotted a stripped-down wreck of a pickup truck. Scattered windshield glass crunched under my running shoes. All the wheels were gone and the engine was missing.

Weary, I tossed my bedroll into the truck bed and used my backpack as a headrest. Safely away from rattlesnakes, I laid back. I lowered the brim of my cap over my eyes and expected to drift into a peaceful slumber. Instead, I began to get chilled. The temperature dropped fast in the desert night. I rolled up tight in my bedroll but was restless from the cold air in the back of that old wreck. This was nothing like sleeping next to an open fire with Dusty by my side.

Somehow I finally fell asleep and dreamed of flying over fields, buildings, cars and people. At first, I'd be walking along a busy street, then I'd just take off and soar above the clouds. It was such a freeing sensation of being weightless and looking down at the world below. This seemed to be a recurring unconscious story that came to me often in my youth. It was my private world.

I awoke before dawn and sat up in the back of that wrecked truck. Famished, I rummaged through my gear and dug out some hardtack that Dusty gave me. I looked at it, then tapped the biscuit on the metal side. It clunked like a rock. So, I poured water over it, yanked with my teeth and slowly chewed on a piece. In those quiet moments before early light, I realized how grateful I was even for something this undesirable. After I ate one, I packed up and stood on the road again.

Soon, the sun began to peek above the eastern horizon, and the far-off Superstition Mountains were bathed in a pink summer glow. I eagerly waved my thumb. Two cars whizzed by. I waited. It seemed like no one cared. Desperate, I stepped out further, danced my own bizarre version of cha, cha, mashed potato and twist all rolled into a cry for help.

Being a young man of dreams, I imagined a red convertible would pull over, and a beautiful blonde with ruby lips and low neck line would greet me with a flirtatious smile. Instead, a clunky gray tow truck stopped just ahead of me.

Back to reality, I eagerly ran to the passenger side door. When I looked in, a big grizzly red, puffy-faced driver said, "Hop in."

I climbed aboard and shuffled my feet through a pile of trash on the floor. Without a word, he shoved the stick into first gear, and we were back on the highway. "Thanks," I said.

His fat hands gripped the wheel. A cigarette dangled from his mouth while ashes dropped in his lap. "Where ya headin?" he asked, then coughed. With a loud, gross hacking sound, he quickly rolled down his window, spat out a yucky, yellow gob and rolled up the glass.

"Casa Grande." I choked from the smoke and a strange lingering smell, like old gym socks. Several soda cans rolled against my feet.

"Me too." He nodded and more ashes splattered on his round belly.

Overwhelmed by the stench, I rolled down the window and

tried to breath outside air. It was hot but I didn't care.

Finally, he drove into Casa Grande. Relieved, I asked, "Where's the Sheriff's office?"

He pointed to my right. "Over there."

"Thanks, I'll get out here."

He pulled over, and I gladly got out. When the truck left, I inhaled deeply and blew out air, relieved that I finally made it.

For a moment, I looked across the street at a beige one-story building. I thought of the dead guy I found lying in a pool of blood and began to worry. How was I going to explain all that I'd been through since I left home? A bright sun glared in my eyes and the heat burned my skin as I stood on the sidewalk. It had to be over a 115 degrees at least.

Overwhelmed by the temperature and uneasy about going in to see the Sheriff right away, I strolled around the town. I came to a shaded sidewalk of the old Southern Pacific Railroad Depot, took several sips of water from my canteen and cooled off slightly. Relieved, I walked along the archways that provided a refreshing breeze on my sunbaked flesh.

This gave me time to think of the best way to tell my story. With my mind clear, I headed toward the Sheriff's office and wondered how the law would respond. I was about to find out.

5 KARMA

I lowered the brim of my cap to block the sun in my eyes. A sweaty shirt clung to my body. It was time to face the law and the unknown reception that awaited me behind closed doors. I ran across the street, stepped into the Sheriff's office and a cool breeze greeted me from two fans.

Behind a chest-high counter, a deputy wrote on a notepad while talking on the phone. I waited and stared at wanted posters on a dingy gray wall. One faded picture had a bald man with a broken nose and pock-marked face. Wanted for murder, it said. Reward, 1,000 pesos. Another showed a smiling, happy-go-lucky handsome pretty boy with a large X scribbled across the face. The word, "Deceased!" was stamped on his forehead. Amused by this, it reminded me of an old-western movie, and I thought this had to be a joke.

As I waited, I glanced at the deputy. He finally hung up the phone but still ignored me and continued to write something on a pad. Unable to hold it in any longer, I anxiously stepped forward and blurted out, "I'm here to report a murder!"

Immediately, he dropped his pencil and stared wide-eyed. "A what?"

"I found a guy dead at a gas station," I spat out the words, "then my car was stolen by the murderer and he tried to kill me and…"

"Hold on, boy!" The deputy interrupted and opened a side gate at the counter, "Get in here." He pointed to a wooden chair. "Sit down."

Another officer stepped out of a back office and asked, "What's going on Sam?"

"This kid's going on about a murder."

"Okay, I'll handle it." The tall man nodded. Then he smiled at me with a neat row of white teeth. His black handle-bar mustache wiggled like a caterpillar. "Come on in, young fella."

When I walked inside, he sat on the edge of his big oak desk and pointed to a chair. "Have a seat and tell me about it." His right leg dangled, as he leaned forward.

I sat down, glanced at the plaque beside him and saw his name, "Sheriff Bill Toliver." When I looked up, there was something about his sky-blue eyes that helped me to relax. It was like gazing into a tranquil mountain lake.

"Well, I was on my way to Flagstaff four days ago, when I stopped to get gas at a station just south of Kofa Wildlife Refuge. That's when I found the dead guy." I paused, as the Sheriff stood up and sauntered over to a water cooler.

He filled up a small paper cup and handed it to me. Realizing I was thirsty, I gulped it down. His friendly hospitality was nothing like I expected.

Then he calmly asked, "May I see your ID?"

"Yes sir." I took out my driver's license and handed it to him.

He studied it and read my name out loud, "Richard Thomson." He tilted his beige Stetson back on his forehead and handed the ID back to me. "So you're the one who left the note. We've been looking for you." He paused and studied me. "We were beginning to think you were dead, too."

"Yes sir, I tried to get here sooner, but I was kidnapped by the murderer. He stole my car, tried to kill me and left me to die in the desert."

"Well, by the looks of you, I can see that you've been through a lot out there, son." The Sheriff went over to his wooden office chair, sat and leaned back. He looked straight into my eyes. "Fortunately, that's all over now."

"What do you mean?"

"He's dead." The Sheriff folded his arms across a broad chest and sighed with a look of satisfaction. "Yep, you had a run in with an AWOL Army private by the name of James Willard. He slit his sergeant's throat and left him to bleed to death. When he took off, the Feds were hot on his trail. They wanted him real bad. Finally, they caught up with him near the Mexican border.

He was gunned down in a hail of bullets!" Toliver grinned, "Yep, I didn't have to lift a finger." His silver star glistened in the overhead light. "Hell, that saved the taxpayers a lot of money."

Relieved and surprised, I stood up and asked, "What about my car?"

He shook his head. "Sorry, son. In that shoot out, they hit the gas tank. There was a fire and explosion. Not much is left."

Shocked by the loss of my beloved red '56 Chevy, I plopped in the chair and groaned, "Ah, geez! I still got payments on it!"

The Sheriff's chair creaked as he stood up and squeezed my shoulder. "Sorry, young fella. I reckon it all happened fast. The Feds managed to drag Willard out before your car blew up, but he died of severe burns on the road a short time later."

I looked up. "Well, that's interesting."

"What's that?"

"That scum tried to set me on fire." I paused to think about it. "Then he winds up getting fried himself!"

"Some of them hippy folks call that karma, son. I reckon that about tells it like it is. Come on." He nodded. "After what you've been through, the least I can do is buy you lunch. We'll talk more."

We walked across the street to a place called, Taco Bandito and slid into a red-cushioned booth. "You hungry?" He leaned his elbows on the table. With his hands clasped just below his chin, he smiled again.

"Yep, I'm starving."

Later, while I chowed down on a massive beef burrito, I remembered how I survived with the help of my desert friend. Eagerly, I gulped, took a drink from my soda and wiped my fingers with a napkin. "Man, that's good! If a guy named Dusty hadn't saved me, I wouldn't be alive to enjoy this right now!"

Sheriff Toliver looked up as he was about to eat his taco and grinned. "You met ole Dusty?"

"You know him?" I asked.

"Yep. Out here, everybody knows Dusty." The Sheriff's eyes lit up and he laughed. "He's a legend. That man is the best damn tracker around these parts." He leaned forward with an enthusiastic grin. "He's saved so many people out there in the desert, I lost count."

"Oh." I pulled out the note and bag of silver from my back pack. "We found an old prospector named, Sonoran Jack. He died of a snakebite on his cheek. We buried him out there." I handed over the piece of paper. "Jack asked me to write this down before he passed away." I also set the bag on the table and waited to see his reaction. "I'm supposed to give this to you."

Sheriff Toliver read the note, glanced at the silver, shook his head and sighed. "Poor ole Jack. I warned him that he oughta give up his crazy prospecting while he had a chance." He glanced at the paper again. "I didn't even know he had a wife." Looking perplexed, he shoved it in his shirt pocket. "Now, how the hell am I supposed to find somebody named Linda, who may or may not live in New York?"

"That reminds me." I set the burrito down on my plate. "I need to call my parents. They're probably worried sick that I haven't contacted them."

"No problem." The Sheriff waved a hand in the air and smiled. "You can use a phone back at the station."

An hour later, I sat in the back of a Greyhound bus as it headed toward Phoenix. I was so weary from my ordeals that I lowered the baseball cap over my eyes and leaned back. While I rested, I thought of my call home. When I told Dad what happened, I was surprised that he handled the news so well. Mom didn't take it so lightly. She cried and insisted I head right back to the safety of our family and stop this nonsense.

I assured her that I would continue on to my uncle's ranch. "Come on, Mom," I pleaded. "It's my last chance at freedom before I either get drafted or join the Navy."

Fortunately, Dad backed me up and calmed her down. "He's right, honey. The Vietnam War is heating up."

While Mom cried in the background, I said, "Dad, just give me a few more days to get a feel for the land. Then I'll go to the ranch.

If I have to get into this crazy war, I need to know what I'm fighting for. Okay?"

"Alright, son," Dad agreed. "Just be careful out there."

While I thought of that phone call with my parents, I glanced around the bus. One pregnant woman, two rows in front of me, stood up and rubbed her belly. She stretched and sat down, while her toddler peeked over the seat. The girl had curly blond hair that was just below her little ears, and she stared at me curiously with big blue eyes. She smiled with two front baby teeth and rosy cheeks. I was smitten and waved. She giggled and wiggled her tiny fingers back at me. Such innocence was so pure, I soaked it all in my memory like a sponge.

"She's a cutie," said an Army corporal across the aisle from me. "She reminds me of my baby sister"

"Yeah, I was just thinking the same thing." I nodded. "Except my sister is going on 17."

He reached across the aisle and we shook hands. "My name's John." He smiled. "Everybody calls me Johnny."

"I'm Rick." I smiled back, and we made friendly eye contact. "I'm heading to my uncle's ranch north of Flagstaff. How about you?"

"Phoenix...going home to my family." A duffle bag was on the window-side seat, and it began to fall against him. He groaned. With his right hand, he reached awkwardly to push it back over but continued to struggle.

That's when I noticed that he had no left arm. I got up and grabbed the bag. "Here, let me help you." I shoved it back against the window and wondered if he got wounded in Nam.

He straightened himself in the seat and sighed. "The surgeon says I'll have phantom pain for a while." He rubbed his left side as though his arm was still there.

"Sorry, Johnny." I didn't know what else to say.

"Don't be." He smiled. I still got my good right arm." He reached into his shirt pocket and pulled out a piece of paper. "You want a good laugh?" Johnny handed me the note.

I took it and asked, "What it is?"

"Go on, read it for yourself." He leaned over and grinned as though I was about to see a good joke.

I unfolded the note and started reading it to myself. It said, "Dear John, I'm sorry, but I decided I don't want to get married when you get home. I don't mean to hurt you, but I found someone else. Debra."

"Ouch. That must've hurt." I winced and handed back to him.

He chuckled again and stared at me. "Don't you get it? I know guys in my platoon, who got their dear John letters." He chortled at his own sense of cynical humor. "Let's see...there was Mario, Billy and CJ. Man, this blows my mind. I'm the first dummy to get a dear John with the correct name." He leaned back in his seat and exhaled. "How's that for laughs?"

"Sorry, man."

"Don't be." He turned and looked at me. "I'll be home soon. Got my Mom, Dad and the whole family waiting for me at the bus depot."

"You seem to be taking this well."

"Sure...why not? I'm still alive. They can't send me back to that hell hole." He grinned. "Besides, I plan to get me an education on the GI bill. Maybe I'll become an accountant." He held up his right hand. "I can still use this. My chaplain says I oughta be grateful for what I've got. Right?"

I reached across the aisle and we shook hands again. "You're okay, Johnny. I like the way you hang loose, man."

For a moment, Johnny stared straight ahead as though he was in deep thought. Finally, he looked over with a serious expression. "Don't get me wrong, man. I'm still pissed." He paused and kept his gaze on me. "Truth is, I tried to kill myself when I was in the hospital." A male nurse stopped me from slitting my throat with a razor. That's how screwed up I got, man. Then the chaplain set my mind straight. He looked me right in the eyes and said something I'll never forget."

"What'd he say?" I asked.

"The padre squeezed my face in his hands real hard and asked, 'Is this how you want your family to remember you, son.' That shook me up. After that, I figured I'd better make the best of it. You know what I mean?"

"Well, I really don't know, Johnny." I tried to understand and intently studied his eyes. "I could get drafted any day. I'm scared as hell, man. What's it like over there?"

Johnny stared back at me with a stoic face. "Rick, all I can do is repeat the two words you just said. "Scared and hell, that's part of what it's like. There's a lot of waiting for something to happen. The not-knowing whether you'll be dead in the next split second can tear your guts out with fear and doubt." He leaned the right side of his face against the seat and sighed. "The rest you'll have to find out for yourself."

For the next half hour, we talked like old buddies. When the bus arrived in Phoenix, Johnny got up and struggled with his duffle bag.

I reached over and tried to help. "Here, let me give you a hand."

Johnny paused with a light-hearted grin. "Okay, you take the rear end." He gripped the sling along the side and started to walk with a limp.

I tried to hold the canvas bag under belly as best as I could with one hand, and together, we awkwardly squeezed through the narrow aisle and down the steps. "Geez...they need to put a handle on the butt end of this thing to make it easier."

"Make a report." He laughed and added, "Be sure it's in triplicate and send it to the Pentagon."

"Roger that."

"While you're at it, tell those damn generals to shoot straight. I've seen enough friendly fire to last a lifetime."

Just as we set the duffle bag on the ground, I heard a woman yelling out, "Johnny!"

Suddenly we were surrounded by his parents and a whole loving mob of kids, aunts and uncles. After all the hugs and kisses, Johnny looked over, as his mother still clung to him and smiled warmly. "Come on, Rick. You can stay at our place tonight."

"No thanks, Johnny. I think I'll go sightseeing and take another bus out later.

He reached out and we shook hands. "Okay, suit yourself." As he started to walk away with his family clinging to him, he glanced back and said, "Take care of yourself, Rick."

"You too, man." I watched him get into a car with his family, and they drove away. That was the last I saw of Johnny.

When I left the bus depot, I walked down the street and saw my reflection in a men's clothing store window. My scruffy brown hair was below my ears, and my skin looked grimy. I had three holes the size of dimes in my raunchy T-shirt, which now had a five-inch cut along the faded words, Pacific Beach across my chest. Another slice was on my right side where I got jabbed with a knife. It had been over three weeks since I last shaved after high school graduation, and the beginning of auburn whiskers shined in the bright sun. I thought, man, I look like a bum on the street. I took a whiff of myself and that did it. I had to get fresh clothes and a shower.

I went into that store and bought a new pair of jeans, two polo shirts, socks and underwear. When I paid the snooty gray-haired male clerk, I asked, "Where can I get a shower around here?"

"Across the street." He looked down through thick glasses with his chin tilted up. "Out the door. Go to your right about three blocks. There's a YMCA on the corner."

After I showered and changed into my new clothes, I looked into the mirror and was pleased. This was the first time I could actually grow whiskers, and I wasn't about to shave it off. All through high school, I worked 20 hours a week pumping gas and struggled to keep my grades up. I earned the right to have that beard, and no one was going to tell me otherwise. Except the military brass. They were nipping at my heels like a raging mad dog drooling to get more bodies in combat.

I strolled down the street with my bedroll and backpack slung over my left shoulder, ready to take on the world. Then, just as I turned the corner, I saw a beautiful sight. Immediately, I stopped and gawked at her. I could not believe my eyes. She was a Woody station wagon parked in front of a Woolworth store.

In awe, I stroked my right hand along the wood panels and admired a shiny green hood.

"Woody," I whispered to myself. I was in love and I examined every angle. Well, I lost my '56 Chevy. Now, I longed for a car with finely crafted wood panels. Ah, yeah...after this war madness is over, I could live along the beach and drive around in one just like this. The California girls would flock around me. I'd be the envy of all surfers everywhere. Not that I was great on a board. I just wanted a Woody.

I thought, what an easy name for people to remember--Woody. Immediately, it struck me. My nickname is now Woody. That's so cool! I chuckled and remembered how Dusty said it would come to me when I was ready for it. Cocky, I strolled down the street and could not wait to try it out on the first person I had a chance to meet.

I wandered around Phoenix for a couple of hours and my mood changed. I was overwhelmed with all the buildings and crowded streets. After I spent several days in desert solitude, the noise and fast pace was too much for me. Everywhere I turned, my ears ached from loud car horns, screeching tires and roaring truck engines echoing off tall buildings. All these structures held in the heat, and it felt worse than being in the desert with Dusty. Even the stench of sweltering asphalt and exhaust irritated my senses.

Desperate for relief, I searched for a place to cool off and get away from the hustle and bustle of a big city. It was so hot that my shoes burned right through to the soles of my tired feet. I had to get out of this madness. But where could I go?

6 GIRL ON THE RUN

I wiped the sweat from my brow and ducked under the shade of trees and awnings to get out of the heat. When I stepped into an ice cream shop, I ordered two scoops of chocolate on a cone. Half-way through the first scoop, I noticed a girl standing by the outside window. She nervously glanced around and appeared to be frightened about something.

Long raven hair flowed to the small of her back. Ruby lips and mysterious eyes accentuated her exotic Asian face. She wore a white blouse with a blue skirt that draped elegantly just above her knees. A gold heart-shaped locket nestled in the V of her neckline.

I stared with my cone still in my hand. Strangely, without even thinking, I pushed the door open and stepped outside. Less than 10 feet away, I observed the girl, who was about my age.

She turned toward me, and our eyes met. At first, I thought she would dart away and hide. Yet, she gazed back at me. She looked sad and scared.

"Um." I stepped closer with sticky, melted ice cream dribbling and dropping tiny puddles of chocolate on the hot sidewalk. I blurted out, "Hi."

She glanced around nervously, then looked at me again. "Hi," she said in a breathy voice. Her sadness was obvious, though, and this worried me. I had no idea why since she was someone I had never seen before. She adjusted the long strap of a brown leather purse on her right shoulder. A yellow tote bag hung from her other side. Her breathing was heavy as though she had been running.

"Would you like some ice cream?" asked stupid me with sticky fingers that held a cone without the scoop.

The girl glanced at my messy hand, giggled and looked at me.

"No thanks." I expected her to turn away and that would be the end of it. Instead, she kept her gaze steady.

Embarrassed, I realized my foolishness and tried to compensate for my clumsiness. "Oh," I chuckled and quickly tossed the cone in a nearby trashcan. "I mean...I'd like to buy you an ice cream, if that's okay."

The girl cocked her head. "Why?"

Feeling like a complete idiot, I tried to wipe my sticky fingers with a thin napkin. "Well, I just thought you might like to have something cool."

"I never heard a pickup line like this before." She studied my awkward expression and glanced around as though she was prepared to run. To my surprise, she said, "Okay."

Relieved, I gripped the door handle with my icky hand, and we stepped in the cool air conditioned-shop. When we stood at the counter, I asked, "What flavor do you like?"

She had been looking toward the door as though she expected someone. Then she turned and said to the soda jerk, "Strawberry...two scoops, please."

Since I already had ice cream, I nodded to him and said, "I'll have a root beer."

While a young freckle-faced kid prepared our cool delights, I noticed that the girl moved to my side and away from the entrance. When he handed our treats to us, she turned and pointed to a spot in the back. "Let's go sit over there."

Deep in the corner, there were no windows. Immediately, she slid into the vinyl bench that faced toward the front, and I sat opposite of her in the booth. Once we were settled, she handed her cone to me and whispered, "Hold this for me, please."

As I sat with her ice cream in my hand, I watched her rummaging through a small yellow tote bag. She pulled out a red paisley bandana, gracefully adorned her hair with it and tied the ends under her chin. "Okay," she reached up and said, "I'm ready." She mysteriously leaned to my side and glanced toward the entrance again.

Although this seemed odd, I was in awe of her every subtle gesture, and I placed the cone in her slender fingers. I watched her slowly, gracefully licking the ice cream. Her tongue had a red tint, while she savored it in a way that I had never seen before. Enchanted, I felt like I did on my first date with a girl back in the eighth grade. I slurped root beer from a straw and I wondered why she looked so sad, and yet, she had a poise about her every move.

"My name's Woody." There, I said my new nickname for the first time, and I was proud of the cool sound of it. "What's yours?"

With her eyes still focused on her ice cream, she licked, daintily, daubed her lips with a napkin and said, "Asia."

Wow, I thought. Her name sounded so exotic, and it reminded me of all the far-off places I wanted to explore. I daydreamed of places like Japan, Korea, India...on and on. I saw myself climbing the Himalayas or backpacking into the jungles of Borneo, all in a long pause. I was lost in my own fantastic adventures.

"Earth to Woody?"

I snapped back to the present. "What?"

Asia laughed. "I asked you a question. You didn't hear a word I said, did you?"

"Oh." I shrugged like it was no big deal. "I was just thinking about your name, Asia." I sighed and gazed into her eyes. "That's unusual, but I like it." Then, I boldly asked, "Where were you born?"

Asia shook her head and giggled. "Now you're asking me a question." She seemed to look right through me. "Okay, you really want to know, so I'll tell you. I was born her in Phoenix." Now you answer my question. Do you live near here?" She glanced over my shoulder toward the door again.

I shrugged and waved my hand up. "Nah, I'm a wanderer. I go wherever I please." I was surprised that I came up with it like I didn't have a care in the world. Wanting to impress this fascinating girl, I had no intention of saying I planned to work at my uncle's ranch north of Flagstaff.

Asia peeked over my shoulder again and exhaled. She seemed

to be in deep thought about something, and she had a strange worried expression. Her ice cream cone had been eaten to within an inch of her delicate fingers but she ignored it. Then she lowered her gaze, winced and rubbed her lower back. Deeply touched by her troubled manner, I wanted to understand and tried to think of something to say.

Finally, I leaned forward, "Something is bothering you. I'd like to help, if I can?"

She looked up with red, moist eyes and feigned a smile of assurance. "I'm fine."

"You didn't finish your ice cream."

"Oh." She scooted her chair back, walked several paces to a trashcan and dumped her left-over cone, then returned to our table. "I'm not hungry." Asia sat down again and wrapped her arms tight across her chest, peeked around my left side and glanced at the entrance again.

"Are you expecting someone?"

Instead of answering my question, she pulled the strap of her purse on her shoulder and stepped away from the table. Worried that I would never see her again, I stood up. "What's wrong?"

"Nothing." She took her tote bag and turned away. "I'll be right back." She walked over to a restroom, went inside and closed the door.

Hoping I still had a chance to learn more about this mysterious girl, I sipped from my straw and waited. Eagerly I glanced at my watch. It was 2:06. By 2:25, I stared at the empty cup. Why was she taking so long? Was there a way for her to sneak out? Would I ever see her again?

Finally, Asia came out, and I noticed that she had changed into tan capris. She wore a white scoop-necked blouse with red flowery designs, and her long raven hair was in a pony tail. The gold locket still elegantly graced her smooth creamy flesh. She looked toward the door, quickly slid into the seat and exhaled as though she had been holding her breath.

"Um, you look nice." Unsure of what else to say, I studied her moist eyes. "Is everything okay?"

"Yes, I'm fine."

"I'm glad." For a moment, we gazed at each other. "Asia, I'm worried about you. Is there anything I can do to help?"

"Yes." she inhaled deeply. After a brief pause, she puffed out air. "I have to get out of here!" She took out a yellow wide-brimmed floppy hat and tucked her pony tail under it. "Let's go together!" She put on sunglasses. "Okay?"

"Sure." Just as that word flew out of my mouth, I thought, what am I getting into? I don't even know this girl.

For the next two hours, we casually strolled around an indoor mall to get out of the heat. All the while, she held my arm, and I liked the intimate feel of it. "You thirsty?" I asked.

Asia smiled. "Yes, I'm hungry, too."

"Okay, we can get something over there." I pointed to a small fast-food place across the street.

We each ordered cheeseburgers, fries and two large root beers. As we sat at a booth, I watched Asia while she slowly unwrapped one as though she was opening a present and wanted to take her time on every detail. She reached to the side and took a plastic mustard bottle, and with slight artistic flair, she squirted yellow lines in circles on a slab of beef. Then she did something completely unexpected. She bowed her head in silence for a few seconds, looked up and asked, "Aren't you going to eat?"

"Uh, sure." I was so taken by her subtle, graceful moves that I forgot to unwrap my burger. So, being the ravenous young man that I was, I dove in, took large bites of beef and chewed massive pieces with my cheeks bulging.

Asia giggled, and her eyes widened. "Wow. You are hungry." She reached over with a napkin and daubed a streak of mustard from the side of my mouth and whiskers. "You're a mess."

Embarrassed, I tried to act like I knew exactly what I was doing as a macho guy. "Well, I make sure I fill up before I head out."

Asia became serious again. "So, where are we going?"

Since I always liked to put on a little show to act like I was cool, I slid out the straw from my drink with a funny squeaking sound and held it up. "See this?"

Asia leaned her elbow on the table, rested her cheek in her palm and sighed with a bored expression. "Okay. Is this supposed to impress me?"

"You'll see." I bent one end about an inch down and laid the straw on the table. "Now, I'll spin this around and we'll go in the direction of this half-arrow point." I flicked the straight end, but it shot right off the surface and landed on the floor. "Uh, that didn't go the way I planned." I started to pick it up, but Asia tapped my arm.

"Forget it," she said with a smug look. She slid the straw out of her cup. "Okay, let's give it a girl's touch." She bent one end, set the straw down and slowly waved her hand over it like she was doing a magic trick. She looked up with an air of superiority and said, "Now, watch and learn." With a delicate, slender finger that had purple polish on the nail, she tapped the straw. It spun around, then stopped. "Looks like we go that way." She pointed over her shoulder.

Impressed with her style, I laughed and forgot all about my pride. "Okay." I smiled. "We head north." I decided to stop clowning around and tell her my real travel plan. "Truth is, I'm going up to Flagstaff anyway. I plan to work on my uncle's ranch for the summer. Maybe we can hang out together."

She didn't respond. Instead, she kept looking out the window.

"Asia, I know we just met, but something is bothering you. Do you want to talk about it? Maybe I can help."

"Not now. Maybe later." She scooted her chair back, stood up, winced in pain and rubbed her lower back. "I need to wash my hands. I'll be right back."

Moments later, Asia returned to our table and asked, "Do you want to catch a bus to Flagstaff?"

"Sure, that's what I planned anyway."

"I'm coming with you." She turned and headed toward the door. "Hurry."

"Okay." I stood up and noticed that she left a half-eaten burger on a napkin. "Aren't you going to finish eating?"

She glanced over her shoulder and said, "I'm not hungry. Come on."

I shrugged, picked up what was left of the burger and held it in my right hand. "Suit yourself." While I strolled out, I took several bites and chewed without hesitation. Since I had no idea when or where the next meal would come from, I devoured it.

When we walked over to the bus depot, suddenly Asia gasped. She grabbed my right arm and looked terrified as she stared into a crowd of people.

"What's wrong?"

She pulled my arm and whispered, "Let's get out of here!"

"Not until you tell me what's going on."

"I can't." She turned and darted through the crowd.

I ran and caught up with her. Unsure of what to make of this, I took her hand and we kept running down the street. Finally, we stopped under the shade of a store-front awning three blocks away. Asia was trying to catch her breath while looking back as though someone was following us.

"It's okay, Asia." I put my hand on her shoulder and tried to calm her down. "Something scared you back there. What was it?"

"I saw him!" Her eyes were wide with fear.

"Who?"

Asia squeezed my hand and said, "Please, Woody. I'll tell you later. It's too dangerous! We have to get out of town!"

Confused, I said, "That's why we were at the bus depot."

"No, we can't now." Asia pleaded with her eyes. "We have to find another way out. He's waiting back there."

"Who is?"

Asia glanced down the street again. "I'll explain later."

Seeing her frightened expression, I nodded. "All right. I must be crazy, but how can I help you?"

"Get me out of town."

She looked so desperate, I decided to take a chance. "Come on."

I held onto Asia's hand. We ran to the main highway and stopped at a busy intersection.

"Now what?" Asia breathed heavily and looked at the traffic.

"We hitch a ride." I smiled at passing drivers and wagged my thumb back and forth.

A four-door black sedan pulled alongside, and we eagerly ran to the passenger side door. A man in his mid-twenties was at the wheel and a woman sat next to him.

Bright sunlight glistened in her short auburn hair as she smiled through the opened window. "We're on our way to Flagstaff," she said and nodded to the back seat. "Hop in."

"Thanks." I opened the back door and liked her friendly demeanor.

When Asia scooted in, the driver turned and looked at her. "Wait!" he spoke with a gruff voice. "Hold on there! I don't want no slant-eyed girl in my car!"

"Honey!" The woman glared at the man in shock. "What is wrong you?"

He puffed out air and pointed his finger in Asia's face. "I didn't fight in Nam to put up with that kind of breed!"

"Larry!" The woman glanced at Asia and glared back at him again. "She's not your enemy. You're acting crazy!"

He groaned and rubbed his forehead. "Now I've got a splitting headache again." His watery eyes turned red with hate. "Get that gook out of my car! Now!"

Stunned, I opened the door and grabbed Asia's hand. "Come on."

We barely got out when the car sped off and left us choking in a black plume of smoke alongside the road. Traffic whizzed by. Tears streamed down Asia's face, and I put my arm on her shoulder.

I glanced to my right. "There's a park over there. Let's go." We walked over to a bench hidden from the highway by trees. Just as we sat, Asia broke down and sobbed in my arms. All I could do was hold her. I had no idea how to handle this strange situation.

"It's okay, now. That guy was just crazy." I brushed back

strands of hair away from her damp face.

Asia sighed, rummaged through her purse and pulled out some tissues. "I should be used to it by now." She daubed her eyes and said, "Some people are so full of hate. I just can't get over it."

Surprised, I asked, "You've been through this before?"

"Of course." Asia lowered her gaze to the dirt at her feet. "Many times! That's because I look different from most round-eyed white people." Her voice was like a whisper that seemed to vaporize into the hot Arizona heat. "My mother was Okinawan and her ancestors were a mixed race with the Chinese. She was not pure Japanese and my Dad was an American Marine."

Confused by this, I asked, "Why would that make a difference?"

Asia let out a deep sigh. "Okay. How can I make it clear to you?" She focused sincerely into my eyes. "I lied to you, Woody. I wasn't born in Phoenix."

"That's all right." I smiled and tried to comfort her. "I haven't been completely honest with you either. My real name is Rick Thomson but I decided it would be fun to be called Woody. I think it's cool for a guy to have a nickname. Don't you?"

She giggled, wiped her tears and sniffled. "I like the sound of Woody." She kissed my cheek. "You know something, Woody?"

"What's that?"

"Although we've just met a few hours ago, I feel safe with you. You're not like other guys I've met."

"Well, as soon as I saw you, I worried that you were in trouble. I wanted to help in some way."

"I know." She kissed my cheek again. "I feel that I can be completely open with you, Woody. So, here it is. I was born on the island of Okinawa when my father was stationed there after the war. Villagers rejected my mother for getting pregnant by an American service man."

I looked into her sad eyes and listened.

"My father brought us to the states when I was two. By the time I was in first grade, I noticed that my mother and I were treated differently. We were not accepted by most people in his home town of Charleston, South Carolina." Asia daubed her eyes. "It was very painful for her. I wasn't Japanese, nor an American. Instead I was labeled Amerasian. A half-breed."

"I'm sorry you had to go through that, Asia."

"About six months ago, my mother was diagnosed with lung cancer." Asia looked up at the azure sky and cried softly. "Oh, I prayed so hard that she would get better but she got worse. It was terminal. She only had a short time to live." Asia took off her floppy hat, and a subtle breeze fluttered hair in her face.

I gently brushed the silky strands away from her eyes with my hand. "If there's anything I can do, I'd like to help."

"Thanks." She wiped tears away from her cheeks with a tissue. "I have to get this out, Woody. If I don't talk to someone, I'll burst." She gazed into my eyes again. "You're the only one I can talk to."

Overwhelmed with her sorrow, I wanted so much to help her. Yet, all I could say was, "Okay." My voice cracked.

"The doctor suggested that we move to a warm, dry climate so my mother could breathe easier. We moved to Phoenix, and I took care of her when I got home from school. Although she was weak, she was there for my graduation. But the next day, she was rushed to the hospital and died that night. I went numb. I couldn't believe it."

Hearing her words, I didn't know what to say. Instead, I listened in silence.

Asia looked into my eyes and exhaled. "Ever since I can remember, my dad drank a lot. He'd get mean and slap us sometimes. When she died, he got worse. Every night, he just sat there on his favorite lounge chair and listened to sad Blues records over and over until he passed out drunk."

For a moment, Asia said nothing, and it seemed like she held her breath. Then, suddenly, she gasped for air. "Oh, Woody!" She leaned her head on my shoulder and sobbed in my arms. This was extremely difficult for me but I held her tight. Finally, she calmed down, sniffled and wiped the tears away again. "I...I have to tell you one more thing. Okay?"

"All right." Uneasy, I braced myself for more drama.

"After my mother died, our neighbor, Robert came over to check on my dad, who continued in his drunken stupor. At first, I was glad that he stopped by every day this past week. But then, he kept staring at me and became obsessive about my every move. He followed me everywhere and even lurked outside the house."

Not liking the sound of this, I said, "Asia, you don't have to say anymore."

"Please, Woody." Her voice was firm, "I need to get this out!"

"Okay."

"This morning I woke and heard a noise. I looked up and saw Robert standing by the bed. He got on top of me. He was so strong, but I fought back. I couldn't get him off me, so I grabbed the clock on the lampstand. I hit him on the side of his head. He fell onto the floor."

Asia stared wide-eyed. "At first, he didn't move. I got up and tried to call the police but the phone cord had been cut. I grabbed my purse and tote bag and started to run but he grabbed my arm. He kept beating my lower back with a clothes hanger. It hurt so bad! Finally, he stopped and said that no one would see the bruises there. I was to be his slave! I kicked him in the groin and hit him over the head with my tote bag. While that creep moaned on the floor, I ran to my dad's room. He was face down on the bed. I shook his arm to wake him up but he was still drunk and unconscious."

"Asia, I..."

"I heard footsteps," she interrupted. "He came at me with a knife and yelled, 'I'll kill you!' I pushed a lamp on the floor! He tripped over it! I ran out of the house and kept running until I stopped at the ice cream shop to catch my breath!" Asia lost control and sobbed in my arms again.

I stroked her soft black hair. "It's okay. Your safe now."

Asia lifted her head and gazed into my eyes. "Oh, Woody! When I first saw you, I don't know why, but I felt you were there to help me."

Her words surprised me. I didn't know what to say. I was no hero. I wanted to console this sad girl, but I was getting way over my head.

"I saw him at the bus station," she blurted out. "He had to be looking for me there! He swore he'd kill me! Oh, Woody! You 're the only one I can trust. Please help me."

Realizing how dangerous this was becoming, I gently placed my palm on her cheek and tried to calm her down again. "Asia, we need to get the police involved."

Her eyes widened in terror. "No!" She leaned in and wrapped her arms tight around me. "I'm scared, Woody!"

"Asia..." I gently released her grip and faced her. "Look at me."

She tried to focus with red, watery eyes.

"We have to call the police. Do you understand?"

She exhaled and nodded.

"Alright." I took her hand.

When she tried to stand up, she winced and rubbed her lower back. "Oh."

"Are you okay?" I turned and looked. "Is that where he hit you?"

"Yes," she said as tears streamed down her cheeks. "I'll be alright."

Sickened to think that a man had hurt this sweet girl, I gently squeezed her hand. "Let's get some help."

When we walked back to the highway, a heavy flow of traffic streamed by. The sun was setting low to the west. I looked down the street and noticed a gas station a few blocks to the north. "Maybe there's a phone booth over there." I pointed in that direction.

Suddenly, Asia grabbed my arm. "Woody!"

I turned and she pointed to the other side of the road. "It's him!" She was shaking and terrified.

"Where?" I looked at dozens of people walking along the side walk.

"That big guy in the brown shirt!"

Just as she spoke, I spotted a large muscular man looking right at us. Cars whizzed by. He darted through traffic and headed right at us. We had no time to think. He came closer!

Asia screamed. I swore. He was coming at us fast! We darted back into the field, down a side street and through a long alley. I knocked over one metal trash can after another with loud clanging, hoping the noise would draw attention. Dogs barked. I held onto Asia's hand. I wasn't about to let go.

Still, no one came out to see what was going on. Finally, after running through side streets, I halted and peeked around a vacant building. I saw him climbing over a fence with a knife still in his hand and heading toward us.

I looked at Asia, "You okay?"

She breathed heavily but nodded. "Let's go!"

We held each other by the hand and continued our mad dash through an endless maze of streets and alleys. All I thought about was to get as far away as possible. With just one look at that guy, I knew he was more trouble than I could handle. Adrenaline pumping through my veins, I sensed we were on our own. We had to get help. But where?

7 HIDING OUT

W e ran and hid behind one building after another. Off to the west, the sun dipped below a ridge. Just when I stopped to catch my breath, that big crazy guy darted around a corner. He spotted us.

"Geez!" I grabbed Asia's hand, "He's like a rabid dog nipping at our heels!" We took off again.

Why was this guy so dead-set on catching us? I had no time to think. Soon, the heat of day gave way to coolness of night. Finally, we lost sight of him as we came upon an empty school field. Closed for the summer, it was the perfect place to hide.

Weary, Asia plopped on cool grass far out in center field. "Now what?"

"We rest here." I sat beside her and looked around. "It's dark. No one can see us from the street lights out there." I pointed to the perimeters. "We have a clear view. To the east, I scanned dimly-lit campus buildings. "We'll be safe in this spot."

I spread my bedroll on the grass, and we laid side by side. Bright stars twinkled above the field, far away from street lights. The air was chilly, and I covered us with another blanket as we snuggled to keep warm. She was quiet until I heard crying.

I lifted my head and tried to see her in the darkness. "What's wrong?"

"I miss my mother. Why did she have to die?"

I held her close, and she cried in my arms. Overwhelmed with her grief, I had no words to comfort her. Exhausted, she drifted off to sleep. I didn't want to move and awaken her. Gradually, my arm became numb, so I slid out and let her rest.

On high alert, I stood up with hands firmly planted on my hips and scanned the darkened field. Shivering, I walked around to keep warm. I thought of the irony and whispered to myself, "Oh look at me standing like a sentry. What a fool. I could get drafted and wind up in Vietnam. Now here I am scared like I'm already at war."

I scanned the perimeters of that field and tried to spot my unseen enemy, then my weary mind began to tell stories. What if that madman sneaks in while I'm asleep? How would I defend myself and protect Asia? I had no weapons and no military training to fall back on. Deeply troubled with my overactive imagination, I paced like a frightened deer cornered by a hunter. "Okay, that's it," I whispered to myself. "I'm calling the cops in the morning."

I remembered the wounded Corporal I met on the bus. I asked, "What's it like in combat?"

Johnny looked at me and said, 'The not-knowing whether you'll be dead in the next split second can tear your guts out with fear and doubt.' I dwelled on his words and shivered from a cool breeze.

"Woody!" Asia called out to me in the darkness.

I ran and knelt beside her. "What's wrong?"

She reached out and pulled me to her. "Oh, Woody, I had a dream about my mom. She looked so cold." Asia shivered in my arms. "When I awoke, I couldn't find you."

"It's okay," I whispered and snuggled under the blanket with her. "Go back to sleep. I'm not going anywhere."

I awoke to the glare of a rising sun and shaded my eyes with the bill of my cap. Next to me, Asia stirred and sat up. For a moment, she paused and rubbed her lower back.

I rolled over and looked at her. "Do you still feel sore?"

"Yes." She lifted her blouse a few inches from her waist. "This is where he beat me with a hanger. Can you look at it for me?"

I examined half-dozen red welts that were about six inches long. "Well, at least it didn't break the skin. You need something to soothe it, though." I remembered how Dusty used honey on my wound, and I rummaged through the pack he gave me. "This should do the trick." I opened a small tin can.

"What is it?"

"Honey." I scooped out a small amount with my fingers. "This is a great healing agent." I rubbed it on the welts of her back, then lowered her blouse. "How's that?"

"Feels good." She felt the back of her blouse "It's sticky, though."

"Yep," I licked my fingers. "Tastes good, too."

"Okay, Mr. Gooey," she said with a slight giggle in her voice and laid on her side. "I think I'll rest a little longer." She curled into a fetal position and covered herself with the blanket again.

While she faced away from me, I looked for a place to relieve myself. Great, I thought. There I was in the middle of a grassy field with no place to go. Off to my left, I spotted a grove of trees along the fence line and hidden from traffic. "I'll be right back," I said.

I hid behind a tree as best as I could. Relieved, I ran back, just as Asia stood up. "How are you doing?" I asked.

She shivered, grabbed her pack and stood up. "I need to find a restroom."

"Uh, you can go behind some trees over there." I pointed toward the fence, but my arm lowered as I realized how dumb that sounded.

"Well, that might be fine for a guy, but a girl needs a lot more privacy." She quickly turned and walked fast toward a coffee shop across the street.

I grabbed my gear and met up with her. While we entered the cafe, Asia rushed into a restroom, and I looked around for a safe place to sit. Worried that the madman could spot us from the front windows, I turned and noticed a better location outside.

When Asia came over to where I was standing, I nodded to a patio in the back and said, "Let's have breakfast out there."

She smiled and seemed happier as we opened the door and stepped into a fenced-in secluded area. It had six round metal tables under the shade of large green umbrellas. We scooted two chairs and sat down while the steel legs scratched loudly on the concrete surface.

A waitress came out with glasses of ice water and placed them on the table. "Hi. I'm Tina," she said with a friendly smile. "I'll be right back with some menus."

As Tina left, I looked at Asia. "Do you feel any better?"

"Yeah, now I'm hungry."

Tina quickly returned and said, "Here you go." She placed a menu down for each of us, paused and smiled again. "I'll give you a few minutes to decide."

After Tina went back inside, I sipped from a glass of water. "Ah, this is just what I need. "The sun is coming up and it's already getting hotter."

"Yeah, I might as well start cooling off now." Asia pulled out a cube of ice with her slender fingers, then slowly rubbed it along her forehead, face and neck. Luscious streams of water flowed down her smooth creamy flesh and dribbled along her arms. "Oh, that feels so good." She giggled, and was more animated. "You should try it, Woody." She flicked the droplets at me.

"Hey!" I laughed and was glad to see her playfulness. I wanted to savor this brief moment without all the sadness and fear. "You're supposed to drink the water, not bathe in it."

For the first time since we met, we both had a good laugh together. It was like all the tension just fizzled right out us and a sense of relief took over.

Tina came back out with a pad and pencil, then stood beside the table. "What can I get you?" she asked with a pleasant smile.

Asia focused on the menu and looked at me. "I think I know what I want. What about you?"

"Yep." I glanced at Tina and nodded. "I'll have bacon, eggs, sausage and two slices of toast. Oh, and bring lots of coffee."

Asia set the menu down and said, "I'll have a bowl of oatmeal, a fruit plate and orange juice."

"Okay." Tina smiled. "I'll come back with your order soon."

When our waitress left, I wanted to keep things loose and said to Asia, "That's not a real breakfast." I tossed a wadded-up paper napkin. It landed in her lap.

"Oh, yeah." Asia picked up the wad and threw it back. It

bounced off my nose. She laughed and said, "Don't knock it until you try it. It's good for your digestion."

We continued to relax and tell silly jokes to each other. It was like we needed this time to release the tension that built up over some crazy guy out to get us. Tina brought our breakfast and left.

While we ate, I slowly sipped my black coffee and said, "Ah, that's good." I tilted my head back and laughed.

"What's so funny?" Asia giggled as she looked up from her cup of hot tea and smiled.

"Oh, I was just thinking of how my Mom would not let me drink coffee. She'd say, 'son, you're too young to have that.' Dad, on the other hand, always came to my defense and say, 'it's okay, honey, he's 18 now.'" I laughed at the memory. "Of course, mom had the last word. So, I never had it until this morning."

"Well, that's not a big deal, compared to my experience. My parents tried to erase anything that had to do with my Japanese heritage so I would fit in better." Asia leaned back, smiled and was more at ease. "When I was brought to America, my father, changed my birth name of Sakura to Linda. I was only allowed to speak English, and I had to forget everything about my country of origin."

"That must've been confusing."

"Yeah, for a long time, I tried to figure out who I was...then I decided that if I'm not Japanese, Chinese or American, I must be Amerasian." She shrugged and held up her opened palms to announce, "So, after my mother died, I changed my name to Asia." She leaned forward and grinned with satisfaction. "You like it?"

Since Asia was still in a good mood, I teased, "Well, compared to Linda, I like it a lot. Besides, the only Linda I know has buck teeth, big ears and short curly, red hair."

"Okay then, you are Woody. I am Asia." She playfully waved a hand in the air. "We are free spirits."

"Yep." I laughed. "We'll drift in the wind." In the back of my mind, I thought how silly that sounded. Somewhere nearby, a crazy guy may be hunting for us with a sharp knife and a clear in-tent to kill.

Asia leaned closer, smiled and had a twinkle in her eye, "Okay, my kindred free spirit, where do we go next?"

"Kindred?" I decided to play dumb, "Oh, sure we're kind to each other, right?"

"No, dummy." Asia laughed, cocked her head and looked at me in surprise. "It means we're like-minded, and we connect with each other. What planet did you go to school on, anyway?"

Enjoying her cheerful teasing, I said, "Earth, I think. But when I was in class, I daydreamed about all the adventures I was going to have as an adult. I must've missed a few facts."

"Not me." She slouched and rested her head on the back of the chair like she had all the time in the world and sighed.

Seeing Asia relax more, I realized how tired I was, yawned and rubbed my eyes.

The sun glared slightly at an angle and she squinted, reached in her pack, pulled out sunglasses and put them on.

"Cool," I grinned. "You look like a famous Hollywood star."

"Oh, yeah? Who?"

Seeing her smile, I didn't want these happy moments to end. I had to come up with something real silly to make her laugh. "Uh, let's see." I tilted my cap on my head and scratched my chin whiskers for maximum effect. I snapped my fingers, "I know! Minnie Mouse!"

"What!" Asia burst out laughing, wadded a napkin in her fingers, threw it and bounced it off my forehead. From there, it landed right into my glass of water. This made her laugh even more. "Minnie Mouse!"

"Yeah, except you don't have big ears."

"Well, that explains everything. You like to watch cartoons."

"I can't avoid it," I said with a light-hearted chuckle.

"Why is that?"

"My kid brothers are glued to the boob tube." I made a wide-eyed, goofy expression. "They look like this every time I walk into the living room."

"Well." She giggled. "I wouldn't know about that." She adjusted her sunglasses and leaned back in her chair. "My parents didn't allow it. I had to get straight A's in all my classes."

"That must have been tough." I slurped from my straw and let the coolness of the ice water soak in my mouth. "My dad let me make my own choices."

Asia smiled. "It must've been nice for you." She lifted her sunglasses and stared at me. "I don't get it. Since you had it so good, why did you leave home?"

I shrugged and tilted my baseball cap back. "Well, don't get me wrong. I love my family. I'd like to travel while I have a chance."

Asia lowered her shades again. "What do you mean?"

"I could get drafted."

"That worries you?"

"Yeah, I might wind up in Vietnam." Just as I spoke, it was like pushing an emotional button from high to low. Angry at the thought of the military interrupting my life, I abruptly scooted the chair away and stood up. "I need to wash my hands."

Inside the restroom, I leaned over the sink and stared in a mirror. Weary from lack of sleep, I looked worn out and haggard. I scrubbed with borax soap and rinsed. After I splashed water on my face, I wiped with one of those yucky pull-down cloth towels on a dispenser. "Get with it, man." I glared at my reflection and stormed out of the restroom. I was mad at the thought of going to Vietnam and worried that I'd never have a chance to live my life the way I wanted.

Short-fused, I shoved the outside patio door open and noticed a big man in his 30's standing over Asia. It was that crazy guy. "Hey! Get away from her!" I was too enraged to think about the danger of standing up to this monster.

The beast sneered and chuckled. "Okay, boy." He glanced around to see if anyone was watching.

I kept my eyes focused on him.

He glared. "Careful, kid. You're lucky we're in a public place." He gritted his teeth. "I could easily break you in half!" As he opened the door to leave, he narrowed his eyes. "I'm coming after you, boy." Slowly he stepped outside and glanced at Asia.

"I'll take her once I'm through gutting you like a rabbit."

I watched him through the window as he started to walk away. Suddenly, out of nowhere, three cops stormed over and tackled him to the ground. It happened so fast; I couldn't believe what I was seeing. "Wow!" I looked back to Asia, "Look at that!"

Asia rushed to my side. "What's happening?"

"They finally got him," said Tina as she ran to the window. "I called the police when I spotted that scum. He's wanted for three brutal assaults in the area."

"Wow! They got him." I turned to Asia. "It's over."

She stood there shaking.

"You okay?"

Asia looked pale, and her lips quivered.

"You better sit down." I put my arm on her shoulder and led her to a chair. She staggered and seemed weak as I sat her down.

Tina, our waitress knelt beside her. "You okay, honey?" She placed her palm on Asia's forehead. "Her skin feels clammy."

"Will she be okay?"

Tina kept her focus on Asia. "All right, honey. Just lean your head down for a minute. That's good. Get the blood flowing." She poured water on a cloth and held it on the back of Asia's neck.

I kept my hand on Asia's shoulder and worried.

"Okay let me have a look at you." Tina gently lifted her chin.

"Phew." Asia sat up straight.

"Feel better?" asked Tina.

"I think so." Asia daubed her watery eyes with her fingers. "I was so scared."

I rubbed her shoulder. "You're safe now."

Tina smiled and stood up. "You'll be fine."

"Thank you." Asia looked up with clear eyes. "I'm alright now."

"Good." Tina placed her palm on Asia's cheek and smiled again. "Okay, what you need is a tall glass of orange juice." She glanced at me and said, "I'll get more coffee for you." She paused and looked at us. "Oh, how about some apple pie? It's on the house."

I glanced at Asia. She nodded in agreement, and I said, "We'd like that very much. Thank you."

"You're both welcome."

When Tina left, Asia sighed in relief. "I can't believe it's over."

"Yeah, me too." I sat in a chair and held her hand in silence. For a moment, we both had to process all that happened to us.

Tina came over with a tray, set two slices of apple pie on the table and smiled at Asia. "You're looking better. Here's your orange juice." Then she nodded to me and said, "Okay, I'll get that coffee I promised."

When she returned I was standing by the table with a plate in my hand, and I forked a piece of pie into my mouth, then chewed with pent-up energy. Tina poured the rich black liquid in my cup and looked at me in surprise. "That's no way to eat apple pie, honey. Now sit down, relax and enjoy it." She patted my shoulder and smiled. "You can relax now."

I nodded with a mouthful and sat down. "It's really good."

"I'm glad you like it," said Tina as she turned and walked back in kitchen.

Relieved to finally relax, I sat at the table and I noticed that Asia quietly ate her pie. She had a graceful way of holding her fork while she put a small piece into her mouth. Focused on eating, she placed her utensil beside the plate. Only after she swallowed, did she pick it up and make another gentle move to her supple lips. It was like watching a deer grazing in the forest.

When Asia finished eating, she asked, "Why is Tina so nice?"

Surprised to hear the question, I said, "Well, Tina's a good person. I can tell."

"But she doesn't even know us."

"Tina reminds me of my Mom. She's works part time as a nurse. Whenever anyone needs any comfort, Mom is right there helping out."

Asia leaned forward and kissed my cheek. "I can see where your caring heart comes from now."

"How are feeling?"

"I'm okay." She leaned back in the chair and closed her eyes.

I could tell she was exhausted. So was I. We didn't get much sleep in the past 24 hours and it was nice to just sit together for a few minutes without any worries.

After we paid our bill, I slung my backpack on and said, "Okay, I'll make sure you get home now."

"When we get there, I'll just take a few things, then leave." Asia picked up her purse and tote bag. "I don't plan to stay any longer than I have to."

"Why not?"

"I'm fed up. My mother has passed away. My father stays drunk and lost his job because of it. Besides, after what happened, that place creeps me out."

"What are you going to do?"

Asia adjusted the purse on her shoulder. "I'm not sure yet. All I know is that I'm 18. I can choose to live where I want."

When we arrived at Asia's house, she started to get her key out but the door was partially opened. We heard loud blues music coming from inside. Asia glanced at me and pushed it further. Seated on a lounge chair in the living room was a bald stocky man cradling a whiskey bottle in his arms like a baby.

"Dad." Asia rushed to his side. "Wake up."

He made a low grumbling sound and clung to his bottle.

"Dad!" Asia shook him harder.

She looked at me and shouted over the music, "Turn off the record player!"

I quickly lifted up the needle and flicked the switch.

"What?" Her groggy father opened his bloodshot eyes and glared at Asia. "What'd ya turn off ma music for?"

Asia knelt at his side and pleaded, "Dad, please listen to me. You've got to snap out of it."

"Don't' tell me what to do!" He grumbled, huffed and tried to stand up. Wobbly on his feet, he staggered toward the record player.

Asia grabbed his arm. "Dad, please listen to me!"

"Get out of my way!" Suddenly he slapped her across the face.

She crumpled to the floor.

I rushed to her side and helped her up.

He glared at me and snorted, "Who the hell are you?"

I ignored him and focused on Asia. "Are you alright."

She wiped a bloody lip with her wrist and yelled, "I've had it with him!

"Why you bitch!" He lunged and fell on the floor with the whiskey bottle still in his arms.

"I'm getting out here!" Asia rushed to her bedroom.

Not sure how to handle this bizarre encounter, I stood and watched that pathetic drunk as he laid there in his own filth. He smelled so bad I held my nose and couldn't wait to get out of there.

Asia ran back in the living room with a small suitcase. "Let's go!"

Later we sat in the back of a Greyhound bus, heading to Flagstaff. I glanced at my watch. It was 1:15. Bright sunlight glared off passing cars, and I lowered the brim of my cap. Asia dozed and rested her head on my shoulder while I closed my eyes, then drifted in and out of sleep. Never had I felt so exhausted before.

Sometime later, I awoke. Asia sat beside me and rummaged through her tote bag. I rubbed my eyes and tried to focus. "What are you looking for?"

Asia paused and smiled. "Here it is." She pulled out an envelope and opened it. "My mother saved this for me. I was supposed to open it after my high school graduation. But she passed away before I had a chance to read it."

She unfolded a hand-written note and began to read it out loud, "Dear Sakura." Asia smiled again. "My mother used my birth name, Woody." She nestled the paper like a prized gift.

"That's a nice-sounding name. What does it mean?"

Tears streamed down her cheeks and she sighed. "Cherry blossom."

She continued to read, "'My sweet daughter, I love you so much.'" Asia's voice cracked with emotion and she continued to read in silence.

I turned away and stared at distant crimson mountains. Passing scenes of desert cactus gave way to the rolling verdant hills of Sedona, and the Verde River flowed freely through rich, wild land. Like a master artist, she drew curvaceous lines in the soil. Along these twists and turns were a mix of alder, sycamore and walnut trees all resplendent in the afternoon sun.

I heard a slight rustling and observed the subtle, graceful moves of Asia again.

She took out a colorfully-designed paper with cherry blossoms printed on it. Carefully she unwrapped it and gushed at the sight of cash. "Look, Woody. This is my graduation present." She counted and said, "It's two hundred dollars!"

"That's great. It'll help you to get a new start."

Asia held the gift close to her heart. "Now I understand."

"What?"

"Whenever my mother bought groceries, she'd whisper, 'Don't tell your father.'" Asia gazed out the window as she continued. "The whole time I was growing up, she wasn't allowed to work. Dad gave her enough cash to get food but she had a way of hiding nickels and dimes. Now I realize she was saving it for me."

"Sounds like she loved you very much."

Asia held up her locket that hung from a neckless and smiled. "Would you like to see a picture of my mother?"

"Sure."

She opened the locket and leaned closer. "See how beautiful she is?"

"Yeah, she looks a lot like you."

8 UNCLE JAKE

When our bus pulled into the station in Flagstaff, we both got out. We picked up our suitcases, then I glanced across the street and said, "There's a coffee shop over there."

"Okay, I'm hungry."

We found a comfortable booth inside and put our bags on the floor beside us. I noticed a pay phone on the wall near the back. "I'll call my Uncle Jake and let him know we're here."

"Do you want me to order for you?" Asia asked.

"A cheese burger, fries and root beer will do."

After I talked with my uncle, I called my parents and told them about meeting Asia but left out most of the drama. I didn't want to worry them. Instead, I mentioned how her mother had died and she left home to find work up north. I quickly returned and sat across the table from Asia.

"Did you get through alright?" she asked.

"Yep, my uncle Jake will be here in about an hour."

"He'll pick you up here?"

I nodded as I opened the wrapper of my burger. "He's helping a friend at his trading post east of here. I'll stay there overnight, then he'll take me to my uncle Buck's ranch."

"Is that where you'll be working for the summer?"

"Yep." I paused. "Unless I get drafted. What are your plans?"

"I'll look around. Maybe I can get a job here."

"Is there anything I can do to help?"

"No, I'll be alright. You've done enough already." She smiled and patted my hand. "Thank you."

When Uncle Jake came inside the coffee shop, he grinned. "Is that you, Richard?"

"Yep." I stood up and he gave me a bear hug.

"Well, you're all grown up." Jake stood there and looked me over. "Last time I saw you, I reckon you was about knee-high to a squirrel."

"I was nine, then." I turned and said, "This is my friend, Asia."

"Well, how about that?" He reached over and hugged her. "I didn't know you had a woman."

Asia giggled.

"Don't pay any attention to him," I said to Asia and laughed. "My mom warned me that he's still rough around the edges."

"That's right." Jake had a mischievous expression and grinned. "How's my sister anyway?"

"Mom's fine. She misses the ranch and family, though."

Jake lifted his Stetson and brushed back his red hair. "Well, alright." He adjusted his hat and scratched his beard. "Let's head on out. We'll talk more later."

I turned to Asia and asked, "Where are you going to stay?"

"I'll get a motel room, I guess."

"What?" Jake stepped forward and placed his big hand on my shoulder. "You're going to leave your woman here?"

Asia giggled again.

"Geez!" I shook my head and glared at him. "Stop saying that."

Jake grinned as though he enjoyed his teasing. "Nah. I think I'll have to check this out first. He turned to Asia and said, "Well, young lady, I may be rough around the edges, but I can tell there's something going on between you two. Am I right?"

Asia smiled and looked at me.

Jake laughed and slapped me hard on the back. "See that, Richard."

"He likes to be called, "Woody," said Asia.

I turned and she gazed into my eyes.

"Oh, Woody, is it?" said Jake.

"Yep."

"Well, okay, Woody." He wrapped his arms around both of us. "Asia, would you like to join us at my place for supper?"

"I'd like that."

"Good, we'll figure something out." Jake walked us outside as though he was a big cuddly bear and said, "My wife will be so glad to see you."

"It'll be great to finally meet her," I said.

"Oh, yeah." He grinned. "She's quite a woman, my Maria."

Uncle Jake drove to the side of an old gas station with a pump that looked like it was built about the same time as the first oil strike. "Well, this is it."

We stepped out of his Chevy pickup truck and strolled to the entrance of a store attached to a garage. I glanced at a sign on the roof. In bold red letters it advertised, McDuff's Trading Post.

"Who's McDuff," I asked.

"He's the owner." Jake placed his big hand on my shoulder. "I'm just helping out my friend until he gets back from a trip back east. He's due in tomorrow. We'll head to the ranch later."

"Oh, now that makes sense. When you mentioned that we were going here, I was surprised."

"Yep." Uncle Jake chuckled. "Your Ma said the same thing." He opened a door that rang a tiny bell and we stepped inside.

I smelled the scent of leather belts, saddles and wallets displayed around the gift shop. On the wall behind the counter a sign had the words, "Welcome to the old west."

Asia laughed at a funny poster with a cowboy pointing a shot gun at a fella standing with his hands in the air. His britches were down to his knees. At the bottom of the picture, it said, "Free buckshot to all horse thieves and scoundrels."

"Make yourselves at home." Jake tapped a small round table with four chairs in the corner.

I heard the rustling of beaded curtains and turned to see a Mexican lady in her early twenties. She stepped out of a back room, put her arm around Jake and looked up with an endearing smile.

"This is my Maria." He grinned proudly like he won a prize, then he nodded to me and said, "Maria, I'd like you to meet my nephew, Woody and his woman, Asia."

I heard a giggle and noticed that Asia obviously enjoyed my Jake's unbridled manners.

"Buenas Nochas." Maria paused as though she had to carefully think of her words. "Um...I am so happy to meet you."

Jake chuckled and kissed her cheek. "That's good, honey. You're sounding more like a gringo every day."

Maria smiled warmly and touched her lips with her finger tips, "Um...you hungry?"

"Do you mind if we wait a while?" I asked. "We just ate not too long ago."

Asia asked, "Would it be alright if I freshen up?"

Maria looked up at Jake and whispered, "Que?"

Jake kissed her cheek and said something in Spanish that I did'nt understand.

Maria smiled and gestured to Asia and said, "Come."

Asia followed her through the rustling of beads into the next room.

"Ah, that's my Maria." Jake laughed with a look of pride. "She still struggles with her English sometimes, but she sure makes a fine meal." He shook his head with a sparkle in his eyes and added, "Among other pleasurable things."

While Jake showed me around the store, he talked about our family. "I reckon your Ma told you we inherited the ranch after your Grandpa passed away."

"Yeah, my Dad was in the Navy then," I said. "We traveled a lot, so Mom left it up to you and Aunt Eileen to run the place."

Jake shrugged. "I wasn't ready to settle down. My sister, Eileen and her husband, Buck have been doing most of the work."

Jake and I walked outside, then he showed me the property. A stream flowed about a 100 feet behind the garage, and we listened to the water gurgling over rocks. I told him all about meeting Asia and the struggles we faced over the past two days.

"Now I'm not sure what to do, Uncle Jake." I sat on a boulder and looked up to him. "She's a nice girl, and I like being with her." I let out a deep sigh. "It's just that I don't want to get serious. I could get drafted any day now."

"I know what you're going through Woody." He squatted like we were relaxing around a campfire and tilted his Stetson back.

"I felt the same way before I was shipped out during the Korean War."

I picked up a rock and tossed it in the river. "What the hell are we fighting for anyway?"

"Who knows?"

A capful of wind fluttered nearby alder leaves, and I breathed in the fresh air of Sedona. I thought of that distant war and watched the sun dipping below a ridge to the west. "I don't mind serving my country, Uncle Jake, but why risk my life for a cause that makes no sense?"

"Yep." He gazed at the sun peeking behind a ridge. "Now you got feelings for Asia. You're worried about how she'll get by. Right?"

"Yeah, that's about it," I said.

"Alright then." Jake stood up and looked at me. "Maybe you could ask her if she'd like to come with us to the ranch for a while. You know, meet the family and see how it goes. What do ya think?"

"Sounds good to me." I got up and reached out my hand. "Thanks, Uncle Jake."

He gripped my wrist and pulled me closer. "How about a hug?"

"Okay." I chuckled. "Just don't squeeze the air out of me."

When we strolled back inside, I heard the rustling of beads again and turned to see Asia wearing a green dress with a scoop neck line. "Wow, you look nice," I said.

"Thank you." Asia brushed her damp hair and smiled. "Maria gave me some of her shampoo, and I feel clean again."

"Well, now it's my turn," I said to Jake. "Just show me the way to the cleaning station."

Jake rested his arm on my shoulder. "Alright, follow me out back and I'll hose you down."

After a good meal, we all sat at the round table and hung out together. Uncle Jake made it easy to relax with his jokes and friendly banter. Maria snuggled up to Jake and laughed at his silly gestures. Her shoulder-length black hair swayed naturally as she turned her head to listen to our conversations. Whenever she seemed confused about what was said, Jake whispered lovingly in her ear.

"Oh," she said as her eyes widened and she smiled with a look of understanding. "Si."

Sometimes Asia covered her mouth with her palm and giggled. Her long raven hair flowed elegantly down her back just below the waist and she leaned into me. When she did this, I noticed that she glanced at me with a smile. Her eyes sparkled and she no longer had that sad, lost expression. Pleased to see her happy and at ease, I laughed with her.

During these special moments, I enjoyed a sense of family bonding with Aunt Maria and Uncle Jake. But I still wasn't sure how to handle my growing feelings of affection for Asia.

While I wondered about this, Asia pointed to a large, two-foot tall aquarium on the counter. "Is that a live snake in there?"

Jake walked over to the counter and grinned. "Oh, you mean dragon?" He lightly patted a screen on the top with his fingers. "This here rattlesnake is all part of my friend, McDuff's act."

The reptile coiled itself with its head erect. Greenish beady eyes glared menacingly while a tongue slithered in and out. "Handsome fella, don't ya think?" Jake had a glint of mischief in his eyes.

I stepped closer. "Yeah, how big is he?"

"Oh, about six feet when he's fully stretched out. Here, I'll show you something." Jake leaned in and placed his nose right on the glass side, then tapped, tapped his finger nails on it. Suddenly the snake struck at the inside with clack, but Jake didn't even flinch.

"Wow! Look at the fangs on that sucker!" I gasped in awe.

Asia backed away. "Now, that's scary!"

"Yep. If that big guy could get at you, why you'd be dead in no time at all." Jake leaned closer with a teasing expression. "Okay, nephew. You think you got the grit to do what I did?"

I shrugged. "Sure, that's easy, man."

"Hah! Hah!" he chortled in a deep sand-papery voice. "I knew you had it in you!" Jake grinned with a right-side tooth missing. "Okay, I'll bet you 50 cents that you'll jump like a scared rabbit as soon as that snake strikes!" He held out his huge hand. "Deal?"

"Deal." I grabbed his palm and my fingers were swallowed in an excruciating grip. "Ow!" I glanced at him and laughed. "Okay, give me a minute to get back circulation."

"Now your stalling."

"Alright, here goes." I leaned closer to the aquarium. Not liking the beady eyes of that snake, I hesitated.

"Go on! You can do it!" Uncle Jake egged me on.

I pressed my nose right on the glass. The big snake's tongue slithered as if to mock me. I tapped my finger nails against the aquarium. Nothing happened. I clacked it again.

Clunk! That snake struck the glass head on. I jerked back so hard, I almost tripped on my own two feet. "Ah! Crap!" I chuckled. "Did you see that?"

Jake let out a roaring belly laugh and held out his palm. "That'll be 50 cents!"

I reached in my pocket and plunked two quarters in his hand. "Let me try it again. I'll double it."

"Oh, now you're hooked on gambling." Jake shook his head in mock disapproval. "Your Ma's not gonna like it, nephew."

"Ah, come on, Uncle Jake. I can do this."

Jake grinned and squeezed my shoulder. "Okay, now remember there's no way that snake can get you. Got it?"

After I lost two more bets, he laughed. "Alright, at this rate you'll be broke in no time." He glanced at the snake and said, "I'll give you a hint. If you don't flinch, you'll win it all back. Go on, try it again. Don't do anything until I tell you to."

I nodded and placed my nose against the glass and stared into the eyes of that snake.

Okay, this time think of yourself like you ain't nothin but air. You're light as a feather. Stay calm."

I relaxed my mind and tapped the glass. It struck. I didn't flinch.

Uncle Jake slapped me on the back. "You did it! Just remember to always stay cool under fire." He held out a fistful of coins. "Here ya go." He plunked it all in my hand.

"Thanks," I said.

While the trading post was closed for the night, we all sat on folding chairs out back. The scent of mesquite wood wafted in the air from a stone fire pit near the stream. Our faces were aglow in reddish-orange as the flames crackled in front of us. Maria served glasses of lemonade, then she quietly snuggled up to Jake.

Our voices were low tranquil whispers in a reverent stream of friendly conversations. Far away from the hustle of city life, I relaxed with each moment and there was no thought of past or future. We were together only in the present without worries or regrets.

Beside me, Asia rested her head on my shoulder and I knew she was at peace. A Cheshire cat moon grinned and the stars twinkled like jewels in the vast blackness above us.

Nothing moved until Asia jumped to her feet, "Oh, look! A shooting star!" She giggled and glanced at me. "Did you see that, Woody?"

"Yeah." I stood up, wrapped my arm around her waist and watched two more rocketing to the south.

"Well." Jake yawned. "I reckon we oughta turn in."

I responded with my own inhalation of air as if it was contagious. "Where do you want us to sleep?" I looked at Uncle Jake as he stood up with Maria at his side.

"You'll hunker down over there." He pointed a flashlight beam on a canvas tent near the stream. "I set that up for you this morning."

In the glow of our fire, I saw Maria's humble expression. "Um, sorry."

"It's okay, honey." Jake placed his arm on Maria's curvaceous hip and looked at me. "She's embarrassed about not having room inside for both of you."

Asia squeezed my hand and smiled at me. "I can sleep in the tent with Woody."

"Yeah." I nodded. "We don't want to impose on you."

"I reckon your Ma ain't gonna like that." Jake stood with his arms crossed. "If she finds out I let you two sleep together, we'd both be in a heap of trouble."

"Well, I mean no disrespect but if I'm old enough to risk my life in the jungles of Vietnam, I think I'll be responsible in this situation."

Jake lowered his arms. "Can't argue with that, nephew." He tossed the flashlight to me. "Okay, check out that tent. Shake out the mattress inside. Make sure it ain't buggy. Asia, you go with Maria and she'll give you a few things. I'll be right back."

I unzipped the flap, crawled inside and noticed there was no attached canvas flooring on the ground. Our feet would be in the dirt. While I examined our conditions, Asia peeked through with the bedding, pillows and sleeping bags cradled in her arms, then handed them to me. Several large roaches skittered out from under the mattress, and I hoped that Asia hadn't noticed.

Jake came over as I crawled back out to greet him. "Here, you'll need these." He plunked a crowbar, machete and a long stick on the ground.

"What for?"

He walked away and whispered over his shoulder, "Weapons against snakes, bugs and whatever creeps along in the night."

Asia stuck her head out. "What'd he say?"

"Nothing." I crawled inside, dropped the gear and plopped on the mattress.

For a long time, I laid on my back and stared into the darkness while Asia relaxed her head on my chest. Although I was exhausted, I could not get to sleep. She was restless, too. We listened to an endless stream of music and laughter coming from the back of the store.

"What's going on?" I sat up and groaned. "I thought they were going to sleep."

"We opened the tent flap and saw a light shining from Jake and Maria's bedroom window. Their silhouettes danced around and they laugh together. We both groaned and laid back down on our mattress.

Asia let out a deep sigh and rested her head on my chest again. "I wonder what it's like to be in love." She was quiet for a few minutes, then asked, "Woody?"

"Yeah?"

"Do you have a steady girlfriend?"

"Not now. We broke up."

"What happened?"

"We were getting too serious. I wanted to travel around the country for a while. She wanted me to stay."

"Do you miss her?"

"No, I got tired of arguing about our future."

"Why did you want to travel?"

"I knew I'd get drafted if I waited around too long. Then I'd never get a chance to see the country."

For a while, we listened to the music coming from Jake and Maria's bedroom.

"Woody?"

"Yeah?"

Asia snuggled closer. "Could you hold me for a while?"

I gently embraced her. In the background we heard sensuous music and giggling from Jake and Maria's bedroom. Asia moaned, quivered and we held each other tighter. Instantly it was like we struck a match. Burning flames of desire ignited. Our lips pressed hard together and I began to lose all control of myself.

Suddenly, she pulled back and gasped for air.

"What's wrong?"

"Maybe we're going too fast," she said.

"But I..." Heated by my youthful desires, I wanted her so bad, and I gasped for air. Yet, deep down I knew she was right. I had to keep my cool and started to roll over.

Then she tapped my shoulder and said, "I'm sorry. Please don't be mad at me."

Her hand was hot. I turned and faced her. "I'm not mad at you, Asia." I took another deep breath. My youthful loins ached. "I...I just don't want to do anything to hurt you."

"I know." She sighed. "I trust you." She paused, and in the heat of our heavy breathing together, she exhaled. "Um, do you mind if we just lay close and talk for a while?"

"Okay," I whispered and noticed the music and giggling from my uncle and aunt's room had stopped. I took a deep breath. "What do you want to talk about?"

"I miss my mother," her voice cracked. "I don't know what to do now. I feel so lost and alone."

"It must be so painful for you." I tried to see her face in the darkness as she cried softly. "Is there anything I can do?'

"I don't know, Woody." Asia cuddled up to me and her cheek was moist. "I...I'm so tired." Her voice was like a puff of air fluttering through the trees. "I just need to relax in your arms until I fall off to sleep." She sighed. "Okay?"

"Sure." I wiped the stream of tears from her face with my fingers and tried to comfort her.

She exhaled softly as we faced each other. In the quiet stillness, her sweet breath was fresh and clean after her recent shower, and I savored the aromatic scent of lavender upon her soft skin. I gently rested my hand on the side of her forehead and listened to her breathing. Slowly, her body relaxed in my arms and she fell asleep.

Sometime during the night, I heard a low rumbling like distant thunder. Flashlight in hand, I got out and spotted an odd creature crawling heading right to the tent. I realized it was a scorpion and stomped on it. I lifted my shoe. It still wiggled, so I squished it until I was sure it was dead.

"What was that?" Asia stuck her head out with her flashlight beam shining wildly in my face.

Blinded, I covered my eyes and said, "Nothing. Just stretching my legs."

I was about to go back into the tent when I noticed a bolt of lightning that seemed far off above silhouetted mountains. I stood there and watched as three more strikes lit up the night sky. From this safe distance, I admired the wild beauty of nature at work without any thought of possible dangers ahead.

Before dawn, it was quiet, and I slept peacefully. I dreamed of floating in a tranquil pool of water and drifted without a care in the world. Gurgling and swooshing sounds grew louder.

I heard a scream! Awakened, I realized we were caught in a flashflood. Asia grabbed my arm. We were being carried by an overwhelming violent force that lifted the tent over us. Further downstream we flailed about to catch a handhold of anything solid. We were spinning round and round. Abruptly, we slammed into something hard as the water kept pushing us. It was a chain link fence at the trading post boundary.

I struggled to my feet and grabbed Asia's arm. "Hold on!"

She choked, coughed and spat, but finally stood up. Waist-high raging water pushed our backs against the fence. Desperately we held on for mutual support.

"Are you okay?" I asked.

Asia nodded, shivered and breathed heavily without saying a word.

"Hang on!" Jake shouted.

I turned to see him standing on higher ground about 20 feet away. "Hurry!" I yelled over the roar of rushing water.

"Get ready! I'll throw this rope!"

"Okay!" I steadied myself as the water pushed me against the fence.

Jake tossed the rope but missed by a foot. He pulled it back, stepped closer and threw it again. I caught it while the chain link dug into my back and shoulder blades.

"Good catch," Jake called out again. "Now tie it around Asia's waist!"

I tried to balance myself while using both hands to get the rope around her. After a struggle, I yelled, "Okay! Pull her in!"

Asia grabbed the rope and held on. By the time she reached dry land, I saw Maria running out with a blanket, and she wrapped it around Asia.

Relieved, I yelled, "Okay! I'm ready!"

Finally, I was safely holding onto Asia. I turned and saw a 10-foot wide stream raging right through the backlot. But there wasn't a drop of rain.

Maria helped Asia in the back room of the gift shop while I changed into a borrowed oversized shirt and pants. I asked Jake, "Where did all that water come from?"

"I reckon we had a lot of rain up in those hills last night. Must've caused a flash flood."

Later, we strolled outside to inspect the damage. The stream had slithered away like a snake as though the flood never happened. We found the tent stuck up against a chain link fence.

Jake patted my shoulder and smiled with relief. "That tent must've lifted right over you guys."

"Yeah, it's a good thing there was no canvas flooring attached to it. We could've been trapped inside."

That morning I called my parents and said, "Uncle Jake is taking me to the ranch today."

Mom said, "I'm glad. It'll be a good experience for you to live on the ranch and see how I grew up there."

"Yeah, I'm looking forward to it." I paused to think of how I would mention Asia again. "Um...Uncle Jake invited my friend, Asia to visit the ranch for a while."

"That's good, son," she responded. "Our family has always welcomed travelers into our home."

"Rick," said Dad. "I heard that your friend, Tom just got drafted."

"Thanks for the heads up, Dad."

"You'll be 19 in three weeks. Why don't you come home and apply for college. You could get a deferment, you know."

"Dad, I'd like to travel after I stay at the ranch for a month or so."

"Okay, son. I felt the same way, but the war changed that in '41. History has a way of repeating itself for the next generation. Now it's your turn."

9 BIG ROCK RANCH

We rode in the back of Jake's dust-covered pickup for about an hour with a breeze cooling our faces. Asia and I sat on burlap bags of oat and leaned against two bales of hay for my Uncle's ranch. While we bounced along a dirt road heading north, cattle grazed in a pasture, and I noticed that Asia especially admired the landscape around us.

"Oh, look, Woody! There's a baby calf suckling from its mother." She brushed away strands of hair blowing in her eyes and smiled. "It's so beautiful here."

I placed my arm on her shoulder, leaned in to get a better look. "Hey, check that out." I pointed at two young calves as they jumped around and challenged each other.

Jake leaned his head out the window and said, "We're almost there."

He turned sharply around the next bend, slowed down and stopped abruptly with a squeak of brakes. I stood up to see why he hesitated and noticed a wayward cow standing in the middle of the road.

Uncle Jake calmly got out with a curled rope in his right hand. "Come on, nephew. We're on the ranch now. It's time you earned your keep."

I hopped down from the back and scanned the fence line. "How did she get out?"

Jake paused, then pointed to an oak tree branch that had fallen on sagging barbed wire and left a three-foot-wide gap along the fence. "That's how."

A big black Angus stood there staring at us and a calf suckled from her swollen teat. Uncle Jake slowly walked up to the mother. At first, she was skittish, but he slid the rope over her head and whispered softly, "Alright, that's a good momma.

Come on."

He held the rope and strolled to the opening in the fence and stepped over the bent wire. She followed as the male calf hungrily tried to keep up. Once they were on the other side, Jake removed the rope and tapped her rear. "Get."

While they ran toward the main herd, Jake went back to his truck, grabbed a chain saw and strolled over to the fallen branch. "Okay, hold this end."

I gripped the eight-inch-thick branch with my bare hands as the rough bark scratched my skin. "Ready," I said.

Jake yanked on the cord and the saw roared. Wood chips flew up like flies in all directions. Once he cut a bushy heavy end away from the sagging wire, this released the pressure on a bent fence post. I dragged my side of the branch and dropped it away from the fence.

During this ruckus the startled herd took off toward a river bank. We continued to cut away at the branches, and when we finished our labor, I tossed the smaller pieces to the side. I turned to see Maria sliding out a six-foot-long two by four from the back of the truck. Without a word, she stood with her boots ankle-deep in mud from the previous night's rain and lifted it over to Jake.

He grinned and kissed her cheek. "Gracias, honey."

Uncle Jake wedged the wood at the base of the fence post and said, "Come on, Woody. Let's use some leverage here."

Together, we grunted, dug in our muddy heels and straightened the post. Just as we stood up, Maria handed Jake a hammer. Pleased with her quick actions, he nodded and smiled again.

He pounded a dozen times on the post, then stopped. "That'll do."

Asia was standing behind us and asked, "Can I help?"

Uncle Jake smiled. "You sure can, darlin. There's a crowbar in the back. Fetch it for me." He nodded to Maria and said, "Go with her, honey and take this saw back while you're at it."

Soon, we all pitched in to repair the fence. Not that Asia and I knew what the heck we were doing. Instead, Uncle Jake had a natural way of making us feel we were part of his crew. I admired how Maria worked right alongside her man and she had no qualms about getting dirty. Later I learned more about this hardy woman of the west and her mixed Apache/Mexican heritage.

After another half-mile of driving along tree-lined pastures, Jake slowed down to go over an old rickety wood bridge. Planks thumped, thumped under the wheels and a raging river flowed wildly below us as we drove across. Moments later, we came to a fork in the road and stopped.

Jake leaned his head out the window and pointed to the ponderosa forest on a lush mountainside. "Great view here."

While Jake paused for us to admire the lush landscape, I noticed a short-haired Australian cattle dog running toward us and barking with his tail wagging. The frisky animal halted at the driver's side and looked up with an obvious happy smile, barked twice, sat and eagerly waited for a command.

Jake chuckled, got out and patted the dog as though it was his long-lost friend. "Hello, Shelly! I see you came all the way out to greet us! Ah, that's a good dog!" Jake held up his hand and she looked up with anticipation. "Okay, sit."

Shelly plopped her rear and waited. Jake took out a treat from his jean pocket and gave it to her, then rubbed her head. "Okay, girl," he said. "Lead us home."

She turned and headed down the left fork in the road while barking and wagging a furry tail the whole time. We followed the dog for a couple hundred feet along a fence line. During this short drive, Asia was excited to see the cattle grazing on both sides of us.

"Oh, look," she said. "Two calves are butting their heads together."

"Yeah, like a tug of war," I responded.

We drove through an open gate and a wood sign hanging over it displayed the name, Big Rock Ranch. It's meaning was clear with a massive tractor-sized boulder on the right side as a permanent landmark.

To our left, we passed a large corral where we saw a dozen horses nuzzling and socializing with each other. Asia jumped up and leaned over on my lap. "Look at that, Woody."

"Yeah, I can see you love animals."

Chickens scurried in front of a barn that had a hay loft and a large hook hanging from a thick rope. A two-story ranch house stood a couple hundred feet away. We pulled over to a white-picket fence at the entrance while Shelly announced our arrival by loudly barking and jumping up and down. Asia looked wide-eyed with just as much enthusiasm, and I was delighted to see her so happy.

During all that commotion, a pregnant woman came out of the house, smiled and waved. "Hi Jake and Maria. It's about time you showed up." She greeted them with hugs and kisses.

I hopped out of the back and smiled, "Hey, Aunt Eileen."

She smiled happily and gushed, "Oh, my. You're all grown up, Richard." She hugged me and laughed. "What happened to that nine-year-old skinny kid that was here last time?" She paused to look me over, "You're so tall."

Just as she spoke, Asia came alongside and held my hand.

Aunt Eileen smiled again, "You must be the young lady Richard talked about on the phone." She leaned in, hugged and asked, "Asia, is that right?"

"Yes, Ma'am."

"I'm so glad to meet you." Aunt Eileen paused and seemed to admire Asia. "Oh, you have such beautiful hair!" She turned and looked at me. "My goodness, Richard, where did you find such a pretty girl?"

Before I could respond, Asia boldly said, "I like to call him by his nickname, Woody."

Eileen had a twinkle in her eye, "Oh, you got grit, young lady. I like that." She patted my chest and said, "Well okay, Woody. Now I know what to call out when I want you to do the chores around here."

Jake stood there with a warm smile on his rugged face while

STEVEN S. FOSTER

resting his arm on Maria's shoulder. "That's right, sis. Bark out, Woody! Remind him this ain't no summer camp we're runnin here."

Just as he spoke, we were surrounded by four little kids. One was a toddler and she kept pulling on Eileen's dress. "Mommy?" She looked up and pointed at us. "Who's that?"

Eileen picked up the curly red-haired girl and kissed her cheek. "This is your cousin Woody." She nodded, "And his friend, Asia. My aunt held her daughter close with affection and smiled. "Now tell them your name, honey."

"Summer." She rubbed her little nose and snuggled in her mother's arms.

"How old are you?" Asia asked.

Summer held up three little wiggly fingers and said, "Um, tree."

Eileen set her back down on tiny bare feet. "That's good, sweetie." Then her mother gently patted the heads of the other children as though she was taking inventory. "This is David, my eldest at nine. Tommy, he's seven and here's my other daughter, Spring, who's five now."

Jake gently rubbed Eileen's pregnant belly. "So, I reckon this next one will be called Winter?"

Eileen laughed and grinned at her brother. "That depends on whether it's a girl or boy."

"As you can see, Woody, my sister is a real breeder, that's for sure."

Eileen slapped him on the chest. "Don't say that!"

"Well, it's true." Jake laughed and teased. "You breed a good herd, sis!"

"Geez!" Eileen sighed and glared at her brother. "I'm no cow, you know!"

"Oh, that reminds me," said Jake with that wild, mischievous grin. "Where's that ole bull of a husband of yours, anyway?"

"He's working on that broken-down truck again." Eileen pointed to the barn. "You'll find him in there. He's probably grimier than a pig in a mud hole."

"Sounds like Ole Buck." Jake looked toward the barn. "Well, baby sis, I reckon if he stays busy in there long enough, you just might not get knocked up so much."

"Ah, Jake," Eileen groaned in annoyance. "Get out of here before you corrupt all my kids with your vulgar talk." She huddled her children closer and glanced over at Maria and Asia. "Come on inside, ladies."

Eileen marched off with her entire brood while Maria and Asia followed her back to the house. Once she made sure they were all through the door, she turned and brushed a hand in the air toward the barn. "Well, just don't stand there like a dumb jackass. Go on and tell my husband that supper will be ready in 30 minutes." She started to go back in but stopped and glared. "Make sure he washes up. Uh, you do know what soap is, don't you?"

Jake laughed and shook his head. "Well, I have no idea, baby sis!" Then he placed a hand on my shoulder, and we headed to the barn. "Come on, Woody! Let's go play in the mud for a while!" He chuckled as though he enjoyed all that teasing and sibling banter going back and forth.

When we stepped inside the barn, I saw a big man's butt crack while he leaned over the engine of a flatbed truck. His right bicep bulged, and he tried to loosen a rusty bolt with a wrench. The harder he struggled, the more he cussed, "Gaul damn, sheets a calla..." in obscenities from a mix of Celtic and mid-western ancestry.

Jake looked at me with his lovable mischievous grin and held his finger up. "Shh." Slowly he sneaked up behind my Uncle Buck and yelled, "Boo!"

Buck jerked up, banged his head and swore so loud, two horses neighed and kicked their stalls. He rubbed his skull and yelled, "What the ...!" Cuss words flew out faster than any Irish-American barroom fighter could have expressed himself.

Jake bent over and laughed so hard; I was sure he would bust a gut. "Got ya!"

Buck's eyes widened. "Why you ole sidewinder!" He grabbed

Jake in a playful headlock while his brother-in-law held on just as tight. Boots dug in. Both men grunted like challenging bulls. Cowboy hats landed on the dirt floor. Finally, Buck let him loose and grinned. "I forgot you was comin today."

"I can see why." Jake picked up both hats and gave one to Buck. He laughed as he brushed back red hair and placed his Stetson back on. Then he nodded to the truck and said, "You oughta scrap that pile of junk. Buy a new one."

Buck shrugged and sighed. "I got but two cents to my name and a house full of kids to feed."

"You ole horny bull. Stop knockin up your wife." Jake punched Buck on the shoulder. "Put some cash aside, man."

Buck laughed with a grizzly voice, "It ain't easy. How can I resist such a hot woman?" Buck poked back. "She sure is a baby maker."

Jake tried to look serious and shoved his friend. "Hey! That's my sister you're talking about!" For a moment, he glared real mean like, then busted out laughing again and they both roared with amusement.

Buck glanced at where I stood a few feet away. "Say, where did you get this here young pup?" He reached over and rubbed my hair. "Are you taking in strays now?"

Jake laughed. "Don't tell me you forgot our nephew, Richard was comin to work for us?"

Uncle Buck hugged me. "Nah, I was just funnin ya."

"By the way, he likes to be called, Woody now," said Jake. "You remember what it was like at his age. We came up with wild nicknames and wandered around the country that summer."

"How could I forget!" Buck paused and scratched his dirty brown whiskers. "Let me see now...you called yourself Duke."

"Yep and all them pretty girls called you Bear." Jake slapped Buck's chest. "Now that I think of it, that fits you, man."

Uncle Jake squeezed my shoulder. "Well, Woody here is doing the same thing. And he's even got himself a young chick to keep him warm at night!"

I laughed and shook my head, "Nah, it's no big deal. She needed my protection for a while. Now she's staying with me until she figures out what to do next. That's all."

"Oh," Buck grinned. "Protection, is it? Well, that's a better angle than we came up with those fillies in Wichita!"

"Yeah." Jake held out his hands wide in front of his chest. "How about the one with the big..."

"Pa!" A voice called from outside. "Ma says supper's almost ready!"

Buck shouted, "Okay, Davey! Tell your Ma we'll be there after washin up."

"Ma says to use soap this time."

Buck groaned and shook his head. "All right, son. Now go on back to your Ma!"

"Getting a little henpecked, I see." Jake laughed.

"Well, it's all your damn fault!" Buck splashed water on his face from a bucket. "Every time you tease her, Eileen gets all riled up!"

"Me?" Jake picked up a bar of soap from a shelf and tossed it to Buck. "Man, you're just getting soft."

10 BUCK AND JAKE

W e all sat at a large pinewood table, and Eileen brought in a serving plate filled with roast beef. I savored the steaming aroma and it looked so appetizing that my mouth watered. Jake must've thought the same thing when he reached over with his fingers.

She slapped his hand and snapped, "Get your paws off! You got the manners of a gorilla hanging from a tree!"

Jake pulled his hand back with that familiar mischievous twinkle in his eyes. "Ah, come on, sis."

I tried to keep a straight face while Asia giggled next to me, and I glanced around to see everyone else with grins. Except Eileen, of course. She looked as mad as a hen trying to protect her chicks from a wily fox. Around the table were us adults, and over in a corner her four children sat on a low handmade picnic table that was just right for them. This reminded me of our family gatherings back home in San Diego.

Eileen sat down, paused and held out her hands. "Okay," She nodded to Buck. "Let's say grace."

Buck reached over, and everyone held hands together. With his eyes closed, he prayed, "Well, Lord, we're all much obliged for this food that you provided for our family. Amen."

He started cutting pieces of roast and served each person until everyone had beef on their plates while Maria and Eileen made sure the kids had their food. I watched as there seemed to be a strange mix of chaos and order with the whole meal. Vegetables and mashed potatoes were passed around, and soon we ate quietly together.

Then, as if to deliberately break the silence, Jake held up a fork with a chunk of beef and announced, "Well, Buck, I see McCracken did a mighty fine job of butcherin ole Bert."

This set off five-year-old Spring and she cried, "Oh, pa!"

Next thing we had was bawling kids, then nine-year-old Tommy slammed his fork down. "You killed Bert!"

"Jake! How could you?" Eileen rushed to the children and tried to comfort them. "It's all right. Now go play in the living room while us grownups have a nice chat." She glared at Uncle Jake again.

"Ah, come on, sis! They have to learn where the grub comes from sometime!" Jake forked the beef in his mouth. "Mmm."

Buck nudged his brother-in-law. "I reckon your timing was a bit off!" He looked at Eileen while she herded the kids out of the room. "He's right, honey. Does em no good if they keep thinkin this here's a pettin zoo."

After supper, we all pitched in to clear the table. Eileen, Maria and Asia cleaned a pile of dishes at the sink while talking and laughing. Little three-year-old, Summer, however, was under her mother's feet pulling out pots and pans from a cupboard with loud rattling noises. Although this was chaotic, the women didn't seem to mind as they worked around her.

When I offered to help round up the kids, five-year-old Spring reached up to me and said, "Give me a horsey ride."

"Okay," I lifted her on my shoulders and galloped around the living room. "Hold on tight."

Spring wrapped her arms around my neck and shouted, "Go faster!" She giggled and bounced up and down.

Meanwhile, Tommy and Davey chased each other around the house in a wild shoot-em-up with toy guns. From room to room they shouted, "I got ya!"

After the kids settled down, I walked outside and leaned against a column that held up the porch roof. There, I was content to stand and hang out with Jake and Buck. They sat on wooden rocking chairs and drank beer while Shelly, the cattle dog curled up at their feet.

Asia appeared at the screen door and smiled. "Here, Woody. I brought you some lemonade. Maria made it for us."

"Thanks." I took the cool, icy glass and leaned against the column again while Asia went back inside. It was nice to see her with the other ladies, and it gave me a chance to relax with my uncles.

"She's a nice, girl, Woody." Jake lifted up his bottle of beer and grinned. "Let's all toast to all those sweet ladies in our lives."

All three of us clacked our drinks together. Buck let out a sigh and loosened his belt. "Well, Jake, you sure got yourself a mighty fine woman." He took a sip of beer, swallowed and burped. "Hahh…yep, considering that ugly mug of yours. Salute, Amigo."

Jake laughed, and they both tapped their bottles again. "Yep, Maria's a real keeper, that's for sure!"

Then, I noticed something that I hadn't seen in Jake before. He went completely sentimental on me. His eyes seemed to get kind of watery and he sniffled. "I'll never forget that time down in Sonora?"

Buck shook his head and sipped his beer again. "Yep."

"Phew!" Jake stared off as though he relived a memory so deep and profound. "There I was cruisin on my Harley without a care in the world."

"Yeah." Buck's voice was almost a whisper.

"I raced around that crazy turn. Out of nowhere was a bunch of sheep right in the middle of the road. It happened so fast. I swerved and slammed into a tree!"

"It's a wonder you survived, man."

"Yeah, I sure as hell thought I was dead," Jake said. "I couldn't move."

Surprised to hear this, I plopped on a swinging bench. "What happened, Uncle Jake?"

"When I opened my eyes, a beautiful angel appeared. She smiled and spoke Spanish. I had no idea what she was sayin." He paused and added, "Her voice was right pretty, though."

Buck reached over and rubbed Jake's shoulder. "That's when Maria found you."

"Yep, all I could do was stare at my angel." Jake let out a deep sigh. "I got real woozy like. Must've passed out. When I came to, I was in a little adobe house. And there was my Maria. She took care of me while my three broken ribs healed well enough for me to leave.

"But you didn't." Buck took another sip. "Good thing you stayed."

"Yeah, her Pa, Juan Carlos and his whole family took me in like I was one of them."

"Wow, Uncle Jake, I never knew about this."

"I didn't want to worry your Ma none." Jake sipped his beer. "I worked the land to pay his family back for their hospitality." He glanced at Buck. "I was wild then. But I settled down a bit. I stayed for six months and learned their language."

"Yeah," Buck's voice was like a whisper in the night breeze.

"Been eight months since I met my Maria." Jake sniffled and shook his head at the memory.

"Yep."

Jake nudged his brother-in-law, "You sure made a butt-ugly best man."

"Hell, somebody had to hog tie you during the weddin." Buck waved a hand in the air and said, "Good thing we had it here. Got plenty of rope."

Both men clinked their bottles together again.

I looked on in amazement. Never would I have imagined that these two grizzlies were that sentimental, but I admired them even more. I stood on that porch, drank my lemonade and tried to understand what I just witnessed. Puzzled by all this, I noticed that they seemed to study me in a strange way.

Jake leaned back with his eyes clearly focused on me and nudged Buck, "Well, what do you think?"

Buck folded his arms across his barrel of a chest and stared at me. "I reckon Woody has all the makins of a one-woman man."

I laughed at their teasing. "Ah come on, fellas. I'm going to see the world and date lots of women. I folded my arms and leaned against the column. "You'll see."

They looked at each other as though they were trying to

decide how to respond to my youthful arrogance. "They both shook their heads and said, "Nah!"

Jake got up and slapped me on the back. "Yep. Before you know it Woody, you'll be married and have a bunch of snotty-nosed kids, just like your ole Uncle Buck here."

"Amen, brother!" Buck tilted his head way back and guzzled down the last drop of beer. "Hah..." He inhaled, paused and burped out what sounded like a bullfrog mating call.

"Yep." Jake sat in the rocking chair and relaxed. "It's good to be home."

11 NIGHT STRUGGLE

O n my first night at the ranch, Uncle Buck handed me a leather jacket. "You'll need this."

"Thanks."

Buck nodded to a couch that was kept along the wall of the
front porch. "You sure about sleeping out here?"

"Yep," I said.

Aunt Eileen came out with an armful of extra blankets. "You
don't have to do this, you know."

I sat down as Shelly; the cattle dog hopped on the couch with
me. "It's perfect." I rubbed her fur and she snuggled on my lap.

Eileen smiled and handed me the blankets. "Well, okay. You're
always welcome to sleep on the couch in the living room."

Jake leaned against a pinewood column that held up the porch
roof. "Don't worry, sis. He'll be cozy and dry under here."

When they went inside I laid back and fluffed a pillow. Although the air was chilly on that June evening, the blankets
were warm as Shelly rested her head on my chest. Meanwhile,
Asia slept on a cot in the girl's bedroom. I heard laughter coming
from the extra room where Maria and Jake spent the night. Buck
and Eileen were upstairs, and I noticed strange growling noises.
It was probably Buck snoring, and I wondered how his wife handled all that racket.

Unable to sleep, I worried about getting drafted into the
madness of jungle warfare in Vietnam. Since I was born after
World War II, I had a sense of duty to serve my country. This
was a different war, however. When my Dad joined the Navy, it
was after Pearl Harbor, and everyone rallied behind a common
cause for freedom. Instead, in that summer of 1966, we were
a divided nation without a purpose. Jaded by the threat of nu-
clear war and the assassination of President Kennedy, many of

us guys either dropped out or followed like sheep being led to slaughter.

For me, the pressure weighed heavily on my future plans. Fresh out of high school, I wanted to travel and see the world. The thought of being called up to fight in Vietnam was like a road block that kept me from living out my dreams. I knew I had four options--wait to get drafted, run off to Canada, try for a college deferment, or enlist in the Navy. The second choice scratched against the way I was taught; you don't run away when things get dicey. The last option made more sense. At least I might learn a skill that would be beneficial later.

While the drumbeats of war grew louder in my restless dreams, I tossed and turned like a dog having a nightmare. I saw myself in the heat of battle with sweat dribbling down my face. Bullets pock-marked the dirt. Explosions deafened my ears. I turned and saw the ashen face of my best friend, Gary.

His eyes widened in a blank stare. "You're next."

I awoke and laid there thinking of Gary. He was two years older than me when he got drafted. Gary came home with his right leg blown off after only three months in Nam. He just dropped out after that, and even his parents weren't sure where he was hanging out. Finally, I found him at a loud mind-numbing party one night. He was sitting in a wheelchair, all drugged out.

I knelt in front of him and said, "Gary, look at me, man."

He had a weird blank stare. Haunted by the horrors of war, he tried to silence his demons with heroin, only to become a lost soul.

I put my hand on his shoulder. "Come on, Gary. Let's get out of here."

Through a thick haze, he looked at me in a brief moment of recognition. "You're next."

"Maybe so." I grabbed the handles of his wheelchair. "But I'm not going to let you kill yourself." I rushed him to the VA hospital and visited him as much as I could.

Then one day, a severely wounded vet was wheeled over to Gary by a male nurse. "I've been watching you, man," he said to my friend. "I see you're pissed about losing a leg."

Gary stared at the guy's two stumps above his knees and looked up. Speechless, he focused on the badly deformed vet, who had burn scars on his face.

"Name's Paul." He reached out to Gary.

They shook hands in a moment of silence.

Paul grinned through swollen, distorted lips. "Do you want to trade places?"

"What?"

"Yeah, you take my body, and I'll gladly have yours." Paul laughed at his own twisted humor. "Let's try it for a week. Okay?"

From that moment on, Gary was transformed. Paul stuck with him like glue, and they supported each other in a way that I could never understand.

Then I remembered our next-door neighbor's son, Chap, who had been missing in action for over six months." When I was growing up, everybody in the neighborhood looked up to him. I did too. He was three years older than me, and like an older brother. Before he was sent to Vietnam, Chap worked in the hardware store to save up his money, so he could provide a nice home for his fiancé, Donna. They planned to get married when his tour was over next month.

Why was this happening to such a good, decent guy like Chap? As I tried to make sense of this, I stepped off the porch and walked in a daze. In two weeks, I would be nineteen. Many of my older friends had already been called up. The Vietnam War was boiling in a stew of American blood. Army generals ordered an endless stream of bodies to the front.

I don't know how far I paced along that country road away from the ranch. A cool breeze swooshed in from the north. I shivered. Silhouetted branches swayed in the light of a half-moon and the leaves fluttered. In the pasture, a cow mooed and had lonely forlorn sound as if she called out for her missing calf.

Then it struck me like a bolt of lightning. What if Chap is dead? He will never have a chance to build precious memories with

the love of his life, Donna. They will not experience the blessings of a close-knit family like my parents had while I grew up.
With that realization, my mood grew darker. I was so pissed at
this insane world, I wanted to shout out obscenities.

Instead, I quietly asked for a miracle. "Please bring Chap
home." Not knowing what else to do, I continued to walk further and listened to my footsteps. Clump, clump, skip. I stopped
at a fork in the road and looked up. Stars twinkled above me.
"What now?" I asked.

A breeze whispered in my right ear, "Shh."

"What?" I listened. Only the leaves answered with a swoosh, a
flutter.

"Chap, if you're alive, hang in there, buddy."

I leaned my back against a thick trunk of an alder and looked
up. In the dim moon light, I watched the branches swaying as
the tree pulsated on my spine. It was alive and grounded in the
rich soil. This helped to calm my mind as I thought of all that I
wanted to experience as a young man.

"I need more time," I pleaded to the heavens.

"Shh," answered a breeze.

I inhaled in response. The cool air flowed in my mouth, down
my throat and into my lungs. "Hahh," I exhaled.

"Shh..."

I breathed deeper and with each in and out breath, I relaxed
even more. "I want to see," I whispered as I gazed at the veins of
branches that seemed to reach out beyond my sight.

"Swoosh," a gentle wind soothed my skin.

"I want to feel and taste all that life has to offer."

Leaves fluttered and I smelled the sweet scent of Jasmine in
the night air. I gazed at thousands of twinkling stars and prayed
for Chap's safe return. Then I asked, do I wait to be called up, or
should I enlist?

12 RANCH LIFE

The next morning, I awoke to creaking noises on the porch and sat up. Asia leaned back on a rocking chair with her eyes closed, and I admired the subtle orange glow on her face as the sun peeked over the horizon. At her feet was Shelly curled up in a ball.

I pulled the blanket away, stood up and yawned. Asia opened her eyes and looked over with a smile. "Good morning." She leaned back in the chair. "It's so nice here. Did you sleep well?"

"Yep." I stretched and took a deep breath. "Not at first, though."

"Why?"

"Had a lot on my mind."

Asia reached out her hand. "Were you thinking about the draft again?"

"Yeah." I squatted beside her and savored the smoothness of her slender fingers.

"Me too." Asia gazed into my eyes. "I don't want you to go, Woody."

We were drawn to each other. Our lips caressed.

The screen door squeaked open, and I looked to see Aunt Eileen in the doorway. "Good morning," she said with a pleasant smile.

"Oh." I stood up. "Hi."

Eileen handed an empty basket to me. "Here, take this." She rubbed her pregnant belly and glanced toward the barn. "It's time you both earn your keep. Fetch me a half-dozen eggs like I taught you the last time you were here. Do you still remember?"

"Sure." I took the basket, shrugged and acted like I knew exactly what I was doing.

Asia got up and stood beside me. "Yes Ma'am."

"Thanks." Eileen smiled again and went inside.

While Asia and I strolled behind the barn she asked, "How do we handle this?"

"Just go in and grab some eggs." I shrugged and kept walking. "How hard can it be?"

"I don't know. This is my first chance to be around farm animals."

I pointed to a screened-in shed with about a dozen hens and said, "Let's see now. I was nine when my family came to visit for a few weeks. It's been a while, but I think I can remember how to do this."

Just as we stepped closer, a huge granddaddy of a turkey leaped out from around the corner and charged at us. Asia screamed. I pulled her closer to me. Sharp talons lunged at my face. I blocked with my arms. He jumped up and threw out his claw-like feet directly at my eyes. I covered my face like a boxer trying to protect myself from heavy blows and stepped back. Still, he attacked.

Claws scratched the arms of my long-sleeved leather jacket. He lashed out again and again. I protected my face and retreated backward. Abruptly, I was against the coop. Chickens cackled wildly.

Asia leaned against me and said, "Woody! I'm scared!"

"It's okay!" But it wasn't okay. I was scared, too. I had to protect both of us. With Asia beside me, I blocked with my left arm and glanced around for anything to defend myself. To my right, I spotted a shovel in a wheel barrel.

"Stay close!" I edged along the coop while Asia held onto my belt. That monstrous four-foot-tall creature stopped and glared at me with the killer instincts of his prehistoric ancestors. Poised to attack, he fanned out large feathers to make himself look bigger. I grabbed the shovel and swung hard.

Thump! The blunt end slammed right on its back.

"Ach!" He jerked wide-eyed. Stunned, that turkey took off gobbling and kept running until disappearing around the corner.

Next thing I knew, Asia had her arms around me so tight, and she jumped up and down like I just scored a touchdown. "You did it, Woody!"

"Yeah." With my adrenaline still pumping, I listened to that turkey's ongoing complaints behind the barn. "That was crazy!" I looked to see if he would come back. When I was sure it was safe, I said, "Let's get those eggs."

I unlatched the coop screen door, stepped in with Asia right behind me, then closed it. A dozen hens clucked nervously as I searched the nests. "See any eggs?"

Asia glanced from side to side and shook her head. "Uh...no. Not yet."

"Maybe the hens are sitting on them," I suggested. Overly confident, I tried to reach under one of them. She gave me a sharp peck of her beak. "Ow!" I pulled my hand back. While I rubbed my skin in pain, I noticed that Asia whispered softly. "What are you doing? I asked."

"I'm asking for permission." Asia continued to make low soothing "brup, brup" sounds. She moved slowly and gazed at each hen like they were her friends.

They responded in a low, "cluck, cluck."

She gently reached under the same hen that pecked me and found one egg. After a few minutes of exploring around other chickens, she collected the half-dozen that Eileen requested.

"How did you do that?" I asked while we walked back to the house.

"I just let those hens know I'm their friend." Asia looked at me and smiled. "They probably sensed you were uptight after fighting off that turkey."

Maybe so." I watched Asia gracefully carrying the basket. "Are you sure you've never been around farm animals before?"

"I wish I had." Asia stepped up on the porch. "Now that I'm here, I like them."

Aunt Eileen greeted us at the open screen door. "What took you so long?"

"Ah, we just had a little run-in with some crazy turkey." I shrugged as Asia handed her the basket.

Eileen laughed. "Oh, you mean, Big Grub. That ornery cuss struts around like he owns the place."

"Big Grub did more than strut," said Asia. "He attacked us!"

"I'm not surprised." Eileen shook her head. "He goes after anybody new to his territory. What'd you do?"

Before I had a chance to respond, Asia spoke up wide-eyed with excitement. "Woody took a shovel and whacked him right on the back. You should've seen that turkey run off!"

"Good." Eileen nodded her head. "You showed Big Grub who's boss around here, Woody. Next time, he'll stay away from you."

I glanced around the yard, then asked, "Where's Jake and Buck?"

"In the south pasture."

"Why didn't they let me know?"

"You'll go out with them later." Eileen patted my shoulder. "I need you here for now."

Maria stepped on the porch with a stainless-steel bucket in each hand. "I milk cow."

"Muchas Gracias," said Eileen as she sat on a rocking chair and rubbed her abdomen. "Oh, I just felt my baby." She waved a hand. "Go with Maria, and she'll show you what to do."

"Yes Ma'am," I said as we turned and followed Maria.

Inside the barn, Maria opened the gate to a stall and said, "You watch me."

Maria stepped inside and whispered soothing words in Spanish to a cow. For the next several minutes we observed her method of washing the udder with warm, soapy water and drying thoroughly. While stroking the cow's side, she set another bucket underneath and paused. She gently held the teats and demonstrated how to properly milk the cow.

After Maria collected some milk, she nodded to Asia. "You try."

"Okay." Asia sat and easily added more of the white liquid like she'd been doing it all her life.

"Good." Maria looked at me and waved. "Your turn."

"Sure." I sat on the stool, thinking that if Asia could do it, this would be easy for me. I squeezed, pulled and got slapped in the face by the cow's tail. Maria held that swooshing fly swatter back and encouraged me to keep going. Finally, the milk splatted into the bucket a few times.

Although I didn't get much, Maria tapped my shoulder and said, "Okay. We go now." When I stood up, she opened the gate to the other stall and led a hungry calf over to its momma. Then Maria picked up the bucket, and we headed back to the house.

Later, while we helped in the kitchen, Maria stroked Asia's hair and admired the long, flowing strands down her back. "Oh, so pretty." Maria shook her head and said, "Not good for ranch work." She twirled the hair in a braided pony tail, checked it and smiled. "Better now." She handed Asia a small mirror. "You like?"

Asia smiled at her reflection. "Yes, thank you very much."

Eileen glanced out the kitchen window and said, "I reckon the men are getting hungry out there."

"Si." Maria opened the refrigerator door. "I make something." She set out cheese and lunch meat on the counter. "I take it to them."

"Gracias." Eileen handed Maria a loaf of bread. "You are so helpful."

"Mommy?" said a voice at Eileen's side.

Eileen looked at three-year old Summer, who pulled on her apron string. "Yes, baby?"

"Can I go with Maria?"

"No, sweetie." Eileen picked up Summer and kissed her cheek. "I need you to help Mommy around the house. Okay?"

"Yes, Mommy." Summer squirmed with high energy. "Can I help now?"

"Okay, baby." Eileen set her gently on the floor. "You can sort the pots and pans for me."

Summer pulled utensils out of a cupboard under the sink and scattered them on the floor with a loud, "Clang! Bang!"

In the living room, the other three kids argued and fussed.

"Mommy! Davy stole my doll!" Five-year-old Spring yelled, "Give it back!"

Eileen calmly walked into the living room and announced, "It's nap time."

"Ah mom." Nine-year-old Tommy groaned. "Why me? I didn't do anything."

"I know." Eileen patted Tommy's shoulder. "You're the man of the house while Daddy's in the field. I'm putting you in charge. Make sure they all lay down for 20 minutes."

"Yes, Ma'am," Tommy glared at Davy. "See what you did? Now I gotta babysit you again!"

Summer ran over from the cupboard and looked up. "Mommy, do I have to?"

"Yes." Eileen clapped her hands together, "Now get."

Aunt Eileen watched them all march upstairs with moans and groans. "I'll be up in a minute," she said. "You'd best be in bed when I get there."

I laughed at the way she handled this chaos. "You remind me of my Mom."

Eileen smiled. "She's my sister, alright. I reckon it runs in the family."

Asia stood beside me and smiled. "I like how you care for your family, Eileen. My Dad always yelled at me about everything."

Eileen shrugged and said, "I make a lot of mistakes, but I do the best I can." She paused and rubbed her stomach again. "By the way, I need your help while Maria takes the men's lunch out. You two go to the barn. Clean out the stalls for me. Okay?"

"Sure, not a problem." I nodded and tried to remember what I did when I was nine years old.

"Oh, here." Eileen gave Asia a basket with carrots. "Stop by the corral where the horses are and give them these treats."

We walked over to the corral and looked at six horses all standing in a circle. "What do we do now?" asked Asia.

"Simple." I grabbed a carrot and abruptly went right over to a red roan. The mare jerked her head back, snorted, and her nostrils flared. "Whoa," I watched her ears twitching. "It's alright, girl."

Asia stood beside me, held up a carrot and hummed softly. "Hello, beautiful," She gazed into the horse's dark eyes. "This is for you."

The mare sniffed, opened her mouth, munched and chewed on it like candy. Then a curious male buckskin stepped up to the fence. Asia smiled and said, "Hello, handsome." She stood on her tip toes and rubbed his neck. "Oh, you're so tall."

Just as Asia did this, the other horses stepped over to the fence and lined up next to her. "Oh, you're all such beautiful animals," she said. "Here you go." She handed out carrots to each one with a warm smile.

Seeing how they all gathered close to Asia, I asked, "Are you sure you haven't been around animals before?"

"I went to a zoo once." She glanced at me. "Does that count?" Then she turned and whispered affectionately into a horse's ear, "My name is Asia." She rubbed his neck and left side. "I'd like to be your friend."

Still amazed, I asked, "How can they respond to you so easily?"

"I don't know." Asia continued to stroke the animal's back. "This is the first time I've been up close to any horse." She giggled. "I think he likes me."

"Wow," I spoke softly.

"I don't understand this, Woody. It's like I belong here. Why do I feel so much love for these animals?"

"It's strange," I said. "We've only been on the ranch less than 24 hours and the animals are already responding to you." Drawn to her, I asked, "How is this happening?"

She gazed into my eyes. "I don't know."

"Asia?"

"Yes?"

"I like being with you."

"I feel the same way about you, too," she said.

"Would you like to stay here on the ranch for a while?" I asked.

"I'd like that."

"Okay, I'll ask my Aunt Eileen if you could help around here for the summer. You sure have a way with animals."

"Does that include you too?" She laughed and smiled.

"Yeah." I teased, "I'll follow you anywhere."

The mare whinnied.

Asia turned and patted the horse's neck. "Yes, I know. You want another treat."

"Forget the horse." I held her close. "What about me?"

"Down boy." She giggled and patted my chest. "We've got work to do."

"Oh," I slapped my forehead, "You have a way of distracting me." I spotted a shovel in a wheelbarrow. "It's time to scoop the poop." As I pushed it toward the barn, Asia picked up another shovel and followed me into a stall.

I scooped a pile of manure and dumped it into a wheelbarrow. "Phew."

The next day, my uncles gave us on-the-job training in the barn and corral. I lifted bales of hay out of a pickup truck while Asia fed the horses. With this hard work, my mind cleared and I no longer worried about getting drafted into the madness of war.

Asia was humming softly as she brushed Jake's mare, and the men stopped what they were doing, then listened to the way she talked in a soothing voice. "Be still. I am here."

I stepped over to my uncles and said, "This is what I've been trying to tell you. She's a natural around animals."

Buck looked over at Asia and asked, "Have you been on a ranch before?"

"No." She continued to rub down the horse. "I'm a city girl, I just love animals."

Jake came closer, nodded to Buck and they stepped away from the stall. "I'm curious," Jake whispered. "How about letting Asia look at Blacky's rear hoof?"

"Yeah, I was about to check on that myself," said Buck. "I noticed he was a little edgy when we rode in."

Buck turned and asked Asia, "Can you walk my horse for a minute?"

"Yes sir." Asia stepped over and patted Jake's buckskin. "Oh, you're so handsome," she said to the horse as she slowly walked the buckskin outside with keen interest. Then she stopped and looked at the hind quarters. "He's limping. Is it okay for me to lift his leg up?"

"Sure." Buck stepped beside her and patted the horse's rear. "I'll keep em steady."

Asia lifted one hoof, set it down and examined the other with interest. "Looks like a rock is stuck in his shoe." She gently rested its leg back in the dirt. "I think it hurts."

"Yep," said Buck. "How'd you figure out what was ailin him?"

"I don't know." Asia gazed into the horse's big eyes and stroked its muzzle. "I just sensed it."

Buck pulled out a pocket knife and lifted the horse's leg. "Okay, young lady. You watch and see what needs to be done."

Asia eagerly leaned closer and observed how Jake gently scraped until a small rock plopped to the ground. "Oh," she said. "That's better."

Both my uncles glanced at each and smiled. Jake nodded to Asia and said, "You catch on fast, young lady."

"Yeah," said Buck. "We could use a hand like you around here."

That afternoon, Jake and I chopped wood behind the barn. We both worked up a sweat, took our shirts off, then gradually we got into a rhythm of chopping, cutting and hauling, and my muscles began to ache. Tiny specks of sawdust were sticking to my heated skin, and even then, I enjoyed the chance to labor alongside my rugged uncle.

While the sun baked down on our backs, Jake wiped his brow with a bandanna and said, "Bring us some water."

I lifted the strap of a canteen that hung from a shady tree branch and brought it to him. Jake took several good swigs, gulped and streams of water dribbled down his red beard. "Ah, just what I needed." He smiled and handed it back to me. "Go on, nephew. It'll cool ya down."

"Thanks." Proud to share a drink with my uncle, I quenched

my thirst.

Back in the barn, Jake, Buck and I tinkered on the old broken-down flatbed truck. While I replaced a spark plug, it was kind of fun to work with them and smell the grease and oil. Of course, I could've gotten along just fine without being so up close and personal with our combined sweaty arms rubbing against each other.

Uncle Buck leaned over to tighten a rusty bolt and farted out a green gas cloud that I was certain would've killed us all. Jake and I stumbled outside gasping and choking as ole Buck continued to battle that bolt like nothing ever happened. Meanwhile, his cussing and swearing seemed to add more to the toxic fumes.

Jake squirted water on his head with the hose, glanced over at the barn and laughed. "I don't know about you, but there's no way I'll go back in there!"

"Good idea." I soaked myself for dear life and desperately tried to get that rotten egg smell off me. "I'm going for a walk to air out."

Nearby, Asia stepped out of a fenced-in garden with a basketful of tomatoes as a chicken scurried around her feet. "No, Carol." She brushed it away with her hand. "This is not for you."

"Carol?" I stopped and watched. "So, you're naming the animals now?"

Asia kept walking toward the ranch house and said, "Of course. That's Carol, the chicken."

13 MULE HEADED

On a sunny afternoon, Uncle Jake gave a lesson on the proper handling of a horse. Before we began our workout, he made sure my leather gloves fit right. "Okay, looks good."

Next, he gave me a knife in a sheath and said, "Keep it on your belt when you're working out here." He held up a lasso to illustrate his point. "If you ever get this tangled up with a big animal, you'll be able to cut your way free."

"Does that happen often?"

"Nope. But if it did, you'd get dragged in the dirt by over a thousand pounds of brute force."

Uncle Jake continued to explain the importance of staying alert and using common sense. We started by walking alongside his Appaloosa mare in the corral. I learned to stand by the left shoulder and this kept me in a good spot to safely guide her around. While I held the rope with my right hand about six inches from the bit, Jake patiently showed me how to lead his animal.

"That's good, nephew. Now, hold up a minute." He examined the way I held my lead rope. "Keep this other end to your side."

"Got it," I started to loop it around my left hand.

"No," Jake spoke firmly. "Not like that. If a horse pulls back or rears up, you'll get hurt real fast."

I unwrapped the rope and held it loose. "Like this?"

"Almost." Jake coiled it and said, "Now, hold the whole thing in your hand. In an emergency, you can easily let go and not get caught up. "Okay, now try it."

Our slow, methodical procedure continued, and we walked the horse around. I noticed that his mare seemed to hesitate, so I jerked a little too hard. She reared her head and seemed agitated.

"No." Jake placed his hand on my shoulder. "Just use light, short tugs and she'll go along."

When we finished this part of my lesson, my uncle led the Appaloosa over to a fence post. He took the extra rope and demonstrated how to tie it securely using a figure eight knot. Then he nodded to me and said, "Okay, your turn."

After several attempts, I finally got the hang of it. Satisfied with my progress, he smiled. "Good job. That's enough for now. Let's take Apple back to the barn."

"Apple?" I asked.

"Yep. She likes to eat apples. I reckon the name suits her." He handed the reins over to Asia and said, "Give her a good rub-down."

"Yes sir." Asia guided the horse as though she'd been doing it all her life.

Jake and I paused to watch her graceful moves in amazement, then we walked to another enclosure and began the next lesson. He patted the back of a big mule and looked at me. "You already know ole Gray here."

"Yep, I've been feeding him every morning."

"Good." Jake showed me how to put on a pack saddle and talked about the endurance of this beast of burden. "I've ridden him up to 10 miles or so without a break. These hooves of his are perfect for going over rugged terrain. Gray's skin is less sensitive and more resistant to the sun and rain than any horse," he continued to explain.

I was impressed with all these details until I heard him say, "You'll be riding ole Gray."

"What?" Surprised, I looked at this long-eared beast and glanced over at the Appaloosa. "You want me to ride a mule?"

"Yep." He removed the pack and placed a riding saddle on its back. "This is how you cinch it down."

I stared at that burly animal again and turned to see the sleek appearance of the Appaloosa. In my young mind, I made a judgement. To me, the mule was like my Dad's Buick. Jake's horse had all the appeal of a Corvette. I lifted my Padres baseball cap and brushed my brown hair back in confusion. "I don't get it."

"Get what?" Uncle Jake turned and faced me.

I pointed and said, "That's a dumb pack mule. Why would I ride this animal?"

"Oh." Jake laughed and shook his head. "Well, first of all, Gray's a lot smarter than you think. Second, if a mule gets stubborn, it's usually because a dumb handler puts em in a risky situation like on the edge of a cliff." He affectionately patted its side and neck. "Yep, he has enough common sense and a strong desire for self-preservation to let you know when he doesn't feel safe."

"But..." I stared at that unattractive animal again. "I'll look silly riding him next to the horses."

Jake placed his palm on my shoulder and looked me directly in the eyes. "Woody, I'm not trying to humiliate you. Ole Gray serves us well on the trail. He's been thoroughly trained. "I've ridden him on many days. We don't have the time to keep him in shape anymore. I need you to take charge."

I let out a deep sigh, "Okay, what do you want me to do?"

"Before we go riding together, you'll need to work with him. Learn his every move. Walk and ride him around the corral. From now on, you are his handler. Respect him and he'll trust you."

"Okay, Uncle Jake." I thought of how I wanted to learn all about ranching and this was part of my training.

He slapped me on the back and smiled. "That's the spirit."

Later, when we strolled back to the house, Jake said, "Your Ma told me you went horseback riding at a stable for practice a few times."

"Yep, I tried to go whenever I could on Sundays." I took my gloves off as we walked. "But I learned more from you today than at any other time." I looked up to my tall uncle. "Thanks."

After supper with the family, Jake took out a box from the hall closet. He opened it and held up a black Stetson cowboy hat with a yellow string along the brim. "Here's something for you to think about." He placed it on a hook above the fireplace.

"What do you mean?"

"That's your trophy," Jake answered. "Once you learn to be a good handler for ole Gray, that will be your reward for a job well done." He reached out his arm with that familiar twinkle in his eye. "Deal?"

"You're on." I shook his hand, then gazed at that cool cavalry-style Stetson and couldn't wait to proudly wear it.

Later, we sat in front of a black and white TV and watched news reports of the war. Reception was poor out there in the country, and I tried to adjust the flimsy rabbit ear antenna. Buck had no interest in getting a color set because there were bills to pay and mouths to feed. In brief flickering flashes we listened to the insane military objective of search and destroy missions. I'd heard this before and it sickened me.

Buck leaned forward on the couch with his hands firmly planted on his knees. It was the first time I saw him angry as a Korean War veteran. "Damn generals!" he fumed. "Is this what it comes down to?"

Jake stood up and railed his fist at the screen. "We can't win a war that way!"

"Yep!" Buck got up and paced the living room. "I reckon what it means is they keep a body count. Kill the enemy. Compare their dead with our losses."

"Yeah," Jake agreed. "The top brass likes to brag, we killed 2,000 VC and we only lost 253 of our men!"

"What about the civilians?" I asked while watching a scene of a burning village.

"Collateral damage." Uncle Jake let out a deep sigh and plopped back on the couch. "They lied to us, Woody! That body count includes dead, innocent civilians!"

While I listened, I began to see things more clearly. Victory in Vietnam was not assessed by holding territory. Instead this was a war of attrition. Wear down the enemy by killing as many as possible. Then publicize the body count on national TV.

It was like a light went on in my head. The mission of our military leaders had to be nothing but to kill. Stack up the dead enemy like firewood. Light the burning rage of the troops and kill more of them than they get of us. Startled by my new-found awareness of the truth, I walked out on the porch. How could this be? I grew up thinking that our nation could do no wrong.

Asia stepped out and wrapped her arm around my waist. "You okay?"

"Nope."

"It's about the draft again. Isn't it?"

"It's more than that."

"What is it?"

"People are dying for no reason! It's crazy! How can I fight for something that's morally wrong?"

"Oh, Woody." She rested her head on my shoulder. "I don't want you to go." She trembled in my arms.

I held her sweet face in my palms and looked into her eyes. "It's okay. I'm not going anywhere."

"But, what if..."

"Shh," I whispered and touched her lips with my finger. "We're together. That's all we need to think about now." I saw the fright in her eyes, just like when we first met. She had been running from a madman. This time it was different. She was no longer scared for herself, but for my well-being. In the short time we'd been on the ranch, it was like a refuge for us. "Don't worry. We'll figure out something."

"Okay," she said.

"Would you like to go for a walk?" I asked.

"I'd love to." Asia smiled.

Our arms naturally slid around each other's waists and our hips rubbed side to side as we walked together. No words were needed. Only the steady beats of our hearts mattered. I was older, a little wiser and more confident than the day I left home.

We stopped at the same alder tree where I prayed for my friend, Chap, who was missing in action. With my arm still around Asia, I whispered, "Look up." Together, we gazed at a half-moon blinking through swaying branches. We listened to the swoosh of wind. She began to relax in my arms.

"Let's get comfortable." I took off my jacket and spread it on a patch of soft grass.

When we sat down, she whispered, "It's beautiful here, Woody."

"Yes." I drew her closer. She closed her eyes and pursed her awaiting lips. We kissed as her warm hands rubbed the back of my neck.

A bright moonlight flickered through swaying leaves. My hormones raged and I wanted to make passionate love to her. Our hearts pulsed together, and she responded to my every move. It was like we were falling and floating at the same time.

Just as we were to go ever deeper, Asia gasped for air and breathed heavily.

"What's wrong?" I paused and tried to see her expression in the dim light.

"Woody, I'm scared."

"You don't have to be frightened with me, sweetie."

Asia sat up. "It's not that. I just don't feel right about going any further."

I gently brushed back strands of hair away from her lovely face. "I don't want to ever hurt you."

"I know, Woody. I trust you." She laid back again and we kissed again.

Although I was overheated with desire, I forced myself to go easy. She already expressed her concern and it was my responsibility to keep cool.

Asia shivered in my arms.

"Are you okay?" I asked.

"Sorry, Woody. I'm feeling cold."

"It's okay. Don't apologize." I held her hand and we stood up.

I put my coat on her shoulders and wrapped my arms in front of Asia while I warmed up her back on my chest. "How's that?"

"Much better." She turned and faced me. "Thank you, Woody." She kissed me. "You're always looking out for me."

"I just want you to be happy."

"Oh, Woody. I don't want this night to end."

"Let's enjoy it while we're together. Look." I pointed to the west. "See how the moon is dipping below that mountain peak?"

She looked up. "Time is slipping away."

"We have this moment."

"Yes." She snuggled in my arms. "This will be our special place."

The next morning, a bright orange globe peaked over the eastern horizon. This was my first day of working with the mule. Asia walked beside me toward the barn to begin our chores.

"Uh, oh." She pointed near the chicken coop. "Big Grub is attacking another turkey again!"

"Hey!" I yelled and clapped my hands.

Grub cackled, "Auck!" He skittered, stumbled, half-flew and disappeared behind the barn.

"That ornery Turkey!" I shook my head as we continued over to the barn. "I can't wait to have him for Thanksgiving."

Just as I grumbled those words, I thought of the high probability that I wouldn't be there to enjoy it by then. One way or another, I'd have to face the madness of war. In two weeks, I'd be 19. The draft loomed in my mind. Time was slipping away like a severed lifeline to my dreams of peaceful days on the ranch with Asia.

Unfortunately, I carried my anger with me when I stormed over to the mule. "Okay, dummy." I glared with disrespect for what I thought was a stubborn animal. "Looks like I'm stuck with you."

Gray snorted and twitched his ears.

I ignored the signs that Gray wasn't happy with me either. "Let's go." I abruptly grabbed his muzzle and pulled.

Gray whimpered and dug in like he was anchored to the ground.

"Come on." I groaned.

"Woody! You're hurting him!" Asia yelled from a nearby stall.

"Nah. He's being ornery."

"Well, you showed Gray who's boss." Jake walked into the barn and frowned. "Did you forget what I taught you yesterday?" He waited to hear my answer.

Embarrassed, I released my grip. My rage fizzled out like a deflating balloon. "Uh, sorry, Uncle Jake."

He showed no emotion. Instead, he calmly turned and waved a hand over his shoulder. "Come, nephew. Let's take a walk."

I followed him outside the barn and over to a corral. Jake leaned on a rail and watched the horses while I came alongside of him. I waited to get chewed out. He said nothing. Out here, working alongside my rugged uncles, I learned that words were not always necessary.

For a moment, we both observed the Appaloosa standing with another mare. They stood quietly side by side while facing a slight breeze from the north. I had a sense that these magnificent animals were socializing with each other as their tails swooshed away buzzing flies.

Uncle Jake made a low whistling sound. Apple, his steady horse looked over and walked up to him, then he rubbed her forehead and kept his focus on the animal. "Woody, what do you see here?"

"She trusts you."

"Yep." He turned and faced me. "Okay, you know what to do." Without another word, he opened the gate and stepped inside the corral. "Get to work." He closed it and patted his mare.

"Yes sir." I walked over to the mule and thought about Uncle Jake's handling of my behavior. He didn't go into a long lecture. Instead, he let me calm down, observe the animals and come to my own conclusion.

I had to get back to the basics of showing respect and building trust in my relationship with Ole Gray. This was the simple common-sense approach he already taught me the day before. He had made it clear that the mule was a highly intelligent, sensitive mammal, and it was my job to treat him in a caring manner.

Back in the enclosure, I went quietly over to the mule. Somehow, I wanted to show that I was sorry for being disrespectful. Instead, I hesitated. Gray's ears twitched and he was uneasy with me. I realized that my training was more about getting my mind right and less about the mule.

Asia opened the gate and stood beside me with a worried expression. "Is everything okay?"

"I don't know." I kissed her cheek and looked at Gray. "I messed up. Now I'm not sure how to make amends."

"Here, give this to him." She handed me a carrot. "Maybe it'll soften him up. Your uncle said to just take our time with these animals. Don't rush it."

"That's easy for you." I turned and gazed into her eyes. "You're a natural and they all respond to you."

"You can handle it, Woody." She smiled and placed her warm palm on my cheek. "You just need to relax. I trust you."

Trust, that was the key. I had to show Gray that he could depend on me. It was my responsibility to provide a regular routine that he could feel secure in. He was smart enough to not fall for any reckless behavior by me. I had to show him that I would do no harm.

I held up the carrot to Gray. He sniffed, took a bite and munched it without hesitation. "That's a good fella," I whispered and let him eat the rest of it out of my hand.

Asia smiled again and rubbed my back. "Well, I'll leave you two alone."

"Thanks, babe."

I picked up a brush and began to groom his back and softly spoke, "Sorry about getting rough." I kept brushing and sometimes I'd pat his sides with my left hand. "I'll do my best to treat you right from now on."

I humbly continued the care of his needs and made sure he was fed and given plenty of water. I removed the manure with a shovel and wheel barrel, then I thoroughly cleaned the stall to prevent any possible infections. Asia worked nearby. Sometimes I caught a glimpse of her smile, and I'd get temporarily distracted. She had a peaceful way about her that I could not explain. With each passing hour together, we developed a steady rhythm like the flow of a gentle stream. This helped the mule to relax with me.

Later, Uncle Jake stepped in the barn and waved to me. "Woody, bring out Gray."

"Yes sir." I held my lead rope and the mule calmly followed me out to the corral.

"Okay, let's get started," said Jake. "Remember that Gray has been thoroughly trained for whatever comes about on the trail." He put a blanket and saddle on the mule and continued to teach.

While I listened, Asia came out and joined us. "Can I watch?"

"Of course." He smiled and added, "I reckon you're part of the family now."

Jake looked at me again. "Alright, let's just say that Gray here still needs a lot of work before you can ride him." He faced the left side of the mule. "To get him used to you, it's best to start like this." My uncle put his boot into the stirrup, lifted himself up and stepped back down again. "Take plenty of time. Don't rush it. This ain't the big city."

"So, you're letting the mule get used to your weight?" I asked.

"Yep." Jake lifted himself up on one leg again. He paused and rubbed Gray's side, then stepped down. "You keep repeating this routine until you're sure he's ready for you to mount up for the first time."

"Well, that's assuming he hasn't been trained." I patted the mule and asked, "Since he's ready, do I still take the same approach?"

"Good question." My uncle studied the animal's body language. "He looks steady enough. Just keep in mind that you're new to him. Okay, let's see how well he responds to you. Go ahead, Woody. Put your boot in the stirrup, lift your body weight up and hold for about 10 seconds."

I followed his instruction and counted to myself, then stepped down. Without waiting for further directions, I repeated it one more time. I figured it was enough. So, I abruptly swung my leg over and plopped my rear on the saddle.

Gray's ears twitched. He whimpered. His legs fidgeted.

Jake held the reins to keep the mule still and frowned. "No, Woody. You're rushing things again. Now dismount and rub his sides to calm him down."

This was going way too slow for me and I let out a deep sigh, then got off. We continued our lessons the rest of the afternoon. After a dozen slow repetitions, I finally gained Ole Gray's trust and rode him around the corral with ease. Asia came alongside while slowly riding a red roan mare.

I was more comfortable on the mule, and I noticed that he was almost the height as the horse. Also, his girth was a lot bigger and heavier in appearance. Jake had placed a half-dozen small logs in the circle to let this intelligent animal show off his skills. While I rode him through these obstacles, I saw how he was bred for trekking rugged trails, and I began to have more respect for his steady abilities.

After two weeks of working around the ranch, I was more confident of being Gray's handler. Then one day, as the sun was setting, Uncle Buck rode up to the barn on his quarter horse and dismounted. "Found some fence line bent from a fallen branch," he said to Jake.

"I'll go out with you at first light." Jake nodded to him.

"No, I need you to get some supplies in town." Buck looked at me and said, "Woody, you come with me in the morning."

"Yes sir."

"Can you shoot a rifle?" Uncle Buck asked me with a worried expression.

"I've practiced at a shooting range a few times with my Dad."

Jake looked surprised. "What happened out there?"

"I saw cougar scat near the river north of here."

"Trouble?"

Buck frowned. "Yep. A calf is missing."

14 HARD RIDE

At dawn, I walked out to the barn with Uncle Buck. Before we stepped inside, I noticed a pinkish cloud hovering like a space ship to the east of us. I took a deep breath and savored the crisp, clean country air. This was my first day to ride out on ole Gray, and although I didn't know what to expect out there, I looked forward to being with my rugged Uncle in the vast wilderness.

Buck opened the gate to a stall and asked, "You sure you can handle the mule?"

"Yeah, Uncle Jake taught me everything I need to know."

He tossed a blanket and saddle on his quarter horse, Blacky and glanced at me. "Good. We have a lot of hard riding to do."

"Got it." Although I was a little apprehensive about how well I could handle the mule, I had to show no fear. That was one of the lessons I learned while working around my uncles. "I'll get him saddled and ready."

When I cinched a strap, Buck held up a .22 caliber rifle. "Take this." He gave me a handful of shells and said, "I'm glad you' had been practicing at a shooting range with your pa."

"Yep." I loaded the cartridge. "I wanted to be sure I'd be ready."

"Let's move out." He mounted up and waited for me to come alongside on the mule. "When we go out a ways, we'll stop and practice a few rounds. Got to see if you're as good as your pa says." He paused and gave me a stern look. "From now on, you stay close to me. You do exactly as I say at all times."

"Yes sir."

He pulled the reins to the left and we headed toward the east together. We rode in silence until we came to a grassy knoll.

"Okay, Woody, let's see what you can do." Uncle Buck dismounted and pointed to a tree stump a hundred feet away.

"That's your target."

"Yes sir." My saddle creaked slightly as I got off the mule and tied the reins on the branch of an alder tree.

I loaded my weapon and aimed at the stump. "No," Buck said. "You're too high." He stood behind me and added, "Bring it down a bit."

Again, I aimed and asked, "How's that?"

"That's good." He stepped back and watched.

"Bam!" A piece a of bark chipped off. I hit it.

"Good shot." He patted my shoulder. "Okay. You'll do."

"Yes sir."

"Let's move out. Got hard riding ahead."

We rode on further toward the west. The glare of the sun was in direct line of my sight and I kept the brim of my cap low over my eyes. Without sunglasses, I had a sense of what it was like for my great-grandfather, Clancy Brannigan, who settled in this land almost a hundred years ago. He came out west in a covered wagon with his bride, Claire and carved out a hard life. I remembered the stories I heard of the constant threats of starvation and Apache arrows. We continued up a steep slope, and it was like I'd been transported back in time. Further down in a valley, I listened to the hooves splashing in puddles and the ground was saturated from the rain that night.

I had no idea what Buck planned, but I knew that when he said, "let's go," you follow orders and don't ask questions. As a Korean War vet, he was the silent type.

Dozens of Angus were scattered about and they all seemed skittish. Thunder rumbled far off to the west, and a cool wind blew through the ponderosa. Blacky and Gray both snorted. None of us liked the edginess in the air.

Buck rode on at a steady canter, and I tried to keep up while my bouncing rear ached. His horse halted about several hundred yards away. My uncle waved his hat to follow him toward a southern ridge. I turned ole Gray in that direction while rocks crunched under the mule's big, sturdy hooves.

We headed through a stand of trees. I ducked under a low-hanging branch and stopped at a brown murky pond. Buck had already dismounted and rushed waist-deep to rescue a calf stuck up to its neck in mud. I swung my leg over, slipped and fell several times before I waded out. With my gloved hands planted on its muddy rear I pushed. Buck wrapped his arms under its front legs and pulled on the other end. When the frightened animal began to move forward, the soles of my boots were sticking in the ooze. Worried that I might get stuck in quick sand, I grabbed its tail.

"Hold on!" Buck sloshed back out, mounted up and lassoed around the calf's neck while Blacky pulled us both forward. I clumsily held on until we made it to dry ground.

At the water's edge, a cow looked on and mooed loudly, then her calf ran over. I paused to catch my breath. Buck kept going without a break. He rode to a ridge where we rounded up several more calves lost in thick brush. We tried to maneuver them out of this entanglement of thorns, and I discovered first-hand why Buck insisted we both wear thick chaps on our legs. After a lot of twists, turns and back steps, I also appreciated the skills of our highly-trained animals. Finally, we guided the calves out to other roaming cattle. Before I had a chance to relax, off he went again while I tried to keep up.

Buck slowed down and looked over at a hillside with massive boulders the size of wrecked cars. Above that rugged area, I spotted a half dozen vultures. When I rode up alongside him, I noticed his furrowed brow. "What's wrong?" I asked.

Buck silently dismounted, tied the horse on a branch and climbed up on a boulder. After a half day of working around him, I instinctively followed and didn't say another word. I stood next to him and focused on what he looked at down in a narrow crevice. There, we saw a cow struggling to get out of its tight spot between the rocks. Blood dribbled out of its mouth and nostrils. My gut wrenched as I realized that this poor animal probably had internal injuries. I wanted to ask, what now, but I kept quiet and waited for Buck to respond.

He climbed back down the boulder and returned with a rifle.

I watched in sadness while this stoic rancher aimed and pulled the trigger. "Bam!" One bullet penetrated its skull. That suffering cow was put out of its misery.

We rode on side by side in silence. Finally, I said, "Sorry about your cow."

For a moment, Buck said nothing as I listened to the steady hoofbeats in drying dirt. "No use being sorry, nephew." Another minute passed. He looked straight ahead with his left hand resting on the saddle horn. "It's a hard life out here. You take the bad with the good."

Little did I know his wisdom would be tested soon after we rode along a stream. Blacky neighed and Gray whimpered like they sensed that something was not right. I glanced at Buck while we moved slowly along numerous rocks and boulders. To our right, he focused his attention on a ridge with crevices that made perfect hiding places for predators. I looked off to the left and observed a herd of cattle grazing several hundred yards away.

Buck held up on the reins and pulled out his rifle again. On the ground, we saw a long trail of blood that led in between two boulders. Nothing moved. It was so quiet; I could hear my heartbeat. I didn't like it. I slid my rifle out of the saddle holster, looked over at my uncle and waited for orders.

Buck pointed to the stream. With a few hand signals, he wanted me to move slowly to the water flowing about 50 feet away and wait there.

I nodded, turned Gray to my left and positioned myself further back where I had a wider view of our surroundings. Once I assured him that I was ready, Buck pointed his two fingers to his eyes and back at me. He glanced at the ridge and made a sweeping motion with his hand.

Understanding that I needed to watch the rocks above him, I gave an okay signal. I held my gun ready and focused on the rocks above us. In those tense moments, my senses were on high alert. On a razor's edge of uncertainty, I listened. A fly buzzed nearby. Nothing moved. I scanned the rocks. What was that up on the boulders? A cougar peered down from an outcrop!

I shouted, "Look up!" I pulled the trigger. "Bam!"

Buck lifted his gun and paused. The cougar had vanished.

I scanned the boulder and waited for orders.

Buck dismounted Blakey and signaled with hand gestures to watch the rocks on my right. I turned the mule and kept my rifle ready as I scanned along the boulders.

He nodded and moved to our left. With each step, he aimed the rifle straight ahead. While I focused in the opposite direction, I kept my finger on the trigger. My pulse raced. Somewhere in those rocks, a cougar lurked. Thunder rumbled in the hills above us.

I heard the scuff of his boots and looked. He stood still and lowered his rifle. I waited for his command again. The wind stopped. Nothing moved. With his eyes still focused on the ground, Buck said, "Come here, nephew." His voice was low and direct.

"Yes sir." I rushed to his side and peered into a three-foot wide opening in the rocks. There, I saw the remains of a calf. Chunks of red meat had been torn away. It was fresh kill.

Without a word, Uncle Buck mounted up on his quarter horse. "Move out."

I took one last look at the dead animal. Blood still oozed from its sides. Guts were exposed to the flies. In a split second, I thought of that far-off war in Vietnam. Is this what it's like in combat?

I heard the faint rustling of a saddle and looked to see Buck turning the quarter horse to his left. He rode off.

I mounted up on the mule and followed Buck. Finally, I caught up to him, and we continued to ride north. I heard crackling, rumbling, then a loud boom. A lightning bolt struck the ground about a mile away or so.

"Getting close," I said.

Buck held the reins and kept riding in silence as rain drops pelted us.

"Uh, shouldn't we?"

"Yep." Buck gave a quick boot and yelled, "Hee ya!" The quarter horse took off.

I was right behind him as we both raced toward the ranch. The closer we got, the harder it rained. When we passed by a dozen Angus, their drenched black hides glistened like licorice. A cool wind nipped the back of my neck. My jeans were soaked.

Even in my discomfort, I had a deep sense of being fully alive and I joyfully breathed in the clean, moist air. Lightning flashed over a mountain to the west. I gripped the reins. Hooves splashed. Ahead, was the ranch and safety.

Just as we rode in, a monstrous storm overtook us so fast that daylight vanished into an eerie darkness. We pulled up on our reins in front of the barn, dismounted and rushed our animals inside. Uncle Buck and I had to care for them before we could think of our own needs. They came first. After two weeks of working on the ranch, I was used to taking it all in stride. We wiped them down and provided their feed and water. Outside, it poured, and I heard the rain battering on the roof.

Satisfied, Buck said, "Come on, nephew."

We ran over to the ranch house and our boots splashed in puddles. Up on the porch, we took off our drenched parkas and hung them on wooden pegs. A strong gust of wind pushed us toward the door while we struggled to pull off our muddy boots and dropped them to the floor with a clunk, clunk.

Just as we rushed inside, Asia hugged me. "I was so worried. Are you okay?"

"Yep." I glanced at Uncle Buck and tried to sound hardened like him.

Aunt Eileen kissed her husband while their four wide-eyed kids circled and looked up. "Daddy," said little three-year-old Summer as she reached out her arms. "Pick me up."

Uncle Buck lifted his daughter and gave a quick kiss on her rosy cheek. "Hello, baby girl."

He affectionately put his arm around Eileen and smiled. I realized I was seeing the other side of my uncle. Outside, he was a tough, seasoned combat vet that I followed obediently. Inside with his family, he was a lovable, caring father and husband.

When we all settled in by the fireplace, we waited for the rain to stop. It didn't take long. Soon, the storm raged through like a herd of cattle. Crackling, rumbling and roaring gave way to silence and the air became still. Sunlight peeked into our windows and we all got back to the normal hustle of children running around playing as though nothing out of the ordinary happened that day. This reminded me of my own family life that I left back in San Diego. I wasn't homesick, though. Now I enjoyed being with my relatives tucked far away on a ranch 20 miles north of Flagstaff.

15 CROSSROAD WITH ASIA

I sat on the porch swing with Asia and we observed a steady dripping of water off the eaves. Each droplet hung and shined like diamonds in the glare of a setting sun and gravity pulled them downward into glittering puddles.

Asia rested her head on my shoulder, and I was content to have her beside me. I leaned closer. She turned her head and our lips caressed.

"I like being here with you, Woody." Her voice was low and breathy. "I feel safe in your arms."

I responded with another kiss and we lingered in the warmth of each other. Inside the house, we could hear the pattering of little feet. Children giggled and played in the background. Strangely, it was like soothing music in my ears. For the first time in my young life, I wondered what it would be like to settle down someday with a girl like Asia. Was she the one for me? What an odd thought. Why was I thinking this way? I had the whole world out there to see and it wasn't a good idea to get serious with her.

Just a few nights ago, we savored our passionate hours under a tree together. Realizing that I was going out of my mind for this girl, I quickly stood up and leaned against the damp porch rail.

"What's wrong?" Asia came alongside and wrapped her arm around my waist.

"Nothing." I looked toward the setting sun over a distant mountain. Clouds were turning a bright red, and I was embarrassed and tried to get a grasp of my emotions. What was happening to me? Although my hormones raged inside me it was more than a lustful desire to make love to her. I sincerely wanted to be with her in a way that I never thought I'd experience at this time of my life. It was happening too fast. I turned and gazed into her eyes. I couldn't speak.

Asia placed her warm hand on my face and asked, "What is it, Woody?"

My response was an abrupt, "I'm going for a walk." I stomped down the steps of that porch and headed toward the barn. "I need to think."

"Wait!" I heard her running to me. "I want to go with you."

I stopped and faced her. "No. I need to be alone." I turned and walked away.

"Go ahead, then!" Asia shouted. "I don't want to be with you either!"

Hearing her sharp words, I wanted to go back and explain about my conflicting emotions boiling inside me. Instead, I walked down the country road away from the ranch. What the heck was wrong with me? I had no idea. I heard the sound of each step crunching in gravel and sloshing in left-over puddles from the storm. Down a side muddy path, I continued on and headed into a pasture. Twilight settled in fast, and I knew I had to get back. I stopped and looked out from a grassy knoll. Darkness was just moments away.

Disoriented, I was angry at myself for not paying attention to where I was going. I saw a faint orange glow to the west. The ranch had to be in that direction. I started the long walk back and knew I had to be careful in the dark. What a damn fool I was to think I could go off half-cocked like an ill-tempered school boy. Why did I do such a crazy stunt? My mind was cluttered with thoughts and worries about my future.

I stopped and asked myself, how did I get here? I gazed into the heavens and saw a great expanse of the cosmos. Above a faint pink horizon, I saw flickering stars beyond the division of light and dark, and it all seemed to shrink my presence in the grand scheme of the universe. I stared at all those stars and wondered about my existence. Why was I put on this planet in the first place? What is the meaning of all this? Does my young life really matter?

My eyes had adjusted to the darkness, and I could make out

trees in the dim light of a waning moon to the west. In the stillness, I listened to my steady breathing and thought of Asia again. From the first moment I saw her, I was captivated by the look in her eyes. She appeared lost and scared then. The next thing I knew was that we were being chased by a madman. For two days we had been on the run. During those nights, we huddled in each other's arms. In that time, I had a strong desire to protect and take care of her.

Perhaps it had to do with how I was raised. As the eldest son I was expected to look out for the family. Asia's life was different. She grew up around an abusive, domineering father. Her mother died and she was all alone. Here on the ranch, she had been welcomed with open arms by the family after I told them about her struggles. They all observed how well she looked after the kids whenever Aunt Eileen needed help around the house. My uncles were impressed with the way she cared for the animals, and everyone accepted her.

While I thought of all this, I realized that I wanted so much to be with this girl. Whenever I saw her coming toward me, I loved to see her face and the way she smiled. Wait a minute. Do I love her? No, that can't be. I'm too young to get caught up in such a deep emotion. I've got to see the world and go on wild adventures before I settle down.

I scratched my whiskers that had grown thicker and tried to think. Okay, maybe I am falling in love with Asia. Now what? I remembered the calls for men to fight in Vietnam. This was getting even more crazy. It was like being squeezed between peace and war at the same time.

In that darkness, I was lost in three ways. First, I couldn't see how to get back to the ranch without falling into a hole. Second, I had no clear direction for my future. Uncle Sam was determined to make that for me, and I sure didn't like being pushed around. Third, I wanted to be with Asia, and I couldn't see any way of living without her.

"Okay, God." I scanned the stars. "I'm lost. Help me."

A bright light peeked over a ridge. Surprised, I looked to see headlights bouncing along the country road. It came closer, and I tried to cover my eyes with my arm from the glare. When the vehicle stopped alongside of me, I recognized it as Uncle Jake's truck.

He leaned over and pushed the door open. "Hop in."

I slid in the seat. "Thanks," I said. "I was on my way back after a walk."

Jake put the stick shift in first gear and turned around. "Yep." He drove in the direction of the ranch. As we bounced along he said, "Asia was worried about you, nephew."

"No need to worry." I tried to make light of my going out alone in the dark after a storm. "Just needed time to think."

"Yeah, I reckon it's good to do that." He made a sharp left turn to swerve around a three-foot-wide puddle in the road. The right wheel dipped and splashed water on my side window.

I gripped the dash with my right hand, as he adjusted the steering wheel again. "Uncle Jake, can I ask you a question?"

"Go ahead." He smiled with his usual easy-going sense of humor. "I may not have the answer but fire away."

"What's it like to be in love with Maria?"

"Why?" He laughed and glanced at me. "She's already taken, ya know."

"Uh, well…" I responded awkwardly. He had a way of throwing me off kilter with his ridiculously funny remarks.

Uncle Jake smiled and pulled the truck over. "I know what you mean, nephew. Just kidding with you. Come on, let's talk." We got out and stood 10 feet away from the front bumper. "You know…" He paused. "I'm not much for words. How can I put this? I've been with other women, but Maria's different. When I'm away she's all I think about. I can't wait to see her face and hear her voice. When I'm with her, I can't stop looking at her."

"Uncle Jake, that's how I feel about Asia." I folded my arms across my chest and groaned. "This is lousy timing. I can't get serious now. What am I going to do?"

"Take it slow. Don't rush it. Enjoy the time you have with your woman." He placed his big hand on my shoulder. "See how it all plays out."

"I'll probably have to leave the ranch soon. I could get drafted. Or I'll have to enlist." I looked up and saw his red-bearded face in the headlights. "I worry about Asia."

"She'll be safe here. As long as she wants to stay, this'll be her home. Your Aunt Eileen already spoke to Asia about it. We're her family now."

"Thanks, Uncle Jake."

"You're welcome." He took a deep breath, exhaled and added, "Besides, we all can see the way she looks at you. If that ain't love, I don't know what is. Yep, she's a real keeper. No matter what happens, she'll be waiting for you."

We got back in his truck and headed to the ranch. I was glad to have this talk with my Uncle Jake. Since he was the younger brother of my Mom, I had a close bond with him. He always had a joke; a warm smile and he became my mentor. I had a different relationship with Uncle Buck, who was married to my Aunt Eileen, my Mother's sister. He was more stoic and managed the ranch with a stern hand.

That night, I wanted to talk with Asia, but she was getting the kids ready for bed. She had wiggly Summer in one arm while chasing after five-year-old Spring. "Come on," she said with a giggle. "Let's put the toys away and we'll go up to your room."

I could tell she had fun with them as I rounded up the boys and herded them into their bedroom upstairs. Out on the porch, Uncle Buck sat with Aunt Eileen on the swing. Her baby was due in a week and they talked about preparing for the fifth addition to their growing family. Uncle Jake had gone out to the barn and checked on the animals before we all settled in.

Later, I tried to sleep on the couch so I could be ready for a busy day with my uncles. We planned to hunt for the cougar at first light, and none of us were in the mood for killing, but we had to prevent the loss of more calves. I kept fluffing the pillow and tossed around like a restless dog. It was quiet upstairs, and

I wanted to talk with Asia. The thought of her being mad after I walked away nagged at me.

I couldn't stand it any longer. "Okay," I whispered to myself. "You might as well get up."

Out on the porch, I paced back and forth. I couldn't get Asia out of my mind as I remembered the precious moments we had over the past several weeks together. I kept seeing her smile, hearing the way she giggled and savoring her soft skin. Hours ago, she blurted out words in anger while I walked away. Neither one of us had a chance to smooth things over. It was driving me crazy.

I stopped and sighed. "Okay, I'll just have to wake her up and apologize."

I went back inside, and just as I started to go upstairs, I discovered that Asia was standing at the bottom step. She was so close, I almost bumped into her. Before I could say a word, she reached out and surrendered in my arms. I lifted her up and held her tight.

"I'm sorry, Woody." Her voice had that breathy sweetness again. "I don't want to be mad at you."

"I'm the one to apologize." I gently set her down and took her hand. "Let's talk." We sat on the couch, and I tried to explain my reason for walking away earlier. I stumbled for the right words that never came out. Instead, I said, "Asia, I want to be with you." I hesitated.

"What are you trying to say, Woody?"

"Um, I really care about you." I squeezed her hand. "I don't know when I'll have to leave. If I do, would you like to stay here with my family?"

"Yes." She wrapped her arms around me and whispered, "We'll work it out together."

We cuddled on the couch until we heard little Summer crying upstairs. We looked at each other and hoped that the beckoning of a child would stop. It didn't.

"I better check on her." She stood up, but my hand still held on tight. "I have to go," she said.

"I know." I released my grip and watched her go up the steps. Asia went into the bedroom where she usually slept with the girls. More like a nanny, it was her responsibility to look after them while Aunt Eileen rested during the night. We all eagerly pitched in to keep the family happy and thriving.

As I laid back on the couch, I thought of how that had been our way since my ancestors first settled this land a hundred years ago. They worked together and built homes out in the wilderness. Before they headed west, they were a proud, hardy people, who immigrated from the Scottish Lowlands and fought against the British during the Revolutionary War.

My mother grew up here, and she told me about our family. The longer I stayed on the ranch, the more I was a part of this rich heritage, and I was determined to stay. The Vietnam War raged on and I wondered how long I could hold out.

16 COUGAR HUNT

From where I had slept on the couch, I awoke in the darkness to a hand shaking my shoulder. I saw Uncle Buck towering over me. "Get dressed," he ordered. "We're heading out after breakfast."

"Yes sir." I pulled on my jeans and prepared to hunt for a hungry cougar that already mauled a calf. We had to kill it before we lost another one of our animals.

I downed two slices of toast smeared with blueberry jam and a strong cup of black coffee in the kitchen. Maria sang a peaceful song in Spanish while she and Asia set out our packed lunches on the counter.

"Where's Aunt Eileen," I asked.

Uncle Buck took a sip of his coffee and set the cup down. "She's resting upstairs. Our baby is due this week." He picked up his lunch and nodded to me. "Let's go."

Asia handed me a sack lunch and said, "Stay safe."

"Thanks." I gave her a quick kiss and wanted to say more, but we had to go.

Jake took his bag from Maria and paused in an affectionate hug, then said, "Love ya."

I rushed out to the barn with my uncles as our flashlight beams lit the way in a quiet darkness. Our boots sloshed in thick mud from last night's fast-moving storm, and thousands of bright stars peeked through parting clouds like holiday decorations. We made sure the animals were well-fed and given plenty of water in anticipation of a long day ahead. I saddled up the mule and my uncles got their horses ready.

Buck gave me a rifle, then handed me a box of shells. "You did good yesterday." He placed his hand on my shoulder and studied me. "Remember cougars are known to attack from behind. Stay alert."

"Yes sir." I loaded the chamber and secured my weapon in my saddle holster.

I opened the flap of my pack on the mule, slid my lunch inside, and walked him out of the barn. With my left foot in the stirrup, I swung my right leg over the saddle, then glanced toward the house. Asia stepped onto the porch and waved under the glow of lights by the door. I responded by lifting my cap up and nodded. In the past three weeks this had become a habit of ours and it was like we were gazing at the same morning sunrise.

I turned and straightened my neck to focus on the mule's ears. Although the view was not as attractive, ole Gray knew exactly where he was going. My uncles were a hundred feet ahead of me. In the twilight, I rode by the grassy knoll where Asia and I liked to sit under the alder tree. We had promised to make this our special place to meet. I also thought of my friend, Chap who was still missing in action, and I whispered a prayer for his safe return while riding out.

I heard Buck and Jake talking as I rode up alongside. Since they tended to ride in silence I was curious and asked, "What's going on?"

Uncle Jake said, "This morning we heard on the radio that more troops were being sent to Nam."

"That damn war is heating up," said Uncle Buck.

Jake spat on the ground. "Yep, them fools in Washington are calling for more of our boys to fight in that crazy war."

"I reckon it's only a matter of time before you get drafted, nephew." Buck rode alongside me and our mounts were neck and neck. "We were hoping this madness would all blow over, Woody." He paused and listened to the clop, clop of hooves. "We're both worried that time's running out."

"Yes sir, I'm just not ready to leave this place."

"Yep." Buck nudged Blacky and turned away.

We rode on in silence. None of us had an answer to the uncertainty of my future. We had to focus on our present objective of hunting down that cougar. Out on the range, I learned a man had to handle the grittiness of his chores even though he had no stomach for killing. You did what needed to be done without hesitation. That was the way of our ancestors, and we had a deep connection to their rugged spirit. This kept us alert to a change of wind or the behavior of our animals.

While I followed the lead of my uncles, I studied the landscape and watched for any unusual signs that the cougar could be close by. Then I noticed a dozen head of cattle had dashed away from a rocky slope. Surprised to see this sudden movement, I yelled, "Hey! What's going on over there?"

We took off in that direction and by the time we arrived, the cows had stopped to graze as though nothing had happened.

"Something must've spooked them," said Buck while he got off his horse and studied the ground for cougar tracks.

Jake scanned the terrain with binoculars. "I don't see anything." He slid the glasses back in his saddle bag. "What do you think, Buck?"

"Head to them rocks." Buck got on Blacky, took off his hat and wiped his brow with a bandana he usually wore.

I noticed an ugly four-inch scar along the back of his neck. He quickly put it back on and tied it. This was his way of keeping the wound out of sight, and I wondered if that was from combat in Korea. We all knew he had a purple heart although he never talked about it.

We pulled on the reins and rode in that direction. I followed on the mule and traversed across a pebbly stream with ease while their horses hesitated until they were coaxed by my uncles. We reached the same hillside where we last saw the cougar. Massive car-sized boulders provided hiding places among cracks and crevices. To our left, we stared at the half-eaten bloody remains of another calf. It looked like a recent kill.

"The cougar must've picked up our scent," Uncle Buck said.

Jake swung his leg over and dismounted the Appaloosa. He pointed the barrel of his gun at the ground and paused. "Okay," he whispered to me. "We'll have a look see. You stay back and keep your eyes peeled."

I nodded, pulled out my rifle and scanned the rocks. Fresh blood dripped from the rocks as though the cougar had just carried a mouthful to a narrow opening above us. I didn't like the looks of it. That wildcat was close by.

Jake and Buck handed me the reins of their horses and climbed on the rocks with their weapons ready while I sat on the mule. My senses were on high alert. Time slowed down. A slight breeze cooled my sweaty back.

Jake worked his way to the top of the rocky hillside while Buck edged along the base and peeked in one crevice after another. With so many places for the cougar to hide in, I began to wonder how we could ever find that wild cat. I spotted movement to my left. A skittish field mouse ran between boulders. False alarm, I thought. Or was it?

Maybe the cougar spooked it. I snapped my fingers twice. My uncles looked over, and I pointed to the spot. Buck nodded and moved 20 feet to my left while Jake positioned himself from above. This gave us an overall view of our surroundings. We waited in silence. I kept my rifle aimed where the mouse had been. Nothing moved. I needed to be patient. Young and cocky, I was not good at it. I ached to see that cougar run out.

Buck came over and glanced in the crevice where I aimed my weapon. "What'd ya see?"

"A mouse ran out from there." I adjusted my sore rear on the saddle and the leather creaked. "Thought you should know."

"You did good." Buck studied the rocks again. "My gut tells me that cougar is still hiding in those rocks."

"Yes sir." I stood up on the stirrups to get a better look on the rocks above us. "I don't like it."

"Hold it." Buck held up his hand. "Did you hear that?"

"What's up?" asked Jake as he stepped off the rocks and came alongside of us.

"Shh!" Uncle Buck cocked his head. "Listen."

"Meow."

"Sounds like a kitten," said Jake.

Buck climbed up a 10-foot-wide boulder to our left and knelt at a narrow gap between the bloody rocks. He shook his head, frowned and slid back down on his rear. "I heard something scurrying down there."

"Damn it!" Jake took off his cowboy hat and brushed his fingers through scruffy red hair. "I reckon that cougar's a momma with her kittens."

"Yep." Buck stared at the terrain. "Got no stomach for leaving a bunch of hungry orphans in that lair."

Surprised to see these tough ranchers expressing concern for the safety of baby wildcats, I asked, "So, are we going to let her go then?" I glanced at the blood stains on the ground."

"Nope." Buck stared at the same spot where the entrails of a calf were strewn on the ground.

"Got no choice." Jake shook his head. "We'll flush her out." He picked up a fist-sized rock and said, "I'll make some noise. Maybe she'll run out to try and divert us away from her kittens." He climbed up the boulder and tapped loudly on the granite slate.

We waited and watched. Nothing happened. Buck said, "Try it again. I'll fire a shot in the air."

Jake pounded on the rock again and dropped it into a two-foot-wide gap in the boulders with a "Clackity, clack" sound.

Buck pulled the trigger. Kaboom! It echoed through the rocky canyon.

To my left, the cougar charged out. "Look!" I aimed my rifle and pulled the trigger.

"Pop! Pop! Pop!" Three shots rang out simultaneously. It happened so fast; I couldn't tell who fired first. That wildcat staggered two hundred feet away and flopped like a rag doll.

No one said a word. Jake and Buck leaped off the rocks, and we rode out to what we hoped was a dead, harmless animal. Instead, we found only drops of blood.

Buck rode ahead of us and we followed in a westerly direction. He leaned to his right side and tracked a trail of bloody spots over rocky terrain until we pulled up at a narrow stream.

"Got a wounded cougar on our hands." He pointed to the edge

of mountain run-off. "She crossed here."

"Yep, she's pissed and meaner than a junkyard dog," said Jake.

Buck turned the reins and Blacky's hooves sloshed in ankle-deep water. Jake and I came in from behind and we crossed over to dry land. We knew she was a desperate mother fighting for her survival and the safety of her cubs. Primal instinct drove her to steer us away from the lair and she would do anything to keep them alive. She was dangerous and we took no chances.

The horses snorted and stomped their feet. Gray tilted his head back and whimpered.

"Take it easy, fella." I rubbed the side of his thick neck.

A dark cloud drifted overhead and blocked the sun's bright, warm rays. Our mounts were getting increasingly spooked, and that wildcat could sneak up without warning.

The mule snorted and jerked his head back.

Jake turned his Appaloosa and circled back to me. "It's all right, Woody. I've seen Gray do this before."

I patted the mule's shoulder. "How do I handle him."

"You're doing fine." Jake glanced back over the rocky trail. "Don't worry about getting hit from behind. Just keep him steady and moving forward."

"Yes sir."

"Ya see," Jake whispered. "There's something you need to know about ole Gray here. He killed a cougar two years ago. He stomped on it with those big hooves of his." Jake smiled as though he relived the memory. "That mule bit into its neck and didn't let go until it was as dead as a rabbit in a trap."

"Yeah, I believe it," I said. Gray's teeth chomped at the bit. He was ready for a fight, and I rubbed his shoulder. "Whoa. Take it easy."

"Just remember, if we're attacked, jump off as fast as you can." Jake's voice was low, like a whisper. "He'll stomp the hell of any wildcat faster than a strutting bull moose. That's for damn sure."

We rode on and Buck stopped often to check for signs of blood or tracks. Thick brush made it more difficult, but we trekked on in the rhythm of hoofbeats on rocky slate.

"Hold it." Buck held up his right arm, dismounted and walked his horse along the edge of a small creek, then scanned the terrain. Water gurgled over pebbles and flowed under a fallen mesquite tree.

I patted Gray's shoulder again. "It's okay, fella." A slight breeze whistled in my left ear, and I waited for our next move.

"I reckon she's holed up in them rocks." Buck pointed to the southern edge of a tree-lined ridge.

"Yep," said Jake.

Buck dismounted. "Give em plenty of water first." He stood beside the buckskin while our animals drank thirstily from the creek. We sipped from our canteens in silence.

Satisfied we all had enough, Buck swung his leg up on Blacky. "Jake, you go around them boulders and have a look see. We'll wait for your signal when it's clear."

Jake nodded and rode up to the rocks. Wind whistled in my ear again. I watched his Appaloosa clomp up a steep hill, as he tried to get a good view of the surroundings. He stood tall on the stirrups, took his cowboy hat off and waved.

"Woody, stay close to me." Buck turned Blacky and headed up the ridge on the north flank.

I followed within inches of the Blacky's rear and ignored the lifting of a tail when he dropped poop bombs. We came up to a rocky ledge and the mule snorted. Edgy, I looked up. In a blur, the cougar attacked. Claws and fangs rained down and gripped into Gray's neck.

Enraged, Gray reared up as I tried to hang on. "Hee-haw!" He shook and tossed the cougar in the air.

I flew off. My body slammed into the ground. Adrenaline pumping, I had no pain. I got up, staggered on my feet and stared at the bloody fangs of that enraged wildcat. She growled as red saliva dribbled from her mouth. I froze.

Gray charged, then kicked and stomped on her skull. She twitched and tried to get up, but he mule bit into her neck and shook the body like a torn rag.

"Get back!" Buck yelled, leaped off his horse and grabbed my shoulder.

I stepped away and heard the clop, clop of the Appaloosa riding up fast. Jake pulled her up in a whirlwind of dust, swung his leg over, rushed to the mule and gripped the mule's reins. "Come on, Gray. You've done enough."

We looked down at the cougar's heaving chest. She was dying and suffering.

Uncle Buck walked over, pointed the rifle point blank at her head and pulled the trigger. "Bam!"

Instantly she was put out of her misery.

Buck turned and faced me with the hardened expression of a warrior in combat. "Mount up."

Yes sir." I got back on the mule and rubbed his neck. "Thanks, Gray." I whispered. "You saved my life."

Jake stepped alongside and gripped the muzzle. "Good job, Gray."

Buck glanced at Jake and ordered, "Give me a hand."

Jake released his grip and looked at me. "Keep em steady."

They lifted the carcass onto the mule just behind my saddle and secured it tight with a rope. Gray snorted but didn't fidget. He acted like he knew this was all part of his job as a seasoned trail mule.

Surprised to see a dead wildcat at my rear, I asked, "Uh, what's going on?"

"We're taking it back to the ranch." Jake slipped his boot into the stirrup and swung his leg over the Appaloosa.

"Got to bring it in for the game warden." Buck mounted Blacky and pulled the reins to his left. "Move out."

We rode on while I whispered to myself, "Show no fear. You can do this, Woody." I glanced at the bloody head and sharp teeth. Its eyes stared blankly at me. "If you can handle this, you can do anything."

We headed up a steep gravelly trail in silence. Our mood was somber as dark clouds hovered over us, and we expected it to rain soon. Instead, the air was thick and sticky, and sweat dribbled down my back. I lifted my hat to wipe my brow with a bandana and glimpsed over my sore shoulder at the carcass and saw blood dripping on the rocks. The mule's hooves clopped, clopped in rhythm. It was a long way back to the ranch, and I had to accept the reality of our gruesome chore without complaint.

When we stopped at an island of boulders where the cougar ran out to protect her cubs, Buck dismounted and said, "I heard something. Let's have a look see in the den." He grabbed a flashlight from his saddle bag and climbed up a rock.

"Sounds like a cougar cub." Jake stepped down from his horse and followed him.

While they climbed, up, I got off the mule, held the reins of our animals and focused on the rocks above me.

They knelt at the opening of a crevice and listened. "I hear meowing in there," said Jake.

Buck cocked his head and leaned closer. "Yep." He crawled in and disappeared. Moments later, I saw his hand reach out with a tiny cub by the scruff of its neck. "Here you go, little fella."

Jake took the cub and held it like a ball of fur. "Well, what do we have here?" He laughed and gently stroked its tiny forehead. "I reckon we'll call you Scruffy. Do you have any brothers and sisters down there?"

"That's all I could find," said Buck as he climbed out.

Jake stuffed the cub inside his shirt and snuggled it close. He let out a sigh, plopped his rear on the boulder and said, "Let's relax a bit to make sure there are no strays."

Buck sat beside him. "We'll take it the vet. He'll know what to do."

"Yeah, maybe this here fella will get luxury accommodations at the zoo." Jake had that light-hearted smile again.

I was surprised to see these rugged men soften up to a cub. Earlier they hunted down its mother to prevent anymore killing of their cattle. Now they released their hardness after a long morning of struggle and acted like doting parents.

I noticed another cub scampering out from between two rocks, and it meandered right over to my boots. It looked up at me as though I was its long-lost pappy. I picked it up and said, "Uh, guys. You're not going to believe this."

"That's two." Jake laughed and kept the first cub close to his chest as he climbed down.

"Yep." Buck stepped off the rock and took the other one from my hand.

While I steadied the animals, Jake cut small breathing holes in a burlap sack and slipped the two cubs inside, then he tied it on the saddle horn. "That'll do."

Buck nodded with approval. "Let's get on home."

While we headed back, I had a lot of time to think. When Jake first said I had to be ole Gray's handler, I didn't think the mule was worthy of my attention. Now I respected him. We were foster parents of two cubs from the mother we just killed. She had preyed on the calves as a way of feeding her family.

I thought of how Buck had said it was a hard life out here, and you had to accept the bad and good that comes with living on a ranch. By their somber silence, it was obvious they cared about all life.

When we rode up to the barn, six-year-old David came running over and yelled, "You got the cougar, Daddy!"

Buck dismounted, knelt and hugged him. "We all did, son."

Just as Jake and I stepped down, Maria ran to him, and we were surrounded by the entire family. Four children jumped up with excitement while the women tried to keep them from bouncing into each other.

Eileen rushed through her mobbing kids and hugged Buck. "I was so worried! Is everybody okay?"

Buck kissed her cheek and smiled. "Yep."

Asia squeezed through the kids and we held each other close. "I'm glad you made it," she said with a smile.

"Me too."

"Okay, kids," said Buck. "Take a good look. Here's the cougar that killed two of our calves."

"Did cat die dead for life, Daddy." Little three-year-old Summer gazed up at the carcass.

Buck lifted her up. "Yes, baby girl."

"Wake up cat," said Summer.

"No." Buck nodded to the body. "It's dead."

"No, Daddy!" Summer whimpered, sniveled and began to cry.

Seeing this emotional breakdown, Aunt Eileen took Summer and held her close. "It's okay, baby." She glared at Buck and said, "Why'd you tell her that?"

"Honey, this is a ranch. She's got to understand the facts of life." Buck frowned and added, "How else are the kids going to learn."

"Meow." A cub peeked out of a hole in the burlap bag.

"Oh, Daddy!" Summer cried out. "Can we keep kitty?"

Before Buck had a chance to respond, Jake held up the other cub. "We've got two kittens for you kids to see."

"No, you don't!" Eileen stepped between her over-excited children and the two men. "Are you both out of your mind? Those are wildcats!"

"It's okay, sis," Jake said. "We'll get the vet to take them to a zoo. Now go call him."

"Okay." Eileen groaned. "When Doc shows up, I want them cubs out of here." She started to round up her children with Maria's help and looked back. "I don't want the kids to be so attached they can't see straight."

Asia stepped over with a blanket and said, "I'll take care of them." She wrapped them up and headed into the barn.

"Thanks." Buck untied the rope on the carcass and ordered, "Woody, get the tarp on the rack and spread it out here."

"Yes sir." I brought out the cover and laid it on the ground.

"Jake, grab the hind legs," said Buck as he held the cougar's head and shoulders. "Okay, one, two, three, lift."

After we placed the body down, we folded the ends of the tarp and carried it over to a workbench. "Wrap it up tight." Buck took some rope and handed it to Jake. "I'll find out when the vet can get here."

I glanced at the bloody carcass with its fangs protruding from a gaping mouth and covered it.

17 BIRTHDAY DELIGHTS

I relaxed on the porch through a cool night, and with my couch against the wall, I was comfortable in a warm sleeping bag. I enjoyed this spot on those summer evenings at the ranch while the air was crisp, clean and filled with the sweet scent of jasmine.

As I breathed in the fragrant aroma, I listened to mating calls of crickets along with the occasional burr-up of a bull frog. During this serenade, I drifted into a peaceful sleep and dreamed of slow-dancing with Asia. This was my heaven, and I wanted to stay there forever.

Unfortunately, I awoke to reality. I rolled on my side, fluffed the pillow and hoped I'd be transported into my dream again. Like a forlorn moose in rutting season, I groaned in the darkness, "Asia, what are you doing to me? I can't get you out of my mind."

"That does it!" I sat up, and Shelly, the border collie placed her paw on my knee and looked up as though she sensed that something was wrong. I patted her head and she nudged with her nose for more attention. "Okay," I said. "Let's go for a walk." I quickly dressed, slipped on boots and put on my leather jacket.

We strolled along the road away from the ranch house. At least I had someone else to talk to besides myself. "You, know, Shelly, I'm having these dreams about Asia almost every night."

Shelly continued to walk with me, and I realized she was a great listener.

"I'm falling for Asia and it's a bad time." I paced back on forth. "This is crazy. I can't get serious now."

My boots crunched along a gravelly path, and I thought about the past month on the ranch with Asia. When our chores were done we usually ran outside holding hands and frolicked like two school kids on our own personal playground. I chased her behind the barn while she screamed and giggled. Almost every evening we had our walks to a grassy hill by the alder tree where we talked openly and honestly as we cuddled on a blanket. I taught her how to ride a mare named Flower, and we enjoyed brilliant splashes of red and orange sunsets.

It was nothing like my dates with a steady girl in San Diego. Usually we went to a movie, or to parties, then we'd make out in the backseat of my '56 Chevy. In this secluded rural area, we were happy to have simple romantic getaways on our walks and horseback riding. This was the closest thing to paradise, and I looked forward to each moment we had together.

During those days, we learned a lot about each other. She understood that I wanted to travel and see the world in all its splendors, but the possibility of getting drafted was always on my mind. I discovered more of her love for animals and it was especially obvious after the cougar cubs were brought to the ranch. When the veterinarian arrived, he was impressed with the way Asia nurtured them.

"You're a natural with these animals," he said. "Have you thought about becoming a vet?"

"No." Asia snuggled the cubs in her arms and looked up. "Do you think I could do that?"

"Yes." He smiled and added, "I'll get some college brochures for you to look at."

This gave Asia hope that she could do something worthwhile and have a good career. Doc Langley stopped by twice a week to check on a calf that seemed to have difficulty weening. That's when she learned more about animal care and she developed a passion to become a veterinarian.

As for me, however, I had only questions and doubts about my future. The next day I would have my 19th birthday, and I was ripe for the draft into the Vietnam War. Tortured with the drip, drip of worrisome thoughts, I couldn't take it any longer. I blew out a steam of frustration like a locomotive at the end of the line. To keep myself busy, I went out to the barn and brushed the mule.

"Well, Gray, how's your love life?" I saw his tail lifting up as he dumped more crap for me to clean up. "Doing anything exciting besides, eating, sleeping and pooping?" I held my nose. "Phew."

I dwelled on my future plans again. "One thing is for sure," I said to the mule. "I want to hang out here with Asia." I paused. "You know, learn all I can about living on this ranch for another month or so." I continued brushing his sides. "Then I'll hit the road and travel. Maybe even take her with me. How's that sound?"

Gray turned and looked at me with his big black eyes. I could tell he was more interested in the rub-down than my endless chatter.

"You don't talk much, do you?" I shook my head and rambled on. "Maybe Asia will go off to college. Anyway, the way I see it, the Army is offering a ticket to hell. Hang tight, they say. You're number will be called up soon. Isn't that nice of them?" I brushed harder.

Gray snorted.

"Oh sorry." I stroked a little softer. "Yep, Uncle Sam offers the deal of a lifetime." I clicked my heels and saluted. "Yes sir. The Army says we'll send you on an all-expense-paid trip to Vietnam. Get friendly with the locals. We'll even throw in free burial just for your participation. Oh, and thank you for your service."

Just before dawn, I was about to go stir-crazy when Asia opened the barn door and greeted me. "Happy Birthday, Woody." Her smile was like awakening in the sunrise.

I was so happy to see her, I was speechless. My young mind replayed the dream of her dancing and beckoning to me.

"Why are you looking at me like that?" she asked.

Unable to control myself, I drew her into my arms and with one long kiss I tasted her sweet lips. She responded by rubbing the back of my neck and held tighter. Breathing heavily in the doorway, we had to get out of sight.

"Come on." I took her hand, then we climbed up a ladder to the hayloft.

She giggled, laid back and her fingers dug into my shoulders as she pulled me closer. In the ruffling sounds of rolling in the hay, we kissed again and savored our passionate moments together. Nothing else mattered. Just like my dream, I didn't want it to end.

But early morning ranch life was already stirring as the family began their chores, and a rooster crowed, while hens clucked and horses whinnied in their stalls. Then we heard footsteps down below, and we knew our time was short. Still, we just wanted to hide in the hayloft, and we peeked through wooden rails to see Maria coming in with two pails. While we watched from above, she began to milk the cow.

"Squish, splat, squish, splat," white liquid echoed in the stainless steel bucket.

To us, it sounded funny as we hid in the hay together. Asia covered her mouth and made a muffled giggling sound while I tried to keep from laughing. We were so happy in our cuddling, it seemed like the whole world was filled with wonderous joy.

When Maria left, we rolled to our sides and gazed into each other's eyes like we had done so many times since we first met. It was natural to us.

"Hi," she said in that sensuous breathy voice that I adored.

"Good morning." I kissed her lips and fondled the curves of her body as though I was still dreaming.

Her arms pulled me closer. Heated by our desires for each other we snuggled until we heard footsteps again and peeked down to see Buck looking around for something, then he left.

"We should go," she said. "He's probably trying to find us. We've got work to do."

"Yeah." I stood up and held out my hand to help her up. "The fun police might find us."

Asia got to her feet, buttoned her blouse and giggled. "Then we'll get arrested for unbridled passion."

We walked hand-in-hand toward the ranch house, and I looked

up at a crystal-blue sky. "It's a beautiful day."

"Yes," she said. "Not a cloud in sight."

We paused at the porch steps and faced each other again. I brushed back several lovely strands of black hair away from her eyes. Her face was flush. I noticed straw dangling just above her right ear and gently slid the piece into my fingers, then placed it in the side of my mouth. "Shall we go in?

"Uh, huh," she whispered and smiled.

When we walked into the living room, Maria sat on the floor with my nieces, three-old Summer and five-year-old Spring. While the girls used crayons to draw stick figures on papers, the two boys ran downstairs and shouted, "Happy birthday, cousin Woody."

Jake, Buck and Eileen came in from the kitchen and smiled. "There you are," said my Aunt. "We've been waiting for you."

The whole family sang, "Happy birthday to you!" It was off-key, and we all laughed together.

"Thanks." I nodded with a smile that seemed to be permanent on my face. My arm was still around Asia's waist, and her curvaceous hip was still warm on my hand.

Jake lifted the black Stetson cowboy hat hanging on the wall above the fireplace and held it up. "Well, I promised you this once you learned to handle ole Gray." He placed it on my head. "Since it's your birthday, I reckon this is the best time to give it you."

I felt the rim of my hat settling just right. "Thanks."

Buck slapped me on the back and smiled. "Yep. You are now a mule handler."

Aunt Eileen hugged me and said, "We're proud of you, Woody."

"Thanks." I lowered the brim of my Stetson and glanced toward the kitchen. "I'll get my breakfast and be ready to head out soon. Are we still mending fences in the south pasture this morning."

"We are," responded Buck.

"You're not." Jake squeezed my shoulder. "Take the day off and go have fun."

Buck smiled at Asia. "You better go with him."

"Yeah, make sure he stays out of trouble." Jake had his usual mischievous grin again. "Maria will look after the kids. Now get."

Wide-eyed, Asia said to me, "Let's pack some lunch and have a picnic."

We quickly filled a tote bag with sandwiches, fruit and whatever else we could without checking off a list. We just wanted to get out of there.

"Come on, Asia," I said. "Let's ride over to that lake I told you about." We rushed out the door so fast, it's a wonder we didn't trip on the way out.

After we saddled up her horse and my mule, we rode toward the east, up a steep trail, then down into a green valley. Finally alone, we got off our animals to admire the view of mountain peaks reflecting like a mirror on still water.

"It looked so inviting, Asia said, "Let's go for a swim."

"Yeah." I pointed to some bushes. "We can change in there."

"Okay," she said. "I'll go on this side."

When I stripped down to my shorts, I glanced over to where Asia discreetly undressed and saw her hand reaching out to drape her white blouse on a tree branch. Eager to get wet, I tossed my pants and shirt on a log and dove in. Although cold at first, I quickly adapted while slicing through the clear water, turned and swam back near the shore.

"Wow!" I shouted. "That feels so good."

Asia dove in, swam over to me and smiled. "Oh, the water is so clean and refreshing."

"Yeah." I noticed she wore panties and a bra below the surface. "The view's nice too."

"Oh, I know what you're thinking, but this is all I have to wear," she said.

"I'm not complaining."

Asia smiled as she looked at me. "I see you're wearing boxer shorts."

"It's all I got." I kept my gaze on the underwater curves of her body.

She splashed water in my face and laughed. "Catch me."

"Hey!" I laughed and wiped my eyes. When I looked up, she was gone.

Enjoying how she liked to play, I dipped my head below the surface and saw her sleek figure swimming away. I took off after her and came alongside as she smiled at me, then we swam close together with our bodies twisting and turning in our own aquatic ballet like two fun-loving dolphins.

Weightless and free, we continued our twirls across the lake that mirrored tall mountains. Way out beyond the shoreline, we treaded water and observed two golden eagles circling overhead.

"Oh, they're so graceful," said Asia.

"Yeah, it's cool how they skim the surface and grab fish in their talons."

"They're flying over those trees," she said. "Where are they going?"

"They're probably heading back to a nest somewhere. I heard eagles stick together."

Asia rested her arm on the back of my neck as we treaded water. "So, they mate for life?"

"Yep."

She kissed my wet cheek. "I like that."

"You do, huh?"

"Uh, huh," she said in her sensuous, breathy voice, then pushed down on my shoulders and we dipped below the surface.

In the quiet stillness, we gazed at each other. Asia's long black hair floated around her lovely face, and I admired the curves of her body through an aquatic haze. Then we held hands while swimming together in our underwater world.

After drifting and savoring our precious moments together, I asked, "Are you hungry?"

"I'm starving."

Let's go in and dry off."

"I'll get out first." She swam toward the shore.

I gave her a couple of minutes to get dressed, then I swam over to my spot. While I dried off and slipped on my clothes, I realized how shy we were out there. We had no problem swimming in our underwear, but we were modest in getting dressed behind the bushes.

Asia stepped out while wearing her blue jeans and white shirt, then walked to her horse. "I'll get the picnic bag."

"I heard there's a waterfall on the other side of this lake," I said as I strolled over to her.

"Let's go find it," she smiled while wiping her hair with a towel.

"Okay, we'll eat there." I held her horse steady while she lifted her leg over the saddle and the leather creaked slightly. For a moment, I paused and admired the way her hair blew in a gentle breeze.

She giggled and leaned toward me. "You've got that silly look again."

"Asia, do you realize how beautiful you are?"

"No, but I like to hear you say it." She smiled again and rested her hands on the saddle horn.

I mounted up on the mule and turned his reins toward an east-facing ridge. We rode along a narrow path and stopped at a stream on the opposite side of our lake.

"Do you hear that?" I asked.

"Yes." Asia looked to her right. "It sounds like a waterfall just beyond those rocks over there."

"Let's check it out."

We dismounted, then hiked further up the trail and climbed onto a car-sized boulder. From there, we looked down into a gorge where a waterfall splashed and gurgled into a pool below us.

"Let's sit for a while," Asia spoke louder over a roar of raging water echoing through canyon walls.

While a soothing mist cooled our faces, we sat cross-legged on our blanket, scanned the slopes above us and noticed something we didn't expect to see. "Oh, look, Woody." She pointed to a deer scampering along a tree-lined ridge."

"Yeah, there's a fawn right behind her."

Asia leaned back and inhaled the fresh air. "I love the scent of pine."

"It's nice here." I breathed deeply and watched the sure-footed animals climbing further up the trail, then they blended in with conifer branches.

Asia leaned closer and squeezed my arm. "I'm so happy here with you, Woody."

I kissed her lips and she responded with her hands pulling me into her.

We paused, listened to the waterfall and watched the water splashing onto rocks. Asia smiled and said, "Since we've been together, I've never felt happier."

"Me too."

"I feel safe with you." She stared at the swirling pool as though she was in deep thought. "I don't want to ever go back to where I was before."

I held her close and said, "You're free now."

She looked at me and smiled. "I'd like to get a college education and maybe I could be a veterinarian someday. What do you think?"

"You'd be great at it."

"I know you want to travel," she said. "I'd like to do that too." We gazed into each other's eyes again and it was our way of connecting deeply with each other. "If you had a choice, where would you go first?" she asked.

I shrugged. "It doesn't matter. Uncle Sam will probably decide that for me."

"It's not fair, Woody." Asia squeezed my hand. "Why is the government pushing so many guys into that war madness? It's tearing the country apart."

"Well, all I know is Uncle Sam says he wants me." I laughed. "I say I want out."

"Forget that old codger," she said with a giggle. "I want you."

"Yeah," I kissed her again and we laid back on the warm blanket. "You're a whole lot prettier too."

"Well?"

"Well, what?"

"Let's run away to Canada."

Surprised to hear her say this, I sat up. "I can't do that."

"Why not?"

"I was taught to never run away." I got to my feet and stared at her. "You know I can't go off and leave my country."

Asia stood up and wrapped her arms tightly around my waist. "Come on, Woody." She pleaded with her eyes. "Let's go now. You're always worrying about getting caught up in that crazy war."

"Forget it." I groaned and tried to change the subject. "Come on. Let's have our picnic."

"Okay." She patted my chest. "Think about it."

We walked back to where our animals had been tied on a tree branch. The mule and her horse grazed on high grass and seemed oblivious to the growing divisions in our human society we called civilization. Life was simple for them.

I reached up on the mule's saddle horn and lifted off a tote bag filled with our lunch. "Let's eat by the waterfall."

While we strolled toward the rocks, Asia pointed to a hillside with patches of green and spots of bright red fruit. "Are those strawberries?"

"Yep."

"Can we eat them?" she asked.

"Sure. I remember picking wild berries when I was a kid."

We walked over to get a better look at the luscious plants. "Let's try some," said Asia while she picked two and held them up in the bright sunshine. "Oh, they have such a lovely red color." She put the ripe fruit to her lips and nibbled. "Mmm, that's delicious." She giggled and placed one in my mouth. "Taste it"

"Mmm." I savored the flavor. Delighted with our discovery, I picked more ripe fruit and sniffed. "Smells good, too." I held up one and she took a bite.

I laughed and watched the savory juices dribbling on my fingers and down her chin. Never had I seen such a sensuous sight, and I kissed her sweet, moist lips. Together, we sat and cherished the wild, fresh taste of strawberries in a way that I didn't think was possible until that moment with Asia.

I found myself getting heated again and pulled her closer. "Now I'm really hungry."

"Down, boy." Asia patted my chest. "Eat first." She had that delightful giggle again. "Play later."

I let out a deep sigh and tried to make a sorrowful puppy-dog look and sniffed our lunch bag. "What do we have to eat?"

She laughed and peeked inside. "I'm not sure. We stuffed food in the bag so fast."

"Yeah, I guess we were in a rush to get out of there."

"Oh, we have cheddar cheese and bread." She held them up. "Will that do?"

"No mustard or mayonnaise?"

"What do you expect?" She tilted her head back and giggled. "A smorgasbord?"

I was so happy to see her enjoying herself, I took a mental picture in my mind and didn't want to ever forget these simple, carefree moments with Asia. I remembered how scared she was when we first met, and for a long time she seemed to be trapped in her sadness. Now she was free with me.

"Cheese and bread," I said and held up a slice of rye in my hand. "What more can a wild man ask for?"

Asia took a knife out of the bag and laughed again. "Here, use this on the cheese, my cave man."

I grunted playfully, unwrapped the aluminum foil, placed the palm-sized morsel on a cloth napkin and cut two pieces--one for Asia; another for me. "Woman, you eat," I said with a teasing glance.

She giggled and took a bite out of her cheese on rye. Her eyes widened and she mumbled, "Mmm."

When I finished chewing, I said, "Hey, that's not bad."

"Let's mix things up a little." Asia pulled out an apple, bit into it and added some cheese on rye. After she swallowed it, she said, "That's good." She put some in my mouth and smiled. "Try it."

"Wow. It's delicious."

"I never realized food could taste so good." She looked into my eyes again. "Why is that?"

"Maybe it's because we're together and in our own world." I waved my hand in the air and shouted, "I now declare this land a free, neutral zone and we shall call it Lover's Valley.

"Population: two," she said. "Oh, I forgot, we also have one horse and a mule called Gray."

We laughed together while pretending this was our personal refuge and nothing could separate us.

18 BIRTH AND RENEWAL

After horseback riding in the mountains, Asia and I rode up to the barn, and neither of us wanted our day to end. While we dismounted, the setting sun peeked over the horizon and warmed our faces in a soft orange glow. Since we still had to clean and feed our animals, we used these chores as an excuse to not go into the house.

Asia took the reins of her roan and said, "Come, Flower," then she led the mare into a stall. "I'm so glad Eileen let me use her horse."

"Yep, she knew you would take good care of her." I patted Gray and said, "Go on." The mule was so used to his daily routine, he walked in without coaxing.

"Woody, can you loosen this strap on Flower for me?" Asia stood beside her horse and looked over while I removed Gray's saddle.

"Sure." I stepped in and unbuckled it. In this tight space, our bodies rubbed against each other like two sticks about to ignite a fire. I started to lift the saddle off but I felt her hand on my shoulder.

"Woody?"

"Yeah?" I paused and took a mental picture of her lovely Amerasian features—the subtle upturned lips, small nose, dark pupils and long black hair that flowed elegantly down her shoulders.

"I..." She hesitated and gazed in my eyes.

As I waited for Asia to speak, I admired several tiny freckles along Asia's cheeks. This identified her Caucasian line. My palm caressed the right side of her face and she leaned into my touch. "I like these little spots on your skin," I said. Remembering art classes in school, I added, "It's like a master artist dotted them in with a small brush to add a final touch of your unique beauty."

"Really?" She giggled and said, "I've always thought it made me look ugly. I was teased a lot in school. Usually I heard the kids yelling, 'There goes that freckle-faced, slant-eyed girl.' When you look at me and say nice things, I feel different inside."

"I say it because it's true." I held her closer.

Asia began rubbing the back of my neck as we were magnetically drawn together in a long embrace and lingered in a fiery kiss. When our lips parted, we continued to hold each other and wanted to make our loving moments last into the evening.

"Asia, the thought of being separated from you is driving me crazy. I don't know where I'll be a month from now."

"I know." She rested her head on my chest. "I love you, Woody."

"I love you too."

As we kissed again, her face was hot. "What are we going to do?" she asked.

"I don't know. Neither of us planned on getting serious."

Asia looked up and tried to smile. "It's been a good birthday for you, hasn't it?"

"It's perfect."

"I felt so free today." She naturally giggled and smiled again.

"Me, too. I just wanted to stay at the lake with you and never leave."

"We should go back there someday," she said.

"I'd like that." When I spoke those words, I wondered if we could ever return to our pretend Garden of Eden. The clock was ticking in my head. Either I'd wait to get called up or enlist and take my chances with military service.

We heard footsteps and turned to see Jake coming into the barn. "Woody, your Ma and Pa are on the phone."

"Thanks. Be right there."

When we stepped in the kitchen, Aunt Eileen was talking to my mom on the wall phone. "Yeah, sis. I've been having contractions since this morning. What? No, I don't need to go to the hospital. I've had all my babies at home and this is no different than the other four. Besides, my midwife lives close by." She smiled and waved me over. "Here's your birthday boy."

"Thanks." I took the telephone as my aunt rubbed her pregnant belly, then she waddled into the living room. "Hi Mom."

"Hello Richard. Hold on while your father comes to the phone."

"Sure." Hearing my name, it seemed strange after going by Woody for the summer. To me, that chosen nickname meant I had been cruising along and living free.

"Hi son," Dad said.

"It's great to hear your voices," I responded.

"Happy birthday," they spoke in unison.

"Thanks." I nodded for Asia to join me. "Uh, Mom, Dad, Remember how I told you about the girl I met in Phoenix?" I held the phone close to her ear, and we listened together.

"Yeah," said Dad. "That's all you talked about."

"She's been living and working on the ranch with us, and she's standing here now. Her name is Asia, and I'd like you to meet her."

"Hello Mr. and Mrs. Thomson."

"Hello Asia," said Mom. "How's your stay at the ranch?"

"I really like it here. Your family is so nice to me."

"I'm glad," Mom said.

"Hello young lady," Dad spoke up. "Did you learn to ride a horse yet?"

"Yes, Woody taught me. We just got back from riding over to a lake."

"Oh, that's right. I forgot about his nickname." Dad laughed and said, "Leave it to my son to name himself after a Woody station wagon."

Asia giggled. "I like it."

"You should see Asia with the animals," I said. "Everybody says she'd be a great veterinarian someday. She was a straight A student in high school. The vet says college would be easy for her."

"That's nice, Asia," Mom said. "Maybe you can look into getting a scholarship."

"Son?"

"Yeah, Dad."

"Why don't you come home and get enrolled in college here in San Diego? You might be able to apply for a deferment and keep out of the draft for a while."

"I think it's too late to get in this fall, Dad. Besides, I'm hoping to stay on the ranch for another month. I'd like to do some more traveling after that." I paused. "Maybe I'll enlist in the Navy."

"Just don't wait too long," said Dad. "The Army may decide for you."

"What about you, Asia?" asked Mom. "When do you plan to attend college?"

"I'm not sure yet." Asia glanced at me and smiled. "I like working with the animals here."

While we talked, Asia and I held the phone close and still had our arms around each other. After we ended our easy-going, friendly conversation, she said, "Your parents are nice. I was a little nervous at first, but they made me feel welcomed."

"Yeah, they're kind of fun to be around. When I was growing up, we always had a houseful of neighborhood kids running in and out like a revolving door."

"I don't get it?" Asia sat on a kitchen chair and looked confused.

"Get what?" I asked.

"Why are your parents so nice?" Asia lowered her gaze as though she was remembering something. "They don't even know me."

I had seen that far-off look before, and this worried me. "What is it, Asia?"

"My father hated everybody." She let out a deep sigh and wrung her hands. "You know, if he wasn't so drunk when you came to the house with me that day, he would've killed you."

"That's over now." I leaned closer and brushed back strands of hair from her moist eyes.

"Sometimes he would be okay with my mom and me when he was sober." She made eye contact again like she was trying to make sense of her life. "The more he drank, the meaner he got. When my mom died, he became more unpredictable. I was so scared. There was nobody I could talk to until you found me, Woody." Asia's voice cracked with sorrowful emotion.

"You're safe now," I said.

Just as I spoke, Aunt Eileen walked back in the kitchen, winced and rubbed her belly. "Phew." She picked up the phone, dialed, waited, then said, "Hello, Mrs. Billings. It's time. Okay, see you soon."

She hung up and looked at Jake while he came in with Maria. "Where's Buck?"

"He's in the barn," Jake said.

"Get him."

Jake's eyes widened. "Wow, sis! You're about to bust." He ran out the door so fast, I thought he'd trip and fall flat on his face.

Eileen calmly turned to Maria like this was a routine mail delivery and said, "I'm getting more contractions." She puffed out air. "My midwife is on the way."

"Come with me," Maria said as she helped Eileen and they carefully walked to the staircase.

Eileen held onto her swollen belly as though she carried a large melon over to the stairs. At the base, she glanced up to the second floor. "Phew." She took one step up and groaned. "Oh, I feel it more now. She paused, went to the next level and puffed out air.

Maria kept her arm around Eileen's waist and helped her up the stairs. When my aunt finally made it to the top, she calmly said, "Oh, my water broke."

Uncle Buck stormed through the front door and yelled, "Hold on Eileen! I'll be in after I clean up!" He rushed into the downstairs bathroom and slammed the door.

Jake came in behind him and said to Asia, "Round up the kids. Keep em in the living room."

"Yes sir." Asia ran to the boy's downstairs bedroom and stepped into the open doorway. She clapped her hands and firmly said, "Alright, Tommy and David, it's story time."

"That's no fun." Tommy groaned. "Why do we have to sit with

the dumb girls anyway?"

"Shh." Asia herded them from behind with her hands on their shoulders like Eileen had taught her. "Your Mother needs to rest upstairs."

"Come on, guys," I said, then waved them over to where I sat on the floor beside Summer and Spring. "This'll be fun. I used to do this with my younger brothers and sisters back home. What do you want to hear tonight?" I scanned the children's bookshelf by the fireplace and picked up a copy of the three little pigs. "How about this one?" I held it up for their approval.

"Yeah!" The girls giggled and snuggled on each side of me.

"Aw, do we have to?" My nine-year-old cousin, Tommy plopped down, huffed and crossed his arms. "It's baby stuff."

"Yeah, that's why you can help," I said as I handed him the book. "Since you're the big brother, you start reading, and David will read it next. That way your sisters can learn from both of you. Okay?"

Tommy was about to start when Jake plopped on the couch and laughed. "Well, knowing Eileen, her baby is gonna shoot out like a peanut. Get ready, guys."

Asia looked at Jake and said, "I've never been around a woman having a baby. "How can I help?"

"Just keep the kids occupied." Jake smiled. "Eileen has done this so many times, all we do is wait."

I glanced at the closed bathroom door where my uncle went in and asked, "What about Buck?"

"He's never missed a delivery yet," said Jake. "That ole bull's getting cleaned up before going in to help Eileen."

We heard a knock at the front door and without getting up to see who was there, Jake said, "Come on in, Mrs. Billings."

A robust white-haired woman in her fifties stepped inside and smiled. "Is Eileen in her room?"

"Yep," said Jake. "Go on up."

"Thanks." Mrs. Billings carried a black satchel in one hand and a green tote bag in the other as she walked up the steps like it was her own home. At the master bedroom door, she knocked, paused and entered.

"Is she the midwife?" I asked.

"Yeah," said Jake. She's the wife of Dr. Henry Billings and a fine nurse. She's delivered all of Eileen's babies."

Uncle Buck came out of the bathroom wearing a robe and walked barefoot up the stairs.

Jake looked up and laughed. "Hey, whatcha wearin under there, big guy?"

"None of your damn business." Uncle Buck entered the master bedroom without another word.

"Okay, Tommy." I nodded to the open book. "Let's get back to our story. You start."

Crickets chirped outside when I checked on the boys in their downstairs bedroom. They had been asleep for an hour and must've kicked off their blankets. Up on the top bunk, Tommy laid flat on his stomach with his right arm hanging over the side. David was curled in a fetal position below his brother. A cool breeze blew in from the partially opened window, and I closed it with a slight thumping sound. I held my breath as I thought they'd wake up. Instead, they stirred, rolled over and didn't move after that. With a sigh of relief, I covered them and went back into the living room.

I sat down on the couch and looked at a clock on the fireplace mantel. It was 9:30 p.m. While he flames crackled and swayed among burning logs, I heard footsteps coming down the stairs. I looked up and saw Asia wearing a pink robe, yellow pajama pants and white slippers. Pleased with the sight of her, I took another snapshot in my mind to keep in my private collection of memories.

"The girls are sound asleep," she said with a smile and cuddled up beside me.

"Good. Have you heard anything from Eileen's room?" I asked.

"Yes." Asia rested her head on my shoulder. "Eileen was making strange groaning and heavy breathing sounds."

"Wow. Just think, Eileen will have a baby soon."

"This is so exciting," she said. "Until we came to the ranch together, I never felt like I belonged anywhere. Now I have a sense of being a part of your family."

I laughed. "Yeah, they tend to grow on you."

Asia snuggled and kissed my cheek. "I'm truly happy here with you."

"I'm glad." Her hair tickled the side of my face and she had a fresh floral scent. "You smell nice," I said.

Asia brushed back strands from her forehead and whispered, "Oh, I just had a shower."

"Yeah, I cleaned up when the boys were asleep."

"Uh, huh." She covered her mouth and yawned. "Oh, sorry."

"You tired?"

"Yes." Asia stretched out, laid back on the couch and rested her head on my lap. "I'll just relax while we wait." She looked up at me and smiled. "I'm too excited to sleep anyway."

"Me too," I said. "It's kind of like waiting to open Christmas presents. Will Eileen have a girl or boy?"

"Whatever it is, I know her baby will be loved." Asia smiled. "I never knew what love could be like until I came here with you. Everyone in your family is so caring and thoughtful. Even the men are respectful of their wives. I wish my father had been like that." She yawned again.

"We've had a long day."

"Yes." Asia blinked, closed her eyes and her warm body completely relaxed while she began to drift into sleep.

In that peaceful moment, I gently rubbed her forehead with my palm and was content to observe her lovely features—the closed eyelids, subtle upturned lips that seemed to always smile; the rise and fall of her chest as she breathed. I wanted to capture it all in my memory and not forget even the way she wore a simple robe, pajamas and fuzzy white slippers.

We awoke to a new-born baby's loud screams upstairs and realized that we had fallen asleep on the couch together. I rubbed my tired eyes and looked up. "Did you hear that?"

Asia sat up and said, "Yeah, it sounded like crying."

"Waa!" a baby cried from upstairs.

Jake stepped in from the porch and laughed. "Eileen's had her baby."

Maria peeked out from the upstairs bedroom door, smiled and in a low voice said, "It's a boy."

"Waa! Waa!"

"Whoa," I said. "It's amazing the kids didn't wake up."

Jake smiled and said, "That boy's got strong lungs." He looked at us with that familiar mischievous smirk. "I told ya that baby would shoot out like a peanut."

I stood up, stretched and glanced at the clock. It was 11:45 p.m. "Wow. Looks like he was born just 15 minutes before the end of my birthday."

19 REBOZO WITH LOVE

On a bright sunnny afternoon, Maria ushered all of us in the upstairs bedroom to see the baby for the first time. Aunt Eileen had a mixed look of exhaustion and a special maternal glow on her face as we stood at the foot of her bed.

Buck sat on a chair beside her and proudly cradled his son. "Ga, wah, coo chee." He laughed and continued to make odd baby sounds.

Jake teased, "Well, if you keep that up, he'll be saying dah, dah in no time."

Buck kissed his son's forehead and announced, "Here's Hank James Robertson."

The kids started to rush in for a better look, but Maria held them back. "That's close enough."

Eileen smiled and said, "You'll have to wait until little Hank gets stronger."

"Come," Maria whispered and herded them back out of the room.

I smiled and nodded to my aunt and said, "We'll watch the kids while you get some rest."

A day later, it was still dark when Asia and I were eating our breakfast and planned to go for our usual morning walk before working in the barn. We heard a slight creaking sound coming from the living room and saw my aunt cradling her baby while rocking back and forth on an oakwood chair.

"Good morning," I said. "You're up early."

"I couldn't sleep."

"Oh, he's so cute," said Asia as she knelt in front of Eileen and asked, "Can I get you anything?"

"No thanks." Eileen looked up and smiled warmly. She still had that maternal glow that reminded me of my Mom after she gave birth to my youngest brother, Teddy when I was growing up.

"How are you feeling," I asked.

"Tired but happy to have my son." Eileen discretely covered her baby and began nursing.

I turned away and went back into the kitchen while Asia observed with increasing curiosity. As I poured another cup of coffee, Eileen said to her, "Come sit with me."

I glanced over my shoulder and saw Asia leaning closer as she studied the way Eileen nestled her newborn son.

"I've never seen a baby nursing before," Asia said. "Does it hurt?"

"Not for me," Eileen spoke softly. "It's one of the most natural things a mother can do."

Meanwhile, Maria came down the stairs with a long red cloth draped over her arms like she was holding a sacred offering. "I have a gift for you," she said to Eileen.

"Oh, that's beautiful, Maria." Eileen smiled and placed it on her lap. "What is it?"

"Rebozo." Maria lowered her gaze in a look of gracious humility. "Por favor acepta este regalo."

Eileen smiled and said, "Okay, I think I understand." She paused. "Yes, I accept your gift." She held up the cloth to admire it with her right hand while still cradling her baby. "Muchas gracias."

"Con gusto." Maria tried to translate, "With pleasure." She giggled happily and added, "It is familia...um...how you say?

"Oh, you mean a family tradition," said Eileen.

"Si, I show you." Maria took the cloth and caressed it close to her bosom. "Rebozo. You hold baby." She wrapped the elegant garment and tied it around the back of her neck. Then she pretended to rock a little child in her arms. "Hold baby."

Eileen's eyes widened. "Oh, yes. I understand. It's like a wraparound cloth."

"Si." Maria gushed. "You try."

Eileen stood up with her baby still in her arms. "Okay." She glanced at Asia. "Hold little Hank for a minute while I learn from Maria."

Asia took the infant in her arms and looked embarrassed. "Oh, how do I hold him."

"You're doing fine," said Eileen as she wrapped the rebozo cloth around her neck and shoulders. She looked at Maria and asked, "How's that?"

"Perfecta," Maria nodded and smiled.

Eileen hugged Maria and said, "I will..." She paused. "Um... siempre apreciare tu don." My aunt embraced her again. "I will always cherish your gift. Did I say it right?"

"Si." Maria smiled happily.

"This is wonderful," Eileen said. "We are learning from each other."

"Muy bueno." Maria smiled again. "Very good."

Eileen turned to Asia and took the baby in her arms. "Thank you, honey. You handled little Hank perfectly." She wrapped him in the Rebozo the way Maria taught her and smiled happily as though she'd been given a royal robe.

While I sat at the kitchen table, it was like I also received a gift. From there, I looked through the opened door that framed a beautiful scene of these three women sharing moments of love and understanding together. Somehow they seemed to look at each other in a way that I hadn't noticed before, and I'd been given the privilege of peeking into their world.

20 WHISPERING TREES

In the early morning twilight, I mounted up on Gray and patted his neck. I was eager to show Asia more of the land where my ancestors first settled a hundred years ago. "Are you ready?" I asked.

Asia swung her leg over Flower and smiled. "Okay."

We rode along a gurgling stream that snaked through a lush green valley, and Aspen leaves trembled in a cool breeze from the north. "Swoosh, shish," they fluttered with a whisper.

I pulled up on the reins of my mule. "Do you hear that?"

"Yeah, I've never heard anything like it before." Asia leaned on the saddle and listened.

"Swoosh, shish."

"Now watch the leaves," I said.

Rays of morning sunlight flickered through each leaf while they turned from green to yellow and back again. It was as though nature took a breath, blew out a joyful song and the leaves danced in harmony.

"Oh," said Asia in a hushed voice. "It's so magical here."

"Yeah, I first experienced this when I was nine. My parents brought me out here. Mom called them whispering trees." I paused to admire Asia's lovely smile as she observed the fluttering leaves. "I couldn't wait to show you," I said.

"I'm glad you did." Asia brought her horse closer, leaned over and kissed my cheek.

"Tap, tap," a sound came from the trees.

"What is that?" Asia looked up and listened again.

"Must be a woodpecker."

"Where?"

I searched in the trees and noticed a speck of red. At first, I waited to be sure of what I was seeing and realized it was the crown of a woodpecker.

"Tap, tap," Its black beak pecked into the bark of a thick white trunk.

"There, over to your right." I pointed to the bird as it perched high up on an Aspen tree. "See it?"

"Yeah." Asia smiled. "Thank you for bringing me out here, Woody."

"You're welcome." I gazed up at several clouds drifting in a blue sky. "Just imagine what it must've been like when my ancestors first came through this valley in a covered wagon."

"I guess it was hard for them," said Asia.

"Yep." I stepped down to feel the land at my feet and scanned the rugged valley. Deep grooves were carved in the ground by ancient volcanic eruptions. Streams flowed down from the mountains and enriched the land. "It's strange," I said.

"What's strange?" Asia swung her leg off Flower and came alongside me.

"I don't know. Somehow I sense a presence." Embarrassed for saying it out loud, I said, "That sounds crazy."

"No." She looked into my eyes and smiled. "I just think you're more aware than most people."

"I remember what my mom said." I knelt and scooped up a handful of dirt. "Somewhere in this soil, my great-parents, Clancy and Claire Brannigan buried their two-year-old daughter, Eleanor." I sprinkled the dust back on the ground. "She died in the back of their wagon. Measles, I think. Her grave was washed away long ago."

"Now I understand why you're so connected to this land," Asia whispered in my ear and rested her arm on my shoulder. "When you share these things with me, I feel closer to you than ever."

"That's why I brought you here." We held each other so tight, the curves of her breasts were hot upon my chest as we lingered in a kiss.

Then I took her hand. "Come on. I want to show you a clear view of the mountains just beyond those trees."

After 10 minutes of going up a steep trail, we reached the

base of a volcanic outcrop shaped like an eagle's beak. We dismounted and tied the reins of our animals on a twisted tree branch. I paused to make sure Asia was ready to go on, then I said, "Okay, take my hand."

"Where are we going?"

"We just need to go along this narrow path a little ways." I pointed to massive boulders to our right. "Stay close to this side. Just around the next bend, it'll be scary at first. Don't look down." I studied her face as the sun gave her skin an orange glow. "You're not afraid of heights are you?"

"I don't know." She gripped my palm with both hands. "I've never been up this high before."

"You'll be fine," I assured her. "It'll be worth it. I'll show you a sight that you'll never forget."

We carefully walked along a narrow rocky path until it seemed like the whole sky opened up to a spectacular view of mountains and deep gorges. At first, it took our breath away. If we went about four feet closer to the edge of the cliff, we were at risk of falling a thousand feet to the jagged rocks below.

"Oh," Asia gasped and squeezed my hand tighter. "It's so..."

"Just relax. We both need to get used this height."

"I don't think I can." She stared straight down and shivered.

I turned to face her. "Look at me."

Asia shakily tried to focus in my direction.

Once we had eye contact, I smiled and said, "Now, just put your hand on the rock behind us." I watched as she reached out and felt the solid granite wall. "That's good. Okay, let's just sit here and lean against it."

Together, we sat with our backs against the sturdy boulder behind us. "Now, we'll take our time to soak it all in," I said. We relaxed and looked down at a river flowing through a deep gorge below us. Framed in the background were the San Francisco Peaks about eight miles away. Even in early August, we could still see small patches of snow.

I pointed to the northeast. "That mountain is called Humphrey's Peak. It's over 12,000 feet."

"Wow," she whispered as though she was in a grand cathedral.

For a moment, I forgot about the mountains and observed the way Asia smiled. She wore a cowgirl hat that Eileen gave her and the brim shaded her eyes from the sun shining in the east.

She let out a sigh and looked at me with moist eyes that sparkled in the sunlight. "Oh, Woody, this means so much to me."

I reached over and wiped a tear drop from her cheek with my thumb. "Why are you crying?"

"It's just that I'm so happy."

"I'm glad you like the view," I said.

"I've never experienced anything like this before." She smiled and giggled in a way that was music to my ears. "I feel so alive out here with you, Woody."

"I wouldn't want to share this moment with anyone else." I drew her closer.

Our lips caressed. Like a magnet drawn to steel, we held each other and didn't want to let go. Deeply attracted, we were grounded to the earth on one side while our spirits wanted to fly off like eagles in the sky.

21 THE LOST HORSEMAN

After a good morning of horseback riding, Asia and I rode slowly toward the ranch. Although we had work to do, we were in no hurry to rush back. In these vast open spaces, it was nothing like my fast-paced lifestyle in San Diego where vehicles raced along freeways in a cacophony of roaring engines and beeping horns. Here among tall stands of Ponderosa we listened to birds chirping and the wind whispering in the trees. Each moment together was like watching a sunset and knowing it would soon be night.

"Let's stop here," I said.

We dismounted at a small stream as the water trickled among smooth rocks that glistened in the sun. Gray and Flower drank contentedly, and we stood side by side with the reins in our hands.

"They're thirsty," Asia said.

"Yeah, maybe we should stay a while." I wrapped my left arm around her waist and rested my hand on the curve of her hip. Gray pulled slightly on my right and snorted.

When I turned to see what was going on, I noticed a black stallion walking slowly toward us. "Where did he come from?"

His reins dangled as he lowered his head and staggered toward the stream. Flies buzzed around his body, and he still had a saddle on his back.

Asia rubbed the horse's neck and said, "Oh, you're all worn out." She knelt and examined his front legs. "Look, Woody. He's got scratches and open wounds."

"Yeah, somebody must've ridden him hard." I removed the saddle and set it on the ground.

"I'm worried." Asia patted the stallion's back. "When the vet came by last week, he talked about things to watch for if the animals are stressed." She pinched the skin along his neck and said, "Do you see how it stays up in a ridge?"

"Yeah, that doesn't look good," I responded.

"Doc Langley said healthy skin should spring back in place. This just stays up and he's got a dry mouth. His eyes are dull and he droops his head like he's depressed. Doc taught me these are signs of being severely dehydrated."

I glanced in the direction the stallion came from. "Maybe his rider got thrown off." I mounted up on Gray and said, "Wait here. I'll look around."

"Okay, but hurry." Asia paused and listened to the horse's shallow breathing. "He's in bad shape."

"I won't be long." I scouted along the trail and called out, "Hello! Anybody out there?" I listened, but only heard a breeze rustling through leaves.

After going a little further, I rode back to the stream. Asia poured water from a canteen on the horse's back and handed it to me. "Hurry," she said. "Fill this up. We've got to cool him down."

For several minutes, we relayed more cool water from the stream and splashed it on the stallion. I glanced at a circled S brand and said, "Hey, look. I've seen this mark before. I think he came from the Sonora Ranch, our neighbor to the south."

"Is that very far?

"Yep. Our ranch is closer. Besides, my uncles will know what to do." I noticed the stallion had lowered his head and drank from the stream. "That's a good sign. Okay, let's take him with us."

"Yeah, maybe he'll be alright if we go slow." Asia faced the horse and rubbed his forehead. "He seems calmer now."

"You take the stallion and we'll walk back." I tied Flower's reins on my saddle horn, then I put Gray in the lead, and we headed out.

Asia gently pulled the horse forward and said, "I hope we can get him to the vet in time."

"We'll make it." I looked back to see her worried expression.

"There's a short cut through the meadow. We'll go that way."

While holding the reins, we continued our slow walk, and a gust of wind blew in from the mountains. Lush high grass rolled across the valley like waves and reminded me of the surf in San Diego. That was my childhood home. Now I traversed on the rich soil where my ancestors had settled. Instead of breathing in an ocean breeze, I was inhaling thin air at 8,000 feet.

Asia leaned into the wind as she guided the stallion with both hands and kept her head down to prevent her hat from flying off. When she came over to me, the top button of her long-sleeved shirt had loosened. The collar fluttered open and revealed a lovely smoothness of her skin. She stood there wearing her cowgirl boots and tight blue jeans with an oval-shaped buckle, and I admired the confident way she handled the challenge we faced.

I nodded to the horse. "How's he doing?" I asked.

"He seems okay." Asia stood in front of the stallion and examined his mouth. "At least his breathing isn't as shallow." She took a canteen and poured water into her hat. "Drink up." The horse slurped until it was almost was gone. "Did you get enough?" She rubbed his forehead. "Okay, I'll give you more in a little while."

"I looked toward the west and lowered the brim of my hat to block the sun's glare. "It'll be dark in an hour. Let's mount up and ride. The stallion can walk behind at a faster pace."

When Asia climbed on her horse, she asked, "How long before we reach the ranch?"

"Maybe a half hour or so." I pointed to a well-worn deer path not more than two-feet wide. "We'll go single-file until we get over the next hill. It'll be quicker than going around those rocks to the west of us."

"Okay." Asia lined up Flower behind the stallion.

I took the lead while holding the stallion's reins, and we rode along the narrow trail. A steep ravine was to our right. The other side had a grass-covered slope. Uncle Jake and I had been here while rounding up a couple of stray cows a week ago. From that experience, I knew we just had to ride a little further and we'd make it to a dirt road. Then we could follow it for another 15 minutes to the ranch.

We still had to work our way up the trail, and I wanted to be sure the weary horse could handle it. I pulled up the reins of my mule and looked back at Asia. "How's he doing?"

"Okay." She nodded to the stallion with a worried expression. "We need to get him to the vet soon. I've been watching his hind legs. He's beginning to stagger a little bit."

"Yeah, I can see the way he droops his head down." I pointed to the next hill. "Once we get on the other side, it won't take long to reach the ranch."

We followed a switchback up the hill and this made it less of a strain on the stallion. Just as we started down the trail, I spotted a fallen tree branch blocking us 100 feet ahead. "Whoa." I patted Gray's neck and took stock of our predicament. The trail was still too narrow to get around it. Thick bushes and trees were growing among jagged rocks along the hill. On my other side, was another ravine. I had only one option—keep the animals back and try to remove the twisted obstacle by hand.

"Wait here." I glanced back at Asia and dismounted Gray, then I tied the reins on a tree. While the mule snorted, I grabbed my rifle and started to walk away.

"Why are we staying way back here?" asked Asia.

"It's best you stay up slope where I can keep an eye on your location. I pointed to the branch that blocked our path and said, "Uncle Buck taught me to expect the unexpected. It may not be safe for you and our mounts if you're down there with me."

"Okay." She got off Flower and watched as I headed down the trail.

When I examined the main branch, I was relieved to see that it was only 10 inches thick. I leaned my rifle against a large rock, pulled out the machete from my belt and cut away some of the twisted growth. "That should do it." I grunted as I lifted and dragged the branch to the side of our trail.

Just as I finished, I heard a rattling sound and froze. Slowly I turned and spotted a rattle snake, coiled and ready to strike.

I jumped back. It struck and missed. I stepped up on a boulder and looked down at the thick head of a diamond back rattler. Its beady eyes glared at me.

I glanced over to the side of our path. My rifle still leaned against a rock. It was too far away. "Yeah, I know," I said to the snake. "You're pissed. You want me to leave."

I remembered what I had learned about survival in the wild with my desert friend, Dusty. "Only kill if you have to or for food," he said. "Reptiles serve a purpose."

So, I said to the snake, "The thing is, you're blocking my path."

It struck and missed again. I raised up the machete. As I did, the snake coiled back in a circle again. This gave me an idea to make it easy for both of us. I placed the weapon into my left hand and grabbed a fresh-cut branch with my right. Then I picked up the rattlesnake with the stick and tossed it down the ravine. "Adios."

"Woody," Asia called out. "Are you okay?"

"Yeah, just clearing the trail." I grabbed my rifle, then ran up the path and got on Gray. "Let's go."

When we came to the ranch road, I saw Jake riding up on his Appaloosa. "We've been looking for you two," he said. "Where'd ya get the stallion?" He tilted his Stetson back and leaned on his saddle horn.

"We found him about three miles east of here," I said. "His rider must've been thrown off. He still had a saddle on."

Asia nodded to the horse. "He was all worn out and dehydrated."

Jake got off and examined the stallion's legs. "He's got some wounds here." My uncle frowned and noticed the brand. "Sonora Ranch. Okay, let's bring him in. I'll call our neighbor."

Asia and I had the animals settled in for the night when Jake went into the stall where we kept the stallion. He said, "I finally contacted the owner of this horse. He's on the way."

"Did he say anything about a rider?" I asked.

"Yep." Jake nodded. "Turns out this stallion belongs to the owner's son, Marcos." He furrowed his brow. "The boy came home from a tour in Nam about a week ago. He had a severe head wound and was laid up in a VA hospital for several months. His Pa said Marcos took off early this morning and hasn't returned."

"What about a search party?"

"Your Uncle Buck's on the phone now. We're rounding up as many men as we can," said Jake as he stepped out of the stall.

"How can I help?" asked Asia.

"You've done a lot already." Jake placed his palms on our shoulders as we walked out of the stall with him. "Now you two get something to eat. Got a long night ahead."

Asia looked back at the stallion. "Is it okay if I stay with the horse until his owner gets here?"

"Sure." Jake smiled and left the barn.

Knowing that we hadn't eaten anything since noon, I washed and dried my hands at a sink. "I'll make some sandwiches and we'll eat out here together. Okay?"

"That would be nice. Thanks." Asia cleaned the horse's wounds and wrapped fresh bandages around his legs again.

"That would be nice. Thanks." Asia stepped back in the stall and examined the horse again.

While she cleaned his wounds and wrapped fresh bandages around his legs, I watched her caring moves. "Need anything else?"

"No thanks." She kept her focus on the stallion without looking up.

"Okay. Be right back."

I strolled into the kitchen where Eileen and Maria were already making a large tray of peanut butter sandwiches. "Be sure to eat," said my aunt. "A lot of volunteers will be showing up soon."

"Thanks." I placed a few sandwiches on a plate. "I'll take these out to the barn. We'll eat there."

Eileen smiled and said, "I heard Asia doesn't want to leave that worn out horse."

"Yep. I couldn't pry her away even if I wanted to." I put two glasses of ice tea on a tray with the sandwiches.

"I thought so," Eileen laughed. "That girl's got spunk."

When I returned to the barn, Asia was busy washing her hands at the sink and looked up. Even here among the animals, her smile had a way of lighting up the darkest places of my weary mind. "The stallion seems okay," she said while drying her hands with a towel. "I'll feel even better once the vet examines him."

"Good." I held up the tray. "Have a sandwich."

"Thanks. That was fast."

"Yeah, Eileen and Maria are preparing a lot of food. I remember Jake had said that once people hear there's trouble, everybody pitches in to help."

We just finished eating when we heard several vehicles pulling up and headlights beamed through the open barn door. I covered my eyes and stepped out to see what was going on.

Jake and Buck were already talking with a tall slender man while I walked over to them. He wore a sombrero, and long grayish side burns lined his cheeks. A well-groomed mustache twitched slightly as he asked in a Spanish accent, "Where is my son's el caballo?"

"In the barn." Buck nodded to me. "This is my nephew, Woody. He brought the stallion in."

"Muchas Gracias." The gentleman firmly shook my hand and his smile revealed a row of neat white teeth. "I am Santos Rodriguez Zapatero."

"Glad to meet you, sir."

Buck said, "Come, my friend. Woody will show you the way."

Santos walked into the barn, examined his stallion and smiled at Asia. "Ah, you must be the young senorita the doctor has talked about. He says you have a natural gift with the animals."

Asia looked up in surprise by the sudden attention. Seeing her shyness, I said, "Asia, this is Mr. Zapatero. He's the owner of this horse." I nodded to him. "She's been caring for your stallion."

Santos immediately removed his well-worn sombrero and bowed in respect. "I am honored, senorita. Muchas gracias for looking after him. The doctor says you will make a fine veterinario someday."

"I hope your horse will be all right," said Asia while holding up a bucket of water and letting the stallion drink. "I cleaned the wounds as best as I could. Will the vet be here soon?"

Jake came in and answered, "I just talked to Doc Langley on the phone. He'll be here tomorrow morning."

Santos turned to Asia. "I can see you are taking good care of my son's el caballo. May I leave El Viento here for the night?"

Asia's eyes widened and she smiled. "Oh, yes." She paused. "What does the name mean?

"The wind." Santos looked at us and asked, "Now, where did you find El Viento?"

"Locket Meadow about three miles east of here," I responded.

"Can you find it in the dark?"

"I'll do my best," I said.

"Bueno." Santos pulled out a watch attached to a gold chain from his vest pocket. He looked at it and frowned. "Our search will be difficult, but my son must be found. His war wounds have made him loco. Even suicidal. Let's go."

A dozen men sat on their horses in front of headlights and waited for orders. "We'll follow Woody out to where he found El Viento," said Santos. Sitting on his lap was a small three-legged mutt. "This is my son's dog, El Amor. Maybe it will help to calm Marcos down."

Santos turned to a lean dark-skinned man, possibly of Afro-Mexican heritage with straight black hair just over his ears. "Vicente, I am depending on your tracking skills. No search dogs for now." He looked up at a half-moon. "You take the lead." He nodded to me and said, "You follow him."

Vincente rode off on a tall Leopard Appaloosa with white mottled skin and black patches. He rested a rifle butt on his upper right leg and pointed the barrel skyward like he was on a war party in Apache country. I followed behind him.

Uncle Jake came alongside of me and whispered, "Santos has given you a great honor of riding behind Vincente."

"Who is he?" I asked.

"Vincente is the foreman," Jake answered. "He's been with the Santos family estate ever since he was a 14-year-old boy. One day he just showed up and asked for a job. After 20 years, of working on the ranch, he has become the most trusted man in a crew of two dozen vaqueros."

"Why does he hold the rifle like that?" I asked.

"Vincente has his reasons. Just stay close and follow orders."

After learning more about him, I kept my eye on his every move. He wore a wide-brimmed straw hat low over his forehead. Brown leather chaps covered his legs, and in the stirrups were tan moccasins, instead of the usual sturdy western-style boots.

When we rode to the springs, I couldn't be sure if this was the exact spot where the stallion appeared. With our flashlights glaring, the shadows of trees danced like ghosts in the night. I dismounted Gray while Vincente knelt and studied the ground nearby.

Santos got off his well-bred Paso Fino horse and came alongside me. "Is this it?" he asked.

"I don't know yet." I lifted my hat and scratched my head in confusion. "It all looks so different in the dark. I can't be sure."

"Jefe." Vincente placed his hand on Santos' shoulder. "Look." He pointed to a silver button in the dirt.

Santos picked it up and examined it under a flashlight. "It is from my son's shirt."

The stoic foreman kept silent as he walked his tall Appaloosa and continued to study the ground for tracks. We followed close behind with our mounts in tow for another several hundred yards. In the darkness, flashlight beams bounced off a rocky slope. Vincente halted and knelt with his fingers rubbing into the dirt.

Santos strolled alongside and asked, "What is it?"

"Not good." Vincente stood up and pointed to numerous hoof

prints that seemed to go in all directions. "El Viento ran this way." He waved a hand wide. "Circled back here. Then go up rocks."

"What does it mean?" Santos looked on while still cradling the three-legged dog, El Amor.

"Marcos ran El Viento hard." Vincente tapped his forehead and added, "He's loco."

"Which way now?" asked Santos.

"We go back." Vincente mounted up. "Wait for daylight. I'll round up more men."

22 THE SEARCH

I awoke to the early morning sunlight beaming through a crack in the barn wall. Men and women were talking outside. Engines idled while horses neighed. It was time to get up for another round of searching for a man I never met.

Asia was still asleep with her head resting on my chest. The hayloft was cozy and warm after I had returned to the ranch after midnight. Since she wanted to be near El Viento, we decided to relax together before I had to go back on the trail.

When I tried to shade my eyes with my arm, Asia stirred and lifted her head. "What time is it?" she asked with a sleepy sigh.

"I'll check." I stood up, opened the shutters to the loft door and squinted from the glare of a sunrise. "About six. Sun's just over the hills now."

Asia came alongside of me and placed her arm on my shoulder. "Wow," she whispered. "Must be a lot of people down there."

"Yep," I said. "Neighbors are coming in from miles around to help in the search." I paused. "Look at all those people getting out of their cars and carrying trays of food to that canopy in the front yard."

"I've never seen so many people wanting to help like this before," said Asia.

"Yeah, we had to wait for daylight to get everyone out here." I turned and smiled. "When there's trouble in this open country, neighbors all pitch in to help. Let's go."

Asia and I gave each other a quick morning kiss and climbed down the ladder to get started.

Doc Langley walked in wearing a wide-brimmed straw hat over his white hair. "Okay, young lady," he said to Asia. "I talked with Santos. He said you helped to save his son's stallion. Let's see how well you did." He checked the horse's hide and mouth.

"Good. Skin's normal. Gums are okay." He knelt and examined its legs. "This is amazing." He stood up and looked over his eyeglasses that rested low on his nose. "Asia, you did a great job patching up these leg wounds."

"Thank you." Asia smiled. "You're a good teacher."

"Now, the other thing to remember about animal care is to look for any subtle changes in their behavior." Doc Langley held up a bucket. "If a horse turns up his nose, it may be that he doesn't like the taste. Rinse it thoroughly. If that doesn't work, add a little mint or apple juice to the water."

Asia looked on with interest. "Oh, that's good advice."

I leaned on the stall and watched closely. "Yeah, I never thought of that."

Jake came in and tapped my shoulder. "We're ready."

"Okay, I'll see you later," I said to Asia.

"Bye," she responded without making eye contact and continued to listen to her instructor. I mounted up on Gray and followed behind Vincente in a party of three dozen men. When we came to our last sighting of wayward tracks, we spread out 100 feet apart. Jake maintained his position to my right. Buck stayed back at the ranch base camp to coordinate with volunteers.

Each man weaved a pattern through a stand of Ponderosa trees. A steady clop of hoof beats kept a rhythm like the tick, tick of a clock as we moved forward with our eyes focused on the ground. Wind rustled the leaves. Somewhere out in that vast wilderness of Coconino National Forest was a lost man. We had to find him and hope that he was still alive.

A bright orange solar ball glared like an eye in a crystal blue sky. It was noon. Heat radiated into every pore of my body. Thirsty, I sipped from my canteen and kept riding. Vincente never took a drop. I glanced around at the other men. Some wiped their brows with their sleeves. Others drank eagerly with a thirst that cannot be easily quenched. We rode on in silence.

Streams were crossed; valleys spread out to mountains and the sun dipped further to the west. Meanwhile, Vincente looked for any signs of the missing man. An occasional lizard scampered by and disappeared among the rocks. Horses neighed. Hooves clopped. Sweat dribbled down our backs.

In the shade of Ponderosa trees, we all dismounted to cool off. We stretched our legs and leaned against sturdy trunks that towered over us. Jake stood beside me as we sipped from our canteens. "Where are the search dogs?" I asked.

"Santos is worried they might frighten his son," Jake responded.

"Well, why does Santos carry that three-legged mutt?"

"Marcos found El Amor behind a coffee shop three years ago. She had been eating out of a tipped-over trash can and was so skinny, her ribs stuck out. He brought the pup home and took care of her like it was his own baby. I reckon Santos thinks Marcos will be glad to see her."

Santos heard us talking. "Ah, yes." He stepped over with the dog and did the sign of a cross with his right hand. "With de Dio's help, El Amor will help to save his tormented soul."

After riding for another hour, Vincente dismounted and studied the back and forth hoof prints at our feet. Santos knelt beside him and said, "These tracks go loco." He let out a sigh and shook his head. "Marcos rode El Viento hard."

Vincente stood up and scanned a sea of grass rolling like waves in the valley. A breeze swept in and lifted the brim of his hat. The left side of his mouth turned up slightly. He swung his leg over the Appaloosa and nodded to the men. "Vamonos."

We followed Vincente with our heads bowed in the wind. Each man held onto the reins of his mount and continued on. Ahead were more hoof prints. Santos sat on his saddle with his back straight. The Paso Fino horse's thick cream-colored mane and tail swayed elegantly in a fine melodic gait that made her stride seem effortless.

Vincente stopped and studied the tracks again. Santos came alongside and asked, "What is it?"

"Look." Vincente patted a flattened area in the six-inch-tall grass. "Marcos fell off El Viento here." He waved a hand to the east. "He crawled on his belly that way."

We all turned toward rugged cliffs and saw jagged rock forma-
tions that peered down like monsters hardened in ancient lava
flows. Vincente walked to a clearing, squatted and pointed to
scratches in the dirt. "Marcos dragged his rifle here."

Santos knelt beside him and said, "Bueno. Purrhaps..." He
paused. "My son used it like a cane."

Vicente quietly examined an odd angle of tracks. He walked
further, knelt again and picked up a discarded canteen. He
tipped it upside down. Not a drop came out.

Santos rushed over and grabbed it. "My son!" He set the dog
on the ground and looked at the canteen. El Amor sniffed and
whimpered. Santos smiled and knelt with the mutt. "Ah, bueno,
mi little one. Go on. Find Marcos."

El Amor barked and sniffed the footprints. Although her left
hind leg was missing, she balanced her walk with a hop and skip.
Her little tail waved as if to signal everyone to follow.

Vincente walked his horse and studied the tracks. We kept our
animals in tow. He stopped and scanned a rocky cliff towering
like a dinosaur with jagged teeth. A hawk circled over a ledge
and called out an eerie sound. Our mounts neighed, snorted and
fidgeted. Something was wrong.

Pow! Pow! Shots rang out from the rugged slope.

We all scattered like mice and hid behind rocks. Santos
grabbed El Amor and hunkered down. A dozen Vaqueros cocked
their rifles and aimed at an unseen enemy. Vincente crouched
and leaned against a boulder, while he scanned the rocky cliffs
with binoculars.

"It's Marcos!" Vincente lowered the glasses.

"My son!" Santos stood up. A bullet whizzed overhead. He
ducked behind the rock again. "Why is he shooting at us?"

"I've seen guys go crazy after they returned from Korea," said
Jake. "Marcos still thinks he's in Nam." He stood up, rushed to
his horse, Apple and yelled, "I'll circle around and try and stop
him."

Another bullet whizzed down from the rocks. "Ah!" Jake

dropped to the ground and gripped his leg in pain.

"Jake!" I crawled on my belly to him. "You all right?"

"Yeah." He groaned and rubbed his left foot. "Help me get this damn boot off."

I gripped and pulled it away, and his toes were red with blood.

Jake tilted his head back and winced in pain while Apple whinnied and leaned closer to her rider.

"Get the first-aid kit out of my saddle bag," said Jake.

I stood up and reached for it. Pow! Pow! Two more shots rang out. I ducked as bullets hit the dirt within inches of my feet.

Apple stayed with her rider as though they were inseparable. She whinnied again and rubbed her nose on Jake's shoulder.

"It's all right girl." Jake stretched out his leg and groaned.

I stood up, grabbed the first-aid kit and dropped to my knees. My hands shook as I opened it. "Don't worry, Uncle Jake." I pulled out antiseptic, gauze and bandages. "You'll be all right."

Jake patted my wrist. "Slow down." He looked up with his familiar light-hearted smirk as if to assure me. "I've been through this in Korea." He winced and sighed. "Face your fear." His brown eyes looked deeply like he wanted me to focus. "Got it?"

I exhaled and nodded. "Yep." I tried to keep calm as I cleaned the wound and the blood soaked into a cloth.

"Well, lookee here." Jake held up his boot. "The bullet sliced the top of my boot clean off." He laughed and winced in pain again.

I examined his foot and let out a sigh of relief. "Yeah, must've grazed your toes." I wrapped a gauze and bandaged it as best as I could. "Phew. That was too close."

Vincente stood up and took the reins of his Appaloosa. Then he yelled to Santos, "Jefe, vamonos!"

Another bullet whizzed by and hit a tree.

Santos placed the dog on a saddle and mounted his horse. She neighed and tilted her head back as more shots rang out over our heads, but she stood her ground.

"Woody!" Vincente yelled, while his horse reared up. "Get the mule. Come with us."

"Hey!" Uncle Jake tried to stand up but fell back. "You ain't going nowhere with my nephew!"

"I need the mule to stop Marcos." Vincente nodded to me. "He's the rider."

"It's okay, Uncle Jake." I swung my leg up on Gray. "It's my responsibility."

Another shot zipped over our heads. Men swore. A vaquero ducked and spat tobacco juice on a rock. Hooves stomped. Horses neighed. We turned our reins toward the firing and rode out.

Pumped on adrenaline, every fiber of my being was on high alert. Bullets whizzed by. Strangely, the world slowed down around me. My breathing was loud and clear in my ears. Dust flew in my face. Bright sunlight glared in my eyes. I lowered my gaze and focused on the trail. Sweat dribbled down my face. The shooter had the advantage with the sun at his back. Whatever Vincente had planned, the odds were against us.

Gray twitched his ears, shook his head and whimpered. "Steady." I patted his neck and tried to calm both of us, then remembered Jake had said, "Face your fear."

I gripped the reins and looked ahead. Hooves clopped as we climbed further up the back side of where Marcos had been shooting at us. When we came to a narrow rock-littered path, Vincente got off his horse and studied the landscape.

"No bueno for el caballos. Now we walk." He grabbed the reins of his Appaloosa and the Paso Fino, then secured them to a tree.

A gust of wind whistled through rocky crevices. Both horses stomped their hooves. One moment it had been calm. Then it was like a banshee shrieking out a warning to go no further.

"Woody!" Vincente called out over more eerie howls. "Bring the mule!"

I pulled Gray forward. "Come on, fella." He followed my lead with a trust that came from the bond we'd established over the summer.

Vincente walked in front of me. Santos kept his pace in the rear while still holding his three-legged mutt, El Amor. We continued up a rocky path. A cool wind whistled in my ears again, and I shivered, slipped on a rock, but steadied myself.

Vincente halted and raised his arm. A quiet stillness settled over us like a thin veil that could be rustled at any minute. "Quedate agui," he whispered and held up his hand to stay put. He walked ahead and disappeared around a jagged rock shaped like a hawk's beak.

Santos and I waited and glanced at each other. Neither of us knew what to expect. We had to put our trust in Vincente's leadership without question. This was a lesson I learned from my uncles while hunting for cougar.

Moments later, Vincente returned and said, "Encontre a Marcos."

"You found my son?" asked Santos with a look of surprise and renewed hope.

Vincente placed his palm on Santo's shoulder and nodded. "Si, jefe."

Santos exhaled as though he had been holding his breath. "I want to see him."

"No, jefe." Vincente shook his head. "Marcos holds the rifle. He's loco."

"What now, mi amigo?" Santos pleaded as he cradled el Amor in his arms like a sacred offering to his son.

Vincente glanced at both of us and waved a hand. "Come," he spoke louder as another gust of wind fluttered the brims of our hats and howled in our ears again.

I led Gray forward until Vincente signaled to stop. He pointed at a narrow fork to the right. "Marcos looks the other way. Loco thirsty. Your mule has las cantinas. He needs to get the agua." Vincente looked into my eyes. "Comprende?"

"Yep." I nodded. "Marcus will go for the water."

"Si." He nodded to Gray. "Send him in there." He pointed to an opening between two boulders. "Marcos will not shoot."

I rubbed Gray's neck like I'd done many times and whispered in his ear, "Go on." I patted his hind leg. He walked into a small opening not more than five-feet wide with granite boulders. on both sides.

We peeked around a corner and watched. Marcos wasn't aware of the mule and pointed his rifle toward the men below us.

"They're coming!" He yelled in his war madness and glanced to his left as though he was talking to someone. "Hang on Sarge!" He lowered his weapon and reached out, then touched the rock. "Sarge?" His voice cracked, and he stared at his hand in shock. "Damn it! You promised to get us outta here."

Breathing heavily, he aimed his rifle. "I'll kill you gooks!" Marcos pulled the trigger. It clicked. He gasped for air and looked to his left, then his right. "They're all dead!" He gripped his head with both hands as though he was in excruciating pain. "Please God!" He made the sign of a cross. "I don't want to die!"

Gray snorted. Marcos spun around. His lips were swollen and parched. He stared with sunken eyes at the canteens hanging on the mule's side.

"Water!" he whispered in a raspy voice as the rifle dropped at his feet. He grabbed a canteen with both hands and drank like a dying man in the desert. Water dribbled down his chin.

"Marcos!" Santos called out. "Mi hijo!"

"Papa?" Marcos dropped to his knees. "Help me, Papa."

"Si, I am here." Santos set the three-legged dog on the ground. "Look, mi hijo! El Amor comes to you." The little mixed-breed terrier hopped into Marcos' arms and licked his face. Her tail wagged happily.

"El Amor!" Marcos cradled the mutt. "Where have you been?"

Santos rushed to his side, knelt and hugged him. "Let's go home, my son."

23 PARTY TIME

A soft twilight glow settled over Asia, while we stood outside that August evening. She wore a yellow dress with orange floral designs that draped elegantly to just above her knees. It had a scoop neck and thin shoulder straps that revealed the smoothness of her skin. Her mother's heart-shaped locket nestled on her chest as a sacred heirloom. Long black hair flowed like a waterfall down her back, and a bright yellow daisy had been placed just above her right ear.

Unable to divert my eyes, I said, "You remind me of a flower blooming at the beginning of a new day."

Asia tilted her head back and giggled. "You do realize the sun is setting. Right?"

I held my gaze and smiled. "Oh, yeah. You have a way of making me forget the time of day."

"Well, may I remind you that this is our first date without a horse and mule?" She put her arms around me and looked up with a sparkle in her eyes.

"That part I remember." I drew her in and savored the sweetness of her lips. "Shall we go?"

"Uh, huh."

I opened the passenger side door of Jake's pickup truck, and she turned her legs toward me. As she adjusted herself to scoot over, the hem of her dress slid up a few inches above her knees.

While the door was still open, I said, "It's nice to see you without jeans for a change. I like it."

"Thank you." She brought her legs in and sat up straight. "Your Aunt Eileen took in one of her dresses and hemmed it for me."

"Yeah, she admires you so much, you're like a younger sister to her. Okay, let's go have some fun." I closed the door and rushed to the driver's side.

We drove on a country road heading to Santos' hacienda. Asia leaned close and said, "I'm so glad we've been invited to Marco's homecoming celebration."

"It's party time, babe." I put my arm on her shoulder as I steered with my left hand.

Asia exhaled and snuggled up to me. "This may sound strange, but I've never been to a party before."

"Oh, that's right. Your dad wouldn't let you go anywhere." I drove further and asked, "Did you hang out with friends at school?"

"Yeah, sometimes." She paused as though she was in deep thought. "It was different, though."

"What do you mean?"

"Well, you know. I told you before that most of the kids called me a slant-eyed freckle-faced girl. Don't you remember?"

"Of course I do." I pulled over and braked alongside the road. "It's just that I don't understand why anyone could be so cruel to you." I kissed her forehead. "Especially the guys. Didn't they see how beautiful you are?"

"Well, there was a boy in my junior year." Asia had a far-off look as she remembered something. "His name was Larry. We used to hold hands and make out behind the gym sometimes. He asked me out, and when he came to pick me up, my Dad threatened to kill him."

"That's crazy!"

"By then, my mom was so sick from lung cancer that she spent a lot of time in and out of the hospital." Asia's eyes were moist in the dashboard lights. "When I got home from school I wasn't thinking about dating. I just wanted to spend every moment with my mom."

"I'm sorry you had to go through that, sweetie."

"I don't want to talk about it anymore." She kissed my cheek. "Can we go to the party now?"

"Sure." I revved the engine and floored the gas pedal. "Let's party!" I yelled as we sped out.

Asia giggled and squeezed my leg. "You're a wild man now."

We laughed and joked all the way to Santos' ranch. When we pulled up to his hacienda, the party had already started as couples danced to loud, vibrant rock music. Cars were parked near a barn, and colorful red, yellow and orange lights were strewn along wires attached to poles and trees. Several large barbeque fires glowed on the faces of cooks standing over grills piled with sizzling steaks.

"I didn't expect to hear rock and roll out here." I laughed as I opened the door for Asia.

"This looks like fun."

I held her hand and smiled. "Come on. This is my kind of party."

She looked radiant as we strolled over to the crowd of people. For a moment, we stood and watched the couples dancing, as a DJ played records and the music blared out from large speakers. A man in his early twenties walked up while limping and balancing himself on a cane. He kept his left arm on Santos for extra support, and overhanging lights revealed scars on his forehead.

Santos helped him to sit on a chair and said, "Marcos, it is my honor to introduce you to Woody and his lovely senorita, Asia."

Marcos held up his right arm and smiled. "I'm glad you two could make it."

"Thank you for inviting us." I gripped his palm and we shook hands.

"I've heard so much about you," he said. "Have a seat." He nodded at two empty chairs next to him. "You are my guests."

Santos patted his son's shoulder, smiled and said, "Please excuse me. I must attend to other matters." As he walked away, he waved to a server holding a tray with glasses.

We each took a glass filled with pink liquid and Marcos said, "It's lemonade." He laughed. My father doesn't allow alcohol here. He thinks we'll all turn into drunken fools."

A man sitting next to Marcos grinned through a thick black beard and said, "I have a remedy for that, amigo." He slid out a flask from under his shirt and poured something into our host's glass.

"Thanks," said Marcos. Ice clinked as he tipped his head and drank as though his thirst could never be fully quenched. He leaned closer to me and asked, "You want some?"

"No thanks," I spoke louder over the music being played. "We're fine."

Marcos looked at Asia and changed the subject. "I heard you took great care of El Viento. For that, I thank you."

"I was glad to help," she responded. "How is your stallion now?"

"He's back to his high-spirited self." Marcos lowered his gaze slightly and appeared embarrassed. "It was stupid of me to ride him so hard. I guess I tripped out."

"How are you feeling now," I asked.

"Not bad, as long as I stay on the meds." Marcos took another sip from his glass. "By the way, my father said you helped to find me. If you hadn't showed up when you did, I would've jumped off the cliff." He tipped his glass and clanked it against mine. "Thanks."

"You're welcome."

The smell of alcohol lingered. He had the same far-off look as my best friend, Gary, when he returned from Vietnam. He too, had been severely wounded in body, mind and spirit. It was obvious that Marcos had a long way to go in his recovery.

"So, what's up with you?" asked Marcos.

"What do you mean?"

"Well, you're about ripe for the Army." Marcos paused and studied me with a curious expression. "They need more sacrificial lambs for slaughter, ya know." He took another drink. "What have you been up to?"

"Well, let's see. The day after I left home, a man tried to kill me. He left me to die in the desert. I was saved by a stranger, who taught me how to survive in the wilderness. When I met Asia, a maniac tried to kill us. We ran for our lives and escaped. I've had two months herding cattle with my uncles. Went on a cougar hunt. Then a week ago, you were shooting at me. Meanwhile, I could get drafted any day now."

"Sorry about that." Marcos patted my shoulder and smiled. "Trouble is, I don't remember a damn thing." He had that far-off look again. "I woke up in the hospital three days later and didn't know how I got there." He tapped the right side of his head. "Got a steel plate in my skull. Compliments of the Army."

Marcos gulped his drink and it dribbled down his chin. "You're next," he said.

"What?" These were the exact words that my wounded friend, Gary had said to me about the draft.

Marcos pointed to the buffet line, "Go on. Get some food."

I looked at Asia. "Ready to eat?"

She swayed to the rhythm of a song and watched the people dancing. "Not yet." She tapped her knee and smiled. "I want to hear this first."

A record played through loudspeakers, "When a Man Loves a Woman."

"Do you want to dance?" I asked as I stood and held out my hand.

"I don't know how." She squeezed my palm and smiled.

"I'll show you." I led her over to where other couples were dancing and held her close.

Asia's hair tickled my cheek as she rested her head on my shoulder. Together, we moved slowly, and she relaxed in my arms. "This is nice," she said in my ear.

As a sensuous male voice sang about a man loving his woman, we gazed into each other's eyes and danced. Another song came on by the Four Tops, and we picked up the pace, then I spun her around.

"Where did you learn to dance like this?" she spoke louder over the music.

"School sock hops." I laughed. "Now that I'm wearing shoes, I'll try not to step on your toes."

"Oh." She laughed and smiled.

Guitars twanged to the next song, "My Baby does the Hanky Panky." Asia glanced at other women dancing with their partners. Seeing how they wiggled their hips; she copied their moves and we swirled in a lover's trance. More music played and everyone seemed to disappear as the rhythm revolved around the two of us.

A well-manicured lawn was soft like a horse blanket under our feet, and we danced to the beat reverberating through our hearts and down to our toes. Asia giggled, kicked off her shoes and stepped with more confidence. Her long hair swayed from side to side, and she smiled as though she lived only in that moment. Worries of our future faded away and the music took over.

The Beach Boys sang and the guitars played on.

When that ended, there was a pause, while the DJ prepared the next round of songs. Asia caught her breath and smiled. "Woo, let's take a break. I'm thirsty."

"Yeah, me too." I held her warm hand, then we squeezed through the crowd of people and strolled to our chairs.

"Excuse me," said Marcos. "I need to get some rest." Our host stood up, wobbled, but two of his friends kept him from falling. "Good night," he called out over his shoulder.

"He doesn't look well," said Asia.

"Yeah, I hope he'll be all right."

A waiter walked by with a tray and offered glasses of lemonade. "Thanks." I took two, then handed one to Asia. "This'll quench our thirst."

Asia relaxed on the chair and sipped from her glass. "I'm having so much fun." She smiled. "I feel like I could fly."

"Yeah, I can tell the music is in you." I took another mental picture and savored the way she sparkled. "I like to see you happy."

In the background, synchronized male voices sang about a girl having fun until her daddy takes her T-bird away.

I glanced over to the buffet table and asked, "Are you hungry?"

"I'm starving," she said.

After we filled our plates with steaks, we sat and enjoyed our meal while the music played on. Overhanging red lanterns bathed Asia's hair in streaks of crimson and her skin was awash in a smooth tint of creaminess. A large bonfire heated the center of our dance area, while barefoot dancers twirled in a display of colorful orange, yellow, purple skirts and low-cut blouses. Their partners, wearing blue jeans and open-collared shirts spun them in a merry-go-round of sensuous energy.

When we finished eating, I asked, "Do you want to dance?"

She smiled again and held up an empty glass. "I'd like more lemonade first."

"Sure." I glanced around to find the waiter and spotted him at a serving table. "There he is. I'll be right back."

When I picked up two glasses from a tray and headed back to Asia, a tall, thin man handed her a paper cup. To her left, were four other men standing around with smirks on their faces. They were gesturing among themselves and watching her, as she took the cup. I had seen this sinister maneuver at a wild party in San Diego. On high alert, I set the glasses on a table and ran to her.

"I'll take that!" I grabbed the cup from her hand and glanced at the fizzing liquid. A strong smell of alcohol wafted in the air, but something else must've been added.

I turned to the stranger. "Thanks," I said with a smile. "But we're just leaving."

"Hey, man!" He glared at me. "I was only giving her a drink."

"It's cool." I handed him the cup. "But we gotta go."

When we drove away, Asia crossed her arms and huffed. "That was rude. I wanted to stay longer."

"I know." I gripped the steering wheel and looked straight ahead. "I did too, but I didn't like the way things were changing after Marcos left."

"Oh, I get it." She puffed out air. "You're jealous because a guy came over and talked to me."

"No." I glanced at her. "I don't care who you talk to." As soon as I spoke, I realized that it didn't come out right.

"Oh, so that's it. You don't care about my feelings at all." She glared as though daggers were flying out of her eyes. "Do you?"

"What are you talking about? You're crazy." Oh, that didn't sound right either. "Look." I let out a deep sigh. "I just wanted to..."

"You're just like my father!" she interrupted and kept her arms wrapped tight across her chest.

"Wow!" I pulled over to the side and slammed on the brake. "You've got to be kidding me."

"Well, what was the harm in talking to that guy?"

"Nothing." I flicked on the overhead light and faced her, but she continued to pout. "Look, you told me that you've never been to a party before. Well, back home in San Diego, I went to a lot of them and had fun. But there was one time when people got hurt."

"What happened?"

"Last year I took a girl to a wild party at a beach house. There were so many people, it was standing room only. All kinds of booze and drugs were being passed around like candy."

"So?" Asia continued to stare ahead with her arms crossed. "What does that have to do with me?"

"Just listen to me. Okay?"

"Who's stopping you?" She still frowned and wouldn't look at me.

"Anyway, we were in the kitchen. I got a couple of beers out. When I turned around to give a can to my date, some guy already handed her a paper cup. Since we'd already been drinking, I didn't think it was a big deal. Later, she started hallucinating. Several others got sick. It was crazy."

"Oh." Asia turned and faced me with wide eyes. "What happened to them?"

"Ambulances rushed my date to the hospital along with two guys and three other girls." I leaned back in the driver's seat and stared at my reflection in the rearview mirror. "Turned out they had a mixed bag of drugs in their systems. They're okay now."

"I still don't understand what that has to do with me." Asia sighed. "This was our chance to get out and party together. Now we're sitting on the side of this road with no place to go."

"Don't you get it?" I glanced at my reflection again and turned away in disgust. "The point is, I promised her dad I'd get her home safely. I failed. After that, I guess I've been overprotective sometimes."

"Well, what now?" Asia took a sip of water from our canteen and looked at me. "I don't want to go home yet."

I started the engine and drove back on the road. "We'll have our own private party." I turned on the radio as it played more rock music."

She giggled and squeezed my shoulder. "Where are we going?"

"I'll show you."

I drove to a secluded lookout and left the radio on, then I opened her door and said, "Let's dance."

"Here?" she asked as she squeezed my hand, stepped out and looked around at the dirt parking area.

"Sure." I pointed to the stars. "We've got party lights that'll sparkle all through the night."

On the radio, a deep male voice sang, "Hey, babe. You ready?"

"Oh, I know this one." Asia smiled and sang along, "Yes, I think I'm ready."

I placed my hands on her hips and danced. "You are?"

She giggled. "I think so."

Then we sang in unison, "Let's fall in love."

After dancing to several more songs, we leaned against the truck and gazed at the stars. With our arms around each other, we savored each moment as the music played on the radio. But the night air began to get colder, and we shivered and stomped our feet to keep warm.

"I'm freezing." Asia cuddled up to me.

"I'll get our jackets from the truck," I said. We slipped them on, then faced each other as we rubbed our bodies to keep warm. "How's that?"

"Better as long as we stay close." Asia's lips quivered and she snuggled in my arms.

"Oh, you're still cold." I reached behind the truck seat and pulled out a blanket that Jake kept for an emergency. "Here, hold this."

Asia held one end, while I wrapped it tight over our shoulders.

She kissed my cheek and said, "Now I'm getting warmer."

"Me too." I looked up at a Cheshire cat moon smiling down from a cloudless sky. "Now that's a good sign."

"Uh, huh." Asia's whispered like we were in a cathedral, "Maybe the universe is happy for us,"

"Yeah." I pointed to the twinkling stars and said, "It's like they're all looking down and cheering."

"Oh, look," she said. "There's the north star."

"That's amazing. I can imagine what it would be like to navigate by all those glittering lights."

"If you could travel right now, where would you go?" asked Asia.

"Well, I always wanted to see Europe."

"What part?" Asia turned and gazed into my eyes. In the glow of interior lights shining through the open doors, her face was flush in pink.

"All of it."

"Let's go right now." Asia stretched out her arms like she wanted to touch the stars. The blanket slid off our shoulders, then landed on the ground. "We'll fly off and see the world together."

"Okay, let's go." I lifted her petite body off the ground, then I let her feel the wind on her face.

Asia giggled. "Oh, this is my kind of party."

As I lowered her, we kissed and lingered in a long embrace.

"And now to the news," blared a radio voice like a rude party crasher. "The Vietnam War continues to escalate as more men are being drafted. Heavy casualties were reported in…" I turned the dial to another station. "Antiwar protesters were arrested in San Francisco today." I flicked off the radio and plopped in the driver's seat.

"This is crazy," I said. "Even out here, we can't get away from the madness of another war."

Asia picked up the blanket, slid into the passenger side and hugged me. "Oh, Woody, I'm so tired of hearing about the war. What if you get drafted and something happens to you? Why don't they leave us alone?"

We closed our doors in a desperate attempt to shut ourselves off from the world. Our lips caressed and we held on to each other. Passions ignited into flaming desires and fused us together. Heat radiated through our bodies and steamed up the windows.

24 TURMOIL

A bolt of lightning struck a ridge to the southeast of our ranch. Thunder crackled and boomed. A fast-approaching storm was just a mile away. Strong gusts of wind howled in our ears and large raindrops began to splatter in the dirt. We had to get eight horses out of a corral and into the barn before it got worse. A buckskin mare reared up and neighed, as I dug in my heels to hold her steady.

"Whoa." I gripped the reins and pulled her forward. When I secured her in a stall, I ran back out, grabbed the rope of another mare and brought her in.

Meanwhile, Asia and Maria helped to get more skittish horses settled. Dark clouds rolled over us like a blanket and blocked out the afternoon sun. Spooked by this sudden change in the weather, a young quarter horse ran in circles. I tossed a rope, lassoed and tried to pull him toward the barn, but he reared up in fear.

"Steady, Rio."

Torrential rain gushed out of the sky like opening the floodgates. Soaked and cold, I struggled to get him out of the downpour.

"Come on." I held tight with my gloved hands. The more I pulled, the more he dug in.

Maria ran back out and led an older stallion alongside, and this calmed Rio down enough to follow us into the barn. Then Asia took the reins of Maria's horse and said, "I'll take care of him."

"Gracias." Maria patted the steed's hindquarters and ran back to the house.

Day had turned to night so fast that I flicked on the barn lights, while horses neighed and fidgeted in their stalls. Lightning flashed in the sky and thunder roared as if to remind us of the storm's unpredictable nature. Safe inside, we continued to work with the animals.

"It's all right," Asia spoke in a soothing voice as she patted the younger horse.

Raindrops pounded the roof. I stood safely away from the opened barn door and noticed a stream flowing through the front yard between the house and us.

"We'll have to hunker down here for a while," I yelled to Asia.

"Yeah, we made it just in time." She walked over and stood beside me. "We've seen a lot of storms come and go this past summer, but this one's the worst."

"Wait," I said. "Did you hear the phone ringing?"

Asia cocked her head and looked to the back of the barn. "Yeah, it stopped. Eileen must've picked it up in the kitchen."

"I don't like the looks of it," I said. "Jake and Buck drove out to Flagstaff early this morning for supplies."

"Did they say when they'll head back?" Asia stood beside me with a worried expression.

"Before dark, if all goes well." A flash of lightning lit up the sky, and thunder rumbled like beats of a drum.

"I wish they'd hurry back." Asia observed the turmoil outside and shook her head.

"Yeah, it's getting worse out there."

We stood with our arms around each other and looked out at raindrops splattering in large brown puddles. The stream continued to flow from a ridge and through our front yard. An hour before this, it had been dry and dusty.

"Woody!" Aunt Eileen called out from the house and waved from the porch. "Your Mom's on the phone. It's urgent!"

"Okay," I yelled back. "I'll take it in here."

I lifted the receiver. "Hi Mom."

"Son," her voice cracked. "Your Dad was in a car accident."

"What?" It was like a gut punch. I couldn't breathe. A lump was in my throat. I tried to swallow. "Not Dad." My eyes watered up. "Is he…"

"He's in the emergency room. You need to come home."

"Okay, Mom. I'll take the first flight out."

"I have to go. A nurse just came out. I love you, son." The phone clicked.

Asia looked over and asked, "What happened?"

"It's my Dad. He's been in an accident."

The phone rang again, and I picked it up. "Hello."

"Rick, I'm glad I caught you." It was the high-pitched voice of my 17-year-old sister. "It's Dad!"

"Kathy? What happened?"

"Dad was driving home when..." her voice cracked. "A car swerved into his lane. Hit him head-on." She broke down and cried.

"Kathy, listen to me."

She sobbed.

"Kathy?" In gut-wrenching agony, all I could do was listen to her crying. "Kathy, please talk to me."

Finally, she sniveled and said, "I'm sorry." Her voice cracked again. "Dad's in ER. We just got here. Everybody's running all over the place. No one's talking to us."

"What hospital?"

"Balboa Naval. When can you get here?"

"I don't know. There's a thunderstorm. I'll leave as soon as I can."

"Hurry! We need..."

"Hello?" I looked at Asia. "We got disconnected."

"Maybe she'll call back." Asia looked out the barn door as rain blew sideways. "Let's get in the house and wait there."

We ran across the yard and splashed ankle-deep in the stream. Our boots sloshed in puddles and clumped up the porch steps. Just as we stepped inside, a bolt of lightning struck an oak tree near the corral. Thunder exploded like cannon fire.

In a whirlwind of anxious thoughts, I packed a suitcase and dropped it in the living room. Everything was happening so fast; I had no time to think clearly. My family needed me, and I had to get home.

"I want to go with you," Asia said as she came running down

the stairs with a suitcase.

"Good." Seeing her beside me, I exhaled and remembered to breathe. "I need you with me."

She reached out and held my hand. "What now?"

"Well, all we can do now is wait until the storm blows over. Looks bad."

Strong winds blew a sheet of rain across the yard and vibrated against the walls. "I'd better close the shutters." I started to step out on the porch when the sky lit up. Thunder rumbled, crackled and boomed again.

"Whoa! That was close." I moved away from rain-splattered windows.

"It's getting dark in here." Asia pulled out a flashlight from her tote bag and flicked it on. Shadows danced on the walls, as she looked around the room.

"Yeah." I took mine out of my backpack and shot a beam over at the ticking grandfather clock. "It's after five already. Shouldn't Jake and Buck be here by now?"

"They'll be fine," said Eileen while she stepped in from the kitchen. "Most likely, they're sitting on bar stools at the Big Horn Tavern, drinking beer and waiting for the storm to pass."

Following behind her were my four cousins, Tommy, Davey, Spring and Summer. They were all talking at the same time. Three-year-old Summer reached out her little hands and wiggled her fingers. "Mommy, I'm scared."

"It's all right." Eileen set the light on a mantle, lifted up Summer and kissed her rosy cheek. "Daddy and Uncle Jake will be home soon."

Maria came down the stairs with a lantern that helped to brighten up the room. "Come," she said to the kids. "Let's play a game."

"Ah, mom," groaned seven-year-old Davey, as he stepped closer to the living room window. "I wanna watch the storm outside."

"No." Eileen frowned. "Get away from there. You know better than that. I've told you all before to stay away from windows and doors when there's a thunderstorm."

Davey lowered his head and dragged his feet. "Yes mom."

"Go with Maria to the playroom," said Eileen as she put Summer down.

The kids marched down the hallway and Summer followed behind with a handmade cloth doll snuggled in her arms. Just as it was quiet, baby Hank began to cry from his basinet in the living room, then he kicked and his toes stuck out from under the blanket. Tiny hands raised up and wiggled around with increasing energy.

"Well, now," Eileen spoke softly as she picked him up. "You finally woke up after all that ruckus."

Asia laughed and said, "It's funny how he can sleep through so much noise. Then, the minute it gets quiet, he wakes up."

"Yeah, now he's hungry." Eileen sat on the oak rocking chair and nursed her baby while she sang a lullaby.

Heavy rain battered the roof and powerful winds rattled a loose shutter outside. More lightning flashed across the sky. Thunder roared, crackled and boomed.

Asia and I huddled together on the couch, and all we could do was wait for the storm to blow over. Worried, I was on the edge of my seat. "This is driving me crazy! I can't do anything."

"I know." Asia patted my shoulder.

"I have no idea what's going on back home." I puffed out air and shook my head. "I should be at the hospital with my Dad right now. How bad is he? If I only knew what's happening."

"Whoa." Aunt Eileen looked over. "Take it easy. You're acting like a wild buck tied to a short rope."

"She's right." Asia kissed my cheek and rubbed my back.

"Well, what am I supposed to do?" I stood up, paced back and forth and slammed a clenched fist into my palm.

"Feel better?" asked Eileen.

I stopped and glanced at her warm smile. In that moment, it was like looking into the eyes of my mom. Eileen had the same wise expression as her older sister. "No, not really," I said. I shook my hand and laughed. "I think I hurt myself."

"Well, since you're stuck here anyway," Eileen spoke softly. "Maybe you oughta try a different way of handling all that caged-in energy."

I sat down and puffed out air like a train coming to the end of a track. "Like what?"

"We could pray together." Eileen put baby Hank on her shoulder and patted his back. He lifted his wobbly head and burped.

"Well, I'm not much for words." I scratched my beard and glanced at Eileen. "You and Mom are good at praying. How about I just listen and you say something?"

"Okay." Eileen smiled and got up from the rocker. "Let's sit together." She sat beside me and held out her right hand, while the baby rested in her lap.

I took Eileen's hand and Asia squeezed mine.

"I'll start," said Eileen. "If you want to add anything, go ahead." She closed her eyes and continued, "Lord, we're all scared. Please give us peace during this painful time. We ask for healing of Robert. Help Woody and Asia to get home and care for his family."

Raw emotions built up, and I blurted out, "Please don't let my Dad die."

Asia began to cry and released her hand from mine. "I can't do this." She ran into the kitchen.

"What's wrong?" I rushed after her.

Asia sat on a kitchen chair sobbing.

I knelt and placed my hand on her shoulder. "It's all right, sweetie. We'll get through this."

"No." She cried. "Don't you see?" She picked up a napkin from the table holder and wiped her tears. "God doesn't care."

"Sure, he does." I brushed back strands of hair from her face with my hand. "We just have to believe and trust him. That's all."

"No, it's not enough." She sniffled and lowered her gaze. "When my mother was sick, I prayed so hard, but she got worse. I begged God to save her. Nothing helped. She died in my arms laying in that hospital bed."

"I know," my voice cracked as I tried to comfort her.

"While my mother was dying, my no-good father was drunk at home. He didn't even bother to show up at the funeral. I had to face it by myself."

Asia sobbed in my arms. Words were not enough to comfort her. I let her cry until the tears dried.

When all the pent-up emotions drained out, she said, "I'm sorry, Woody." She looked into my eyes. "I want to believe, but I can't."

"You don't have to be sorry or do anything." I held out my hand. "Would you like to go back in the living room and relax on the couch? It's warmer by the fireplace."

Asia took my hand. "Yes, I'm feeling cold in here."

While we sat on the couch, Eileen placed her baby in the bassinet and covered him with a blanket. "There now." She smiled and tucked him in. "All snug as a bug in a rug."

Asia looked over and tried to smile. "He's so cute. I like being around your family."

Eileen relaxed in her rocking chair and said, "Well, young lady, I want you to remember that you're part of our family now."

I put my arm on Asia's shoulder and teased, "Yeah, you're stuck with us."

"Thanks." She kissed my cheek. "I feel at home here."

By ten that evening, the storm had raged through the valley and headed east over Mogollon Rim. Asia was in the kitchen with Eileen and Maria. The kids were in bed and it was quiet around the house until a tea kettle whistled on the gas stove. Maria turned off a burner and poured steaming water into three teacups. Without electricity, the women sat together by the light of candles and talked in low voices.

When I walked in from the living room, I was glad to see them gathering in their usual manner like nothing had happened. Although they were different in so many ways, they had bonded not by blood, but with a deep respect and affection for each other.

"Do you want some tea?" asked Asia as she looked up and smiled at me.

"No thanks." I picked up the phone and dialed the number to my home in San Diego. This was one of many attempts to find out about my Dad. After it rang a dozen times, I hung up. "Still no answer. I'll call the hospital again. They wouldn't tell me anything last time."

I started to call, but I noticed bouncing headlight beams coming up the road. "It's Jake and Buck."

We all rushed out on the porch to greet them as tires splashed in puddles and their pickup truck stopped in front of the house. After quick hugs, we sat on chairs, while rainwater dribbled off the roof. Anxiously, I told my uncles about my dad's accident and the urgency of going back home. "We need to catch a flight out," I said.

"Sorry." Uncle Buck shook his head. "We barely made it across the bridge down our road."

"Yep," said Uncle Jake. "The river flooded and washed out part of the bridge. Some of the wood gave way just as we drove over to our side."

"We'll have to wait until daybreak to fix it," said Buck.

"How long will that take?" I asked.

"Couple of hours." Buck glanced at Jake. "That about right?"

Jake nodded. "Give or take."

The phone rang in the kitchen. "I'll get it." I ran in and grabbed the receiver. "Hello."

"Son," Mom answered. "Kathy said you're waiting for the storm to pass."

"Mom, how's Dad?"

"He's still heavily sedated." She paused. "He has a broken leg, a collapsed lung, two cracked ribs and a concussion."

"Is he going to be all right?"

"Yes, I think so. But the doctor says he has a long recovery ahead."

"That's a relief."

"He's too stubborn to give up," Mom said. "In fact, we saw an encouraging sign already."

"Tell me, Mom." I wanted to keep listening to her voice. "What happened?"

"He looked bad. Tubes were stuck in him. Loud monitors beeped. He was covered in bandages and his face was swollen. I was scared he might not ever wake up; even when the doctor assured me that your father would be all right. The longer I waited, the more it seemed like the room grew darker."

While Mom tried to speak calmly, Asia came alongside me and put her hand on my arm. I kissed her forehead and held the phone close.

"I tried to pray," Mom added. "But I couldn't breathe. I felt like I was dying with my husband." Her voice cracked. "Somehow, I lost hope."

Her doubtful words sent waves of sorrowful emotions through the phone line. A thick lump clogged my throat and my eyes watered up.

"Son?"

"I'm here." I wiped my eyes with my long sleeve.

"While your father laid there unconscious, all I could do was wait. Each minute dragged on. Suddenly, he gasped out so loud, it startled me. I looked at him, thinking this was it. His eyes widened. Then, he called out your name. After that, he drifted off to sleep again. The doctor said this was a good sign."

"Really?" I gripped the phone tighter. "When was that?"

"A few hours ago."

"Mom."

"Yes."

"That must've been the about same time I was praying for Dad."

"Oh Richard." Her voice choked up. "I'm glad you told me. In a split second, I went from despair to hope. For the first time, I felt God's presence in the room." She paused and asked, "When are you coming home?"

"I'm sorry, Mom. The bridge was partially damaged. We have to wait until dawn to repair it."

"I know what that's like," she said. "It happened to us when I was growing up on the ranch. Just do your best and keep praying. It'll all work out with God's help."

"Mom, there's something I need to tell you."

"Yes?"

"Asia's coming with me."

No response.

"Did you hear me?"

"Yes, I heard you." She paused. "It's just that I didn't expect this."

"I know."

Asia started to walk away, but I squeezed her hand. She turned, and we gazed into each other's eyes like we had done so many times before. "Stay," I whispered to her. She hesitated, then nodded and leaned closer.

"Well, what brought this on?" asked Mom.

"I want you and the family to meet her."

"Sounds like you two are more serious than I realized." She paused again. "Is Asia pregnant?"

Surprised to hear Mom ask that question, I looked at Asia's reaction. She rolled her eyes and shook her head.

"No." I spoke firmly in the phone. "I don't get it. The last time we all talked on the phone, you and Dad sounded as though you really liked Asia."

"We still do. It's just that we thought she would stay on the ranch. At least she can get a little on-the-job training with the vet, while caring for the horses."

"Well, the vet thinks Asia should apply at one of the veterinarian colleges in San Diego."

"That makes sense. There are a lot of opportunities here."

"Yeah, she could start classes at the community college," I agreed.

Asia tapped my shoulder and pointed to the phone. I nodded and said, "Mom, she wants to say something."

"Well, put her on then."

"Okay." I held the receiver closer.

"Hello, Mrs. Thomson."

"Oh, Asia. I'm so glad to hear you want to pursue your education."

"Me too." She glanced at me with moist eyes. "Um, I'm sorry about your husband."

"Robert will pull through. He's too stubborn to let this get him down."

"Yes." Asia was silent and fiddled with the telephone cord. Finally, she said, "I would like to meet you and your family, if that's okay."

"Yes, I'd like that too." Mom added, "Well, I need to get back in the room. Robert's been sleeping. I want to be there when he wakes up. We look forward to seeing you both. Love you. Goodnight."

"I love you too." I leaned the phone closer to Asia, so we could both hear.

Asia held my arm tight with both hands, while I hung up the wall phone. She looked at me and her eyes glistened like dew drops at dawn. "I wish..." She hesitated.

Seeing her sorrowful expression, I asked, "What is it?"

"I wish my father wasn't such a miserable person."

"I know."

"Let's go sit by the fireplace for a while," she said. "I don't want to talk about it anymore."

"Yeah." I nodded. "No more talk about the past. Now that the storm is over, we can relax and plan for our trip tomorrow."

25 HURRY UP AND WAIT

In a morning twilight, Asia and I stood on the porch and looked toward the west. We were anxious to take a flight out for San Diego, and see my dad in the hospital, but the bridge still needed to be repaired. Just 24 hours before, we had no thought of leaving this beautiful ranch. It was our refuge away from a fast-paced city life and the constant bombardment of news about the Vietnam War. Now I just wanted to get home and check on my Dad with Asia at my side.

Jake drove up and parked his Chevy pickup truck in front of the house. "I got a better look at the damage on that bridge," he said.

"Can we repair it?" I glanced at my watch. "It's 5:30."

"Yep. We just need to replace a few planks, and we'll get you to the airport."

"I nodded to the barn. "Buck went out back to get that broken-down flatbed truck started again."

"Good. We'll need it to haul wood," said Jake.

When we walked over to the truck, Buck had it running, but then it sputtered and died. He frowned and said, "Still needs work."

Jake shook his head and closed the hood. "What we need is a new truck."

"Can't afford it."

"I reckon so." Jake took his hat off and brushed back his red hair. "Woody, hitch the wagon."

Asia patted my shoulder and said, "While you guys work on the bridge, I'll take care of the horses one last time."

After I hitched Gray and another mule to the wagon, we loaded up wood and tools, then hauled them out to the bridge. Clouds sailed above us in a sea of blue, while Ponderosa trees swayed in the wind. At the riverbank, we examined the main frame that still looked sturdy.

"At least the river's gone down a few feet," said Jake as he pointed to the bridge. "We'll replace five planks in this section. Okay, let's get to work."

Jake slid out a 12-foot-long beam from the wagon, then I gripped the other end while I balanced myself on a narrow cat-walk, and we carried it across the bridge. Wary, I glanced at the fast-moving water below us.

"Don't look at the river, Woody." Jake lined up the board. "Just watch your step and we'll set it down here."

Once we put the board in place, we went back to the wagon while Buck slid out the next one and handed it over. We continued this relay between the three of us, then filled in the gaps with wooden beams.

Meanwhile, I kept glancing at my watch. "How much longer?"

"Soon." Jake patted my shoulder.

We finally shored up the surface when Buck examined eroded areas where the ends of the bridge were supposed to connect with land. Cracks had opened up during the storm. He frowned and said, "This'll never work."

"Yep." Jake picked up two fist-sized rocks and dropped them into a crack. "We'll have to fill it in with a mix of stones and mud."

I anxiously glanced at my watch again. "Man, this is crazy! It's after 11:00 now. I've got a three o'clock flight out of Phoenix, and I'm still stuck here."

"It is what it is," said Buck as he added two more rocks and looked at me. "Get the shovel." He glanced at the muddy ground. "Start digging and dump it in the cracks. We'll pack it here."

A cool breeze blew across the river and nipped the back of my neck. I took a shovel from the wagon, scooped up mud and dumped it where my uncles continued to set the rocks in place. Without a word, we all worked on our hands and knees to fill in eroded areas at both ends of the bridge.

Finally, Buck stood up with his gloved hands caked in mud.

"Looks good here."

"Yep." Jake walked along the bridge and inspected the surface. "That'll hold. Let's get cleaned up and head to the airport."

We climbed on the wagon as the noon sun glared overhead. When Buck slid on the seat beside me, I asked, "How long will it take to drive to Phoenix?"

Buck shrugged. "Couple of hours or so."

Jake stood behind us and held on to the back of our seat. "Could take longer."

My knuckles tensed and I gripped the reins. "That's cutting it close." I snapped a whip with a loud crack and yelled, "Hee ya!"

Our mules pulled us forward and the wagon wheels bounced along ruts in thick dried mud. I tried to go faster. The animals took it slow. It didn't matter that we had a tight schedule. All I could do was listen to hoof beats and stare at bobbing heads with their pointed ears.

When we arrived at the house, it became a whirl wind of us rushing to get out. After a quick shower and change of clothes, I hugged everyone, then said goodbyes a lot faster than I planned. Time was short. We had to make it to the airport on time or miss our flight. Jake carefully drove his pickup truck along curvy one-lane roads littered with fallen branches from the storm. Asia sat in the middle and I was on the passenger side.

Gradually we descended from a pristine mountain elevation of 8,000 feet to the Red Rocks of Sedona. Cool breezes blowing through stands of Ponderosa trees gave way to desert cactus and dry, hot air. When we made it to the highway, we speeded up. Telephone poles and billboards whizzed by our windows.

Still, I looked at the dashboard clock and sank in my seat. "It's 2:35 now."

"Yep." Jake turned on the AC, and we rolled up the windows. "We still have 40 miles or so before we get there." He glanced at me. "Sorry, nephew. I reckon you'll miss the flight."

"Might as well drop us off at the airport anyway," I said. "Maybe we'll catch a later flight."

Resigned to this reality, I stared at the long, straight highway. Ahead was a hitchhiker standing alongside the road with a bulky duffle bag at his feet. The tall slender man wore an Army uniform and one stripe on his sleeve. Sunbaked, he had a tired look of desperation as he waved his arm and stuck out a thumb.

Seeing this, Jake pulled over on the shoulder, and the hitchhiker ran to my side as I rolled down the window. Hot air blasted in like opening an oven, and I looked at the soldier's haggard, sweaty face.

Remembering my lonely hitchhiking days, I asked, "Where ya heading?"

"Phoenix." He wiped his sweaty brow and revealed the stains on his underarm. "Going home. It's near the bus depot off the highway."

"Hop in the back," I said. "We'll take you there. Just tap on the window when you're ready to get out."

"Thanks." He tossed his duffle bag in the truck bed and climbed aboard.

Jake put the stick shift in gear and drove on. I looked over my shoulder, and for a moment, I watched the soldier leaning back and resting his left arm on the side. His black hair blew in the wind. Although his face was turned away, he must've had the same worn-out sensation that only a fellow hitchhiker understands. You're tired, hungry, thirsty, and you just want to reach your next destination in one piece.

This was a time of unrest, and our generation had been jaded by the assassination of President Kennedy. The Vietnam War raged on. Men were being called up by the thousands and thrust in combat or sent off to distant bases, while awaiting orders. They were passing in an endless stream through cities and towns; on trains, buses and planes. Meanwhile, bloody battles were seen by millions of people on TV screens across the country. Young, disgruntled men and women rose up in greater numbers to protest the madness of another war.

When we arrived in Phoenix, the soldier tapped on our back window and pointed to a corner house. Jake pulled over, and the man climbed out, then grabbed his duffle bag. "Thanks." He slung the gear over his shoulder and walked up to a simple, two-story house with an American flag hanging from a pole on the porch railing. It was nothing fancy, but it reminded me of my family home in San Diego.

Jake started to turn the steering wheel when I said, "Not yet. I'd like to see this first."

For a brief moment, we watched the soldier as he knocked on the front door and waited. A woman in her mid-40's opened it and looked surprised. She smiled, hugged the young man, then they went inside.

"I reckon he's home now," said Jake as he drove back on the highway. "We'll be at the airport soon."

"I'm glad he made it." Asia sighed and glanced over her shoulder one last time.

"Maybe he's home on leave," I said.

When we arrived at Phoenix Sky Harbor Airport, Jake gave us a bear hug and said, "I ain't much for goodbyes. I reckon I'll see ya soon."

"Thanks for everything, Uncle Jake." I shook his hand. "You taught me a lot. I won't forget it."

"We had some good times." Jake placed his big hand on my shoulder with a worried expression on his face. "The war's heating up. Don't wait to get drafted in the Army. You got some choices like enlisting in the Air Force or Navy."

"Yeah, I know. I'll look into it."

"All right." Jake gave us a quick hug and said, "Take care of yourselves." He got back in the truck and drove away.

We grabbed our bags, opened a door and cool air drew us in. People milled about the busy terminal with weary traveler's eyes, all waiting to depart. Near a window, two Marines were stretched on the floor with their heads resting on heavy gear.

In the rustling crowd of people, Asia asked me, "Where do we go?"

"Look for American Airlines," I yelled over my shoulder.

Loudspeakers blared out, "Bonanza Airlines flight 106 to..."

A military plane roared down the runway and muffled the

announcement. In the confusion, I stopped to figure out which way to go.

"What'd they say?" An Air Force Sergeant looked up from his seat. A cigarette dangled from his mouth and hot ashes sprinkled down his shirt and pants. He brushed off the sizzling debris and swore in a strong New Jersey accent.

"Hell, I don't know," said another Airman in a southern drawl sitting beside him. "All I heard was that damned C-97." He looked up at me and asked, "Could you make that out?"

"No," I said while standing next to him. "Something about Bonanza, I think."

"Nah," the Airman shook his head. "Ain't ours."

I glanced out the window and noticed a TWA landing on the runway while loudspeakers announced, "All military standby personnel report to the tarmac."

"That's us," said the Sergeant as he stood up with his buddy.

While they headed out to a gate, I looked at signs pointing in different directions. One said, "Arizona National Guard" with an arrow pointing to the right. Another read, "197th Air Transport Squadron. Then I spotted an American Airlines counter. "There," I said to Asia.

We squeezed through uniformed men as they ran passed us. Then we stopped at the back of a long line of people, and I glanced at my watch. It was 3:55. After waiting in line for 30 minutes, we finally stepped up to the front, and a well-dressed lady greeted us with a smile.

"Can I help you?"

"Yeah," I said. "We missed the three o'clock flight to San Diego."

"Do you have tickets?" she asked.

"No. We planned to pay here. When's the next plane leaving?"

"Sorry. The earliest flight out won't be until 11:00 tomorrow morning."

"Wow. That's a long wait." I turned and looked at Asia. "I guess we're stuck here."

"Let's check on another airline," she responded. "Maybe

they'll have something."

"I doubt it," said the clerk. "But it won't hurt to try."

"Okay. Thanks." I stepped out of line with Asia.

We went to other airlines and found nothing available until the next day. Everywhere we looked in that busy terminal, people waited or streamed in and out; all hoping to go somewhere. Frustrated, we sat among the crowd and weighed our options.

"All right," I said. "We can wait here all night or find another way out."

"Oh, I have an idea. Remember the bus we took to Flagstaff?" Asia asked with a twinkle in her eye.

"Yeah, I see that look and I know what you're thinking. That's when we snuggled in the back seat together."

"That was cozy." She kissed my cheek and smiled. "Well, let's take a bus to San Diego."

"Okay." I drew her closer. "We'll take the bus on one condition."

"What's that?"

I whispered in her ear, "We'll cuddle way in the back again."

"Oh, I'd like that." She smiled and adjusted the tote bag on her shoulder. "Let's go."

26 TRYING TO GET OUT

We strolled out of the airport terminal to an intersection and waited for a red light to change. Heat radiated off asphalt while cars and trucks whizzed by. Horns beeped from impatient drivers, and a delivery van spewed black fumes in our faces. When the signal flashed to green, we darted across the street with a dozen people rushing to their homes or the nearest cool bar after work. Everyone was in a hurry to get off the street and into shade. On the other side, a tall building blocked the sun and provided temporary relief as we kept walking.

When we made it to the Phoenix station, two buses idled rumbling engines and passengers boarded. The smell of exhaust lingered around the entrance and we ran inside; only to breathe in cigarette smoke that stuck to our clothing. We waited in another long line and finally stepped up to a round-faced middle-aged man behind the counter.

"What time does the next bus leave for San Diego?" I asked.

"Well, let's see." He lifted a page on his clipboard and said, "Got one leaving at 8:05 tonight." He looked over the brim of his reading glasses resting at the edge of a bulbous red nose. "That'll getcha there by 5:45 tomorrow morning." His thick gray mustache twitched like a hairy caterpillar.

"We'll take two one-way tickets." I said.

He nodded. "That'll be 10 bucks."

When I opened my wallet to get the money out, Asia tapped my shoulder, then handed me a five dollar bill. "Here's my half."

"Thanks." I gave it to the clerk.

Once we had our bus tickets, I said, "There's a phone booth. I'll call home."

"Okay." Asia nodded and sat on a bench. "I'll wait here."

I stepped inside a stale-smelling booth littered with cigarette butts on the floor and kept the door opened to get air. After I dialed the home number, I waited as it rang.

"Yeah. What do you want?" answered someone in a high-pitched voice.

"Oh, sorry. I must've gotten the wrong number," I said.

"Is that you, Richard?"

"Uh, yeah." I stared at the receiver in confusion. "Who are you?"

"It's me, dummy! Don't you recognize your Aunt Emma Lou's voice?"

"Oh, yeah." I continued to hold the phone away from my ear. "My dad's sister." I rolled my eyes and glanced at Asia while she fiddled in her purse. "How could I forget?" Just hearing her annoying voice brought back memories of a pecking hen dominating the roost. She had a way of showing up unannounced and staying for weeks at a time. This was trouble. "Uh, what's going on?"

"Well," she huffed. "That should be obvious. My dear brother is in the hospital. God knows if he'll ever pull through! After his horrible accident I had to fly all the way out from Mobile and take charge here."

"Oh, okay. Where's my Mom?"

"Your Ma's at the hospital visiting my brother. God rest his soul." Aunt Emma Lou puffed and fumed as though my dad was already dead. "Now I'm minding these no-good-for-nothin kids of your Ma's. The house is filthy. I'm tired of cleaning up after them, but somebody's gotta keep order around here."

There she goes again, I thought. "Yeah, well, I just called to say we're taking a bus. Should be there by 5:45 tomorrow morning. Can you ask my Mom to pick us up?"

"What do you mean, us?"

"I'm talking about my girlfriend, Asia." I said. "She's coming with me."

"Now you listen to me, boy. You ain't a gonna bring no tramp here. We got enough troubles."

Her crappy tone was so toxic, I had enough. "I have to go." I slammed the phone before I could say what was really on my mind. "Bitch!"

It was like I'd been exposed to deadly germs. I needed a hot shower to cleanse myself. Instead, I walked over to Asia and smiled like nothing happened. How was I supposed to tell her about my Aunt from hell. I had to break it to her gently. "Let's get something to eat before we catch the bus."

"Good." She stood up and took my hand. "I'm hungry."

We strolled down the street and found a hole-in-the-wall place called Bella's Bistro. When we stepped inside, an attractive silver-haired lady greeted us with a warm smile and sparkling blue eyes. "Welcome." She gestured with an open hand to a small round table and two red-cushioned chairs. "Would you like to sit here?"

"Sure, thanks." I waited for Asia to have a seat, then I sat across from her.

"My name is Bella." The waitress handed us menus. "I'll be right back with some ice water."

"This is so quaint," said Asia.

"Yeah. I've never been in a place like this before." I looked around the narrow dining area and wanted to release the tension inside me. "Hey, check out that cool sign above those pictures of sailboats. It says, Boston Harbor."

I paused to take in the scenes. "After I graduated from high school I planned to see places like that. Now look at me. I'm heading right back home to my family."

"I know." Asia squeezed my hand. "I always wanted to be a concert pianist and travel the world." She held up her slender fingers. "That changed while we lived on the ranch this summer. Now I'd like to be a veterinarian and care for animals."

When Bella returned with our water, she held an order pad and pencil ready. "Did you see something you like?" she asked in a New England accent.

"I don't know. Everything on the menu seems delicious." Asia looked up and smiled. "You have a very cheerful restaurant here. It feels like we just stepped into a place along the east coast."

"Thank you. I'm a retired music teacher." Bella nodded toward the kitchen. "My husband, William was a traveling salesman. We decided to try something different and settled here a few months ago."

"That's nice." Asia smiled and observed our elegant waitress. "You remind me of my piano teacher in high school." She paused. "I miss her."

"Well, anytime you need practice, come to my studio out back. I still teach."

"Thank you for the offer, but we're on our way to San Diego." She focused on the menu again. "Oh, I know exactly what I want. I'll try the crab cakes since I've never had them before."

"I'll have fish and chips," I said.

During our quiet moments of hanging out over good food, we relaxed in this tiny refuge surrounded by a bustling city where people were coming and going from all over the country. It was like time had slowed down again, and we could hear each other's voices. No radio blared out news of antiwar protests or the body counts in Vietnam.

"I'm hearing classical music coming from somewhere." Asia turned her head and listened.

"Yeah. Must be a recording in the kitchen."

"Sounds like Mozart." Asia closed her eyes. "He was my favorite composer in class." She waved her hand to the rhythm like a conductor.

"I was probably in machine shop then." I laughed. "No music there." I noticed the way she tapped her fingers on the table as though she played a piano. "Funny, I wasn't into classical music. Seeing you, I kind of like it." I leaned back and observed her easy-going style. This girl has real class, I thought. "That reminds me. You had said you were a straight-A student in high school. Right?"

"Yes." She kept her eyes closed and listened to the record playing. "I like to learn about everything."

"That's what I love about you."

Asia opened her eyes and giggled. "Oh, so you love me for my mind?"

"Among other things." I leaned in. She met me half-way and we kissed. While we held hands I said, "I think you should definitely get more education somehow."

"Well, I'd like to get a part-time job and take a couple of courses at a community college first. Besides, I can't afford to get a Veterinary degree at a university. I'll figure out something."

"I want you to stay at my family's home," I said. "It'll be like living with my Aunt Eileen's family. That'll make it easier for you."

"I don't know about that." Asia looked up with a worried expression. "Your Mom didn't sound too thrilled about my coming with you."

"I'll admit she didn't say, I'm cool with that." I wanted to tell her about my crazy Aunt, but I was wary of discouraging her. "Oh well." I tried to be positive. "At least my Mom warmed up when you got on the phone. That was a good sign. Right?"

"Maybe, but you'll still have to leave home anyway."

"Yeah, I'll probably have to enlist and march off to that stupid war. Geez this is crazy." I held her hand tighter. "Like a crap shoot. The longer I wait, the greater my chances of getting drafted."

"Woody, I love you, but I don't see how this is going to work."

I leaned closer. Her eyes appeared moist. Not liking the sound of her voice, I asked, "What are you talking about?"

"You know." She looked like, hey, wake up. This is serious. "Us," she said in a firm tone. "You'll have to go into the military. We won't see each other," her voice cracked with emotion and tore into my heart. "What if you get yourself killed?"

"This is crazy." I puffed out air to relieve tension. "Asia, I love you so much, it hurts. When I was out working with my uncles, I couldn't stop thinking about you. Even in my sleep, I dreamed of us together."

"Oh, Woody, I felt the same way. Still do."

"What's happening to us?" I leaned back in the chair and crossed my arms. "I'm not supposed to fall in love now."

"Me neither." She sighed and looked at me with a worried expression. "We can't help the way we feel. I'm so confused." She gazed into my eyes. "All I know is I'm happy being with you."

"Yeah, it's like we belong together." I brushed my fingers through her soft hair. "I know everything is happening so fast, but I'll go nuts without you."

She tried to smile. "I guess we're crazy then. Now what?"

"We stick with our plan," I said. "First, we'll visit my Dad in the hospital. Make sure he'll recover. Then we'll see my family." I squeezed her hand. "Okay?"

"All right," she smiled. "I want to be with you as long as I can."

I glanced at my watch. "It's 7:30. The bus leaves at 8:05. Better hurry."

We paid our bill and rushed to the depot, then stood in line as people started to get on the bus. The driver tossed each piece of luggage into the storage compartment with a loud clunking sound. Slowly we inched forward one step at a time. Finally, we boarded and went to the back of the bus. When the Greyhound bus left the station, overhead lights dimmed while the engine vibrated our seat, and we snuggled together.

After a few miles, I said, "There's something I need to tell you." I hesitated to bring up the bad news about my aunt from hell.

"What is it?"

Well, my aunt Emma is staying at the house." I sighed. "We may have trouble."

"What do you mean?

In the darkness, I told her about my phone call with my crazy aunt.

"Oh," said Asia. "That sounds bad."

"Don't worry. I'll handle it."

"How?" she asked.

27 AUNT FROM HELL

When we stepped off our bus in San Diego and looked around the depot, a cool ocean breeze greeted us. Asia brushed back strands of hair from her face and said, "Oh, the morning air feels cool here."

"Yeah, we're not far from the beach," I agreed. "Hey, there's a pay phone. I'll call my mom to find out if she can give us a ride."

Asia glanced at her watch and shook her head. "It's only six o'clock."

"Everybody's wide awake by now." I opened the phone booth and expected to hear warm words of welcome home as I called.

Instead, a blustery voice blurted out, "Yeah! Who's this?" It was Aunt Emma Lou.

With my right ear burning, I winced and said, "It's me, Richard. Just got into the Greyhound Bus Terminal. Can you put my mom on the phone please?"

"Your ma's sleeping." She huffed and said, "I swear that woman spends all her time at the hospital. Then she comes home, rests and goes right back out again. I've only had a couple of short visits with my brother. I'm always stuck in this filthy house minding these kids."

My aunt's tone was irritating as usual, but I tried to keep my cool. "Well, I'm sure my mom needs her rest," I said. "Is my sister there?"

"Nah, that girl is sleeping in again," growled Emma Lou. "Ever since I've been here, she stays in her room. I swear these teen-agers now a days are no good. Can't get em to do a damn thing."

"Okay. I just wanted to see about getting a ride home." I looked over at Asia while she stood by the open door with a worried expression. "Never mind. I'll call a taxi."

"No you ain't." She puffed out like releasing gas. "I have to do everything around here, so I'll drive your ma's car and pick you up. Which station?"

"Uh, it's the one on Trolley Avenue, but you don't have to do that. I'll..."

"Somebody has to," she interrupted with rustling sounds in the background. "Oh, here they are on the kitchen counter. Got the keys. On my way." Click.

"Ah, man." I groaned and slammed the phone. "My aunt's coming to pick us up."

Asia backed away and looked wary. "I don't want to upset your family." She sat on a bench and clutched the tote bag in her arms. "I'll wait here while you talk to your crazy aunt first."

"No." I sat down and put my arm on her shoulder. "Let me handle this. It'll work out. I promise."

"You sure? That aunt of yours sounds like she could be a lot of trouble."

"True." I kissed her cheek. "But there's no way I'm going to let her ruin our relationship."

"Well, maybe I should just stay away."

"Don't worry. If anybody leaves, it'll be her." I stood up and took Asia's hand. "Let's go wait outside. She'll be here soon."

"I'm kind of nervous," said Asia as we walked toward the entrance. "How should I act around everybody?"

"Just be yourself."

When a green 1965 Chevy Impala station wagon pulled up along the sidewalk where we waited, I recognized my mom's car. Behind the wheel was my aunt from hell. As usual, she had her gray hair so tightly wrapped in a bun that she looked tense, intimidating and not a welcoming sight.

I tried to make the best of a bad scene and smiled. "Hello Aunt Emma Lou. Thanks for picking us up."

"Well," she huffed. "It's about time you showed up. Your pa's been deathly ill in the hospital for more than two days now."

"Couldn't help it," I said. "We had a storm and..."

"I don't want to hear your excuses, boy." She got out of the car and walked right up to me—toes to toes. "What do you have to say for yourself?" She glared up at me like a short, round drill Sergeant bullying a recruit.

Bizarre childhood memories flashed in my mind. She was about to lash out in another scolding of how irresponsible I was as a kid. This time she seemed smaller. After a summer of riding roughneck on the ranch, I saw right through her domineering ways and stood my ground. I looked my aunt right in the eyes, smiled and said, "I see you haven't changed."

She crossed her arms and stared back at me. "Mmm." She rocked her stocky frame back and forth like a prized fighter trying to size me up. "I reckon you've grown a lot taller since the last time I saw you."

"Yep. It's been three years."

"Who's the girl?" She nodded with a look of disdain.

"Oh, Aunt Emma, I'd like you to meet my girlfriend, Asia."

"Hello." Asia warily held out her hand.

My aunt stared without reaching out to her. "Where you from, girl?"

"Phoenix." Asia lowered her arm and glanced at me.

"Mmm." Emma Lou continued to size her up. "I ain't never seen your kind before. You must be one of them half-breed oriental tramps I've heard about."

"Don't talk to her like that!" I put my arm around Asia's waist. "Why are you so hateful?"

"I'm just tellin it like I sees it, boy." She turned toward the car and ordered, "Get in."

"No! Not until you apologize to Asia." I faced her head on. "I'm so tired of your rudeness and disrespect to my family." I fumed and clenched my fists. "Now you insult my girlfriend!"

Aunt Emma Lou glared back at Asia. "She is what she is."

"Wow!" Disgusted by another bigoted remark, I shook my head. "I don't want to hear another word. You'd better sit in the back."

"What?"

"I'll drive." I held my palm out. "Give me the keys!"

"Well," she huffed again and dropped them in my hand. "I went out of my way to pick you up. Then you treat me like this."

"Get in!"

"You should mind your manners, boy." She reluctantly slid into the back seat, and I slammed the door.

"Sorry about this," I said to Asia as I lowered the tailgate and put our luggage in the back.

"That's okay." She kissed my cheek. "I like the way you handled it."

After I closed the back, I opened the passenger side for Asia. "You sit up front with me."

I drove along Mission Bay and glanced in the rearview mirror to keep an eye on Aunt Emma Lou. Her arms were crossed and she glared back at me with such rage I imagined smoke fuming out her ears. At first, she boiled like a tea kettle. It was building up.

Meanwhile, Asia was content to rest her head on my shoulder like she had done on our bus ride. A refreshing ocean breeze blew in from the opened windows. "The weather is so nice here," she said.

"Yeah. It's calm before the storm," I said in a low voice so my aunt wouldn't hear me. "She looks like she'll explode any second now."

Asia peered over her shoulder. "I see what you mean. I'll turn on the radio. Maybe some soothing music will set a better mood."

A song blared, "Bitchy, bitchy Woman." Asia shook her head and said, "Oh, that's not helping." She turned to a country-western with the lyrics, "Watch out, cowboy. She's gonna gitcha."

"Turn off that damn radio!" My aunt from Hell blurted out, "It's too loud!"

"Here comes the storm," I said to Asia.

"Watch where you're going! Don't you know how to drive?" She huffed and puffed again. "Hey! You were supposed to turn left back there. Slow down. You're going too fast! Do you hear me, boy? You're no good."

Asia squeezed my arm. "Shouldn't you do something? She's

really mad."

"Nah. Ever since I was a kid, she's always blown a gasket about everything. Just ignore it."

"Now what are you doing?" yelled my aunt. "Didn't you see that light back there? I swear you are the worst driver I ever did see. You should be arrested." She cackled on and on like a mad hen.

Asia covered her ears. "How can you stand it?"

"I just let her blow off steam. It's better than getting in a fight with her."

I noticed Emma Lou was breathing heavier, then she began to gasp for air. She hiccupped, then burped as her fat face puffed up like a balloon.

"Calm down," I said. "You're upsetting that ulcer again."

"Ahh…I can't…" She couldn't stop hiccupping and burping.

"Take it easy." I watched her bulging cheeks as she kept gasping for air.

Asia looked back and said, "She looks terrible. Can you pull over? I'll try something I learned from the vet." She took a small bottle from her purse. "This lavender oil works great on horses."

"Okay." I laughed as I pulled over alongside the road. "I want to see this."

Asia got out and slid in the back seat. "Emma Lou, I need you to relax and breathe."

Through the mirror, I saw my aunt heaving, hiccupping and burping. "Maybe she needs a horse tranquilizer," I teased.

"Shh." Asia rubbed the oil in her hands and held them close to Emma Lou. "Smells nice, doesn't it?"

"What?" My Aunt turned her puffy face and sniffed the aroma.

"That's good." Asia cupped her palms over my Emma's mouth and nose. "Now just relax and breathe."

Emma inhaled deeply and said, "Oh, that does smell nice."

"That's better." Asia nodded and smiled. She rubbed the lavender oil on my aunt's arms and palms. "Now hold it close to your face and breathe slowly."

Amazed, I continued to watch from the front seat. It was like we were back at the ranch and Asia used her magic touch on what I thought was an untamable beast in our family. She talked in a soothing voice until Emma Lou calmed down enough to keep from exploding.

We drove for another five miles while Asia kept saying, "Oh, you're doing much better. Now imagine you're floating in a peaceful lake."

Aunt Emma Lou leaned back, let out one more loud burp, then closed her eyes. As we headed north to Clairemont Drive, she slowly drifted off to sleep. Surprised, I pulled over and let Asia get in the front seat, then I leaned in and whispered, "How did you do that?"

"I don't know." She looked over her shoulder again. "I just thought the lavender oil would relax her. I didn't expect her to doze off like that."

"Yeah, she gets so worked up, she must've wore herself out."

"Well, at least she's quiet now," said Asia.

"I just saw another reason why I love you so much," I whispered.

"I love you too." She laughed. "Oh, now you're tickling my ear."

"You like that huh?" I kissed her neck.

"Down boy." She giggled. "Keep this up and I'll give you that horse tranquilizer."

"All right, I'll be good." I glanced at my snoozing aunt in the back seat. "We don't want to wake her up anyway." I drove east on Balboa Avenue. "Check out those hills." I nodded to my right. "That's Clairemont Mesa. We're almost home."

28 HOME AT LAST

I pulled into the cul-de-sac that overlooked a steep canyon and pointed to my family's two-story house with a driveway that led to a detached garage. "We're here."

Just as Asia and I stepped out of the car, we heard loud barking. I turned to see Snuggles, our golden retriever heading full-speed with a big slobbery tongue sticking out and ears flapping. She greeted me with her paws on my chest, and I patted her head.

Once Snuggles was satisfied with a doggy welcome, she started to jump up on Asia, but I grabbed the collar. "Get down. Sit."

My dog was so excited to see someone new, I had to hold her tight. "Come on." I nudged her rear. "Sit."

She finally sat with her tongue out and tail wagging, then she barked and panted. I held the collar to keep her from going between Asia's legs like oh this is so cool, I just gotta sniff this person.

"You are so cute." Asia knelt and kissed Snuggles' furry forehead.

"Sorry," I said. "She gets a little excited around people." I opened the car door and peeked in at Aunt Emma Lou while she slept on the back seat. "We're home. You can wake up now."

She snored like a bear in hibernation and laid there in a fetal position. Since she was usually grumpy, I expected her to rear up and lunge at me. I stood back and waited, but she didn't move.

"Good. We'll let her rest for a while." I carefully closed the door and said to Asia, "Come on inside and you can meet the rest of my family."

Snuggles barked, then ran ahead of us, and just as I was about to reach for the front door, it swung opened. Standing in the entryway was my Mom with her arms outstretched and ready for a hug. "Welcome home, Richard." Her hazel eyes sparkled and her auburn bouffant-style hair was aglow in the bright morning sunshine.

"Hi Mom."

After a quick embrace, she stepped back and looked me over. "Oh, my goodness. You're so tall." She squeezed my upper right arm and smiled. "I can't believe you've grown so much. Well, come in."

As we stepped inside, I said, "I'd like you to meet my girlfriend, Asia."

Mom gushed with enthusiasm and gave her a warm hug. "I'm so glad to meet you. I just got off the phone with my sister, Eileen and she said a lot of nice things about you."

"Thank you." Asia smiled. "Woody has talked about you too."

Mom laughed and said, "Oh, that's right, it's Woody now. It seems like everybody else remembers to call you by your nickname." She gave me another hug and patted my shoulder."

My 17-year-old sister, Kathy peeked around the hallway entrance and said, "Oh, it's you, Woody." She rushed over and we hugged. "I've been hiding from Aunt Emma. Where is she?"

I laughed. "She's taking a nap in the car.

"I'm not surprised," said Mom. "She hasn't slept much since she got here two days ago. We'll let her rest a while."

"Good." Kathy turned toward the hallway as her shoulder-length brunette hair swayed to the left and yelled, "Okay guys. It's safe to come out now."

"That's a relief," said 15-year-old Dan as he rushed down the hall and greeted me with a bear hug. "Hey man." He looked up with a surprised expression. "You're a lot taller now."

Meanwhile, my youngest brother, Teddy stumbled in and tripped on his feet. "Yeah, Rick." His 12-year-old voice squeaked, then cracked to a deep tenor. "What happened, man?" he asked in a sudden girly tone. "You been eaten a lot of beef."

"Yep." I laughed and ruffled his scruffy red hair. "Hey, I see you got a zit on your nose."

"Ah man." He slugged my shoulder. "You ain't nothing to look at either."

"Settle down boys," said Mom. "I know you haven't seen each other the whole summer, so don't tussle all at once."

"Oh, sorry about that," I said. "Where are my manners? Guys, I'd like you to my girlfriend, Asia."

"Hello." She smiled while everybody gathered around.

"Hi," said Kathy.

Teddy stepped closer to Asia with a goofy grin on his face. "Hey babe. Where ya been all my life?" He reached out and was about to either kiss her hand or go all the way up and lick her neck. Since puberty had kicked in, he was so clumsy, I wasn't sure what was he up to.

"Okay, get back." I blocked him with my arm. "Asia, this is Teddy."

Asia giggled and said, "Hello."

"That's Dan over there."

"Hi." Dan brushed back his surfer-dude bleach-blonde hair and tried to act cool. "Sorry about my kid brother. He ain't house broken yet."

"Hey!" Teddy pushed him.

Dan shoved him back.

"That's enough," said Mom. "Let's have some breakfast." She put her hand on my shoulder and smiled. "We have a lot of catching up to do. Later we'll visit your dad in the hospital."

"I'll help in the kitchen," I said.

"Kathy looked at Asia with a caring expression. "You must be tired after that long bus ride." She smiled. "Would you like to see my room? You can freshen up in there."

"I'd like that very much." Asia glanced back at me and smiled as she walked down the hallway with Kathy.

I could tell Asia was pleased by the warm welcome. Aunt Emma came in and tromped by us without saying a word. Since she wasn't her usual bitchy self, we were surprised to see her quietly going into the guest bathroom. Man, this was a relief, and we quickly went our separate ways.

After we all had breakfast the next morning, Mom and I went to see Dad in the hospital. He was still unconscious. At first, I didn't recognize his swollen and bruised face with bandages wrapped around his head. Tubes were stuck in his wrist and mouth while a machine beeped to keep track of his vital signs. A sling elevated his right leg wrapped in a cast. The doctor had said his condition was stable and hopeful, but that didn't offset the unease in my gut.

How could this happen? We were told a drunk driver hit him head-on. Unable to do anything, I watched as Mom held Dad's hand and silently prayed. Torn between hatred of the man who caused this disaster and the love I saw in that moment, I struggled to make sense of it all.

Several hours had passed as we sat in that depressing room with no sign of Dad waking anytime soon. For two days since the accident, Mom had spent most of her time there while other family members visited and left. She looked so tired and emotionally drained as this was the third day. I knew she wouldn't leave his side even after I suggested she go for a walk while I stayed with him. This was taking a toll on her and she needed a break.

That came when Aunt Emma showed up and gave us a chance to get some fresh air. True to her gruff nature, she started complaining about how bad the conditions were in the hospital. No one could do anything right, so we were glad to leave and let her think she was taking control of everything. After a stroll outside, Mom and I ate lunch in the cafeteria where I had a chance to talk freely about my aunt's rude behavior toward Asia.

"Why is she so like the wicked witch and bitchy all the time," I asked.

Mom looked up from sipping a strong cup of coffee and smiled as if she was amused by my choice of words. "Well, she wasn't always like that, son."

"Really?"

"Yes, your father told me what she was like growing up. She

enjoyed singing and dancing around the house. Her dream was to be a Broadway dancer when she grew up."

"What happened?"

"The war," said Mom. "Emma had just turned 18 when she ran off and eloped with a handsome Marine. They were so madly in love, but they only had two days together before he was shipped out. He was killed at Iwo Jima."

"Why didn't we hear about this?"

"Your father and I thought it was best to it keep quiet." Mom exhaled and said, "Emma was so heartbroken, she had a nervous breakdown and spent a year in a mental hospital. She wasn't the same after that. Besides, no one wants to admit their relative wound up in an institution."

"So, she's crazy then?"

"We all get a little nutty when we're hurt." Mom had a far-off look as though she had a memory. "Emma was so young and full of passion. Then she lost her husband. Now she tries to control everything around her. After four divorces, she still wants to make life go her way. You see, she's afraid to love and get hurt again."

"Geez, now I feel sorry for her."

"Instead of pitying her, try being more understanding. Even if she doesn't change, we can still love her. Can you do that?"

"It won't be easy. She didn't apologize to Asia for her bigoted remarks."

"Pray about it, son." Mom reached across the table and patted my hand. "Sometimes we need God's help to forgive an unlovable person." She looked at her watch. "It's almost two. Let's get back in case your father wakes up."

When we opened the hospital room door, Aunt Emma was sitting beside the bed with tears in her eyes. "Please, don't die, Robert," she said in a whiny voice. "Don't leave me."

Surprised by the way she was so emotional; I wasn't sure how to deal with this softer side I'd never seen before. For the first time she almost seemed human.

"It's okay," whispered Mom as she knelt beside her sister-in-law. "The doctor says he'll fully recover, but we just need to let him rest."

"What if he ain't coming out of it?" My aunt looked at her with a worried expression. "You sure he's a gonna be all right?"

"Yes." Mom helped her up and smiled with a look of compassion. "Now why don't you go on back to the house? I'll call you when Robert wakes up. All right?"

"No!" Emma blurted out loud. "I'm staying here." She plopped back in the chair and yelled, "You can't make me."

Oh, now she's back to her crazy self, I thought.

A nurse appeared in the doorway with a concerned expression. "Is everything all right in here?"

"Yes," said Mom in a calm voice. "She's just worried about her brother."

"I'm not leaving." Emma folded her arms across her chest.

Mom looked back at the nurse and smiled to assure her. "She'll be fine."

"Okay," the nurse whispered. "Let me know if you need anything." She quietly closed the door and left.

"What?" said a groggy voice. It was Dad looking up with wide eyes.

Surprised, we all gushed at once. Aunt Emma cried. Mom leaned in and kissed Dad's cheek. "Hi honey."

His eyes blinked. "Uh, what's going on?"

For the next half-hour, the room was filled with a flurry of excitement, while the doctor examined him. We all hugged each other, and Dad had an expression like what's the big deal? At first, he had no idea how he got there, nor any memory of the accident. All he knew was that he awoke from a deep sleep. Confused, he looked around the room.

Once Dad realized his broken leg was hanging in a sling he squirmed like a roped steer. "Hey, get me out of this thing."

"Take it easy," said Doctor Peterson as he held his patient's shoulders. "Do you know where you are now?"

"Yeah, how did I get in the hospital?"

"You were in a car accident," said Doc. "Can you remember

anything?"

"Blinding headlights." Dad blinked and turned away as though his memory was coming back. "Couldn't see. I tried to..." He closed his eyes again, and in a low, groggy voice said, "Um, what was I saying?"

"Get some rest," Doctor Peterson said. "We'll talk later." He looked at us and smiled. "He'll be all right."

After we were assured that Dad just needed time to recover, we went home before sundown. This gave us a chance to relax and not worry so much about his condition. A bright orange solar globe began to dip into the ocean, as we all hung out on the patio together. I took his usual role of flipping burgers over the red hot glow of our barbeque grill, and we all pitched in for a laid-back dinner.

My two brothers set up folding chairs while Asia helped Kathy to bring out plates, forks and glasses for everyone. Mom spread out her favorite table cloth with designs of golden California poppies on it.

Aunt Emma was back to her normal grumpy self as she complained about Snuggles being underfoot. I tried to be more understanding of her miserable behavior, but it wasn't easy. Especially during the meal when she sat directly across from Asia and me and gave us that killer stink eye again.

To break the ice, Mom sat next to her like a buffer and said to me, "I heard you got pretty good handling the mule and horses on the ranch."

"Yeah, I learned a lot from Buck and Jake."

She smiled at Asia. "My sister, Eileen says you were a great help with the kids around the house."

Asia looked up from her plate and said, "I had so much fun with them, it didn't feel like babysitting."

Mom leaned in with increased interest. "What is really amazing, though, is the way you cared for the animals like you'd been doing it all your life." She smiled. "You must have a gift for it somehow."

"Well, I can't explain it," Asia said. "I just love to work with animals."

"Oh, that's right," said Mom. "I remember our talk on the phone. You wanted to become a vet. What are your plans now?"

"I'll look for a job, so I can get a place to stay. Then I..."

"You can share my room," Kathy interrupted.

"Yeah, that's a great idea," I said with relief to get this out in the open. I'd been waiting for my sister to bring it up and winked at her.

"No!" Aunt Emma Lou burst out so loud, we all froze. "You ain't a gonna have her kind stayin here. She's not one of us."

"Hey!" I stood up and faced her. "Don't talk like that."

"Son, I'll handle this." She exhaled to relieve the tension and looked at my Aunt. "Emma, I am so disappointed in you."

"What for?" She shrugged like it was no big deal. "I'm just tellin it like I sees it." She glared and pointed a finger at Asia. "Go on, have a real good look. Hell, she's nothin but a half-breed oriental tramp with no ties to us."

"That's enough." Mom stood up and glared at her. "Emma, I've tried to be patient with you, but now you've gone too far."

"You know I'm right." She got to her feet and crossed her arms with a defiant expression. "It does a body no good to mix furin blood with kin folk."

"Emma, I'm only going to say this once. You're a guest in my home. Either you apologize to this young lady and my family, or you'll have to leave."

A hush swept over us. Never had we seen Mom so forceful and clear in her tone. It was like a scene out of a western. Both sides faced each other in a show down. Who would flinch first?

"Sorry for speakin my mind." Aunt Emma turned away, muttering, "It ain't no good to speak the truth around here." She walked away in a huff.

"Wow." I shook my head. "That didn't sound like an apology to me."

"It's the best she can do. Ever since her husband died on Iwo Jima, she's been sick with hatred." Mom sat at the table and let out a weary sigh. "I'll have another talk with her later." She leaned closer and patted Asia's hand. "I'm so sorry you had to be treated with such disrespect."

"Thank you," said Asia. "I don't want to be a bother. Maybe I should leave."

"No." I put my arm on her shoulder. "Please stay."

"Yes,' said Mom. "You're a guest in our home, young lady." She smiled to assure her. "I don't think Emma will be here much longer."

"Yeah." Kathy spoke up. "It'd be fun to share my room with you."

"I'd like that," said Asia.

"Good." Mom turned her attention to me. "Son, you'll have to sleep on the couch for now. Aunt Emma's staying in your old room until she leaves soon."

"Yeah." I laughed. "I noticed the hand-written do-not-disturb sign on my door."

"That'll change." Mom smiled again. "Just remember a simple house rule, you two." She nodded to the both of us. "No sneaking around and no hanky-panky under my roof. Do you understand?"

"Yes Ma'am," Asia and I spoke at the same time.

29 HEART MOVES

For the first time since the accident, Mom went to bed early and had a restful night. She was so exhausted, she decided to wait before confronting her sister-in-law again. We still had to put up with Aunt Emma Lou as she complained about everything. Poor Snuggles took the brunt of her attacks and was dragged outside for shedding all over the house.

Feeling sorry for our whimpering golden retriever, Asia patted her and said, "It's alright now."

While I knelt with them, I noticed she had her finger nails freshly polished pink and said, "That's a nice color."

She smiled. "Kathy made me feel like I was her sister. We listened to cool surfer music in her room and did our nails."

"I'm glad to see you happy."

"Oh, I could never do this at home." Asia sparkled over her new experience. "My father wouldn't allow me to have any friends in the house." She had a soft giggle that I adored. "This was my first time to hang out and do girl stuff."

"Hopefully, it'll get better after the wicked witch leaves."

"Kathy wants me to sleep over on her roll-out bed for as long as I like," Asia said.

"That's great." I sat on a swinging bench and she joined me. Snuggles seemed to agree as she came over and rested her snout on Asia's lap.

We gazed at the flickering stars that could still be seen overhead while city lights blocked out the rest from down the hill.

Asia leaned closer and kissed my cheek. "This is nice."

"Yeah." I turned and savored her lips, then said, "I don't know about the future but at least we have these moments together."

"Shouldn't we plan ahead?"

"Yep." I whispered in her ear. "I want to be with you every day."

Asia giggled. "That tickles." She gazed at me and rubbed my whiskered chin. "I feel the same way about you."

"Well, for now you have a place to stay in my sister's room."

"Looks like you'll have to sleep on the couch like you did on the ranch," she said.

"Yeah." I laughed. "Aunt Emma took over my room and made it into her personal suite. She even stored all my stuff in the garage." I rolled my eyes. "How rude is that? Here we are in a four-bedroom house, and the only place left is the couch." I tried to make the best of it for Asia and joked, "Pretty cool, huh?"

"What? No hayloft?" Asia giggled.

"Nope." I relaxed on the swinging bench as it rocked back and forth. "We'll just have to make out in my Mom's station wagon."

"I'm sure she'd be thrilled with that idea." Asia laughed, then looked up. "What about our plans for the next day and the one after that?"

"Well, let's see now." I paused like I was in deep thought. "Tomorrow I'll go down to the draft board and ask, would you mind taking my name off the list? I'm mentally and emotionally unfit. You see, I'm crazy in love with this girl and it's serious."

Asia leaned on the left side of my chest as if to hear my heartbeats. "How serious?"

I exhaled. "Can you hear that pitter, patter?"

"It sounds like the little drummer boy."

"Yep. I'm nuts about you. Watch out for the men in white coats."

"Now you're being silly." Her soft giggle was like bird song on a new day.

"See, you're my witness. I'm crazy." I tapped my forehead and circled with my finger. "Uncle Sam will see I just want to make love, not war."

"Okay, then what?"

"Well, my next plan of action is to do this." I knelt on one knee and said, "Asia, I want to spend the rest of my life with you."

"What are you doing?" She cocked her head with a bewildered expression and laughed.

"I'm proposing. Let's get engaged, okay?"

"Oh Woody." She let out a deep sigh and stood up. "Why did you have to say that?"

"What's wrong?"

"I thought we were just kidding around. That's serious."

I straightened up and faced her. "Don't you love me?"

"Yes, I love you." She put her arms around me and looked into my eyes again. "It's just that I'm scared. What if you go to Vietnam and get yourself killed?"

"Ah, come on, babe. Don't even think that."

"I can't help it. If something were to happen to you I...I would just die."

"Geez, that's not exactly in my plan."

"This is so confusing. How can we be sure of anything?"

"Yeah, I guess that was a dumb idea." I plopped back down on the bench and knew she was right.

Asia sat beside me. "Please don't be mad, Woody. I love you so much."

"Nah, I'm not mad at you." I paused to admire her eyes again. "All I'm asking is for us to think about getting married someday. Even if we have to wait a couple of years, I wouldn't want to date anyone else anyway. If I have to go off to that stupid war, at least we could write to each other."

"I only want to be with you, too," she said. "It just feels so right whenever we're together."

"Well, since we both want the same thing, why don't we get engaged? We won't have to plan a wedding date or anything. Okay?"

"I'd like that." Asia placed her palm on the side of my face. "But if it comes down to it, can we handle a long-distance relationship?"

"Yeah, I know it would be difficult, but my parents proved it could be done. They were away from each other for two years during World War Two. I've always admired how they kept their relationship so strong all that time."

"How did they do it?"

"They wrote love letters to each other almost every day."

"Sounds romantic." She snuggled closer.

"Yep. Every anniversary they'd bring out carefully wrapped love letters and read them together."

"Really?"

"Yeah." I laughed. "When I was growing up, Mom and Dad usually sat on the couch late at night while taking turns reading. Funny thing is, they thought us kids were sleeping, but I'd peek around the corner from the hallway and spy on them."

"Oh, so you were a sneaky little guy, huh?" She giggled.

"I couldn't help it. They were always so loving toward each other."

"You're fortunate." She sighed and turned away. "My parents weren't very good examples."

"I'm sorry babe." I brushed my fingers through her hair like I'd done so many special moments during that summer with Asia. "You deserve to be happy."

She looked into my eyes again and smiled. "I'm happy when I'm with you, Woody."

"Does that mean you want to get engaged?"

"Oh yes." Her smooth cheek rubbed the side of my heated face as we held onto to each other. "If we have to be away from each other, I'll write you every day. I promise."

"That'll be fun." I laughed with the excitement of knowing we could get married someday. "I'll have so much to say to you on paper, I don't think it'll fit in an envelope."

"Book binders will do," she whispered in a sensuous voice like a warm summer breeze. She sat on my lap, snuggled, and we lingered in a long kiss. Strands of her soft hair tickled my face as she leaned in. "I'm so comfortable sitting here." She looked into my eyes and giggled again. "I'm stuck."

"Good. Just stay right where you are," I said while the swinging bench swayed hypnotically back and forth. "Let me look at you." Her black eyes were like highly-prized gems. Her lips were supple and inviting. "I know one thing is for sure."

"What's that?" Her breath was warm as she cuddled on my lap.

I inhaled her sweet air and said, "I want to see your face every day for the rest of my life."

"That's a long time," she said. "What if I get all wrinkly? Would you still want to look at me when I'm old?"

"Yep. I'll prove it to you."

"How?" She tilted her head with a look of curiosity while she continued to sit on my lap.

"You'll have to get up first."

"Oh." She had a subtle breathy laugh as she stood and straightened her green skirt. "Show me." She smiled like she expected to receive a gift she could unwrap.

The heat of her body still simmered on my chest and loins. "All right." I got up and faced her. Now close your eyes." I held her hand. "Ready?"

"Uh, huh."

"Follow me."

"Okay."

"Don't peek." I led her over to a 20-foot tall Valencia orange tree in our yard. Thick fruiting branches were bathed in a glow of yellow patio lights. "You can open your eyes now."

Asia leaned closer and focused on the tree trunk. "Oh," she gushed while her slender finger felt along the lines of a heart, then read the words out loud. "Woody and Asia forever in love."

"I carved this surprise while you were in Kathy's room today."

"Oh Woody." She gasped as though she had been holding her breath. "It's beautiful."

"There's my proof that I'll always want to see your face no matter how many wrinkles you get. It's my commitment to you."

Asia hugged me and said, "This means so much to me. Thank you." She rested her arms on my shoulders and smiled. "I should give you something too."

"You already have."

"I did?"

"You said yes to my proposal." I kissed her, then added, "You also promised to write me every day if we're away from each other."

"I will always love you, Woody."

"You just gave me another gift." I pointed to the orange tree as we stood there together. "One thing I learned from my parents is that the best present comes from the heart. Dad planted this tree the year I was born 19 years ago. That's why I wanted to carve those words on the trunk."

"I love the sweet citrus scent." Asia reached up and touched a hanging fruit. "Can we pick one?"

"Sure." I plucked off a rich Valencia and peeled it with my fingers. "Here, taste it." I held up a slice.

She placed it to her lips and sucked on the juices. "Mmm. That's delicious."

"Let me try." I kissed and savored the sweetness dribbling from her mouth.

We laughed and sat on the swing again. It seemed like the whole world disappeared, and we lived each moment in our special garden far away from the madness of another war. Nothing else mattered while we enjoyed the fruits of our tree.

When I finished eating the last savory bite of my orange, I said, "Now the next step is to shop for an engagement ring."

"When?" She gushed with excitement.

"How about Tuesday after we visit Dad in the hospital?"

"I'd like that."

"It'll be the perfect time to shop for your ring at a jewelry store near the hospital. The owner, Mr. Washburn, is a long-time friend of my family, and he'll help us out."

"Okay." Asia sighed, and we sat on the swing again. "Maybe we can find a ring that's not too expensive."

"Well, you pick out whatever you like. I want you to be happy wearing the ring."

"Oh," she whispered softly as she snuggled in my arms. "I'll cherish it forever."

Although our future was uncertain, we savored our present moments and let all worries drift away like passing clouds above us.

30 TRANSITION

I awoke in the darkness on my first morning back home in San Diego. Sleepily I shuffled into the kitchen with a flashlight in hand, then flicked on the light and glanced at the wall clock. The minute hand clicked to 4:55. While I made a pot of coffee, I remembered my summer of living on the ranch where I was used to getting up early and Asia joined me. Normally we had a quick breakfast with Aunt Eileen, Maria and my uncles, then we all headed out to work.

Horses neighed, cows mooed, hens cackled, roosters crowed, and the fresh mountain breeze whispered in our ears. Asia kept busy in the corral while I rode out to check on the cattle with Buck and Jake. Maria milked Daisy, and Eileen was upstairs caring for her baby as the kids slept in. This had been our way of life on that now distant ranch north of Flagstaff.

As I sipped from my cup, I looked around our family home and tried to adjust to my surroundings in San Diego.

"Good morning," said Asia when she came into the kitchen. "Coffee ready?"

"Yep." I poured a cup, mixed in a teaspoon of cream the way she liked and handed it to her.

She took a sip. "Thanks."

"You're welcome." I set a plate of toast down next to a jar of strawberry jam, then sat across from her at the table. "Sleep well?"

Asia looked up from her steamy cup and smiled. "Yes. It took a while before I could sleep, though."

"I know you had to get used to a new place."

"It was more than that. Kathy and I stayed up late talking about everything." Asia laughed. "I've never had so much fun with girl talk before. She's really funny."

"I'm glad you had a good time."

She took another sip and looked out the window. It was still pitch-black. "Um, I don't hear a rooster crowing. Where are we?"

We laughed together and realized how much everything had changed during that summer of 1966. Later, when the sun rose and bathed our neighborhood in a soft glow of orange, we went for a walk.

Eager to show her where I grew up, I pointed out my former high school, then took her to the local hang out off campus for cherry sodas.

From there, we strolled to the top of a hill near my family home, where we had a clear view of the Pacific ocean about five miles away. To the east, we looked down into deep canyons filled with a mix of dry browns, greyish-greens and subtle reds on plants like spiky sage and the heart-shaped leaves of buckwheat.

Amazed at the change in scenery, Asia said, "Wow, this is nothing like the views we had on the ranch in Northern Arizona."

"Yep. You won't find any stands of Ponderosa in this area." I turned and faced her. "Can you get used to living here?"

"Yes." She reached out and we held hands while looking into each other's eyes. "Kathy said there are lots of jobs in the city." Asia smiled. "I'll work and maybe I can go to community college when I save up enough money."

"That'd be perfect for you. In fact, with your straight A's in high school, you could get some scholarships and earn a degree."

In that moment, I took a mental picture of the warm sunlight on her creamy skin and the way her long black hair fluttered in the breeze. During the summer, we'd grown accustomed to our pauses without words. "Come on. I'll show you the Little League field where I played as a kid."

"I didn't know you played baseball," she said as we walked along the quiet neighborhood streets of Clairemont Mesa. "I'm learning something new about you."

"Yeah, it was a lot of fun then." We stopped near a field, and

I looked at the base through a chain link fence. I could almost hear loud cheers in the stands. With Asia standing beside me, I said, "I remember how kids taunted the guy on base, "'Hey batter, batter! Swing! You can't hit a thing!'"

She rested her arm on my shoulder like she relived the memory with me. "How old were you then?"

"I was 10-years-old and loved the game as a catcher. It's funny how things change, though. In those days, I dreamed of playing on the Padres team. Now it seems like my life is on hold. How can I plan ahead knowing I could get drafted a week from now?"

"I don't know." With a worried look, Asia squeezed my hand. "It scares me, Woody."

Seeing her expression, I tried to change the subject. "What's wrong with me?" I laughed. "Here we're having a nice time together, and I go spoiling it." On the sidewalk, I noticed chalk marks for a child's game of hop-scotch. "Hey, let's have some fun."

"Are you kidding?" She laughed and took a quick glance over at nearby houses. "What if somebody sees us? We'll look silly."

"Who cares?" I shrugged. "Live it up." I hopped across the 10 feet of squares and looked back.

Asia giggled and followed right behind me. "Hey, that's fun. Let's do it again."

We laughed as we hopped back and forth again. From there, we skipped arm in arm along the sidewalk like two kids bursting with energy and forgot about our worries. When we returned to the house, we both had a freeing sensation in our lungs from all that frolicking around.

"That was so much fun," said Asia as we came in the front door.

While still laughing, I almost hit an ugly wall. Aunt Emma was blocking the entryway with a frown on her face again. I froze. It was like she flicked off an emotional high to a grumpy low. I steadied myself and said, "Oh, hi."

Asia stopped cold and she faced the witch head on. "Uh, we were just..." She glanced at me like what now?

We expected another tongue lashing.

"It's okay, son." Mom stood nearby smiling. "Emma has something to say."

"Yeah?" I looked at my aunt and noticed loose strands of gray hair dangling from a usually tight-fitting bun.

She took a deep breath and exhaled. "Your Ma says I oughta apologize for my remarks to you last night. I ain't much for sayin such things, but if I want to see my brother, I best get on with it." She tried to smile but couldn't quite get her stiff lips to move upward and just stood there without saying anything.

I glanced at Mom and back to my aunt. "Uh, get on with what?"

"You know..." She paused and looked awkward about what to say next. "I'm sorry for disrespectin ya." She held out her hand but didn't make eye contact.

This was so different from her normal bitchy self that I had to look over at Mom to make sure I understood what was happening. She smiled and nodded. I responded with a handshake and noticed my aunt's face. She seemed a little softer. "I accept your apology," I said.

Aunt Emma puffed out air like relieving gas. "I reckon that's settled." She turned and started to head down the hallway.

"Emma, you forgot something," said Mom.

"What?" My aunt froze without looking back.

"You need to apologize to Asia," said Mom.

Emma stiffly turned around like a tin soldier. I could see she was trying but it was painfully difficult to change her ways. She hesitated, then lowered her gaze. "You mean the girl there?"

"I'm talking about the young lady," said Mom in a calm voice. "Her name is Asia. My son's girlfriend. You owe her an apology."

My Aunt tensed up every fatty cell in her already swollen face and puffed out air again like a deflating balloon. "All right." She jerked her arm half-way up and said, "The same goes for you, girl."

Aunt Emma turned and walked back into the guest bathroom like she was constipated. For a moment, we just stood there trying to take it all in and not quite sure how to handle this half-baked apology.

Mom stepped forward and hugged Asia. "I'm sorry, dear. That's the best Emma can do. I made it clear she'll have to leave unless she changed her attitude. She wanted to have a few more visits with her brother in the hospital, so she agreed to apologize to the both of you. At least she tried."

"That's okay, Mrs. Thomson," said Asia. "I understand how difficult it is for you. I grew up with the bitterness of my father. It's not easy to break through the hardness."

"You're right." Mom sighed and tried to smile. "Emma has until Wednesday, then she'll have to leave. All we can do is pray and hope that she'll continue to soften her hardened heart."

"I admire your patience, Mrs. Thomson."

"Call me Lily." Mom placed her palm on Asia's shoulder and smiled.

In that moment, I observed something I didn't expect. Here were the two most important women in my life seeming to bond together like mother and daughter. Surprised to see this connection so soon after Asia and I decided to get engaged, I wanted to treasure it in my mind.

31 FEAR IN ASIA

On a bright sunny morning Asia, and I were on our way to visit Dad in the hospital. This was our third day of staying with my family in San Diego, and her first chance to meet him. While I drove along Balboa Park, she took a compact mirror out of her purse and kept looking at her reflection. She constantly brushed her hair and fidgeted in the seat.

I had never seen Asia act this way before and asked, "Are you all right?"

"I'm kind of nervous." She looked at me with a worried expression. "What if your dad doesn't like me?"

"Relax." I smiled as she sat beside me. "I've had plenty of time to prepare him for this day. He's been more alert. I talked a lot about how we met and our working on the ranch together. Now he keeps asking to see you."

Asia adjusted her blue skirt and white blouse, then sat straight. The gold locket that encased the photo of her late Mother elegantly caressed her neck. "Do I look okay? Your aunt treats me like a tramp. You don't think I have too much makeup on do you? What if your dad gets mad and says terrible things about me?"

"Whoa. Take it easy." I drove to the side of the road and parked. "Dad's not like that." I noticed her eyes were moist. "Don't worry. He cares about people."

"I want to believe that." Asia stared out the window and let out a sorrowful sigh. "My father never trusted me or my mom. He was suspicious of every move we made. We couldn't do anything without getting yelled at or slapped. Now I'm supposed to meet your dad?"

"It's okay." I held her close. "You'll see."

"I hope he's like you."

"You'll be fine." I turned back on the road. "We're almost there."

When we entered the hospital room, Dad's eyes were closed, and he seemed to be resting peacefully. A white bandage still covered his head. We sat in chairs and talked softly as we waited to see if he'd wake up soon. This was his usual time to be more alert. A bouquet of red, white and yellow roses were in a vase beside his bed where Mom had put them the night before.

Asia stood up, inhaled the aroma and smiled. "I had fun with your mom yesterday," she whispered. "It was nice that she invited me to help pick these flowers from her garden."

"Yeah, she likes to share this simple pleasure with everyone in the family," I said in a low voice.

Asia moved the flowers around like she wanted them to look just right for Dad. "It was kind of neat how she said, 'Let's take some time to smell the roses. They will bring you joy.'"

"That sounds like Mom. The other day she held a red rose under Dad's nose. He woke up with a smile on his beat-up face." I pointed to the flowers. "Go ahead, try it."

"Are you sure?"

"Yep, it just takes a whiff." I nodded. "You'll see how he lights up."

Asia picked up a rose and wafted it close to Dad's face. He sniffed, blinked several times and opened his eyes wide. For a moment, he tried to focus on what he was seeing, then he smiled and said, "Oh, I don't think I've met you before."

"Good morning Dad." I leaned closer. "This is my girlfriend, Asia."

"Oh, yeah." He looked up at her and smiled again. "For a minute there, I thought you were an angel." Even with his bruised face, he still had a sense of humor.

"No." Asia giggled. "Far from it."

"Yeah, Dad." I laughed. "You're not in heaven." I patted his hand. "How are you feeling?"

He yawned. "Tired. I keep dozing off."

"Are you thirsty?" I asked.

"Yeah." He nodded to a pitcher on a tray. "Water's there," he said in a whisper.

"I'll get it." Asia poured some into a small plastic cup, held it close and bent a straw at a slight angle to help him drink.

Dad took a few sips. "Thanks."

"Would you like some more water?" Asia had that same caring expression I grew to love during our summer on the ranch together.

He tried to clear his throat and nodded. "I'm thirstier than I thought." He sipped from the straw but had a shallow cough, and water dribbled down his chin.

Asia grabbed a napkin from the tray and daubed the moisture away from his face.

Dad looked pleased while he gazed at Asia. "You're a good nurse."

"I took care of my mom when she was sick." Asia put the cup on a tray again. "After four months of caring for her, she passed away. I learned a lot then."

"I can see why my son raves about you."

Asia glanced at me with a relieved expression. She had been worried about what he would think of her, and now she realized there was nothing to fear.

We stayed and talked for another half-hour while Dad focused his attention on her. "So, tell me about your piano playing. Woody says you love it."

"Oh, yes." Asia's eyes lit up like the beginning of a sunny day. "Whenever I touch the keys and play Haydn's music, I feel like I could fly."

"Ah, that's beautiful, young lady." Dad paused to look at her. "You have a nice voice. Do you sing too?"

"No." Asia had a soft giggle and lowered her gaze. "I let the piano sing for me."

Dad smiled. "That's nice to be so gifted. I hear you're pretty amazing around animals too."

Although he seemed tired, he still kept his gaze on Asia as they continued to talk. Meanwhile, she looked over at me like she was happy to see everything going so well.

Later a nurse came in and said, "Okay, Mr. Thomson, it's time for you to rest now." She had a nice smile as she glanced at us. "I'll give you another five minutes to visit."

When she closed the door and left, Dad looked up at me and said, "Before you leave, I need to tell you something."

"Yeah?"

"I love you son."

"I love you too. Okay, get some rest. We'll come back tomorrow."

Then he looked over at Asia and held up his right hand. She smiled and placed her palm in his.

Dad's eyes seemed to light up even more. "I'm so glad to meet you, Asia. I hope to see you again." He kept his light grip and smiled.

"I look forward to it." She leaned in and gently kissed his cheek.

I snapped this pleasing sight in my memory of the two connecting in a moment of understanding together. "See you later, Dad."

"Yep," he said with a slight grin that showed his ongoing light-heartedness. "I'm not going anywhere." He patted his left leg in a cast.

When the nurse came in, we left the room. While Asia and I walked out of the hospital and headed to the car, I asked, "How are you feeling now?"

"Relieved." Asia glanced back at the entrance. "Your Father is so kind, I don't know what to say."

"Happy?"

"Yes. It's just that my Father was so cruel and filled with bitterness, I..." Asia hesitated, then said, "I thought all men were like him." She smiled. "Until I met you. Now I see where your caring heart comes from. It's your Dad."

"I'm glad." I stood there admiring the way her eyes shined in the sunlight. "Do you know what I'd like to do right now?"

"What?"

"I want to take you out to a nice lunch at a Mexican place that's just a few blocks from here. Then we'll go to my friend's jewelry shop to pick out your engagement ring."

"Oh Woody." She wrapped her arms around me tight. "I love you so much. I can't wait to go there."

"Let's eat first." I held her hand. "Come on. I'll treat you to the best tacos in town."

32 BLUE SAPPHIRE

W hile we sat in a booth and ate our lunch, I told Asia about the owner of the jewelry shop. "Bill's a long-time friend of my dad. They both survived a kamikaze attack on their destroyer during the Battle of Okinawa. After the war Bill helped with the reconstruction in Japan. That's where he met his wife, Emiko. I told her about our engagement. Now she wants to help you look at rings."

"I'd like to meet them," said Asia.

"Good. Bill and Emiko specialize in helping Navy couples with their rings when they get engaged or plan their weddings."

"But you're not in the Navy."

"Well, they also serve family members of veterans. Dad's a re-tired Master Chief Petty Officer. Besides, after talking with him in the hospital, I realized he's right. I can't wait any longer. I'll enlist as soon as I'm sure you'll be settled here with my family."

"When will you have to leave?" Asia looked worried.

"Maybe a week."

"How long will you be away?"

"I don't know." We held hands across the table. Neither of us wanted to let go. "Boot camp takes seven weeks. After that, I'll probably head out for more training. A ship maybe. Could be six months to a year."

Asia squeezed my hand tighter. "I'll wait for you no matter how long it takes." Her black eyes glistened like gems soaking in a pool of fresh water. "I promise to write letters to you every day."

"I'll write you, too." I wanted to cheer her up and smiled. "We'll do like my parents did."

"Yes," she whispered. "We'll have tons of love letters."

"I still need to make sure you'll be living comfortably with my family while I'm gone."

"I'd like that. Maybe they can show me how to stay strong for you."

"Yeah, it's good to talk about this now." I took a napkin and daubed tear drops from her eyes. "You need to know what to expect. As a Navy brat, I had to get used to Dad being gone. Each time, he'd say, 'son, you're the man of the house until I get back.' I remember one tour that was the hardest for me. He was away for nine months."

"When was that?"

"During the Korean War. I was four."

"Oh." Asia winced like she'd been struck with the emotional reality of what I experienced. "You were so young. Sounds painful."

"It hurt to see him go." I paused as I remembered Dad leaving in a taxi. "I cried a lot. Then I tried to be tough like Dad. I'd strut around the house wearing a paper captain's hat. Everything had to be shipshape."

"You mean you were acting like a man of the house?"

"Yeah, I had to make sure Mom didn't get too sad while Dad was gone. I kept trying to cheer her up by telling stupid knock, knock jokes."

"You were worried about her."

"Couldn't help it. Sometimes I heard her crying."

"That must've been difficult."

"Yep. I was a bit confused. One minute I'd run around the house like a normal kid. Then I'd be under her feet trying to make her happy again."

"Oh, that explains why you're so protective of me."

"Uh, oh." I laughed. "I probably get too carried away."

"No." She giggled. "That's one of the many things I love about you."

"It's important that you feel safe and happy with my family." For a moment, I focused on the way she intently looked at me. "So, now you know what it might be like when I get in the Navy." I paused to let the truth soak in. "Do you still want to get engaged?"

"Yes." She gazed into my eyes and smiled. "I'd like us to shop for my ring now."

"That's my girl." I glanced at our bill and placed cash on the table. "Let's go."

We left the restaurant and strolled down the street. Asia squeezed my left arm tight with both hands as we headed toward the jewelry shop. Although she worried about our uncertain future, she kept a brave, steady pace alongside me without saying another word.

When we stepped inside the jewelry shop, Bill greeted me with a strong handshake and a warm smile as usual. "Hello Richard. Oops, I mean Woody. I have to get used to your nickname."

"Bill, I'd like you to meet my fiancée, Asia."

"Ah, yes." The lens of his glasses reflected her Amerasian features. "Woody talked a lot about you on the phone." He held out his right hand. Old burn scars covered the sides of face, neck and arms. A permanent reminder of a kamikaze attack during the Battle of Okinawa. "I'm glad to meet you."

"Hi." With a relaxed smile, Asia reached out to him as though she hadn't noticed his wounds.

Bill shook her hand, then pointed to a glass display case filled with a selection of rings. "I have some pieces you might like. Feel free to look at these, and I'll get my wife, Emiko."

While he went in the back, we admired the glittering jewelry on display. "Oh, there's so much to choose from," she said. "They must be expensive."

"Don't worry about the prices." I drew her closer with my arm on her shoulder, and we leaned into the counter for a good look. "Let me handle it," I said.

Just as I spoke, Bill came in with Emiko. Seeing them together was like watching a basketball player standing next to a Japanese doll. The contrast could not be more obvious. He was tall, lanky, balding and had thin gray sideburns. She, on the other hand, stood just five feet of pure, sweet energy and a ready smile. Fully immersed in our American lifestyle, she wore a yellow dress with red floral designs that flowed to just below her knees.

Emiko rushed toward me, then stopped, looked up and said, "Oh my goodness gracious, Thomson San. You are big man now."

"It's been awhile," I said.

"Too long." She shook her head as if to disapprove, then laughed while covering her mouth with her palm. "You should come see us more often."

"I'll try." I paused to admire the way Emiko looked up with an endearing smile. I had known her since I was two-years-old. Through my childhood, she had been my adopted Auntie, and I loved her as though we had the same blood flowing in our veins. "Obasan, I'd like to introduce you to my fiancée, Asia."

"I am so happy to meet you." Emiko kept smiling and bowed slightly. "Thomson San has told me so much about you on the phone."

"Hello." Asia returned the polite gesture. "He has spoken fondly of you too."

"Oh, I see that look of excitement in your eyes," said Emiko. "You want a very special engagement ring that says to the world, "I am Thomson San's lady." Obason gushed like she was the one getting the ring.

"Yes." Asia squeezed my hand, then looked at me with a familiar smile that drew our hearts into one synchronized beat.

"Well, let's see what we have for you." Emiko's shoulder-length greyish hair swayed forward as she leaned closer to pick out rings for Asia. "Here's a lovely blue sapphire that's perfect for you." She held up the ring. "Would you like to try it on?"

"Oh, yes." Asia looked up to me again and smiled.

Seeing Asia's delighted expression, I said, "Here, let me do this, babe." I took the ring and slipped it on her finger.

"It's beautiful." She held her hand up to admire the elegant oval cut. "What do you think, Woody?"

"It's perfect."

"I don't know if we can afford such an expensive ring." She kept her gaze on it. "I really like it but..."

"Oh, you must not think that way," said Emiko in a hushed

voice. "Such a blue sapphire will bring you good health, a long life and many children."

I laughed and kissed Asia's cheek. "You just heard the wisdom of my Obason."

"That's right," said Bill. "Woody and I already discussed our family payment plan on the phone."

"Yep." I whispered in her ear, "Is this the one you want?"

"Oh yes." Asia continued to admire the engagement ring and smiled. "It feels so right."

"Good." I turned to Bill. "We'll take it."

While I finalized the generous credit arrangements with Bill and signed the papers, I kept looking over at Asia. Seeing her face all lit up in a subtle warm glow of sunshine peeking through the store window, I wanted to hold that moment and not let go. Soon I would have to enlist in the Navy. Time was fleeting.

I snapped the scene in my mind as Emiko and Asia stood there talking and laughing together. This was an encouraging sight. Besides my family, Asia would need the support of other lady friends after I had to leave for boot camp.

"I know what you're going through," Bill interrupted my thoughts. "I've seen it many times. A man has to go fight another war and leave his fiancée or wife behind." He placed his hand on my shoulder. "I left a girlfriend during World War Two. Then I had to be away from Emiko while Korea blew up." He paused to watch the ladies again. "Now we're sending more young men out to Vietnam. It never ends."

"How did you handle it?"

"I had to let go of my worries and trust Emiko." Bill nodded. "Do you see what's happening?"

"What do you mean?"

"They're bonding."

"Yeah."

"It's good for the both of them." He paused to watch them talking together. "Women are tough and resilient."

"I agree. I've seen Asia handle a lot of challenges this past summer."

"Good." Bill patted my shoulder. "Hold those memories. Do what has to be done. If you have to be away from each other for a long time, stay committed. Keep the lines of communication intact. Got that?"

"Yes sir." I laughed. "You talk like I'm already in the Navy."

"Can't help it." Bill grinned with a far-off look as though he remembered his past. "I served 20 years. When I retired, I realized the sea still flowed in my veins."

"Now you sound like my Dad."

"Yep. We have a lot in common. Since we served on the same destroyer escort together, we're brothers." Bill gave me a signed agreement to pay off the ring in installments and smiled. "You're all set. I'll go visit your Dad in the hospital after I close."

"Thanks." I shook Bill's hand.

Just then, Emiko came over with Asia, smiled and gave me a warm hug. "Oh, Thomson San, I am so proud of how you've grown up as a man."

Asia glanced at her blue sapphire and held my hand as we lingered together with my adopted aunt and uncle. Then we said our goodbyes while not knowing when we would see each other again. Little did I know what was ahead.

33 STANDING FIRM

I drove north on Morena Blvd., and bright rays of sunlight glistened over Mission Bay. Colorful red, yellow, green sails puffed out in the wind and well-crafted sloops sliced through the blue shimmering water with ease.

The warmth of the sun was on the left side of my face. A song played on the radio, and we listened to the sensuous lyrics, "By the sea we shall be. Making love. You and me."

To my right, Asia kept looking at her engagement ring as though she never wanted to take it off.

"I'm glad you like it," I said.

"Oh Woody." She gushed and kissed my cheek. "Being engaged to you feels so right."

"Yeah, it's like we're supposed to be together." I drove past Garnet Avenue and headed north to Clairemont Mesa. "After I graduated from high school, I just wanted to travel and see the world. That changed when we danced at the lookout after the party."

"Really?" She lifted her head from my shoulder. "We argued that night. Remember?"

"I just recall how we made up in the pickup truck that night."

"Oh." Asia snuggled closer again. "You mean the steamy windows?"

We laughed over one of our many memories that summer. For the rest of the drive up the hill, we talked about our working together on the ranch. We also relived our horseback rides in the mountains and swimming at the lake on our days off.

"We had so many good times," said Asia in that smooth breathy voice again. "Do you know what impressed me the most about you?"

"What?"

"That Sunday morning on the ranch when you tried to make breakfast for me."

I laughed at the memory. "Burnt toast."

"Soggy scrambled eggs."

"Strong black coffee."

"It looked like oil," she added.

"Tasted like it too."

"You wanted to do something special for me."

"I couldn't take my eyes off you."

Asia let out a sweet sigh. "I loved you for trying."

"Hey, I just realized something." I reached over and put my arm on her shoulder. "Out of all our memories we made together, we think of waking up and seeing each other at breakfast."

"Oh, look Woody."

"What?"

"There's a sign that says Millie's Dog Grooming Service." Asia pointed to a large ranch-style house. "Can you pull over?"

"Sure." I parked in front of the building.

"I see a note in the window. Help wanted." Asia opened the passenger side door and stepped out on the sidewalk. "Maybe I could get a job here. I'll check it out."

"That'd be perfect for you." I turned off the engine. "I'll wait here."

"Okay." Asia walked up to the front door with a welcome sign and went inside.

While I waited, I realized that it was only about a mile from our house, and Asia could easily walk to work. She'd have a chance to earn money and pitch in for room and board while staying with my family. I glanced at my watch. It was 3:50.

A gray-haired lady came out cradling her fluffy white-haired poodle and drove away. Other dog owners came and dropped off their animals, then left. It looked busy. Restless, I left the car and paced with a hunger for good news. I kept glancing at my watch, expecting Asia to rush over at any minute, and the hour hand ticked to 5:00. This had to be a good sign.

Finally, Asia stepped out the front door and walked toward

me. I held my breath.

"Well?" I asked.

"I can't believe it," she burst out wide-eyed. "I got the job!" She wrapped her arms around me so fast, I had to steady myself.

"Ah babe." I exhaled to relieve the pressure. "I'm so happy for you." I stood there holding her and didn't want to let go. "Tell me all about it."

"I met Millie, the owner. After I filled out the application, she asked a lot of questions while giving me a tour of the place. I told her how I worked with animals on the ranch and what I learned from the vet. She had me observe a groomer trying to get an anxious dog into a bath. When the collie saw me, she jumped in my lap and calmed right down."

I laughed. "Well, naturally."

"Millie had me walk several dogs around the backyard and watched to see how I handled the different breeds. She liked the way I worked so much, she offered me the job. I won't have to start for another week. That's when one of her groomers plans to quit."

"Great! It'll give us more time together before I have to enlist."

"Yeah, I still have to bring in my high school diploma and references to make it final."

"Perfect. Eileen, Buck and Jake will be happy to add their names to the list."

"Uh, oh." Asia looked at me with a worried expression.

"What?"

"We still have to announce our engagement to your family."

"You're right." I scratched my whiskered chin and tried to imagine my parent's reaction. "It'll be a shock to Dad and Mom at first. They'll probably say we're too young." I opened the passenger side door.

Asia slid into the seat and looked up. "It's your Aunt Emma I'm worried about. She glares at me like I've have the plague."

"She'll be leaving soon." I rushed to the driver's side and got in. "We'll show her what love is all about." I leaned in and we kissed. "Maybe we'll soften her up."

"I hope so."

"Okay. Let's break the news," I said as we headed home.

When we stepped inside the front door, our golden retriever greeted us. I patted her forehead and said, "Hello, Snuggles."

Asia knelt and rubbed behind Snuggles' ears. "Oh, you're such a good dog."

Our official greeter responded with happy face licking, and Asia laughed like she adored our retriever's affectionate welcome. Seeing the way she delighted in being with our dog, I captured the scene in my mind and didn't want to let go of the moment. I'd have to leave soon.

"Damn it, girl!" bellowed Aunt Emma. "Stop rollin around with that filthy mutt." She huffed and shook her head in disgust.

"Ah come on," I said. "Lighten up.

"Oh, it's alright." Asia kept brushing her fingers through thick fur, then Snuggles rolled over to get a good tummy rub.

"No, it ain't!" Aunt Emma fumed and glared at Asia. "You come tramping in here with those slant eyes like you own the place." Her cheeks puffed out like she was about to explode. "Why don't you go back to your own kind?"

"Hey!" I stepped in front of her. "Don't talk like that to my fiancée."

"You're what?"

Snuggles growled. My sister, Kathy peeked out from her bedroom door.

"You heard me," I said. "We're engaged."

Asia patted our dog. "It's okay, girl." She stood up and calmly faced Aunt Emma. "Why do you hate me?"

Emma froze. Her cheeks bulged. "Well, I..." Tightly wrapped greyish hair looked as though it would all twang out from a bun on the top of her head. Stunned by the question, her brown eyes widened.

"Well?" Asia stepped closer. "I'm waiting for an answer."

My Aunt gritted her teeth, held her breath and fumed. "You!" she puffed.

"I never did anything to hurt you." Asia took another step toward her.

"Don't you dare come any closer!" Emma's eyes narrowed. She folded her arms across her round chest.

"See this?" Asia held up her hand to show her blue sapphire ring. "Woody and I love each other. We're engaged."

Emma's face contorted. "No!" She turned and glared at me. "Can't you see?" She nodded toward Asia without making eye contact. "Wake up, boy! She ain't one of us." Her arms dropped to her sides and her fists tightened. "I told you before. That girl's a half-breed."

"Hey!" I resisted the temptation to curse back at her.

"I'm a human being." Asia stepped to within a foot of her. "Take a good look. I'm flesh and blood just like you."

Emma raised her hand like she was about to hit Asia. "You!" She kept a clenched fist in the air but didn't strike.

"Go ahead." Asia calmly stood her ground. "It won't change a thing. Woody and I will always love each other no matter what you say or do."

Emma huffed, stomped down the hallway and slammed the bedroom door.

"Are you okay?" I placed my hand on Asia's shoulder. "You're shaking."

"Am I?" She looked at me with fire in her eyes. "I'm so angry. All through school I was bullied by the other girls. I guess I got tired of it."

"I'm proud of you."

"Me, too," said Kathy as she came from down the hall. "I've been too scared to stand up to her." She looked at us with a surprised expression. "Are you really engaged?"

Before I could respond, Mom came in from the back door with a handful of freshly cut red and yellow roses. "I picked these for your Dad. Do you guys want to go to the hospital with me?"

"Yeah," I said. "We'd like to talk with you and Dad anyway."

"Good." She placed the flowers in a glass vase and smiled. "Let's go."

34 COMING TOGETHER

While Mom drove her station wagon, I sat in the back-seat with Asia. Kathy was in the front holding the bou-quet in her hands. Mom's eyes reflected in the rearview mirror as she glanced at me. "Your Aunt Emma was banned from the hospital this afternoon."

"What did she do this time?"

"She refused to leave when visiting hours were over." Mom turned right on Balboa Avenue. "Emma had taken a cab there and ran late. When she was told to come back this evening, she yelled at the nursing staff. They tried to calm her down, but you know how she can get."

"Yep." I said. "Let me guess. She was escorted out of the build-ing by security, right?"

Mom rolled her eyes in the mirror's reflection. "Oh, yeah."

"That explains how angry Aunt Emma was after we came home," I said.

"Yeah, I told her to pack her bags." Mom slowed down and braked at a red light. "She was getting ready to leave for the air-port when you got there."

"That's so cool." Kathy laughed. "We should celebrate."

"No," said Mom. "This is nothing to be happy about." She glanced at Kathy. "Your aunt is a very sick person. I've tried to help, but her emotional outbursts are more than I can handle. All we can do is pray and hope she gets some kind of counseling."

"How's Dad taking it?" I asked.

"He's all right now." Mom turned into the hospital parking lot. "But Emma made it difficult for him to relax. She kept hovering like an overprotective mother hen."

"So, he's relieved?"

"Yes." Mom parked her car and turned off the engine. "Now he can rest easier without his older sister pestering the nurses all the time."

While we all walked to the hospital entrance, Mom said, "By the way, your Father keeps watching the news about the buildup in Vietnam. He's worried that you might get drafted."

"That's one of the things I want to talk about." I held Asia's hand as we went through the door.

When we entered the hospital room, Dad was propped up and sitting in bed. The bandages were still wrapped around his scalp and reddish, purple bruises reminded us of the accident caused by a drunk driver. Although he had a right to be angry, he was in good spirits as usual.

Glad to see us, he smiled. "Hey, there you are." His eyes lit up as Mom leaned in and kissed him.

"Hi honey," she said. "How are you feeling?"

"Great. Doctor Peterson will remove the stiches tomorrow."

"Before you know it, you'll be back home with us," said Mom.

Kathy set the flowers on a lampstand, then stepped closer. "Hi Dad."

"Hey, there's my princess." He hugged her as she kissed his cheek. "You're looking more like your Mother every day."

"Thanks." Kathy brushed back her shoulder-length brunette hair and glanced at Mom.

Dad looked pleased to see everyone and said, "Hello, Asia."

Asia smiled. "Hello Mr. Thomson."

"Call me Robert."

"I like the sound of that," Asia said. "Thank you."

Dad looked at me and shook my hand. "I'm glad to see you, son."

"I couldn't wait to get here," I said. "We have a lot to talk about."

"We sure do." He looked into my eyes with a serious expression. "Did you hear about the casualties in Vietnam?"

"Yeah."

"It's getting worse." Dad frowned. "More young men are being called up. It's only a matter of time before you get drafted."

"I know. That's why I decided to enlist in the Navy. I'll go into the recruitment office in a few days."

"Good." Dad leaned back on the pillow and let out a deep sigh. "You've got good sense." He gripped my wrist as he kept his gaze on me. "It's a crazy war, son."

"I know."

"This is nothing like what we went through after Pearl Harbor." His bruised cheeks tensed up.

I patted his hand. "I know, but you need to relax. You're getting too worked up again."

"Maybe so." He exhaled. "We knew the enemy was out to destroy us then. We had to fight. This time nobody attacked us. Damned hawks in Washington! They've stirred up another bloody war."

"Take it easy, Dad."

"I can't." His grip grew tighter on my wrist. "It's tearing our country apart. People are angry. Blood-thirsty generals! They're playing a devil's game of killing by the numbers. Damn it! They don't care about our boys over there."

"I agree but you need to get well."

Mom leaned in and kissed his cheek. "He's right. Now relax and we'll talk about something else."

Dad leaned back on the pillow and sighed again. "Well then, what do you want to talk about?"

"Asia and I just got engaged," I blurted out.

She held up her left hand to show off her blue sapphire ring and smiled.

"What?" Mom's eyes widened. "You're too young to get married."

"It's okay," I said. "We're not thinking about wedding plans anytime soon."

"That's right." Asia slipped her hand into mine. "We're making a commitment to be faithful to each other."

"Yeah, once we get more settled a year or so from now, then we'll figure out when to get married," I added.

"That's a big step," said Dad. "You'll both meet other people.

Things could change."

Mom frowned. "You've only known each other for the summer."

"That's true." I nodded. "But you and Dad got engaged two months after you first met. It worked out well for you two. Right?"

Dad laughed and patted Mom's hand. "He's got us there."

She still had a worried expression. "I know, but we had to work hard at it."

"I understand." I looked at Asia as she turned to face me. "But we love each other."

"Yes." Asia kept her gaze on me. "Our love will make it work. I got a job today, so I'll be able to support myself."

"You could live with my family," I said.

"Do you see how they look at each other?" Dad asked Mom.

"Yes, I know," said Mom. "It brings back memories."

"We were just 18 then."

"Nothing was certain," Mom said.

"The war was on. I had to leave soon."

"We were so much in love."

"I still feel the same way," said Dad.

"Me too." Mom paused and shook her head. "But they're just kids."

"So were we."

"Now it's their turn." Mom stood up and placed her hands on our shoulders. "We just want you both to be happy." She smiled and hugged Asia. "It would mean a lot if you were to live in our home with us."

"I agree." Dad reached his arms out. "Welcome to our family."

Asia leaned over and they embraced again. "Nothing would make me happier. Thank you."

Relieved, I hugged my parents. "I knew I could count on you guys."

"Cool." Kathy smiled at Asia. "We'll be like sisters together."

"I'd like that."

"Great," I said. Pleased with the way things were coming together, I added, "Now we just need to call Eileen and her family at the ranch. I know they'll be excited to hear about our engagement."

"How about calling them when we get back to the house," asked Mom.

"Yeah," I said. "We can all take turns on the phone."

"That'll give me a chance to update my sister, Eileen about your Dad's improving condition." Mom smiled with a look of satisfaction. "Your brothers will be home from the San Diego Padres ball game by then."

"Okay," said Dad as he relaxed on the pillow and closed his eyes. "While you guys do that I'll get some more rest."

Asia leaned over and said, "Here, I'll lower the bed for you." She pushed a button and adjusted it, then asked, "There. How's that?"

"Much better." He looked up and smiled. "Thanks."

Mom gave Dad a quick kiss. "We'll come back tomorrow."

"You and Kathy go on ahead," He said. "I want to talk with Woody and Asia."

"All right." Mom nodded. "We'll be waiting down the hall."

When they left, Dad looked up with a serious expression. "Well, history is repeating itself. Your mother and I got caught up in a war." He reached out and held both of our hands. "Now it's your turn to face the hardships ahead."

"I know it won't be easy." I looked at Asia. "But we love each other."

"Love means being patient and faithful," said Dad. "You may be separated from each other for a long time." He paused to let his words sink in. "It'll require hard work to keep your relationship strong. Do you understand?"

"Yes sir."

"We can do it." Asia looked into my eyes with confidence.

"Good." He smiled at both of us. "You have our blessings and support."

"Thanks." I shook his hand.

Asia leaned in and kissed his cheek. "Good night."

35 EBB AND FLOW

Mid-afternoon sunlight shined on Asia's smooth skin during our stroll along a beach north of San Diego. We stopped to watch a pod of six porpoises arcing in the water and swimming south. Seagulls divebombed a fishing boat to get their fresh catch of the day. A dozen sandpipers danced with the ebb and flow of surf while pecking at bubbling holes in the sand. One caught a wiggling crab in its beak, then quickly devoured its meal.

Our hearts seemed to beat in a rhythm of the sea as we talked about our lives together. Asia's hand was warm in mine. "It's so beautiful here," she said.

"Yeah, I'm glad we have this time along the shore." I picked up a small round rock and tossed it in the breaking waves.

Her eyes sparkled in the sunshine as she looked at me. "It was so nice to talk with your aunt and uncles at the ranch last night."

"I agree. Now everyone knows we're engaged."

"Your aunt Eileen wasn't surprised when we called and told her."

I stopped to admire Asia's smile. "Yeah, I think she could tell that we were getting serious weeks ago."

"Jake said the same thing." Bright sunshine drew out a subtle auburn tinge in Asia's black hair as she spoke. "He was very happy to give me a good reference for my new job."

"So was Buck," I said. "He'll get a signed letter from the vet too."

We held hands and paused to gaze at the ocean as the sunshine lit up the cresting waves in a rich turquoise glow.

Drawn to the sea, I asked, "Would you like to go for a swim?"

"Yes." Asia smiled. "I'm well-prepared." She took off her green shorts and yellow blouse, then revealed a navy blue one-piece swim suit. "I'm ready."

I stripped down to my green and yellow surfer shorts. "Let's leave our towels and stuff over there." I nodded to a large black rock imbedded in the sand.

After we set our belongings down we held hands, then stepped in the rolling surf. As the tide flowed back out, our toes sank in the sand, and we were caught off balance.

"Oh, I'm not used to all this motion," she said while grabbing my arm. "It's cold."

I laughed as I steadied myself and took her hand. "We'll get used to it."

"This is fun." She laughed as another wave splashed us. "It's the first time I've ever been in the ocean. This is nothing like the pool in my Phoenix high school." She glanced at me and asked, "How old were you when you learned to swim?"

"I practically grew up in the ocean. When I was three, Dad tossed me in the water at Mission Bay. I trusted him completely. He jumped right in and helped me to relax, then taught me to float."

Asia hesitated as she looked out over the ocean. "I'm a pretty good swimmer, you know."

"Yeah, I remember how well you swam at the lake."

"This is different though."

"Waves are trickier," I said.

She took a deep breath and exhaled again. "Okay, here I go." She stretched out her arms and lowered her head like she was ready to dive in.

Just then, a wave slapped our faces. "Whoa." I laughed as we tried to keep from falling backward. "Well, there's only one thing to do now."

Asia wiped her eyes and spat out salt water. "What's that?"

"Dive in." I sliced into the arc of a wave, swam out, then looked back.

She was swimming up fast and came alongside of me. "Oh, this feels so good."

"See, nothing to it."

"Yeah. Next time, I won't hesitate." She wrapped her arms around the back of my neck and we treaded water together. "This is nice," she said in that breathy voice I grew to love during our summer together.

"Are you warmed up now?"

"What do you think?" She lingered in a long, passionate kiss."

"Wow." I caught my breath. "You're definitely warmed up."

Our legs kept swaying in rhythm under water as we held hands and breathed in the fresh ocean air. It was like our hearts were synchronized into one harmonious flow of living in the moment and all worries about the future just floated away.

When we swam in, we let the waves carry us ashore, then stumbled out as the surf pushed against our backs. While the swells rolled in, we stood in the warmth of a bright sun long enough to dry out our suits. A dozen small fish appeared in the crest of a wave, then vanished below the surface. Red and orange sails billowed in the wind as a dozen sloops raced south.

"Would you like to walk up the beach?" I asked.

"I'd love to."

While we gathered our stuff, I glanced to the north. "There's a cove I'd like to show you about a mile from here."

"Good." She smiled. "We'll work up an appetite."

Holding hands, we strolled along the shore as the surf rolled in, and our toes sank in wet sand. Then a cool ocean wind blew in from the north and reminded us that summer was almost over. Soon I'd have to leave, and we wanted to make the most of our time together.

When we came to the cove, I said, "This is one of my favorite spots."

"It's beautiful here."

With our arms around each other, we observed black pebbles rolling and clacking through gentle waves lapping on the shore. Small crabs skittered on wet boulders and tiny fish swam in tide pools that glistened from the afternoon sun.

Asia spread out our towels and a breeze fluttered the fabric like a sail. "This is perfect."

For us, it wasn't the kind of date at a fancy restaurant. Instead, we ate peanut butter sandwiches and sat on towels cushioned in the sand. This was all we needed and we were young, full of passion for life and deeply in love.

Each moment belonged to us as the water flowed onto the sand, then oozed between our toes, and we laughed freely without the worries of a chaotic world. A simple touch from Asia made me long for more, and her eyes beckoned me closer. I wanted to be with her, not just for one day or a night, but always.

We had the cove all to ourselves until a group of six teenaged guys and girls sat nearby, then turned on a transistor radio tuned to rock and roll. Guitars played along with smooth voices about love by the sea, and reminded me of last summer with my high school friends when we gathered together. Couples sat around listening to music without a care in the world.

Since then, my rugged experiences had all come together to slap a youthful cockiness right out of me. I was thinking more like a man, and all I wanted was to live my life with Asia. Blocking that desire was the Vietnam War, and it was like a great wall that could separate us for a long time. I was about to enlist in the Navy.

Content to be with Asia in that moment, I looked out over the ocean as she sat beside me. We listened to the beat of Surfer Stomp and watched the waves roll in, and her eyes sparkled in the sunshine.

"Oh, I love that song," she said.

"Me too."

We were blissfully happy until a voice on the radio blared out, "The latest figures are still coming in for this year," said a reporter. "More than 4,000 American soldiers have been killed in action."

The tiny speaker scratched and squeaked with poor reception, then continued, "Vietcong casualties are much higher. More than 40,000 VC have been terminated during the same period. The Pentagon claims this kill ratio as a victory. To continue their strategic seek out and destroy missions, they estimate over 380,000 young Americans will be called up by December."

Dad was right, I thought. They tallied body counts like pawns on a chess board. Hatred had sucked out my loving moments with Asia. I could not breathe. Powers beyond my control were demanding a call to action. To me, the message was clear. It's us against them. Fight to the bitter end. Wipe out the commies before they destroy us.

Deep within, I asked, "Why must it be this way?" I had no answer. I looked at the teenagers on the beach and wondered; do they really understand? How strange. It was like they had ears but couldn't hear. Innocent and unaware, they sat on a blanket and listened to rock-and-roll while hiding behind dark sunglasses.

"Not again." Asia covered her ears.

"Come on. I know another spot."

We picked up our towels, clothes and picnic basket, then strolled to a quiet inlet with towering cliffs behind us. Away from all the noise of a world gone war mad, we settled in the sand again. Beams of sunlight from the western horizon speckled the blue waves like glittering jewels. An easy-going ebb and flow of surf lapped the shore. Nestled on three sides by boulders, it was like a refuge where we could talk and relax again.

"How's this?" I asked.

"Much better," she spoke in a soft whisper while snuggling up to me. "I'm glad we have this time alone."

For the rest of our afternoon, the sun warmed our bodies as we talked and laughed like we needed to live fully in each breath. While the hours passed, a bright orange globe began to hover above the horizon.

"I love being with your family," Asia said.

"I'm glad."

"It was always tense at my home." She sat up and exhaled like she needed to let go of the memory again.

"I know." I sat up with Asia and held her close. "That's over now."

"Yes." She smiled. "Now I can relax and just be myself."

"That means a lot to me."

"I like the way your parents are so caring around each other."

"Yeah, me too."

"It's been such a relief to be around you and your whole family."

"Yeah, well, we're far from perfect." I laughed. "Sometimes my brothers and I will argue over the dumbest things. If my sister gets involved, you'll hear a lot of yelling and slamming of doors."

"Now that should be interesting to see." She looked surprised. "I've never had siblings to tumble with anyway."

"Interesting?" Amused by her word choice, I had to laugh again. "It's more like watching a three-ring circus with clowns bumping into each other."

"I'm looking forward to it." Asia gazed at the setting sun. "Next week I'll start working at Millie's Dog Grooming. I can't wait to get started."

"Good. Working with the animals on the ranch was a great experience. Then with all you learned from the vet, you'll get promoted to supervisor before you know it."

"Do you think so?"

"I know so."

Asia's face had a warm glow as she smiled. "Oh, Woody. I've never felt so happy. Being here with you is the best thing that's ever happened to me. I love you so much."

"I love you, too." For a moment, we kissed. "If only we didn't have to be away from each other."

Just as I spoke, a chop-a-chop sound invaded our private territory. We looked up. Overhead a Marines helicopter flew in fast and low like we were its intended targets for war games further north at Camp Pendleton. Within seconds, it flew over the cliffs and disappeared. Leaving in its wake; a reminder that the Vietnam War was flaming out of control.

Startled by this reality, Asia gasped and held onto me. "Oh, Woody. The war's closing in on us."

"I know. It's crazy."

"Can't you stay out of it?" Tears streamed down her face.

"I don't have a choice."

"You could get killed."

"Take it easy, babe." I wiped her tears with my thumb.

"You could be away for a long time," she said.

Cold, hard reality of separation sank in. Asia shivered as a cool breeze blew in from the ocean. I did the same, and I spread a beach towel over both of our shoulders.

"At least we have this moment," I whispered in her ear.

"Yes." She leaned the side of her face on mine. "Look. The sun is setting."

We huddled together and watched the sun dipping into the ocean. A stream of silvery sparkles flowed out on the water and seemed to point directly at us. Blue horizon was like a painter's canvas while an invisible artist held a brush and made broad strokes across the sky. Orange, red, and yellow streaks mixed into purplish clouds.

Gradually the sky grew darker, and a cool ocean breeze nipped at our legs again. Night fell upon us. Time was short. We held on to each other and didn't want to let go. Shivering, we had no choice. It was time to leave. We stood up and gathered our stuff. With our hands full, we strolled back to the car as the sand squeezed between our toes. Ahead were the bright city lights of San Diego.

When I opened the passenger side door for Asia, I asked, "Would you like to find a place to eat along the boardwalk?"

"No, let's go home. I need to wash my hair and get cleaned up first." She slid her legs in and smiled. "Okay?"

I leaned in and kissed her. "Yes, home. I like how you said that." I rushed to the driver's side and drove up the hill.

Thoughts of war invaded my mind. I stopped at a red light and said, "It's no use putting it off any longer."

"I know." Her hand squeezed mine as though she understood what I'd say next.

"I'll enlist tomorrow."

275

Somewhere over Colorado, I tried to see out the rain-splattered window of a DC-9, while a lightning bolt flashed across the twilight sky. Instead of thunder, I heard the deafening roar of twinjets mounted on the tail. Powerful updrafts tossed the commercial plane around like a tin can.

Beside me sat a well-dressed man in his forties. He wore a black suit; gray tie and he was drunk as a skunk in a brewery. Out cold and snoring, he was oblivious to our up and down roller coaster ride. His empty glass vibrated on a tray in front of him, and a smoldering cigar butt wobbled in the ashtray on his armrest. I reached over and snuffed it out. Cigarette smoke wafted from the guy sitting in front of me, and I coughed and missed the fresh ocean air of San Diego.

In my hand was a love letter from Asia. I had given her mine before I left, and our plan was to write each other every day. For relief from the stench, I held her letter under my nose and inhaled the fragrance of orange blossoms. She had packed the envelope with dried flower petals from our tree in the backyard. My seat vibrated too much for me to open it and read her words, and I had to wait until things settled down.

Just two hours ago, I had rushed up to a gate at the San Diego Airport with Asia by my side. She wanted to see my off. It was happening so fast, we barely had time to kiss and say our goodbyes. Behind us, Mom and the rest of my family waved and smiled. Except Dad. He was still recovering in the hospital.

I ran and boarded the flight to Denver. This meant a two-hour layover in the mile-high city before I could take another plane to Chicago. There, I had to get on a bus to Great Lakes Naval Training Center for boot camp. I thought I was supposed to train in San Diego, but they sent me back east instead. Although disappointed at first, I looked forward to seeing a place I'd never been before.

When the jet began to take off, I looked out the window while Asia waved and smiled. I took one last picture in my mind and cherished it.

The plane flew higher, and somewhere over Colorado, we were going through a storm. While bouncing up and down in strong updrafts, I thought of that past summer. In the beginning, I planned to travel and see the world. Instead, I found Asia and fell in love. I got as far as the ranch north of Flagstaff, then back to San Diego.

Now I was at the beck and call of the U.S. Navy. Then it dawned on me. I could still see exotic places after all. Just as I thought of this, the plane bounced up and down. Thrilled with the excitement of adventures ahead, I braced myself for a wild ride into the unknown.

Wherever I traveled, Asia was always be on my mind.

ABOUT THE AUTHOR

Steven S. Foster

After Steven S. Foster served in the U.S. Air Force, he earned a BA degree in communications. He also wrote numerous magazine articles and gave presentations in schools for nonprofit organizations. While he refined the art of studying human behavior, he settled into a career in customer service. Now retired, he works full-time as a researcher and author of fictional stories that inspire and encourage his readers.

ACKNOWLEDGEMENTS

I am grateful for my son, Scott Foster, who designed the cover of Summer Passage of '66, and my first novel, Spirit of an Eagle. His positive attitude has been inspiring to me, and I can always count on his support through my writing projects.

Also, I am grateful for the encouragement of the Hawaii Writer's Guild and our local writer's support group.

www.ingramcontent.com/pod-product-compliance
Lightning Source LLC
Chambersburg PA
CBHW020417260626
47156CB00007B/2424